Praise for
The Intimacy Experiment

"Danan's book is at its very best when it's connecting faith, trust, strength, and desire in complex ways. . . . An ambitious and rewarding story."　　　　　　　*—The New York Times Book Review*

"This follow-up to Danan's steamy 2020 debut, *The Roommate*, is filled with humor, healing, and heady good times (and yes, that is a naughty pun)."　　　　　　　　　　　　*—Vulture*

"Rosie Danan has a staggering gift for subverting expectations. . . . *The Intimacy Experiment*, on the whole, is a blessing of a book—tender, bruising, sexy, and transcendent."　　*—Entertainment Weekly*

"I could cry about how much I love Naomi and Ethan. Rosie Danan's writing brims with compassion and wit, and there's a tenderness that runs underneath everything—even when her characters are positive they're not falling for each other. A stunning, subversive romance that made me proud to be Jewish."
　　　—Rachel Lynn Solomon, *New York Times* bestselling author of
　　　The Ex Talk

"*The Intimacy Experiment* by Rosie Danan is effervescent. It is the perfect combination of endearing vulnerability, swoon-worthy romance, and scorching chemistry. Rosie Danan brings us a charming exploration of the intersections of sex, love, faith, and identity in a fiercely feminist novel that will leave you breathless."
　　　　　　　—Denise Williams, author of *How to Fail at Flirting*

T0037480

"*The Intimacy Experiment* delivers on every promise: humor, steam, and an 'unlikely' couple that readers will not only fight for but admire."   —Felicia Grossman, author of *Dalliances and Devotion*

"Focusing on prejudices and preconceived notions people may have about both sex workers and Jewish folks, this book brings patience, love, understanding, and high heat to the budding relationship between two apparent opposites who find themselves extremely attracted to each other."   —Book & Film Globe

Praise for
The Roommate

"One of the steamiest romances of the year. . . . A downright revolutionary story about modern women owning their desire."   —PopSugar

"Rosie Danan's *The Roommate* is seriously sexy, seriously smart."   —Helen Hoang, *New York Times* bestselling author of *The Heart Principle*

"Genuinely, swoonily romantic."   —*New York Times* bestselling author Rachel Hawkins

"What an incredible debut! Danan gives us strangers to annoyed roommates to kinda friends to angsty pining to finally lovers with humor, wit, and just a hint of pathos. Josh and Clara are easily my favorite 'smash the patriarchy' couple, and *The Roommate* is easily one of my top romance reads of 2020!"   —Jen DeLuca, *USA Today* bestselling author of *Well Met*

"Rosie Danan not only created characters who you'll think about long after you're finished reading, but she wrote a powerful, feminist book that makes you laugh as hard as you cheer. *The Roommate* is sunshine in the form of a book. I can't wait to see what Danan brings us next!"
　　　　　　　　　　　　　—Alexa Martin, author of *Snapped*

"*The Roommate* is laugh-out-loud funny, bananas sexy, and deeply romantic. Danan's voice is fresh and sharp, and the romance between Clara and Josh is both sizzling hot and heartwarming. Everything I want in a romance."
　　　　　　—Andie J. Christopher, *USA Today* bestselling author of *Thank You, Next*

"Nuanced, funny, super steamy, and surprisingly tender, *The Roommate* raises the bar for rom-coms in 2020—a smashing debut, and I can't wait for more by Rosie Danan!"
　　　　　　—Evie Dunmore, *USA Today* bestselling author of *Bringing Down the Duke*

"*The Roommate* is unapologetically sexy as hell. Danan's writing, like her characters, is funny, seductive, and full of heart. You're gonna love this book."
　　　　　　—Meryl Wilsner, author of *Something to Talk About*

"Fresh and different; a special, superbly written slow burn."
　　　　　　—Sarah Hogle, author of *You Deserve Each Other*

"A deliciously fresh romance with strong characters and feminist themes."　　　　　　—*Kirkus Reviews* (starred review)

"Red-hot and fiercely feminist."　　—*Publishers Weekly* (starred review)

TITLES BY ROSIE DANAN

The Roommate
The Intimacy Experiment
Do Your Worst

Do Your Worst

ROSIE DANAN

BERKLEY ROMANCE

NEW YORK

BERKLEY ROMANCE
Published by Berkley
An imprint of Penguin Random House LLC
penguinrandomhouse.com

BERKLEY and the BERKLEY and B colophon are registered trademarks of
Penguin Random House LLC.

Library of Congress Cataloging-in-Publication Data

Names: Danan, Rosie, author.
Title: Do your worst / Rosie Danan.
Description: First Edition. | New York: Berkley Romance, 2023.
Identifiers: LCCN 2023013973 (print) | LCCN 2023013974 (ebook) |
ISBN 9780593437148 (trade paperback) | ISBN 9780593437155 (ebook)
Subjects: LCGFT: Romance fiction. | Novels.
Classification: LCC PS3604.A4745 D6 2023 (print) | LCC PS3604.A4745 (ebook) |
DDC 813/.6—dc23/eng/20230331
LC record available at https://lccn.loc.gov/2023013973
LC ebook record available at https://lccn.loc.gov/2023013974

First Edition: November 2023

Printed in the United States of America
2nd Printing

For Ruby Barrett.
The beginning and end of it is, having you as my friend
makes everything better.

Do Your Worst

Chapter One

While other women inherited a knack for singing or swearing from their grandmothers, Riley Rhodes received a faded leather journal, a few adolescent summers of field training, and the guarantee that she'd die alone.

Okay, fine, maybe that last thing was a slight exaggeration. But a unique talent for vanquishing the occult, passed down from one generation to the next like heirloom china, certainly didn't make dating any easier. Her matrilineal line's track record for lasting love was . . . bleak, to say the least.

Curse breaking—the Rhodes family talent—was a mysterious and often misunderstood practice, especially in the modern age. Lack of demand wasn't the problem. If anything, the world was more cursed than ever. But as the presence of an angry mob in any good folktale will tell you, people fear what they don't understand.

To be fair, Gran had warned Riley about the inherent hazards of curse breaking out of the gate. There was, of course, the whole physical danger aspect that came part and parcel with facing off against the supernatural. Riley had experienced everything from singed fingertips to the occasional accidental poisoning in the name of her calling.

As for the personal pitfalls? Well, those hurt in a different way.

She'd grown up practicing chants at recess and trying to trade homemade tonics for Twinkies at lunch. Was it any wonder that, through middle school, her only friend had been a kindly art teacher in her late fifties? It wasn't until tenth grade when her tits came in that guys decided "freaky curse girl" was suddenly code for "performs pagan sex rituals." Riley had been almost popular for a week—until that rumor withered on the vine.

It was like Gran always said: *No one appreciates a curse breaker until they're cursed.*

Since she couldn't be adored for her talents, Riley figured she could at least get paid. So, at thirty-one years old, she'd vowed to be the first to turn the family hobby into a legitimate business.

Still, no one would call her practical. She'd flown thousands of miles to a tiny village in the Scottish Highlands to risk life and limb facing down an ancient and unknowable power—but hey, at least she'd gotten fifty percent up front.

Hours after landing, strung out on jet lag and new-job nerves, Riley decided the village's single pub was as good a place as any to start her investigation into the infamous curse on Arden Castle.

The Hare's Heart had a decent crowd for a Sunday night, considering the total population of the village didn't break two hundred. Dark wood-paneled walls and a low ceiling covered in crimson wallpaper gave the already small space an extra intimate feel. More like an elderly family member's living room than the slick, open-concept spots filled with almost as many screens as people that Riley knew all too well back home.

Hopefully after this job put her services on the map she could stop picking up bartending shifts in Fishtown during lean months. For now, her business was still finding its feet. The meager income she managed to bring in from curse breaking remained firmly in the "side hustle" category—though it was still more than anyone else in her family had ever made from their highly specialized skills. Riley had always thought it was kind of funny, in a morbid way, that a family of curse breakers could help everyone but themselves.

Whether out of fear or a sense of self-preservation, Gran had never charged for her practice. In fact, she'd kept curse breaking a secret her whole life, serving only her tiny rural mountain community. As a consequence, she'd never had two nickels to rub together. She and Riley's mom had weathered a few rough winters without heat, going to bed on lean nights—if not hungry, then certainly not full.

Riley had never faulted her mom for ditching Appalachia and the family mantle in favor of getting her nursing degree in scenic South Jersey. It was only because she'd never been good at anything practical that Riley found herself here in the Highlands, hoping this contract changed more than the number in her bank account.

If word got out that Riley had taken down the notorious curse on Arden Castle, she could go from serving small-time personal clients to big corporate or even government jobs. (She had it on good authority they'd been looking for someone to remove the curse on Area 51 since the seventies).

Perching herself on a faded leather stool at the mahogany bar that divided the pub into two sections, Riley had an excellent vantage point to observe the locals. Up front in the dining room, patrons ranging in age from two to eighty occupied various farm tables brimming with frothing pints and steaming plates.

Her stomach growled as the scent of melting butter and roasted meat wafted across the room. After ordering a drink, she'd ask for a menu. As much as Riley didn't mind charging into battle against mystical mysteries, she was terrified of plane food, so she hadn't eaten much in the last sixteen hours.

Next to her, a middle-aged man with face-paint-streaked cheeks bellied up to the bar to speak to the hot older woman pulling pints.

"Eilean, come and sit with us." He thumbed at the more casual area in the back of the pub.

Over her shoulder, Riley followed his direction to a cluster of rowdier guests on the edge of their seats in a haphazard cluster of well-loved armchairs. They all had their necks bent at uncomfortable angles to watch a small, shitty-looking TV hanging from the wall.

"We need you. The game's tied and you're good luck."

The bartender—Eilean—waved him off. "Even if that were true, I wouldn't waste it on you lot and that piss-poor excuse for a rugby club."

She smiled at Riley when he turned tail back to his buddies, but her eyes held the kind of guarded interest reserved for interlopers at a place that served almost exclusively regulars. "Can I get you something?"

Without hesitating, Riley ordered an aged local scotch on the rocks, hoping the quick, simple order would convey that she came in peace.

While she waited, the face-painted man and several of his buddies took turns heckling the sports teams onscreen, their impassioned shouts cutting above the dining room's steady din of conversation.

Riley smiled to herself at the colorful insults delivered in their thick Scottish brogues. A similar disorderly air erupted in her mother's living room every time neighbors and friends gathered to get their hearts broken by the Eagles. Even though she'd never traveled abroad before, suddenly Riley felt a little more at home.

"You've got good taste in scotch." Eilean placed the highball glass of amber liquid in front of her. "For an American," she said, warm, teasing.

Apparently, in a village this small, even a few words in her accent stood out. Riley raised her glass in acknowledgment before taking a sip.

She savored the sharp, smoky flavor of the smooth liquor, a subtle hint of spice lingering on her lips after she swallowed. Good whiskey tasted like indulging in bad decisions—that same satisfying burn. This job might kill her, but so close to Islay, at least she could enjoy single malt without paying shipping markup or import tax.

"I'd ask what brings you all the way out here," the silver-haired bartender said, "but there's really only one reason strangers come to Torridon." Almost imperceptibly, her gaze strayed to a couple tucked in at a corner table wearing a pair of what looked like homemade novelty T-shirts reading *Curse Chasers*.

Riley winced. Reminders that her real life was someone else's sideshow circus could make a girl feel cheap, if she let them.

Accustomed to using people's drink order as a bellwether for their character, out of habit, her eyes fell to check what they were drinking. Riley groaned.

"Not mojitos." Far and away the most tedious cocktail to prepare. She revised her previous analysis of their threat level. To make matters worse, their table held the remnants of several rounds.

"All that muddling." She rubbed phantom pain from her wrist.

Eilean barked out a laugh. "You've spent some time behind a bar, then?"

"More than I'd care to admit."

They shared a commiserating sigh.

"Do you get a lot of gawkers?"

"Not enough," Eilean pursed her lips. "The Loch Ness monster is obviously a big draw for bringing supernatural enthusiasts to the Highlands, but unfortunately for us, the curse on Arden Castle scares off more tourists than it brings in." She grabbed a rag to wipe down the bar where a bit of beer had splashed. "The latest land-lords have promised to make a big investment in turning the castle into a vacation destination that will 'revitalize the whole village,' but we've heard that promise enough that we try not to get our hopes up anymore."

"Maybe these guys will surprise you." Riley pulled a card out of her wallet and extended it to Eilean. No one really used business cards anymore. Even though she'd gotten them on sale, they'd been an irresponsible purchase. But they added an air of legitimacy that her unconventional offering still required.

"At the very least, they hired me." Based on what Riley could tell from their website, her new employer, Cornerstone Investments, was a land developer based in London. The latest in a long list of investors both public and private who had inked their name on Arden's deed, they were a relatively young company with eager, if green, staff.

"A curse breaker?" Eilean arched a finely crafted eyebrow. "No wonder that weedy project manager looked right pleased with himself last time he came in here."

Considering how frazzled and desperate he'd been when they spoke on the phone a week ago, Riley took that as a vote of confidence in her abilities.

"Still." As Eilean handed back the card, her voice took on a new note of gravity. "Arden Castle is no place for the faint of heart."

Riley's ears perked up at the first hint of a lead.

"You believe in the curse, then?" Not always a guarantee, even among locals.

"Oh, aye"—Eilean laughed humorlessly—"and anyone who thinks I've had a choice in the matter hasn't been here long. I've seen enough people broken by that curse over the course of my lifetime to know that land doesn't want to be owned and the curse ensures it won't."

When a guest at the other end of the bar held up two fingers, the bartender nodded and began pulling a pair of fresh pints while simultaneously finishing her warning. "I hope you know what you're getting yourself into."

"I'm a professional," Riley assured her firmly as she slipped the card back into the pocket of her jeans. Part of the gig was projecting confidence in the face of the unknown. Gumption, as Gran called it, was an essential trait for curse breakers. "But the more I can learn about the curse, and quickly," she said with a meaningful head tilt, "the better my odds."

The little time she'd had to research in the short period between receiving the assignment and arriving in Scotland had left her with more questions than answers. Arden Castle didn't attract the same obsessive analysis and "eyewitness account" forum fodder as other Highland supernatural stories. A cursory Internet search hadn't turned up many hits.

Maybe it was like Eilean said, that the close proximity of Loch Ness, or even the standing stones at Clava Cairns, simply drew interest. Or maybe it was because castles, cursed or not, were a dime a dozen in the UK. Whatever the reason, Riley knew she would have to tap into the firsthand experiences and folklore of locals like Eilean—people who had grown up in the castle's backyard—to get this job done.

"Very well." Eilean's mouth pulled to the side. "I suppose it's better you hear from me than the sensationalized tales of these hooligans." She raised her chin toward the armchair crowd from earlier.

Riley eagerly pulled out a pocket notebook and pen from her purse. "Start at the beginning, please."

It was curse breaking 101: pin down the origin.

In their most basic form, curses were uncontrollable energy. And power stabilized when you completed a circuit back to the source. Riley's first task was always uncovering specific details: who, when, why, and how.

"Now, I'm not a historian, mind you." Eilean popped open a jar of olives and began to spear them in pairs while she spoke. "But based on what I've always heard, the curse started roughly three hundred years ago."

Riley leaned forward. An origin date somewhere in the eighteenth century was a broad window, but it gave her something to start with in terms of timeline.

"A land war had broken out in Torridon between the Campbells, the clan who held the castle at the time, and the Graphms, who controlled the region to the east." Eilean kept one eye on her customers as she spoke and patiently spelled out the Gaelic version of "Graphm" when Riley jotted down the names.

"The fighting was so bitter and so deadly that it nearly wiped out both clans."

Already the set pieces were starting to make sense. Gran had taught Riley that curses came from people, born out of their most extreme emotions—suffering, longing, desperation—feelings so raw, so heavy, that they poured out and drew consequences from the universe.

A blood feud made the perfect catalyst. All that burning hatred, the sheer magnitude of anguish from so many lost loved ones.

"The tale goes that when both clans' numbers had dwindled so far that it looked like the castle might soon belong to no one," Eilean said, her low, lilting voice weaving the story like a tapestry, "one desperate soul went into the mountains, seeking the fae that lived beyond the yew trees, determined to make a terrible deal."

Ah, the infamous Highland fae. Riley loved a good fairy tale, especially when they were real.

"But which side did the person come from?" By the sounds of it, a member from either clan would have enough they stood to win or lose.

"The name is lost to legend, I'm afraid." Eilean frowned. "Whoever it was, they made a bad bargain, because the last lines of both clans fell, and the castle lay dormant for years before a lieutenant from the Twenty-First Light Dragoons purchased the place in 1789."

The bartender paused to hold up the bottle of scotch from before.

With a smile, Riley tapped the bar next to the glass, accepting the offer of a refill.

"Whatever that sorry soul was promised by the fae remains unfulfilled"—Eilean delivered a generous pour—"and the curse persists as a consequence, driving any- and everyone away from that castle."

Riley bit the inside of her cheek while the bartender went to help another customer. She knew there were tons of regional nuances to curses, but even though popular lore cast the fae as tricksters and mischief-makers eager to make deals with desperate humans, Gran's journal didn't say anything specifically about their influence.

Whatever Riley was up against here, she had her work cut out for her.

A bell chimed over the front door of the pub, pulling her attention from the first stirrings of a mental pep talk.

Holy shit. Her breath caught in her throat at the sight of the man who entered.

Everything from the harsh line of his jaw to the broad stretch of his shoulders pulled tight with a specific kind of tension that seemed . . . tortured. Even though that didn't make sense. The expression on his face was perfectly neutral; he wasn't limping or dripping blood.

As he walked in and moved toward the bar, Riley had the sudden, visceral memory of a painting she'd seen once. She was far from a fine art lover, but back when she was in the sixth grade, her whole class had gone to the Philadelphia Museum of Art on a field trip.

Riley had found the whole day unforgivably boring—none of the work moved her. But then she'd come to this one massive canvas, and it was like her feet sprouted roots into the marble floor.

All these years later, she still remembered how the artist had captured an angel suspended midfall. She'd felt the momentum of that still image within her own body. The way anguish strained his face and form until his plunge became like ballet, like poetry.

She felt it again—the painting feeling—now, looking at this stranger. Heat licked up her spine, as swift and sudden as wildfire.

Looking back, that painting had probably been some kind of sexual awakening. For even though the man at the bar was fully dressed, coat and all, the angel had been naked, his modesty preserved in profile.

Riley had found herself fascinated by his body, the high contrast of strength and vulnerability. Sharp ribs and taut thighs versus how tender the pink soles of his feet had looked. How those massive indigo wings had folded as he fell.

Looking at this real-life man who reminded her of an artist's rendering, Riley realized something new about the painting.

It wasn't the despair in the pose that had drawn her in. It was the defiance.

It was that even in the act of falling, the angel had flung up one arm, fingers curling, reaching for the only home he'd ever known, refusing to go quietly, while the other arm remained tucked to his breast, protecting his heart.

The man with his dark head bowed over the bar looked similarly braced for impact. For the fight that inevitably awaited a fallen angel on land.

What did it say about Riley that his weary resilience called to her? Probably something twisted.

Since she was someone trying to make curse breaking into a career, it wasn't a great secret that Riley wanted to save people, but she feared the parts of herself that wanted to be saved in return.

"Who is that?" She hadn't meant to speak the words out loud, but Eilean heard and answered anyway.

"Oh. *Him.* He's been causing quite the fuss ever since he came to town."

Wait, that guy lived here? Forget the curse; *he* should be Torridon's new claim to fame.

Though if the unimpressed look on Eilean's face was anything to go by, she was seemingly immune to this guy's whole thing.

Riley leaned forward, lowering her voice. "What do you know about him?"

"He's English." Eilean moved to restock some napkins. "Like the land developers who hired you, though blessedly he doesn't work for them. He comes here most nights, so he probably can't cook. And he's an archaeologist hired to—"

"An archaeologist." Riley's ears perked up. "Oh, that's perfect. I just watched a movie about archaeology on the plane!"

Eilean's slate brows came together. ". . . So?"

"So, that can be my in!" Riley didn't remember all the details of the film—she'd nodded off a bit in the middle—but it had been based on a true story. The main character was ripped directly from the pages of a best-selling memoir after some major film studio purchased the guy's life rights.

"Wait." Eilean stopped working. "You're not going to hit on him, are you?"

"I mean, yeah," Riley said, "but, like, respectfully."

She didn't make a habit of picking up people in bars, but she certainly didn't have a problem striking up a conversation with someone she found attractive. And this guy was hot like burning—even dressed in the repressive layers of a Ralph Lauren ad, with a button-up under his sweater and a tweed blazer over top.

"I don't think that's such a good idea." Eilean began to shake her head. "The assignment you took—"

"Oh, don't worry." Riley could already tell that Eilean saw everyone under this roof as her responsibility. "I'm not on the clock until tomorrow morning."

She didn't mix business and pleasure at home, but that was mostly because she didn't want to pollute her potential client pool with former flames. Since her first trip to Scotland was likely to be her last, that didn't seem like an issue here.

"Do I have anything—" She bared her teeth at Eilean.

"No," Eilean said after a quick glance, and then, crossing her arms, "I suppose, in your line of work, you know your way around trouble."

"Huh?" Riley had gotten distracted looking at the guy again. Before tonight, she hadn't even known they made cheekbones that sharp.

"Never mind." Eilean ushered her forward. "Good luck to you, curse breaker."

Chapter Two

When Clark Edgeware grew warm across the back of his neck upon entering the Hare's Heart, he simply assumed the pub's radiator had gone to pieces in keeping with the rest of his life.

After shrugging out of his wool coat, he ordered a beer, ready to chalk today up as another with nothing to show for the job he shouldn't have taken in this village that resented his presence.

But then, a few minutes later, when the flush wouldn't go away, he turned to his left and saw her.

"Hi," the woman descending from one of the neighboring barstools said in an American accent.

Clark's first thought was that she was loud. Not her voice, but how she looked. Everything about her demanded attention. From her blond hair, so bright it was almost silver, to her eyes, heavily shadowed, as if she'd smudged charcoal across the lids, to her impossibly plush lips. And that was just her face.

Even without letting his gaze fall, his body was aware of the decadent curves of hers.

Truly, someone who worked here should do something about the thermostat.

"Umm, hello." He tried to lean casually against the bar.

"I'm Riley." She stuck out a hand as pretty as the rest of her, sporting a fine-lined tattoo—a starburst above the third knuckle on her ring finger.

He wanted to ask about it. He also worried that his ears were ringing.

On a delay, he accepted the handshake. "Clark."

He knew he was looking at her too intently, but nothing had cut through the monotonous haze of his life in so long.

Ever since Cádiz, he'd been relentless with himself, trying to earn back his reputation. The few things he did outside work, he did merely to sustain himself so he could work more, harder—eat, exercise, shower, sleep. He couldn't remember the last time he'd done anything simply because it felt good. And looking at her did.

Thank god, she didn't seem to mind. In fact, she looked back, flushed herself, like the lousy radiator had gotten to her too. It wasn't unusual for people to stare at him, but it was unusual for Clark to feel seen.

"Listen." She released his hand. "I don't want to disturb you if you're waiting for someone . . ."

"I'm not." He'd taken every meal alone for the last month. And even before he'd come to Torridon, he hadn't met mates at the pub in ages. He was poor company, even before the scandal. And Patrick—who had always smoothed the way for him socially—had gone.

"Okay, then," Riley said, stepping a little closer, close enough that he got the whiff of a fragrance he couldn't quite catch, something that made him think of summer even though the leaves had begun to change in Scotland, daylight growing scarce as autumn took hold. "Eilean, over there"—she raised her chin toward the bartender he recognized from his frequent visits—"said you're an archaeologist?"

That threw him. He'd thought—had hoped—he read a different kind of interest in her approach.

"That's right." He changed his posture to better suit a professional inquiry. "Are you in the market for one?"

She curved her obscenely pretty mouth in a coy, closed-lipped smile. "Maybe."

"Well." He cleared his throat, trying to get ahold of himself. If she was looking to hire someone, he'd need more information about her objectives. "I specialize in ancient Roman civilizations in the Mediterranean region. There are a lot of different kinds of archaeologists, commercial, industrial, forensic . . . it depends on what you need." He didn't have the strongest set of contacts these days, but he'd do his best to get her a reliable referral, if he could.

"Oh, okay, no." She brought a curled finger to her mouth, seeming to find something amusing in his answer.

Even though he didn't know what it was, Clark liked the way her eyes lit up.

"That was my attempt to . . . I don't actually know anything about archaeology," she confessed. "I just watched this movie on the plane, *Out of the Earth*."

"Oh." Clark stiffened. Dropping his eyes to the bar top. Of course.

"Have you seen it?"

He grimaced. Was she joking?

"Not personally," he said after a pause.

There had been a premiere, multiple actually, but Clark had only had to beg off the one in London. His father hadn't put up a fuss. He wanted Clark there in theory, but in practice, this was cleaner. No whiff of scandal to take away from his big night.

"It's about this famous dig from the 1970s—"

Wait. His eyes shot back to her face. Did she seriously think he didn't know what *Out of the Earth* was about?

"—where they found this entire ship buried on some fancy English lady's property."

She looked sincere. A little nervous, speaking quickly. As if worried she'd bore him with the recap.

"I thought you might know about it because the main character, the archaeologist, is based on a real person—a British guy, and he's still alive, I'm pretty sure." She snapped her fingers. "Shit, what was his name . . . something with an *A*."

"Alfie Edgeware," Clark finally supplied, stumbling a bit on the vowels of his own last name.

"Yes!" She pointed and almost poked him in the chest in her eagerness. "That was it. Have you ever met him?"

This was surreal. People brought up his dad to him all the time—especially since the film came out—but not like this.

Clark took a deep breath. "I have."

Even people who didn't care about archaeology got weird when they found out he was related to England's second-favorite scientist (after Sir David Attenborough—who, Clark had always heard, was actually nice).

"Really?" Riley's eyes widened. "Okay, that's amazing. What are the odds? I guess the circle of British archaeologists isn't that big. Can I . . . do you mind if I ask you something about him?"

"Sure." He could be polite. It wasn't her fault his dad was a tosser.

"Is he . . ."

As she paused to pick her words, Clark braced himself for the adjectives he encountered most frequently—brilliant, charming, *single*.

Better Clark than his mum at least, fielding that one.

Riley leaned in, lowered her voice to a self-conscious whisper. ". . . kind of a jerk?"

"Pardon?" He coughed, choking on nothing but air.

"Sorry." She bit her bottom lip. "I know he's supposed to be the real-life Indiana Jones—and I guess he's like best friends with Oprah ever since she picked his memoir for her book club—but he seemed really insufferable, even before he found the boat."

The laugh built like a volcano in his belly, his chest. Until it was taking everything Clark had not to let it out.

"—and then after, it's like, why doesn't he give more credit to his team?" Riley continued, oblivious to how good it felt to hear someone, anyone, say what he'd been thinking for most of his life. "There's no way he would have found the mast if that woman Emory hadn't recognized the change in soil structure the day before."

"Excellent observations." Clark grinned like a fool.

"Sorry, again"—her blush was exceedingly becoming—"if he's your friend."

"He's not." Clark would have defended his dad against serious slander. He loved him, for all his flaws. But he felt confident Alfie would have found secret delight in such an incisive character assessment—though, to be fair, not as much as Clark.

He wanted to say, *Who are you?* Because her name wasn't enough. But that didn't make sense, so instead he said, "Can I buy you a drink?"

"Uh, yeah," she said with a laugh.

The sense of relief that washed over Clark was as good as if he'd done it himself.

"I would really like that."

He waved for the bartender.

"Wait." Riley caught his arm, and that felt loud too, her hand on him. High volume. Everything else in the room—people shouting at the telly, glasses clinking, the hum of the radiator he'd developed a fondness for in the end—all muted.

"Actually, I'm sorry." She grimaced, dropping her arm. "I shouldn't have another drink. It's not you," she rushed to assure him before his brain could even go there. "Like at all." Her eyes fell to his mouth and lingered a moment.

He wet his own lips, confused, but not enough that his body could ignore how close they stood to one another.

"You're really se—" She cut herself off, opening her eyes like she hadn't meant for them to fall half-lidded. "What I mean to say is, I would really like to accept, but I just had two generous pours of scotch on an empty stomach."

Clark couldn't get over how much he liked the way she spoke. Not just the accent, but the decisiveness of her statements. It was so refreshingly straightforward. So not English.

He thought for a moment. "In that case, would you let me buy you dinner?"

"Dinner?" She tilted her head. "That's a pretty big commitment for someone you just met."

He shrugged. A gesture that was as unfamiliar to him as inviting a stranger to join him for a meal. "I've got a good feeling about you."

Her gaze softened. "You do?"

"Is that a yes?"

She was so pretty, especially when she smiled.

"Yes."

They got a table, and a server brought them menus. Clark pointed out a few of the dishes he liked best, since he'd come here pretty often over the last month. Whenever he didn't feel like cooking in his cramped camper kitchen.

"So," he said, once they'd placed their orders and gotten their drinks. "You're obviously not from around here. What brings you to Torridon?"

Riley bit her lip, studying him. "I'm a little nervous to tell you."

"How come?"

"People tend to look at me a little differently when they find out."

Clark tried to rack his brain for something that would make him not like her. "Are you in fracking?"

She shook her head. "You've heard of the curse on Arden Castle, right?"

Ah, so she was a tourist. It made sense. Clark had encountered a few people visiting Torridon because of the local lore. He didn't blame her for being embarrassed about putting any stock in the silly fairy tale; the idea of a curse on the castle was as outrageous as any of the local legends about mythical monsters.

"I have, yes."

He certainly wasn't going to tell her that the curse was just one of many things making his path to professional redemption harder.

"I looked into the history of Arden Castle quite a bit before coming to Torridon." Reaching into his briefcase, Clark pulled out one of the books he'd gotten on special order from a local university press and extended it to her. "You might find this interesting."

Riley took the book eagerly, studying both the cover and back copy with care before leafing through the pages.

"This is fantastic." After a few more moments of careful inspection, she handed the book back with obvious reluctance. "Thank you for showing me. It's harder than you think to find research on Arden."

"Keep it," he said impulsively, handing it back. He wouldn't dampen her sightseeing vacation by sharing that even Historic Environment Scotland, the preservation group tasked with protecting heritage sites, didn't think Arden Castle was worthy of proper excavation efforts.

He guessed they were a poorly funded, resource-strapped government body. But still, they'd been more than happy to let upstart land developers purchase the historic property with the meager stipulation that they bring in a contract archaeologist to check for any "salient" artifacts remaining in the crumbling castle before they turned it into a tourist destination to rival Nessieland.

After everyone suitable had turned them down, the HES didn't even care that Clark specialized in a totally different time period and region. As long as they could say they'd sent someone with the bare minimum of qualifications, they could wipe their hands of the entire matter.

Clark tried to do a good job anyway, to bring whatever semblance of process and procedure he could to the assignment. He hoped, however fruitlessly, to find something worth studying. Something he could publish, really, so that the only journal articles with his name on them weren't the—now retracted—ones on Cádiz.

"Are you sure?" Riley looked down at the book again, flipping it open to run her fingers reverently across the pages.

"Absolutely." Clark had finished it, and besides, he had plenty of others.

"Thank you." She placed the book carefully in her lap, spreading out her napkin to protect it. "Curses are always hard to pin down in documentation. They're difficult to visualize, and half the time, people who have experienced a curse are too afraid or ashamed to write anything down."

Wow. She seemed to have spent a lot of time thinking about curses.

"You genuinely believe in this stuff, then? You're not having me on?" Clark supposed it wasn't that different from his mom getting into astrology a few years ago. Apparently, he was a textbook Capricorn. Whatever that meant. He certainly didn't put any stock in pseudoscience, and Riley's interest in the occult seemed to him a similarly harmless misconception.

"Oh, no, I'm a firm believer." Riley carefully moved her water, making room as the waiter delivered their food—a pair of burgers and fries. "I guess you could say it's sort of an obsession for my family. My grandmother wrote a whole book about it."

"Really?" Despite himself, Clark was fascinated.

Though he didn't ideologically align with the subject matter, he knew from colleagues how difficult it was to both write and publish a novel. And on such a polarizing topic. She must have been a very gifted storyteller indeed.

"That's certainly impressive."

"Gran was one of a kind." Riley popped a fry in her mouth, then licked a trace of salt off her thumb.

Clark momentarily forgot how to chew.

"I spent every summer with her in the mountains—and she tried to teach me as much as she could about curses—but she passed when I was nine." Her voice held traces of a sadness still raw after all these years, but her eyes remained clear. "I still wish almost every day that I could ask her a question, get her advice."

"She sounds very special." Clark certainly couldn't begrudge Riley for holding on to stories shared by a beloved grandmother.

While they worked to clear their plates, the woman across from him continued to surprise him, to make him laugh. When he asked about her hometown, she described the place simply by enumerating its local culinary delicacies—soft pretzels, roast pork sandwiches with broccoli rabe, water ice (pronounced *wooder ice*, and which was neither water nor ice but instead some kind of in-between slush), and something called Tastykakes, which sounded truly appalling—and proudly talking about how her city's sports fans were some of the most hated nationwide. To his surprise, she didn't think much of cheesesteaks, though she insisted that if he did have one, he should go to Woodrow's.

She asked him about himself too—about growing up in Manchester and how he'd chosen his specialization in archaeology and whether people had made a lot of Superman jokes when he was growing up, dark haired and square jawed (yes).

The night passed like a dream, everything but Riley blurred into soft focus, the pub emptying around them as visitors went home to prepare for the week ahead.

He paid, though she sincerely tried to get him to split it, suggesting they settle the matter in a thumb war, an offer he indulged purely for the chance to hold her hand. His life could do with an influx of whimsy.

By the time they stepped outside, the sky above was dark as pitch.

"Whoa," Riley said, tipping her head back. "Get a load of those stars."

Clark stopped and looked up too, at a scattering of constellations winking down at them. He alternated his gaze between Riley's rapt face and the wonders above, his belly pleasantly full, crisp air against his hot cheeks.

"I'm really glad I met you tonight," he said, as if her boldness had rubbed off on him during the meal. Clark didn't believe in destiny or anything like that. His father had made sure he didn't believe in anything but determination and grit. But even he could admit this felt—*different*.

She turned to him, the breeze tugging at the strands of her blond hair. "Do you wanna kiss me?"

Fuck. More than he wanted to keep breathing. But something held him back.

"It's late," he said, but didn't move away.

"Kissing doesn't have a curfew." Her voice came out frayed at the edges.

"You don't know me." Clark stared at her bee-stung lips, for what felt like the thousandth time and the first, swallowing thickly. "I could be a terrible person."

"Are you?"

"Sometimes," he whispered without meaning to, and then, more dryly, "but in any case, you can't take my word for it."

This time when she laughed, Clark couldn't resist. He reached up, slowly, carefully, to cup her jaw. And as her eyes fluttered closed, he closed the distance between them, bending to kiss her. Her lips were petal soft and so warm in contrast to the night air.

Riley dropped her hands to his shoulders and swayed forward, until they were pressed together from the knees up. Clark groaned into her mouth at the contact, the way her body molded to his, tugging her closer, moving one hand to her waist, the other sliding up to curl into her hair.

A moment ago, he'd been able to hear the vague sounds of people stacking chairs inside the pub, the whistle of the wind, but now kissing her drowned out everything else. There was nothing but the growing harshness of their breaths, Riley's tiny gasp when he sank his teeth softly into the impossible fullness of her bottom lip.

Only the sudden clang of the bell above the door startled them apart.

"Sorry," Eilean said, looking anything but. "I was worried if I left you out here any longer, you'd freeze together like horny statues."

Riley laughed while Clark flushed, glad that his long coat hid exactly how much he'd enjoyed that kiss.

"I should get back to the inn and try to go to bed," Riley admitted. "I'm sure I'm already gonna get rocked by jet lag tomorrow."

"Right," Clark said, and Eilean ducked back inside, leaving them to their goodbyes. "How long will you be in town?"

"It's kind of hard to say." Riley pressed her lips together, drawing Clark's eyes back to them until he forced himself to look just over her shoulder for fear of trying to pull her back into his arms. "At least a week."

A week. It was more than he'd hoped for from her trip to such a small village. "I'd like to see you again, if you—"

"Definitely," she said before he could finish. "Here." She reached into her pocket and pulled out a piece of card stock, sliding it into his palm. "My information's on there."

"Great, thanks." He watched as she headed back toward the inn, the entrance close enough down the road that he could see it from here.

It wasn't until she'd slipped inside, looking back once to wave, that Clark lowered his gaze to examine the paper.

Riley Rhodes, he read, *Curse breaker for hire.*

Chapter Three

Riley hurried down the footpath to the castle the next morning, stumbling on wet cobblestones while chilly mist beaded across her forehead and cheeks. Who knew Scotland was so wet? Her phone's weather forecast for the week was downright depressing—a solid wall of weeping clouds. Apparently, she was committing to the dewy look for the duration of her stay.

Her meeting with Martin Chen, the project manager who'd hired her, started at eight. A hasty look at her watch read quarter past the hour. Not exactly a great start for someone looking to prove she could handle the big leagues.

Hopefully he'd attribute her tardiness to charming eccentricity. Usually Riley could get away with a fair amount of flightiness by virtue of her occupation. No one trusted an occultist who seemed too put together.

The inn was only about a mile from the castle, but she'd had to hoof it the whole way, paying the price for hitting the snooze button not once but twice this morning. *Blame Clark*, she thought, smiling to herself. He was worse than the time difference for her sleep schedule. She'd been up half the night, lying in bed with cartoon hearts circling her head. Thinking about his falling-angel grace. How quick he'd been to offer her a book when he learned she was interested in something. She sighed. The way her name sounded in his accent.

It was embarrassing, honestly, going to jelly over a random guy she'd met at a bar, but at least it was the safe sort of mistake. How much damage could a harmless little fling across the pond really inflict on her life?

Finally, she got across the footbridge—the place had an actual moat. Nestled on a cliff overlooking the North Sea, Arden Castle stood majestic and imposing even after centuries of neglect. Fortified by four towers, one on each corner, the castle was basically a giant rectangular outline protecting an open-air inner ward. Somehow, she'd accidentally come in at the back.

Riley didn't have time to stop and admire the lush crop of wildflowers in the high grass. *Later*, she promised herself, slipping through a section of stone that looked to have been blown away by cannon fire at some point. Riley planned to learn all of this castle's secrets.

As soon as she crossed the threshold, the scent of the curse hit her nostrils. A combination of smoke and metal and earth—ozone—buried beneath other, stronger odors. Wet stone and moss, the slightly sweet odor of decay.

Tracking was a learned skill like any other. One of the first tricks of the trade that Gran had introduced by hiding cursed objects sourced from all over the world for Riley to find. They'd started inside her tiny cottage, then later gone out into the forest, where there were so many more competing scents.

"It's like hide-and-seek," Gran had promised.

And it was—the same thrill of the hunt, the rush of discovery. Even now.

That training, her finely honed attuning to the scent of power, was how she knew a curse waited in this castle, banked but burning. Riley rubbed at her arms, trying to rid herself of sudden goose bumps as Arden Castle called to something deep in her blood.

Light refracting off the remaining stained glass in a series of windows sent colors glittering across the floor like the inside of a kaleidoscope. She held her breath as she tilted her head back, looking up and up and up to the vaulted ceilings where the skeleton of a chandelier swayed with the breeze. This must have been some kind of great hall.

"Hello?" Her voice echoed in the cavernous room. "Mr. Chen?"

The castle remained tomb silent. Layers of dust muted her footfalls as she wandered farther in, each step kicking up clouds that swirled and settled in her wake. It was easy, looking at the remnants of wooden benches withered to matchsticks, to imagine how many people had passed through this room, none of them withstanding the curse long enough to leave more than fading footprints.

As she got to the edge of the hall, she caught notes of conversation coming from somewhere down the corridor. Martin must have brought along a colleague to welcome her.

Picking up her pace, she managed to make out the next sentence.

"I can't simply give her the boot," someone argued. "She's come all the way from America."

Oh shit. Immediately, Riley hugged the wall, keeping an eye on where her shadow landed. She was a world-class eavesdropper.

"Come off it," another voice objected. Both speakers sounded English, which made sense given the holding company's London headquarters. "Have you been to her website? All those phony testimonials? The merchandise? Frankly, you should be embarrassed for having hired her in the first place."

Riley dug her nails into the meat of her palms.

"I came here as a professional scientist, expecting to find a productive work environment." The man's voice pitched so low it was practically a growl. "I have a PhD from Oxford, for Christ's sake. I refuse to allow a con artist to jeopardize the possibility of legitimate research. If the board of trustees from Historic Environment Scotland knew about this—"

"Respectfully," the other voice cut in, "the HES contracted you to survey the site for artifacts a month ago, and so far, you haven't turned up anything more than shards of broken pottery."

"I know it may not seem like it to you, but I'm making progress," the protestor grit out. "Extenuating circumstances have caused unexpected delays."

Extenuating circumstances. Unexpected delays. Yeah, sounds like a curse, jackass.

Riley shifted her position, trying to catch the speaker's reflection in the opposite window without giving herself away, but all she saw was a slice of someone's back as they paced.

"I apologize that we didn't alert you ahead of time." The first speaker tried to console his companion. "But we're all eager to see the castle cleared out and ready for development. Surely having her on-site can't hurt?"

Wanna bet? Riley had heard enough. Time to give these jerks the verbal smackdown of their lives.

"Good morning." She made a show of leaning against the doorway. "Sorry I'm late."

Both men swiveled as one. The first she recognized as Martin from his headshot on the Cornerstone website. The second was—

"Riley," Clark said, dropping his folded arms. He really did have a face made for looking pained.

Her stomach sank to somewhere down around her knees.

Because there was no mercy in this world, the hunter-green sweater he wore brought out his eyes.

She played back the conversation she'd just overheard like a slow-motion car crash.

"You work here?" Riley directed her question at Clark, even though Martin had stepped forward with a big smile that said he hoped to avoid a scene.

Clark winced. "I—"

"And you're trying to get me fired?" For all her puffed-up anger of a moment ago, her voice came out traitorously weak. The same man who had made her laugh last night, who had bought her dinner and kissed her under the stars, had just called her a con artist with so much venom in his voice, Riley could still feel the sting of the bite.

Did he really hate her that much? Already?

She closed her eyes against bitter memories of her dad packing his bags the week after Gran's funeral. He'd found the journal in her drawer while putting away Riley's laundry and the whole family secret had unraveled like so much yarn.

I always knew your mother was heathen, backwoods trash. For nine summers you let her pollute our child with this voodoo shit?

Get out, her mom had said calmly in response to his vitriol. Even though she'd never picked up a charm or practiced a ritual. Had left the mountains the moment she turned eighteen.

Riley hadn't touched Gran's journal for twenty years after that. She'd tried to forget about it, only pulling the book from storage when her thirtieth birthday dawned and she decided she didn't want to spend the rest of her life as a bartender.

"You don't understand," Clark said, voice imploring.

"Oh really?" Riley's blood boiled in her veins. She'd spent

enough time letting a man shame her into ignoring her skills. "What exactly did I miss? That you've got a PhD from Oxford?"

He had the nerve to look at the ground.

"Do you lie to all your dates?" Riley had thought he was so generous, so sincere. A falling fucking angel. She'd practically thrown herself at him last night. Talking about that stupid movie, melting in his arms.

Something that might have been regret flickered across his face, but it was gone as fast as it arrived. "You didn't tell me what you came here to do."

"Are you serious? I told you I came for the curse. I told you my family—"

"Right. I thought you were a sentimental tourist, not someone running a scam."

He hadn't even asked her. Hadn't given Riley the courtesy of the opportunity to defend herself, her business. Had she really been that drowsy from jet lag last night? That overcome by attraction? She knew there was more than one way to be wrong about a person, but apparently, she'd stumbled upon . . . just . . . all of them.

"One of us is deceitful, all right, but it's not me." Riley balled her hands into fists as humiliation burned into a more useful emotion.

Sensing the palatable tension in the room, the project manager stepped forward.

"Miss Rhodes, if I may?" Martin ran a hand through his hair. He had the tall, slightly stretched look of someone who'd shot up over a single summer and never recovered. "Thank you for coming. I was just—"

"Getting ready to fire me?" She kept her tone innocent, inquiring.

This wasn't the first time someone had screwed her over. And besides, Riley had thick skin.

"No. No, of course not." Martin reached forward to clasp her hand in his own. "We need you. I fully believe there's evidence of supernatural forces at work on this property. We need this pesky curse cleared up yesterday."

Clark groaned.

"Haven't you yourself claimed to have tools go missing?" Martin scolded him. "And just last week you reported a spontaneous explosion in the room you were surveying."

"I was in the weapons storeroom." Clark gazed critically at the project manager. "There's enough unstable cannon powder in there, it's a wonder the whole place isn't burned to ash."

"Well." Martin released Riley to tug at the sleeve of his dress shirt. "If you're uncomfortable with Ms. Rhodes's presence on the project, you always have the option to walk away."

"I can assure you," Clark said, pinching the bridge of his nose. "I don't."

"Ah." A somber look passed across Martin's face. "That's right, I forgot."

Forgot what? Riley didn't see anything sympathetic about Clark's position.

"My apologies, Dr. Edgeware." Martin dipped his head. "I simply assumed that since your father arranged this assignment, he could— Well, never mind. We're indebted to him for his referral in our hour of need."

"Wait a minute." Riley stepped forward. "Your last name is Edgeware?"

Just like that guy from the movie. The one she'd basically roasted in front of him. "And he just said 'father' . . . oh my god. Is Alfie Edgeware your dad?!"

Clark winced.

Great. Sure, why not add another log onto the Riley-looks-like-a-fool fire?

"And he got you this job?" She laughed helplessly, holding a sudden stich in her side. "Wow. Gotta love nepotism, I guess. Is that why you were in such a rush to get me out of here? Were you that afraid I'd find out?"

To think she'd had a twelve-hour crush on this dillweed.

"Nothing about you scares me." He held her gaze for a long, heated moment.

It felt like a dare. A challenge to see who would look away first.

Riley didn't care if he feared her—the response she'd been craving her whole life was respect, and clearly, she'd never get that from him.

Everything she'd once found beautiful about Clark's face filled her with rage now. Those dark, heavy brows. The sharp, stubble-lined jaw. His thin, cruel mouth.

"How can you be so sure the curse doesn't exist?" Riley couldn't believe she'd let herself be open and vulnerable with him.

"Occam's razor," Clark said. "That means—"

"I know what it means," Riley cut him off.

The simplest explanation was usually the right one. Usually, but not always.

"You know what?" She brushed her palms off on her jeans. "You don't have to take my word for it. I can prove it."

Clark scoffed. "You're going to prove this place is haunted?"

"Cursed," Riley corrected.

Martin held up a finger. "What's the difference?"

"Whether the person fucking shit up still lives here." It was a common enough misconception, and she would have happily explained the nuance in more detail, but right now Riley needed to wipe the smugness off Clark's face before she did something worse.

Martin thumbed toward the door. "I'll just wait outside, then, shall I?"

"Don't go far." Riley closed her eyes for a moment, anchoring herself. "This won't take long."

Again? Gran asked each time one tracking exercise ended, and the answer had always been yes. Until Riley could follow her nose even in the middle of a summer storm.

There. Underneath the smell of her own bodywash and a spicy, alluring sandalwood and citrus scent she was terrified might be coming from Clark, she had it. Faint but present. A trail.

Riley barreled out of the room and headed for a massive, imposing staircase with weeds sprouting up through cracks in the stone.

"Wait." Clark came up behind her, holding out a long metal flashlight. "If you insist on maintaining this farce, at least take my torch."

Despite the chunks of missing ceiling, it was kinda dark in the castle, devoid as it was of electricity. Riley could track at twilight with only the barest sliver of harvest moon. But she'd known that forest. She'd had Gran at her back. Her plans for vengeance would be wrecked if she twisted her ankle or fell through a hole in the rotting floorboards. She snatched the thing reluctantly.

"Don't think this makes up for you pretending to be nice to me last night."

"I wasn't pretending," he protested, following her as she started up the stairs.

"Oh, please. No one does an about-face that quickly. The least you can do is own the fact that you're an asshole."

"Hey." He used his longer legs to get ahead of her, spinning around and drawing her up short. "I'm not the one who makes money by taking advantage of other people's desperation."

Riley reeled. Was that really what he thought of her?

"I do *not* take advantage of people." She charged a fair fee and had a strict moral code about the types of clients she took on. Only a bitter cynic would see it that way.

"How can you say that? I spent hours poring over your website last night. Your only clients are high school kids and desperate singles."

"Okay, first of all." She grabbed the railing for leverage and shoved him aside. "The Cherry Hill Bobcats didn't hire me themselves. Their football coach commissioned me to break the curse causing their ten-year losing streak."

Clark resumed his pursuit. She could feel the heat coming off his body at her back.

"Second of all, there's nothing desperate about wanting to remove the supernatural forces keeping you from finding love. Courtney Oberhausen is an amazing woman! Where else was she supposed to turn after the third Tinder date in a row tried to open up a bunch of credit cards in her name?" That poor lady had been cheated on, ghosted, negged, and scammed to an outrageous degree. Even for New Jersey.

They took the steps side by side now, Riley quickening her pace to match Clark's longer stride so he couldn't pull ahead. The staircase narrowed as they went up, their shoulders brushing as they fought for advantage.

"And besides, where do you get off trying to claim the moral high ground? You kissed me last night and then turned around and stabbed me in the back this morning." Her lips still stung from the press of his teeth.

"You asked me to kiss you." Clark let out a grunt that could have come from frustration or exertion.

"No, I asked you if you wanted to kiss me." Riley pushed herself forward, her thighs starting to burn. *What was this, a staircase to the moon?* "There's a difference!"

"Fine. I'm the villain here." Clark's breathing had gone slightly labored.

"Correct."

Cobwebs hung like lace from the rafters. Riley made a mental note to invest in some kind of hat so the bleached blond of her hair didn't beckon critters the way it seemed to summon fuckboys.

"I did try to warn you," Clark said, so softly she almost didn't hear.

"What, with that poor, puppy-dog-eyed 'I could be a terrible person' bullshit? Please!" Riley wouldn't be surprised if smoke started coming out of her ears. "Next time," she bit out, "try harder."

Clark tilted his head in confusion. "Next time I kiss you?"

What? "No." *Shit.* Her angry walking turned into angry jogging. "Shut up."

They came to a landing. Not the end of the stairs, but a tight little alcove with a big window.

When she stopped to catch her breath, Clark followed suit.

He looked unmercifully good in the natural light. Handsome. Chiseled. He could have been a fabled prince reincarnated. Riley was pretty sure she hated him.

She didn't want him to know he'd hurt her. From this point forward he wouldn't see the vulnerable, striving Riley, the one who didn't have her footing on this assignment, or in life. He'd see what she wanted: someone cool, confident, and put together.

Behind him, out the window, a flash of steel in sunlight caught her eye.

"What is that?" She shaded her gaze. "Why would someone park a camper—"

Clark stiffened.

No. No one was that silly. That ridiculous and eccentric.

"It's convenient." He folded his arms across his chest. "It allows me to stay on-site when I work."

"It's a Winnebago! Parents buy those to take their kids to national parks."

"It saves time and money during a dig," he said archly.

Riley threw up her arms. "But this isn't a dig. You heard the man downstairs. You're a glorified cleanup crew hired so land developers could dodge historical preservation society regulations." She stood on her tiptoes, trying to see more of the camper. "Does that thing even have a shower?"

He smirked. "Awful quick to think of me naked, love."

"Don't call me pet names." She warned him, hoping he attributed her labored breathing to the climb. Unfortunately, nothing got her hot like a challenge.

"Look." Clark put a placating hand on her arm. "Why don't you give this up now, rather than waste both our time? I mean, seriously, what evidence could you possibly produce?"

"Trust me, *sweetheart*. It's like porn." Riley tapped his cheek twice with her palm. "You'll know it when you see it."

Chapter Four

Clark had hoped he might not be attracted to Riley Rhodes after discovering her nefarious business practices last night. Unfortunately, seeing her this morning, pink-cheeked with rage as she dealt him an impressive verbal flaying, proved that at least his body still fancied her.

Indignation rolled off her in waves so righteous that yes, Clark did feel a little bit bad about trying to get Martin to remove her. But just because Riley claimed innocence of any dodgy dealing, he reminded himself, didn't mean he could believe her.

Clark had a faulty internal compass. He'd trusted Patrick in Cádiz even when the initial scans had seemed too good to be true. Because of one exceedingly well-crafted lie, he'd gotten everything he ever wanted. Accolades, praise, invitations to speak on the international stage. His father had taken him to the club and handed him a Cuban cigar. Clark had thrown up in the loo after smoking it, but still. Things had been brilliant. For a little while.

Awakening had come rude and swift. Retractions printed in the journals. Patrick's termination. His father's long, hard sigh.

Clark needed redemption. His career couldn't be over at thirty-two. Arden Castle wasn't a premier assignment, not even close. But it had potential if, this time, he neutralized the charlatan poised to make a mockery of his work.

It didn't matter if his betrayal wounded Riley. Or if watching her eyes go from wide to shuttered when she realized what he'd done sliced at his insides. Clearly, she'd already recovered enough to go in on him about his dad. He had to harden his resolve.

Clark followed her to where the stairs finally ended, at the top of the southeast guard tower. He hadn't surveyed for artifacts up here yet, but at this point he knew the castle's blueprint like the back of his hand.

"Well, here we are." The small, circular space was no more than twelve paces across in any direction. And there was nothing in it. "You've run out of staircase. What now?"

Clark bet she didn't have a plan. Obviously she'd thought she could sneak up here and regroup, but he hadn't given her the chance.

Ignoring him, Riley flicked off his torch and handed it back to him. A single window let in enough light to illuminate the small space, even with strands of ivy choking the bars. Clark put the torch in his pocket for safekeeping.

As Riley began a turn around the room, Clark couldn't help but admire her performance—the way she paused every now and then to close her eyes, furrowing her brow in concentration. He was almost sorry that her charade would soon come to an end.

Suddenly she stopped, pulled her sleeve down over her palm, and extended her hand toward one of the heavy wooden beams covered in carnivorous-looking weeds that fortified the curved stone wall.

"Don't," Clark warned, instinctually shooting forward.

Riley froze but didn't retract her arm. "Why not?"

"Just"—he yanked his gloves from his belt—"here, take these." Her sleeve barely covered half her hand.

When she didn't reach out, he flapped the fabric at her.

Riley looked down her nose at his offering. "Stop trying to give me things as a way to ease your guilty conscience."

Oh, for the love of— She obviously had no idea what she was doing. This castle was a thousand years old and neglected, full of dangers both structural and elemental. Someone had to look out for her. Since Clark was the only other person here, the burden fell to him. It wasn't like he personally cared if she cut herself on the splintering wood or jagged stone. No one could blame him if, through her own carelessness, that cut got infected and she died.

Willing the uneasiness out of his voice, he made himself look bored.

"Do you really want to touch anything in here with your bare fingers?" He watched for a moment as she battled with her decision, weighing her immense dislike of him and any help he might offer with what he assumed was some small degree of pragmatism.

"Fine." Riley snatched the gloves away, spinning on her heel to give him her back.

Which, honestly? *Not a hardship, love.* The woman possessed a heart-stopping bum. All of her was gorgeously curved. Clark had to run a hand over his face, cutting off the mouthwatering view.

How could he lust after her, knowing what he did about her despicable scheming?

No amount of moral superiority seemed to dampen his ardor. This wasn't like him—he never allowed his emotions to ride this close to the surface. Ever since he was a child he'd been ruthlessly even-keeled, always monitoring, trying to make sure no one got upset—a consequence of growing up with a highly emotional parent. Somehow, Riley Rhodes shorted his fuse.

In hindsight, Clark supposed that with the way his luck had been running, he should have been less surprised when she wiped away a thick sheet of vines from the wall to reveal a dagger stuck between two wooden beams.

While she squealed in triumph, Clark's mouth fell open.

How had she— Where did that— "What the fuck?"

Riley turned to smirk at him over her shoulder. "I told you I knew what I was doing."

Clark stepped closer, half hoping the dagger would disappear like a mirage. But no, the metal glinted when a ray of sunshine struck it.

"I don't understand." He'd been through forty-seven of the castle's ninety-three rooms in the last month and found nothing of value. This property had changed hands so many times in the last three hundred years, had suffered wars and looting and the destruction of countless, terrible Highland winters. And she had just . . . found an entire bloody dagger after fifteen minutes?

Had Riley somehow gotten so lucky that she'd randomly picked the one room hiding a highly valuable artifact? It defied the bounds of logic.

Unless she'd somehow known it was there. Perhaps a villager had given her a tip. It was a stretch, but no more outrageous than the alternative explanation—that she really could do what she claimed.

"Who told you that was there?"

"No one. Unlike you"—she gave him a searing glance—"I'm good enough at my job that I don't need to rely on other people."

Without an ounce of hesitation, Riley wrapped one gloved fist around the dagger's handle, pressing the other hand to the vine-covered wood for purchase, and before Clark could stop her, she yanked.

The wood must have rotted through over the years because the dagger came free with so little resistance that Riley stumbled back a few steps, her warm back falling against his chest.

His hands caught her upper arms, moving instinctually to brace her. For a moment they breathed together, bodies flush.

"Let go of me," Riley said, low and dangerous, as soon as she got her feet under her.

Clark released her at once. Next time, he'd simply let her fall on her perfect backside.

The dagger glinted as Riley lifted it, turning it this way and that.

"Wow." She wiped at the layers of muck that obscured the intricate design of the handle. "It's kinda gorgeous."

For once today, they agreed on something.

Judging by the design, it might date back to the eighteenth century. A silver alloy, he'd guess. Extensive filigree marked it as a private weapon, rather than a military one.

Clark brimmed with wild hope. This was the first real clue to the castle's history. A piece like this could be quite precisely carbondated, its makeup studied to reveal so much in each individual component. He eyeballed the length of the dagger, the delicate nature of the blade.

"It looks like it was made for a woman." The craftsmanship was ornate enough, even without jewels inlaid, that it might have been a gift.

"Yeah?" Riley looked so pleased with herself, practically bouncing from foot to foot as she thrust and parried the dagger in some kind of strange celebration. "Well, amen to that."

Clark had known from an early age that his path would be easier if he did anything other than follow in his father's giant footsteps. Yet he'd spent his summers on dig sites. Scraped knees and sunburns and sleeping on the cold hard ground. Clark loved it, but he'd always lived for this—moments of discovery that helped unravel the mystery of people. Sad as it might sound, he found that distance let him understand the dead much easier than he'd ever understood the living.

That dagger had meant something to someone. They'd held it in their hand, in this room, the same way Riley did now, centuries later in the same spot. For a moment, Clark forgot himself and grinned.

He must have looked like a maniac, because Riley's face changed, her own exuberance skipping like a record.

"See?" She dropped her gaze from his. "I told you I'd prove the curse is real."

"What do you mean?" Clark couldn't explain how she'd found that artifact, but it didn't mean he was ready to attribute the discovery to some kind of magical abilities.

Clark refused to be made to look a fool again. Alfred Edgeware might have been knighted by the sodding Queen Mum for his contributions to English culture, but his family was still new money with blue-collar northern accents and a thousand breaches of etiquette stacking the deck against them.

Even before Cádiz, Clark had grown up on the receiving end of disdain. His dad had shipped him off to boarding school in the Swiss Alps as soon as the first big check from the book cleared, trying to make him fit in with the aristocracy. But Clark had always been an outlier among the peerage of gentleman academics. Had always cared more than the sons of earls and viscounts who got degrees with no intention of ever using them.

"It's just a dagger," he said, tone brooking no argument.

Riley's face hardened. "Just a dagger, huh?" She flipped the weapon end over end in the air, catching it neatly by the handle.

Clark took an involuntary step backward. "Where did you learn that?"

Nothing about the glint in her eye made him comfortable. "You didn't think curses went quietly, did you?"

He swallowed. "Well, don't do anything rash."

"Oh, I wouldn't dream of it." The smile she gave him sent a shiver down his spine, the sensation some terrifying combination of emotions he didn't dare name. "But you see, there's something about this dagger." Riley looked contemplatively at the stone ceiling. "It's like the longer I hold it, the more bloodthirsty I feel."

Clark could see where this was going. He'd pissed her off royally earlier. Now that they were without witnesses, she wanted to make him squirm by pretending to be possessed by some kind of evil spirit or other nonsense.

"Ha ha." He kept his eyes on the blade. "Very amusing."

"No. I'm serious, Clark." Riley prowled toward him, twirling the dagger with alarming flippancy, her generous hips swaying. "It's like this red fog is rolling in across my vision." With each step, she cut off his path to the door.

Somehow, his back found the wall.

"You're trying to fuck with me." His brain knew that, even if his body didn't—all his hair standing on end, adrenaline coursing through his veins. "It won't work."

Riley aimed the blade at his breastbone, the tip of the dagger barely prodding one of the buttons on his shirt. "Are you sure?"

With a flick of her wrist, she sent the small plastic circle plinking off the floor.

Clark's breathing stuttered. There was something about this woman. Clark didn't know how to describe it in words. It wasn't just the danger talking—he was pretty sure he wouldn't get hard from just anyone threatening him at knifepoint—it was her. Not just that she was beautiful—plenty of beautiful people left him cold. Riley was . . . more.

This close, every inhale carried the scent of her shampoo—cheap, artificial strawberry. *Like fucking lube.* He bit off a groan.

"What's the matter?" Riley leaned forward to whisper in his ear, her warm breath falling against his sweat-slick skin. "I thought you weren't afraid of me."

"I'm not," he ground out around his straining jaw. Fear-laced lust threatened to buckle his knees.

"No?" Riley raised the dagger from his chest to rest above the hollow of his bare throat. "You look pretty worked up to me."

This was an absolute nightmare. A woman with no sense of right and wrong held a knife half an inch from his jugular—Clark had to shallow his exhales to avoid getting nicked—and all he could think about was leaning closer, death be damned, so he could kiss her again.

"Tell me something, darling," he said in a desperate attempt to distract himself.

"'Darling,' huh?" Riley sounded almost impressed. "Bold of you to offer me endearments from the business end of a blade."

"Let's say that dagger is cursed." He pressed his palms against his thighs to keep from reaching for her. "Shouldn't you, I don't know, *fix it*?"

"Me? But I'm a charlatan." She moved the dagger until it almost but not quite caressed his pulse point. "Unless you've changed your mind?"

"I haven't." Enough of this game. Clark wrapped his hand loosely around her wrist, the one supporting the dagger. Though he was barely touching her, the threat was there.

"Drop it or I'll make you." He could feel the delicate arrangement of her bones, the strain in her tendons.

Riley stared at his hand and bit her lip.

"Go ahead," she said, sounding a little breathless.

Clark squeezed until her hand flexed, controlling the pressure so she'd be forced to release the weapon.

After a moment of her hectic pulse under his thumb, the dagger clattered to the ground.

They stood like that for a beat, Clark holding her wrist, their furious gazes locked, before Riley wrenched free.

"Just so you know, curses don't work like that."

"What?" Clark barely had enough blood left in his head to breathe, let alone think.

Riley shook out her wrist. "A curse can't brainwash someone. Can't alter free will."

Was she admitting she'd made the whole thing up, then? Not just this little murder foreplay act?

"I'm not following."

Riley pressed her lips together. "Do you believe in fate?"

"No." Clark believed in science.

"Okay, me neither," Riley admitted. "But you get the general concept, right?"

He did. "A fixed sentence by which the order of things is pre-scribed."

"Exactly." Riley's eyes fell absently back to the dagger, still lying in the dirt at their feet. "The parameters of a curse are similar. It can't control how people think or feel, but it can manipulate ex-ternal forces, throw obstacles into your path, obscure information it doesn't want you to find."

She made curses sounded like an interfering busybody. "I think I'm going to need an example."

"It's like with that football team I helped."

Clark nodded. The one from her website.

"Their curse couldn't possess the quarterback and make him throw lousy passes, but it could ensure that pages of his playbook blew away or that the road he always took got closed down for con-struction so he couldn't make it to practice."

Fascinating. If she hadn't just admitted to lying to him, Clark might have felt a twinge of interest in her theories about the supernatural.

"And that curse was only around for a decade. Strength multiples with age. Arden Castle's curse has lasted at least three hundred years."

He picked up the dagger. "I have to give you credit. You've put a lot of depth into your deception."

Even though his gloves were huge on her hands, Clark could still make out Riley giving him the middle finger as she left the room. "I'll let Martin know I've found the first cursed artifact."

"I thought we agreed it wasn't cursed?" he shouted after her. Turning the blade over in his hand, Clark didn't feel any emotional shift. He was still angry and confused and turned on—and still angry and confused about how turned on he was.

"Check your hand," Riley called back.

Sure enough, angry red welts had begun to swell across the palm that gripped the dagger's handle. "Oh, fuck me."

Chapter Five

When incessant knocking woke Riley before dawn the next day, she had a feeling she knew who had come calling.

Quickly, she threw on a pair of jeans and an oversized wool sweater, unwilling to confront the enemy in her pajamas.

Sure enough, when she opened the door—

"What the hell did you do to me?" Clark Edgeware stared back at her, his blotchy fist raised.

"My, my." Riley tsked, not bothering at all to hide her mounting glee. "Someone's grouchy this morning."

She'd ask how he knew where she was staying, but this town had one inn with ten rooms. And she'd learned almost immediately upon arrival that the proprietor enjoyed running his mouth as well as the front desk.

Clark's nostrils flared. "You'd be grouchy too if you'd spent half the night trying to make sure you didn't spread a burning itch to your unmentionables."

Riley looked pointedly at the angry red marks covering his hands and winced. "You should really take care of that."

"Why do you think I'm here? Tell me what you've inflicted upon me so that I can undo it."

Riley leaned against the doorway and gave him a full-body

once-over. Even discounting the hives, he looked different today. His jawline had gone from barely shadowed to full-on ebony stubble. *Must have forgone his morning shave in his rush to come over here and glower.*

With that face, and the type of clothes she'd seen him in the night they met—simple but impeccably tailored, reeking of money—Riley had figured he was too vain. But apparently a visit to her bedroom wasn't worth the effort.

"I'm sorry you're unwell, *Dr. Edgeware.*" Getting to mess with him after he'd mocked her and the curse felt so fucking sweet. "But I simply can't be held responsible for your actions."

It was his own fault, really. Clark had sealed his fate through false chivalry. If he hadn't insisted on giving her his gloves, she would have been the one to wind up splotchy, her sleeve insufficient protection against the stinging nettle wrapped around the dagger.

She'd immediately recognized the leaves sprouting perpendicular to each other in pairs, dark green and oblong with tapering tips—and accepted the risk of retrieving the cursed artifact.

Her grandmother instilled in her early the value of plants and herbs—to help or to hinder—and she'd been studying them ever since.

He looked down his nose at her. "You're claiming a cursed dagger did this?"

"Not exactly." There wasn't a doubt in her mind that the dagger was cursed. It was drenched in scent signature. But she couldn't exactly have said, *Here, smell this,* yesterday without Clark thinking she was even more ridiculous than he already did.

It didn't matter that she knew she was right. No tool existed to populate the kind of evidence he would believe. She had nothing to point to, no way to make him understand what she knew in her bones.

If he wouldn't take her word for it that the dagger was cursed, why should she tell him it had been covered in nettles? She knew he'd reach for the artifact eventually, and had decided to extract a little payback of her own in the meantime.

Honestly? She'd gotten lucky the hives appeared as quickly as they did. Clark appeared to have sensitive skin.

"Charging into a cursed castle and denying the existence of said curse is a textbook way to get your ass handed to you." Riley abandoned the doorway. She'd wasted enough time on Clark Edgeware already.

"Is that what your textbooks said?" He stepped forward onto the paisley-printed carpet, sidestepping Riley's suitcases. Evidently he'd taken the fact that she hadn't slammed the door in his face as permission to follow her inside. "I suppose I shouldn't be surprised, considering the appalling underfunding of the American education system."

Riley popped open a tube of lipstick and leaned toward the mirror over the desk. "It's amazing that you can manage to reek of superiority so soon after getting incapacitated by a common weed."

Riley raised the deep raspberry color to her mouth while reveling in the reflection of the scowl he gave her.

Let him watch her get ready if he wanted to so badly. She certainly wasn't going to entertain him just because he'd invited himself in.

While Clark attempted to melt her with his eyes, she took an obnoxiously long time tracing her lips, blotting, and reapplying until the shade was perfectly vampy.

It wasn't until she'd finished and replaced the cap that she caught a flash of movement out of the corner of her eye. Clark walked over to the corkboard that hung where there had previously been a benign landscape of a field of heather.

"Why have you installed a murder board in your room?"

"It's not a murder board." Though Riley had to admit she saw the similarities. She'd divided the big rectangle into four columns using string—*WHO, WHEN, WHY, HOW*—and then tacked Post-its with ideas and potentially relevant information about the curse underneath each corresponding section.

Marching over, she reached for the Post-it he'd plucked carelessly from its pushpin, but he dodged her at the last second.

"'Clark suggests dagger made for a woman,'" he read aloud, spinning to avoid her. "Is this your professional curse-breaking strategy? Writing down things I say?"

Riley ducked under his arm to snatch the note back, accidentally knocking the metal lipstick tube she still clutched into his knuckles.

Clark hissed, cradling his raw, red hand to his chest. "Ow. Fuck."

She should leave him to suffer. See how many days it took him to work out the right combination of hydrocortisone and antihistamines to clear up the swelling.

But even if said person lived so far up his own ass that he couldn't see daylight—Riley didn't like seeing anyone in pain. She marched into the room's en suite to rifle through her army of lotions and potions, looking for a small brown jar with a homemade label.

It was one of her best concoctions. Adapted from a recipe in Gran's journal, tweaked after reading her mom's old nursing school study guides. Riley had played with the formula for years, swapping St. John's wort for calendula, adding and removing rose, then peppermint.

After finding it at the bottom of her bag, she stared down at where she'd marked the ingredients and the date it was made. Riley knew firsthand this salve helped soothe everything from swelling to irritation in record time—but Clark would probably scoff at anything she gave him.

Well, she told herself, if he did, that would be twice he'd brought about his own misery by underestimating her.

"Here." Coming back into the bedroom, she gently handed him the jar. "That will take the sting out of the welts and reduce the redness until it heals."

Clark traced a thumb across her peeling label, probably finding her handwriting wanting. "You made this?"

Riley nodded. She'd always found the medicinal applications of plants interesting—had even thought about becoming a nurse, like her mom, after high school.

But she hadn't ended up finishing more than two semesters of college. Her mother had wanted her to go, had taken out the loans to make it possible, but Riley saw the way the mounting bills—not just tuition but textbooks and lab supplies—stressed her out. How she sat at the kitchen table after the late shift at work, doing the math on an old yellow legal pad over and over.

I didn't like it, Riley had said, casually mentioning that she'd dropped out on an average Tuesday. Her mother hadn't said anything in reply, just kissed her hair on her way out the door as she headed back to work another double.

Clark took the top off the jar and stuck his nose in, wrinkling it after a moment. "Smells like a candy cane."

"Then don't use it." Riley reached to take it back, but once again he eluded her. *Damn his superior wingspan.*

"Now, wait a moment." Clark studied her reaction while he held the mixture out of reach. She had a feeling he treated everyone like slides under a microscope. "That was a neutral observation. I haven't rejected your act of mercy."

"Yeah, well." She exhaled heavily through her nose, reminding herself that she was trying to appear calm and unaffected. "Don't get used to it."

"I won't," he said softly, looking down at her offering in his hands. "But thank you." He raised his gaze to meet her eyes. "You didn't have to do this. I appreciate it."

It wasn't even praise, not really, but something in her warmed anyway.

He won't lose sight of the battle, she reminded herself. *He'll look for the first opportunity to undermine you again.* He hadn't even agreed to let her take the dagger she had found back to the inn so she could study it. Martin had made them compromise by keeping anything either of them uncovered at the castle in one of Clark's firesafe boxes.

"On second thought, you know what, never mind. Please go ahead and let this interaction lure you into a false sense of security before we both make our way back to the castle this morning."

Clark gave a low laugh. "I suppose I'll see you there."

Riley experienced a moment of mourning for the man she'd met in the pub—the one who had seemed entertained by her eccentricity rather than annoyed by it.

He almost made it to the hallway before tripping over the strap of a bra gone rogue from her half-unpacked luggage.

At least it was one of her nicer ones.

Clark's face flushed to complement the hot-pink lace. Crouching to remove it from his ankle brought him eye level with her jeans. "You're not planning to wear those trousers to work in the castle, are you?"

"I was." Riley ran her hands down the front of her pants, checking for stains or holes she might have missed, but no, they were fine. "Why? What's wrong with them?"

"You can't be serious." He stood up, scowling. "Look at the state of the cuffs."

"Ummmm." She guessed they were kind of frayed.

"The castle is dangerous. There's loose stonework, insufficient lighting, overgrowth-obstructed ledges." He made a beeline for her dresser. "What else have you got?"

"Excuse me." Riley rushed forward to press her back to the wooden drawers, keeping them closed. "There's no way in hell I'm letting you root through my clothes."

The depths of his arrogance were astounding. Only someone born with a silver spoon in their mouth would dream they were entitled to tell others what to wear.

Clark ran his fingers through his dark hair, looking harassed. "What if I ask nicely?"

Riley snorted. "Not even if you got down on your knees."

They both stilled. *Why had that come out sounding like an invitation?*

"I—ah . . ." When Clark bit his lip, looking not altogether opposed to the idea, Riley rubbed absently at her wrist, finding the heightened kick of her pulse and an echo of the firm clench of Clark's fingers. The way he'd applied pressure had been so measured, even as his eyes had devoured her. Just hard enough to make her feel it.

Under her sweater, her nipples tightened. *Shit.*

"Don't even think about it," She might have been talking to herself, but he didn't need to know that.

Clark cleared his throat. "If you're so desperate to keep this job, at least put a thought to the risks."

"Call me desperate one more time." Riley gave him the smile she reserved for men who thought they could tip their way into her pants.

He pressed his hand to his chest, rubbing, as if the next words came carved from his skin. "I'm just trying to keep you safe."

No, she told the part of herself that wanted to sag against the dresser at those words. *Don't listen to him.*

Riley didn't blame her mom for turning away from curse breaking—mostly she didn't—but sometimes she wished someone had her back on these assignments. Wished for more guidance, more comfort than the curling pages of Gran's journal could provide.

She loved curse breaking, critics be damned. But her calling came at a cost. It meant she was alone. Not just here, so far from home, but in life. Always removed. Othered.

It was a cheap shot from the universe, the way Clark looked at her. So handsomely earnest.

"You can't try to get me fired and then claim to care about my well-being." If he really gave a damn what happened to her, he wouldn't have decided his ambitions mattered and hers didn't.

"Fine." Clark clenched his jaw. "I knew you'd make everything difficult."

Ugh. Her blood heated.

"You're the one who invited yourself into my bedroom!" She hadn't asked for a fashion consultation any more than she'd asked to have her emotions chewed up and spit out from the moment they'd met. "I'll have you know that these jeans have survived eight-hour shifts slinging pickleback shots for irate Philadelphia sports fans. That's right, for the guys who threw snowballs at Santa Claus."

Clark tilted his head. "Are you saying you're a bartender?"

Oops. *Way to go, Riley.* Why not hand him fresh ammunition for his "she's a fraud" campaign? He would reach for his phone any second now, ready to dial Martin.

"Look." She folded her arms. "Not that I need to justify anything to you, but the curse-breaking business—not the practice, but the actual charging-people thing—is kind of new for me. And it's not so lucrative yet. Especially with British jerks trying to get me kicked off assignments."

Clark lowered his chin, just slightly, in acknowledgment.

"I pick up shifts when I need to, and the bar is actually a great place to find curse-breaking leads. More than one of my clients started as a customer coming to drown their sorrows without realizing their repeated problems had supernatural origins. I'm starting to build a pretty robust referral network."

"I see," he said, but his dark brows drew together. "Actually, no. I don't. You're obviously enterprising. Why would you place your bet on curse breaking?"

Right. Her choice must seem silly and shortsighted to him.

But the answer to his question was complicated, messy.

Part of Riley pursued curse breaking to honor the Rhodes women who raised her—alone—with limited means and without the luxury of a safety net to fall back on. Another part wanted to help people, to protect them, give them a path to healing.

Some of the individuals she worked with suffered the consequences of a curse for years while well-meaning friends and family told them their experiences came down to nothing more than coincidence or chance. When she took their fears at face value, Riley saw in their eyes, their posture, that they were grateful simply to be believed.

But there was a last part, one she could only admit to herself on dark days—a selfish need to be special. Someone who could do what others couldn't.

Riley liked who she was when she broke a curse. Powerful, useful, respected. Needed—even if only temporarily.

Yet in her gut, Riley knew none of those answers would appease Clark.

"I think we both know nothing I say will make you see what I do as anything more than a scam." Clark had already proven that he'd never believe something he couldn't understand.

"Perhaps you're right," he said eventually, but then, as if he couldn't help himself, added, "But you must know you're facing an uphill battle. If money is a concern, surely there's something else you could do? An easier path."

Riley almost wanted to laugh. How like a man to think he could waltz into her life and provide the solution she'd failed to see hanging right in front of her face.

"You know what? You're right." She slapped her forehead. "I should just do something easier. *Thanks so much for bringing that opportunity to my attention.*"

"Ah." Clark grimaced, looking genuinely regretful. "That was clumsy of me. I wasn't trying to insult you."

Wasn't he?

"Right." Riley scoffed. "I'm sure it's just a consequence of growing up a sheltered snob who's built a career trading on Daddy's name." Her job was dangerous enough without getting repeatedly bulldozed by the last person she'd kissed.

Clark's face went white and then crimson.

But she hadn't said anything that wasn't true. Riley let the fumes of her anger drown out any traces of guilt.

"Let's be clear about what's happened here. You did your very best to undermine me in front of my employer." She stepped forward so they stood toe-to-toe. "You've insulted my character, my work ethic, and now my intelligence."

He shook his head. "I didn't mean to—"

"If you had even an ounce of honor," she said over his interruption, "you'd pack up your shit and go home. Because I promise I'm not leaving, and if the opportunity arises to pay you back, I'm going to take it."

"Despite what you think"—his tone was tight, his hands folded behind his back—"I can't afford to abandon this job."

Riley recognized the words he'd fed to Martin.

"My career hinges on making something of this mockery of an assignment, but—" His words lost their razor edge. Clark ran his hand through his hair, looking frustrated, like she kept getting in the way of his plans. "It doesn't have to be a battle between us."

Ha. Easy for him to say. They might both have something to prove professionally, but without the security of Clark's father's money and connections, Riley would always have more to lose.

"I promise you," she said, feeling the potential of this assignment to make or break her, knowing that Clark's soft mouth could cut her down as sure as the dagger they'd found, "it does."

"Very well, then." His posture changed, hardened, as any attempts to be conciliatory gave way to challenge.

Riley might have done the noble thing, declaring her intentions, but the wicked glint in his eyes said she'd come to regret it.

"Enemies it is," Clark said, all crisp consonants and barely leashed scorn. "Do your worst."

Chapter Six

For the record, Clark knew something like this would happen.

Ideally, after throwing down the gauntlet outside Riley's room, he could have stormed off, metaphorical cloak swishing. But in actuality, they were both headed to the castle—both leaving at the same time—so what transpired was an incredibly awkward walk over. He had a few minutes' advantage and did his best to hurry without looking like he was hurrying, but he never really managed to pull more than a kilometer or two ahead of her.

"I'll be working in the music salon today," Clark told her when they both reached the front gate. "All I ask is that you don't get in my way."

"Whatever." Riley waved him off. "I'm taking the dagger for the morning."

"What do you plan to— You know what, never mind." The less he knew, the better. Clark needed to maintain plausible deniability for whatever calamity she undoubtedly caused. "Just try not to damage it." It pained him to allow her to handle any historical artifacts, but thanks to the HES's apathy and Martin's refusal to see sense, he didn't exactly have the jurisdiction to stop her.

Once they'd parted ways, heading down separate wings, Clark set up shop. He unpacked his tools and his trusty solar-powered

Bluetooth speaker, as well as some battery-operated lanterns to supplement the low light coming through the dusty windows.

With a mixture of gratitude and trepidation, he applied the salve Riley had given him, letting out a deep sigh as the fragrant mixture soothed his irritated skin. Assuming the concoction didn't eventually turn his hands purple or something, it had been nice of her to offer it. Surprisingly nice, considering he'd done nothing but piss her off over the last twenty-four hours. He still had no idea how she'd managed to cause the irritation. Perhaps he had an allergic reaction to something in the tower and she'd merely taken advantage of convenient timing.

Despite her acerbic pronouncement that they were at war, he did hope some degree of civility could be maintained during their shared time in the castle. Ignoring her would be a challenge, but if Clark simply kept to his system, he might finish his work here with minimal additional interruption.

He wanted to do a good job even though his assignment was a sham. As Patrick had pointed out somewhere around sixth form, Clark had always been desperate for approval. Still, this poor, maligned castle deserved better than to fall to capitalist wolves without proper attention worthy of its legacy. Arden had been shaped and sieged, burned and reclaimed, from a thirteenth-century fortress to a fifteenth-century clan seat, until it was finally made into a manor house at the end of the 1700s.

Rumors of an alleged curse contributed to ownership of the estate passing like a hot potato between minor aristocracy and private investors over the last few centuries. No one lasted long enough to finish anything they started. Everywhere he looked he found scaffolding, half-laid floors, peeling wallpaper, and faded frescoes.

On the bright side, this room was in better shape than most of the others. Though water damage had turned a formerly white ceiling brown, and the wood frames of the walls—bent and warped—were now held up by metal beams from previous, abandoned restoration efforts, partial remains of moldings and golden sconces hinted at former grandeur.

This wasn't a proper excavation—he didn't have license to dig—but Clark still segmented each accessible room with gaffer's tape and a digital measuring device, adapting a survey method to make sure he searched for artifacts in the closest proximity to a scientific process as he could. It was why, in addition to the random mishaps Martin had mentioned, he was taking longer than projected to complete the contracted review.

Carefully, he sifted through piles of detritus and debris. Other scientists might have rushed this job, and the HES even seemed to expect him to—certainly Martin would have preferred it—but this work was about more than professional redemption for him. Clark needed to prove to himself that he could work without Patrick—that he was fine—*look how fine he was*—after the betrayal, the months of despondency that followed.

He would make the best of a bad situation. As it turned out, solitary work suited him. The sudden end of invitations, both personal and professional, had troubled him originally. But now he found isolation no more painful than a fading bruise, an affliction that only hurt when he pressed on it.

In the six months since the scandal broke, Clark had grown a tolerance for loneliness—had learned to fill the silence with classical music, concertos so frenetic, so transportive, he lost himself in the notes. Accompanied by Johann Sebastian Bach, he could fix this mess of an assignment. And himself. Soon—any minute now—he'd stop feeling like the only person who had ever really liked him must have lied about that too.

At first, when the second Brandenburg Concerto cut out, he

assumed the batteries on his speaker had died. The castle had given him a hard time since he got here. Nothing at the caliber of a "curse," mind you—all sites had their challenges and quirks. This one was simply more . . . tenacious. But then . . . a new song began, a sort of vaguely familiar drumbeat.

Had his phone somehow shuffled to another random playlist? Clark's face folded in confusion. Then the lyrics started—

> *I've known a few guys who thought they were pretty smart*
> *But you've got being right down to an art*

What in the name of . . .

> *You think you're a genius, you drive me up the wall*

Marching over, Clark picked up the speaker and, sure enough, it read, *Connected device: Riley's iPhone.*

He made a noise alarmingly reminiscent of a chicken. This kind of tomfoolery—this lack of respect for a professional working environment—was exactly why he hadn't wanted that woman on his site. Hijacking his speaker was so completely juvenile. And her song choice. Some people had no taste at all.

> *Oh-oh, you think you're special*

Hold on . . . Surely, the lyrics weren't specifically directed at him? No. She wouldn't. Would she?

Clearly Riley had chosen a song to annoy him—a cheerful girl-power ballad—but it wasn't like she thought he was—

The song switched abruptly, the next opening with a set of unmistakable strings.

Clark stared down at the speaker with mounting dread, waiting for the singing to start.

You walked into the party like you were walking onto a
  yacht

Oh, for Christ's sake. He wasn't even vain!

Growing up he'd been nothing special. Overlarge ears, puppy fat. He'd thinned out when his delayed growth spurt finally deigned to arrive—two years too late. Around the same time he'd finally grown into his teeth.

Clark knew what he looked like now, knew some people liked it, but he didn't take any particular pleasure in his appearance. In fact, he often found his face an obstacle to connection—people were quick to project fantasies onto him that left little room for reality.

As Carly Simon continued to mock him, Clark seethed. He couldn't let this indignity stand. He had no choice but to avenge himself. If her phone was in range to connect—two could play this game.

But what song to choose? He needed artillery against her invasion. Something that showed he wasn't the pompous elitist she presumed. As he scrolled through his playlists, nothing was quite right. Thumbing to the search bar he typed in *vengeful woman*, but all he got were playlists full of Fiona Apple and Taylor Swift. What the fuck? A muscle ticked in his jaw.

Until, finally, he found the perfect choice. He even head bobbed a little to the intro.

American woman
Stay away from me

Clark turned up the volume.

American woman
Mama, let me be

He smirked. Let her come back from that one.

It barely took her until the third chorus, the music once again switching with an abrupt *click*.

Payback is a bad bitch
And baby, I'm the baddest

He rolled his eyes. Who even sang this? Some teenager?

Now you're out here looking like regret
Ain't too proud to beg, second chance, you'll never get

Jesus. Clark barely stopped himself from laughing, muffling the impulse with his fist. He was almost having fun—he had to put a stop to this at once.

Urgently, he hit the off button on the speaker, plunging the room back into silence. He simply couldn't tolerate these types of time-wasting pranks. Setting down the device, he went to find her. They were about to have a very strongly worded conversation.

"Riley," he called, heading through the granary toward the servant's hall. She couldn't have gone that far and still been in range.

A few steps farther and an acrid smell hit his nose. *Was that—* Clark sped up, breaking into a jog when the hint of smoke grew stronger.

"RILEY." Clark burst into the hall to find her with her back to him, standing in front of the hearth. "Tell me you're not intentionally starting a fire."

She arched to look at him over her shoulder. "You want me to lie?"

Was he not due a break? Did he truly deserve these incessant torments? Had he not spent enough of his life picking up the pieces of someone else's recklessness?

His father was gifted and important, and everything else fell to the wayside. Payments to Clark's school he said he'd taken care of, doctor's appointments for Mum. Every family holiday was at the mercy of his career. Clark had learned to double- and triple-check every contract, schedule, and commitment, to pay extra for travel insurance, to remain always, always on guard.

He marched forward. "What could possibly possess you to do something so reckless?"

"I'm using the fireplace," Riley protested.

Indeed, she'd placed a small pile of dried sticks and brush in the blackened hearth and held a matchstick, still smoldering, between her fingers.

Where should he even begin to list the number of problems with that plan? Oh, yes, how about, "That hearth has likely been blocked for a century."

"Oh." She stared at her tiny blaze, the flames merrily dancing in shades of orange and gold, then bent her knees to try to see up the flue. "That's not good."

At least the floor in this room was dirt. Muttering under his breath, Clark began using his boots to kick together a pile large enough to douse the fire.

"Next time you're cold, try putting on a hat."

Seeing what he was doing, Riley began to help using her own boots. "Please. I'm not that delicate."

Her words drew his eyes from her feet up her thick thighs, the wide sweep of her hips, the sweet dip of her waist. Clark dragged his gaze away before he could get any higher.

"I wanted to run a diagnostic on the dagger we found."

A diagnostic? But then why— "Wait, were you going to put the dagger *in* the fire?"

He hadn't thought he could lose his composure any further today, but once again Riley had gotten the better of him.

Kneeling, he began sweeping dirt from the pile into his cupped hands.

"I know Martin said you could examine the artifacts you find—against my advisement, I might add—but that doesn't mean you can treat them so cavalierly, pursuing every whimsical idea that pops into your head."

"I'm not just making things up as I go along." Mirroring him, Riley scooped her own dirt, the two of them beginning to douse the fire. "My gran had a process for curse breaking. A system of analysis and elimination."

Heat from the rapidly dying flames warmed Clark's hands, his arms. "What kind of process, exactly?"

"Why should I tell you?" A scowl sat wrong on her features. Her rosy apple cheeks and softly dimpled chin were made for exuberance. "I don't care whether you believe me or not."

It was starting to seem impossible that they'd ever spent a whole evening sharing drinks without arguing. Let alone just two days ago. At this rate, Riley Rhodes would never smile at him again without malice. It was a shame. She had a remarkable mouth.

Clark thought of the care she'd taken with her website. The business card. How defensive she'd been when she handed him that salve this morning.

"I think you do," he said slowly.

Riley bristled. "Excuse me?"

"Your whole attitude is armor." Clark let the scientist side of his brain take over, giving in to the impulse to read her like a discovery. "Why do you think even innocuous questions sound like insults to your ears?"

"Because you're a dick?" She threw her last handful of dirt into the hearth at such an angle that some blew back on his shirt.

"You care what I think anyway." The blaze dimmed to smolders. Clark removed a handkerchief from his back pocket to clean his hands. "Even though it kills you."

He extended the cloth to her, but with a storm brewing in her eyes, Riley wiped her filthy hands on her denims—the ones he hadn't wanted her to wear.

"You want me to eat crow? Fine." His curiosity about Riley, about the increasingly elaborate folds of her story, persisted like an itch Clark couldn't seem to resist scratching, even as he knew doing so would only make things worse. "Tell me how curse breaking works."

If he had to spend an indeterminate amount of time around her, he wanted to know what she planned to do. Even more, he found he wanted to know how she thought. How she'd built a compelling business proposition out of smoke and mirrors. Worst of all, he'd discovered an unparalleled delight in provoking her. His whole body hummed with anticipation for her next move. Would she strike or parry?

Riley shook her head at the ground, full lips pressed tight together, and Clark thought for sure the game, this game at least, had ended, but then—

"Every curse is different." The hard edge in her voice said she'd make him pay for this, even as she kept talking. "But there are four main techniques, applied in isolation or combination, on an ascending scale of difficulty. Charms, cleansing, sacrifice, and rituals."

"The fire tells you which one to use?" That sounded . . . remarkably practical.

If someone had asked him to describe artificial magical lore, he would have come up with something much more loosey-goosey. The way Riley described curse breaking was almost scientific.

"Sometimes. It depends on the age and origin of the curse—" Her next few words were cut off by a sudden, intense gust of wind, so strong it rattled the remains of the kitchen's wooden shelving.

Both Riley and Clark turned toward the room's set of busted windows, but the source of the current seemed to come from behind them, instead, from the doorway.

"There must be some kind of cross breeze coming from the other side of the castle," Clark said, coughing a bit as the wind caught and carried ash from the hearth, scattering orange embers at their feet.

"You think this is *normal*?" Riley threw up her arms, protecting her face from the gray clouds as another gust tore through, this one seemingly from the opposite direction.

By the time they could both open their eyes, they had other problems.

"Something's burning," Clark said at the exact same moment that Riley looked down and screamed.

The second he saw the flame starting to lick up the loose fringe of her trouser cuffs, he didn't think, just wrapped one arm around her waist and used the other to cradle the back of her skull as he threw them both to the ground.

He landed hard on his back in the packed earth, his teeth clacking together.

"Roll," he commanded, flinging them both bodily to the side, hoping the combination of momentum and the coverage of his body worked to smother the small flame.

For several dizzy seconds he could hear nothing, see nothing, think of nothing but how blankly terrified he was and taste the dirt in his mouth.

They kept rolling until they hit the far wall of the room. Pushing up to his knees, Clark frantically checked to see if her black, smoking hem had gone out.

"Did it get you?" The damaged fabric didn't appear to reach higher than her ankle, and she had on thick boots, but—

"No." Her voice shook a little as she sat up on her elbows. "No, I don't think so."

Carefully, Clark reached for her, tugging up from the untouched part of her jeans to reveal the boots and the tops of her ice-cream-patterned socks, both unburned, as well as the smooth, pale skin of her lower calf.

He should have stopped there, but Clark caught a glimpse of pink scar, and his hand acted of its own accord, shoving the fabric higher toward her knee, heart stuttering.

"That's old," Riley protested, and Clark could see now that it was, jagged and faded. "I got caught in a barbed-wire chicken fence last year, helping a farmer whose crops had suffered several years of blight."

Clark's thumb traced another scar, small and white across her knee. "And this?"

"That was my fault." She stared at his hand on her skin rather than look at his face. "I was gathering blackberries for a cleansing solution, and I knelt on a thorn."

For some reason, Clark's throat hurt, each swallow sharp and tight. "You get hurt a lot?"

"It's part of the gig," she said, finally tugging the fabric back down.

"Right." Clark shoved his hands in his pockets.

She's fine. Look at her, she's okay now.

Everyone had scars. It didn't make sense that he wanted to treat these old wounds as if they were fresh—as if Riley would have let him. She wasn't his dad, coming home with bruises, laughing around a split lip. Telling Clark to grab the first aid kit so he could see to some sutures he'd accidentally torn.

You're too controlling, Patrick had said, scolding at the end of another long day in the sun because he'd insisted on repackaging all the samples after an intern had used the wrong method. It was a weakness. And one of the reasons why Clark had bitten his tongue for so long in Spain.

For years he'd been told he was overbearing, relentless in his expectations for himself and others. Until one day Patrick said, *Relax. Trust me.* And out of love and a desire to be better, Clark had made himself do it.

Not anymore.

"There are rules on an archaeological site." He scrubbed a hand over his face. "In fact, I'm pretty sure there are rules on any job site—*especially when that job site is a giant, ancient, crumbling castle.*"

Riley nodded, the serious look she was going for slightly undercut by the mussed, dirt-laden state of her ponytail.

"I understand that you're upset."

"No." Clark got to his feet. "I'm not upset. I am . . ." Shaken. Unmoored. ". . . irate."

"Oh boy," Riley muttered, standing herself.

"I'll never be able to get my work done"—he tried to instill every ounce of authority he possessed into his tone—"if I'm constantly babysitting you."

"Babysitting? Are you fucking kidding me?" Riley threw up her hands. "How about this—just stay away from me."

As much as he'd like to agree to such a simple suggestion, Clark couldn't. "I won't be able to stop worrying about you."

"You don't even like me." She barely bit out the sentence around her mounting fury.

"That's not the point." It also wasn't completely true. Not that Clark needed her knowing how difficult he found it to write her off. "If we're sharing a site, you have to follow basic safety procedures. It's nonnegotiable."

"Oh really?" She opened her mouth, presumably to tell him exactly where he could shove his demands, but then something seemed to occur to her. "Wait a minute. Maybe there's a way for both of us to get what we want here."

"I'm sorry. What is it that you want?" Besides to send him to an early grave.

"I want your help."

His help? With what?

"I'm afraid I don't have any magical powers."

"Cute." She scoffed. "But what I meant was I want your research on Arden."

In negotiation, Riley had the calm, relaxed air of an experienced bargainer. He could imagine her at a car dealership, wearing down a salesman until he gave her the employee rate. "That book you had at the bar, I read it last night. It's useful, but not enough. I bet there's plenty more where that came from."

She wasn't wrong.

Clark had used the research exercise to pull him out of his Long Winter of Despondency. He didn't just have books and journals, but collections of historical and topographic maps of the region, town and county records, aerial photographs, even soil maps. In the wake of the three dark, numb months that had followed the scandal, Clark had exhausted all available resources on Arden Castle while preparing for his arrival.

He supposed Riley might find his materials useful in her paranormal diagnostics. *Since burning them both to the ground hadn't worked.*

"You have access to stuff I could never get my hands on alone," she continued. "I'll bet your credentials can get you into any university database or private collection you want. Plus, you had the luxury of time."

It was an astute assessment born of a keen eye. Once again, he was forced to evolve his understanding of his opponent.

"All right. Let's say I allow you access to my research. With supervision. What exactly are you offering in return?" Through sheer force of will, he kept his mind blank of any indecent exchange.

"It's simple. Lend me your research, and I'll follow whatever safety procedures you want."

Despite himself, her hook landed. "You'll wear appropriate protective equipment?"

"Sure, if you pay for it."

"And I get final approval over your work outfits?"

"No. Weirdo. But you can give me some general guidelines and I'll consider them."

It was the most insulting deal he'd ever heard.

"So, you get everything you want, and I get to spend money."

Riley Rhodes was dangerous in more ways than he'd ever imagined. She'd seen his vulnerability and shrewdly capitalized on it for her own gain, shoring up her weaknesses as she put herself in prime position to sabotage him.

"True, but you are getting peace of mind." She patted him consolingly on the shoulder. "Can you really put a price on that?"

"I'm getting fleeced." And he didn't feel anywhere close to bad enough about it.

"Does that mean we have a deal?" Her face said she already knew she'd won.

And she had, because Clark's breathing had finally slowed, his vision clearing. He'd have done worse, he realized with no small sense of terror, in the hopes of protecting her from herself.

"We have an accord." Clark held out his palm. "Please don't spit in your hand to seal it."

He'd seen that in a Western once and wasn't entirely sure Americans hadn't maintained it as a custom.

"No need." Her grip was firm, the handshake as easy and confident as her smile. "We've already kissed."

Chapter Seven

As the sun set, Riley entered enemy territory.

"It's a restored Airstream from 1978." Clark opened the door to his camper, gesturing for her to climb in.

He'd insisted she review his research here, in his home, rather than letting her take books back to her own room at the inn. *Apparently* she couldn't be trusted not to damage them.

They entered into the "living room." Against the wall, he'd arranged a merlot two-seater sofa with a floor lamp beside it. There was even a little navy rug over the laminate flooring.

He'd furnished the place in clean, sharp angles and rounded lines. In dark wood and pops of color. He even had art—old, framed maps and a black-and-white shot of a canyon that made Riley ache in that specific way that came from seeing something beautiful that nature made, something that people, with all their tools and innovation, could never quite capture.

"Wow. This is . . . actually nice." Riley didn't know what she'd been expecting—maybe something stark to prove he didn't need comfort or something hopelessly retro, a relic of the camper's previous life, to prove he never bothered to make things his own, but the interior suited him somehow.

"Your surprise is noted," Clark said without smiling.

Against the opposite wall sat a workspace, clearly very much in use. A table folded down from the wall like a Murphy bed, scattered with pens and notebooks, two cameras, and a set of binoculars, as well as playing cards laid out in the middle of what looked like a game of solitaire.

It felt strangely intimate, seeing his home, his things. Like accidentally walking in on someone half-dressed.

An abandoned mug, with a dried tea bag still pressed to the enamel side, sat on a coaster next to a book left face down to mark the page. Riley could picture Clark letting the tea cool at his elbow, distracted by reading some scintillating recap of yet another medieval battle.

"Would you mind taking off your shoes?" Clark bent to untie his own boots, stacking them neatly on a little stand by the door. He wore thick green socks, made of that heavy wool blend that cost a fortune, that you could only find at specialty stores like Patagonia or EMS. Riley had gotten her mom a pair for Christmas one year. She wore them every winter, wiggling her toes in Riley's lap while they watched the Great British Bake Off.

Telling herself to stop staring at his feet, she followed his lead.

Since her second, "appropriately constructed" fire hadn't yielded any indication of the type of curse she faced, as usual, she was flying without a map. Getting access to Clark's research was more important than ever. Even if that meant working under his supervision.

He flicked on a set of recessed lighting that went all the way to the back of the camper.

"Did you, uh, want a tour?"

Apparently those posh British manners would not be suppressed.

"Why not?" Her mom had always said the best way to get over

a crush was to picture them on roller skates. The more Riley learned about Clark, the better her chances of squashing her inconvenient, lingering attraction to him.

It wasn't even like that many horny feelings remained. Her body was just confused from the whiplash of meeting him, kissing him, swearing to exact revenge, and then having him kinda sorta save her from, if not death, then at least disfigurement. It was fine. Just some wonky brain chemicals. All she needed was to see his toothpaste-stained mirror and the pile of dirty socks next to his bed to nip the last of it in the bud.

"This is the kitchenette," Clark said, awkwardly gesturing at the sink and then the small two-burner stove with the mini fridge beside it.

He'd made good use of the tight space, with hanging shelves that held neat glass jars filled with things like rolled oats, dried fruit, whole-grain pasta, and assorted nuts. He probably mixed himself a bowl of muesli every morning—reciting all the health benefits of fiber between bites.

"Would you like a drink?" He opened the mini fridge and peered inside. "I have water, or I could put the kettle on for tea?"

"No, thanks, I'm all right." It was weird, having him be nice to her. Riley knew he resented the bargain she'd gotten out of him, but clearly he couldn't bring himself to be flat-out rude to a guest. "I've got my water bottle in my bag."

Closing the fridge with a nod, he led her forward to the other end of the camper, where he had a queen-sized bed, neatly made with a sober, dark plaid comforter and an impressive four (matching!) pillows. A big step up from the distressingly large number of men she'd slept with who, even into their early thirties, still kept their mattresses on the floor and offered her half of a single bare pillow.

But the bed didn't hold her interest for long. No, it was the bookshelves that arched above it, curving toward the emergency hatch in the ceiling in carefully designed angles that kept the books straight.

"Whoa." She stepped forward to thumb across the spines on the nearest shelf, careful for some reason not to let her knees brush the end of the bed.

Clark had built himself—or more likely paid someone else to build him—a library on wheels. Amid the expected textbooks and journals were pulpy mysteries, the covers worn and fading but obviously well cared for. It hit her then—he was a filthy little hypocrite.

"Hey! You claim not to believe in anything supernatural, but these books, they're all like *Creature from the Black Lagoon* and shit."

Clark folded his arms, leaning his back against the wall between the bedroom and the kitchen. "It's called knowing the difference between fact and fiction."

She had a reply poised like a dart on her tongue, but her gaze snagged in that same moment on something—a picture frame—shoved into the small space between the bed and the bookcase, the only thing she'd seen so far that seemed noticeably out of place.

"Something fell." She reached for it, pulling out the picture—what looked like a hand-drawn sketch of a temple, twin columns guarding the entrance. In the bottom corner was a label.

"What's the Lost Temple of Hercules?"

Clark's breath hitched. "It was once one of the most important sanctuaries in the Western world," he said, voice stilted. "According to ancient accounts, it's the place where Julius Caesar wept after seeing a depiction of Alexander the Great."

He held out his hand and Riley forfeited the frame.

"It's sort of a holy grail for archaeologists. People have been looking for it for centuries." Clark stared down at the sketch. "My dad was obsessed with it when I was a kid." He thumbed across the hastily scrawled label. "He drew this."

"Oh. That's neat." Obviously Riley knew what it meant to share a family obsession. "Did anyone ever find it?"

"Someone said they did." Clark hardened his jaw. "About a year ago, a pair of archaeologists went looking for it," he explained. "They used a newer methodology, digital terrain modeling, to trace a shallow channel in the Bay of Cádiz."

"What's digital terrain modeling?" Was the sharp edge in his voice professional jealousy?

"It's called lidar. It's basically 3D laser scanning." Clark dropped his arm, letting the picture fall to his side. "By targeting an object or a surface with a laser and then measuring the time for the reflected light to return to the receiver, you can create high-resolution models of topography."

Riley whistled. "Sounds fancy."

"It is. The technique gets used a fair amount now in archaeology, especially for environments that are as marshy and hard to access as the bay. But the technology is advanced, and you need specific training for it." Clark swallowed. It looked painful.

"Did you study it or something?"

"No, but my—" He pressed his lips together. "No."

Riley no longer thought the picture had fallen. He didn't speak with the distance of someone who had read about this discovery or heard about it casually through the grapevine.

"What happened? Someone faked the scans?"

"Yes." His face had gone strained, his cheeks hollowed. "One of the archaeologists altered the topography mapping to create the impression that a larger structure had been identified."

He shook his head.

"It was a clever ruse, until it wasn't. Because of the nature of the terrain and the tides, the laser renderings were printed and circulated six months before digging could begin."

Dropping his gaze to the floor, Clark sighed.

"You can do a lot in six months—conferences and press, dinners and donors. Finding an elusive, ancient landmark will make you a hero in certain circles. Someone even my famous father couldn't help but admire. It's heady. When it's finally your name printed on the accolades and invitations—at least until people start to notice your story doesn't add up."

Pieces slotted together. Why Clark had taken this job. Had needed a referral from his dad. The defensive crouch he'd gone into over his reputation when he found out her occupation. "Was it a big scandal, when the truth came out?"

Clark smiled ruefully, looking out the window to the castle. "Career-ruining, you might say."

The bitterness in his tone wasn't just regret. No. There was a deeper wound beneath his words. One that said he'd lost more than his professional status in the fallout. Riley knew she made him uncomfortable in many ways, but what Clark seemed to fear most about her was being deceived.

"Your partner lied to you."

His eyes jerked back to her face. "What makes you think I wasn't the duplicitous bastard?"

And she supposed that should have tracked. After all, look at the way he'd treated her. But . . .

"You kept the picture." Tucked away out of sight, but close enough he could reach for it, even in the dark. "Guilty people don't like reminders of their crimes. But when you get betrayed," she said, speaking from experience, thinking of how breathless she'd been the night they'd kissed, and then again, for a different reason, the morning after, "you can't let yourself forget."

"He broke my heart." There it was again. That look. The one that had always made her ache. A fallen angel reaching, rioting against all he'd lost. All that had been stolen from him for daring to strive.

Riley had never had a friend who understood her work. Who she trusted with her reputation. She had clients, sure, but no co-workers. Not since Gran. But it didn't matter. She had her mom, and she knew what it was like to lose someone you never expected to leave.

"He took a punch for me once." Clark laughed, the sound jagged. "It was at some terrible house party in Oxford. This guy thought I'd hit on his girlfriend. I hadn't—I didn't even know who she was—but he got in my face, hollering about laying me out, and Patrick jumped in to smooth things over." Clark's eyes were the gray-green of a forest after a storm. "The next thing I know, he's on the ground, blood pouring from his nose, asking me if I'm all right."

Part of Riley wished she didn't know this. That she could go back to thinking he was nothing more than a privileged rich kid. It had been easier when Clark was simply an asshole who'd hurt her, instead of someone who'd been hurt—had lost his reputation and one of the most important relationships in his life to a con. She had never lied to him, but she understood a bit more now why he couldn't see that.

Clark bent over his desk, started shuffling papers around. "I'll clean this up so we have a place to work."

Right. Trying to give Clark a moment to collect himself, the way she would have wanted, Riley retreated to the remaining door.

She assumed she'd find some kind of bathroom through here, but she didn't expect the large orange tabby that hissed at her from the lid of the closed toilet seat, as if to say, *Can't you see this is occupied?*

"Oh, god. Sorry," Riley blurted out before she could think better of it. And then, turning to Clark, "You have a cat?!"

"No." He looked up innocently.

"Umm . . . hello?" She swept her arm toward the very large, still-hissing feline.

"Oh." His gaze softened a few degrees. "That's not mine."

"And yet you don't look surprised to see it." The cat licked its paw lazily. It was missing half of one ear. A fellow scrapper if Riley ever saw one.

"She lives around here somewhere." Clark gestured to the surrounding woods. "I feed her occasionally, when I have leftover tuna, and sometimes she naps inside when the weather is unpleasant."

"Uh-huh." Riley closed the door slowly. Clark as a cat person made sense. He too was prickly, standoffish, and arrogantly territorial. Personally, Riley preferred dogs. They were simple and devoted. You always knew where you stood with a dog.

A few minutes later, as she made herself comfortable at his desk—upon closer inspection, she saw he'd missed an opportunity to stack his jack on the queen of spades—Clark started taking down books from different shelves, opening cabinets to pull out maps and blueprints. The task seemed to anchor him, his movements sliding into something familiar. He proceeded to mount all his research in front of her until the pile grew so high, Riley couldn't see over it.

"I've selected a representative sample from among relevant texts for us to start with," he said, unfolding a battered folding chair from behind the fridge to sit beside her.

"A representative sample." Riley stared at the stack and swallowed. "This isn't all of it?"

Clark smiled, as if she were joking. "Hardly."

It felt a bit like homework, which Riley had never been particularly good at. Her grades had been fine, solid, in high school, but she'd spent most of her study time angsting over a series of boyfriends—all of whom treated her like dirt—while painting her fingernails with Wite-Out.

As if sensing her discomfort, Clark pulled out a text for them to start with. "What are you looking for, exactly? I know what a backgrounder looks like for an archaeologist. I assume curse breaking is . . . different?" He tried to keep the judgment out of his tone and missed by a hair. Still, Riley appreciated the attempt at restraint.

"Look for something weird," she told him. "Things or people going missing, mysterious occurrences, unexplained phenomena. Anything that doesn't fit."

They pored over the books and his notes together. She hadn't expected him to help. Had sort of figured he'd sit around and make rude quips while she worked. But Clark showed her the timeline he'd constructed so they could narrow in on any major event that might have occurred on or around the property in the 1700s, and he drew her a sort of clan family tree for both the Campbells and the Graphms when she couldn't keep all the names straight.

Hours bled together, the sun fading behind the tree line.

"What?" Riley said the third time Clark winced when she scribbled an idea on a Post-it note and stuck it inside one of the texts.

"Nothing." He tore his eyes away as if from the scene of a car crash.

Of course, Clark kept all notes in a separate Moleskine with section tabs, where he recorded any ideas or findings with a corresponding label of title, author, and page number. Imagine having the luxury of so much time that you could justify doing something so needlessly slow when sticky notes were *right there*.

Clark argued with himself too, under his breath, "No, that can't be right," while running his finger beneath a passage.

Riley bit her thumbnail, smothered a smile, and didn't say anything as she flipped to the next page.

Occasionally, one or the other of them would get up to stretch.

Clark groaned as he rolled his shoulders.

"You good?" Riley might have some Motrin in her purse.

"Fine." He grimaced in a way that made him look decidedly the opposite. "Tweaked my back when I hit the ground trying to save *someone* from going up in flames."

"Okay, relax. No one asked you to go all Smokey Bear. I could have just as easily stopped, dropped, and rolled without you."

"Since I understood less than twenty-five percent of the words in those sentences"—gingerly, he returned to his seat—"shall I go ahead and assume there was a gracious thank-you in there somewhere?"

Riley rolled her eyes. *Sheesh.* You catch on fire one time, and they never let you forget it.

Eventually, when her stomach growling turned supersonic, Clark insisted on serving her what turned out to be a half-decent frozen pizza.

"Do you want a beer?"

Riley's head shot up. Mr. No Fun had been holding out on her.

As if to demonstrate, he opened the fridge and held up two bottles of some kind of dark ale she didn't recognize.

Her mouth watered. It was a tempting offer after a long, frustrating day. But Riley hesitated.

Having a beer with him felt too casual. Too familiar. Not a business arrangement, but something she might do with a friend.

"No, thanks," she said.

He put them both back and brought her a glass of water she hadn't asked for instead.

Riley took a sip and got back to work.

By nine o'clock, they still hadn't found anything and her eyes had begun to tear from strain. She was already thinking about the route back to the inn when something in an agricultural journal caught her attention.

"Hey." She nudged Clark's hairy forearm. "What about this thing with the angel's-trumpet?"

He knuckled at his eye. "Is that a euphemism?"

"It's a plant." She showed him the illustration.

"Pretty?" he said, obviously hoping that was the answer she wanted.

"No. Look." She tapped the text below the drawing. "A particular varietal used to be native to this region, right around the castle. Usually, the flowers are yellow or pink, occasionally orange, but the ones that grew here were dark blue and extremely rare. Something about the nutrients in the soil. It says here that growers used to make a fortune cultivating it—that it was a show of wealth to have them on display—but then the plant went extinct."

"So?" Clark sketched a literal trumpet in his notebook, a pretty good approximation.

"So," she repeated, "they call it 'the riches of the holding—the jewel in Arden's crown' and it went extinct *overnight*."

Pulling the journal forward, Clark studied the page and frowned. "These accounts are old and likely exaggerated. It wasn't uncommon back then for insects or even a harsh frost to suddenly change the biome."

Leave it to him to come up with the driest explanation possible.

"Yeah—or the castle—and all the surrounding soil—got fucking cursed!"

"An equally likely conclusion," he deadpanned.

Riley didn't care if he wanted to be a dick. This was weird. And weird meant a lead. How could he not see the connection? Her blood pounded. This was something!

"Here." She cross-referenced the timeline. "June third, 1779. Who lived in the castle then?"

Under the table, their knees knocked as she sat forward for a better view.

"That's near the very end of the clan war. Almost no one was left on either side." Clark looked at the list of names, running his finger down the page, looking for someone with a death date later than that. "Philippa Campbell," he said finally. "The clan called her the last daughter. They left her in the castle during the battle at Dunbar and none of her kinsmen returned."

"And you said that dagger was made for a woman!" Riley sprang to her feet. "Oh my god! Do you get what this means? We have a who, and a when, we know why—*hello, she was left desperate and alone with enemies at her doorstep*—we just need a how and we're in business, baby!"

"Am I the baby in that sentence?" Clark said dryly.

"Come on." She smacked the desk. "We found something."

He yawned. "I hope you're not simply reaching for my benefit?"

Riley's momentary elation dimmed. Apparently her breakthrough was boring him. And yeah, that was pretty much the story of her life. Is that why he'd sat here with her for hours, working at her side, to prove to himself at the end that she had nothing to show for it? To watch her play at research when he was a professional?

She'd almost forgotten for a bit that she was alone in this. That was her problem. She wanted something that wasn't on offer—for him to believe her.

"Forget it." She reached over and flipped the agricultural journal closed. "Let's just call it a night."

"All right," Clark said easily, already reaching forward to close other books and gather pens. Obviously he couldn't wait for her to leave.

Of course he can't. He thinks you're a menace, she reminded herself. *You remind him of his deceitful best friend.* Riley couldn't help herself—despite her anger, her embarrassment, she felt bad for him.

Between the famous dad and his soap-opera-star face, it was probably hard for Clark to trust anyone. People must feed him bullshit constantly, trying to get into his good graces or his pants, respectively.

"Sorry," she said when he caught her staring. God, she was exhausted. She'd zoned out there for a second, gazing at him. Creep alert.

"It's fine," Clark handed her a pile of her Post-its. "You don't need to be embarrassed."

"Wait. Embarrassed about what?" Almost falling asleep at his table?

"Being attracted to me," he said, as if that were obvious. "We've spent a lot of time together this afternoon, in close quarters. And it's only been a few days since we . . ." His gaze slipped to her mouth. "It's perfectly understandable."

"Excuse me?" Riley fought not to choke on her own spit. "I am *not* attracted to you!"

Of all the asinine, bigheaded, ridiculous things to assume. Just because he was objectively, face-meltingly hot, and probably had people swooning all over him constantly, did not mean she was sitting here with her tongue hanging out. She wasn't completely shallow.

"Hey, it's not a big deal." Clark had the nerve to pat her hand. "I know it doesn't mean you're fond of me or anything. Anyone could get confused—"

Riley snatched her hand away, flexing her fingers to rid herself of a sudden shock from his touch. "No, it is a big deal. Did you think I was sitting here mooning over you? Because I totally wasn't."

"Okay, fine." He shrugged. "I guess you're not attracted to me. My mistake."

"You don't believe me." His tone had placation written all over it.

"If it makes you feel better," he said, "I believe you don't want to be attracted to me."

Riley could feel a hot flush spreading across her chest, climbing up her neck.

No. Fuck that. She couldn't afford for either of them to have an ounce of doubt that she was in control of her feelings about him.

"When I look at you, all I see is someone selfish and uninspired. In fact, there's no one I could desire less."

"All right, love." Clark scoffed. "Go ahead and tell yourself whatever you need to."

"I'm serious." She racked her brain. How could she display how completely unaffected she was? "You could go full Magic Mike— *XXL*—right here on this table and I wouldn't even blink."

"Well, you'll have to excuse me. I'm afraid I'm not up for gyrating at the moment." Clark rubbed at his neck, once again making a show of how sore he was after his gallant rescue.

Hey. There was an idea. If he wanted to blame her for his back pain, Riley could give him something to really whine about.

"Why don't I give you a massage?" There! Why would someone attracted to him offer to do that? Of course they wouldn't! They'd be nervous and uncomfortable and awkward. Unlike her.

Clark looked at Riley as if she'd sprouted an extra head. "I don't want a massage from you."

"Aha! Exactly." She pointed at him. "See? Because *you're* attracted to *me*. And you're worried you might get overcome."

"I'm sorry." Clark recoiled. "You think you have better self-control than I do?"

"No." Riley smiled sweetly. "I know I do."

"Fine." His nostrils flared. "Give me a massage, then, if it's that important to you."

"Fine!" Was she shouting? Riley didn't mean to be shouting. She lowered her voice to a normal decibel. "I will."

"Great." Clark reached for the hem of his sweater.

"Whoa. Hey. Whatcha doing?"

"Taking off my jumper," he said, his voice deceptively harmless. "That way you can access the muscles more directly. *Since you're not attracted to me*, I'm assuming that won't be a problem for you."

Oh ho ho. He thought he was so slick. As if she would lose her mind at the sight of his bare chest. Or go to pieces because she had to slide her hands down his hot, naked shoulders. Please! Bring it on.

"Of course I don't mind." Riley made a *pshh* sound like a tire with a puncture. "I feel completely neutral, bordering on negative, about your body."

"Great," Clark said. "Glad we're clear on that front."

Riley made herself watch as he yanked his sweater off, two hands at the back tugging it over his head. She made herself not blink, not look away, from the dark hair below his navel, the mouthwatering cut of the muscles that arced from his hip toward his groin, a single vein jumping just above the top of his jeans.

Riley took a breath, a totally normal, not-at-all-shaky breath, as he revealed the smooth, hard planes of his stomach, the broad expanse of his pecs, small brown nipples, more dense hair, and a collarbone that begged for her teeth.

"Riley?"

She snapped her eyes to his face. "Yes?"

He was done, holding his sweater and staring at her expectantly.

"I mean, yep." She waved a hand toward his body. "Just as I suspected. You look . . ." Why did her tongue suddenly feel big in her mouth? ". . . bleh."

"Thanks," he deadpanned. "Do you want me on the couch?"

Okay, he had to be doing the innuendo on purpose. But that didn't stop her from picturing laying him flat on his back. Riding him at a gallop. Hands pressed to that chest, holding him down as she carved her initials over his heart with her fingernail, as he panted beneath her, teeth gritted, asking for more.

Jesus. *Get your head in the game, Rhodes. This is about showing him you're stone cold—or better yet, making him sweat!*

"That works." On only slightly unsteady legs, she got into position, kneeling on the seat behind him once he sat down.

She started with her thumbs at the base of his neck, pushing firmly up and out toward his ears. His skin was pink under her hands, almost red and so warm.

Riley inhaled sandalwood and orange and something spicy like black pepper. His soap probably cost more than her weekly grocery bill—he probably tasted like potpourri. But underneath was the salt of his skin, the base of his hairline just a tiny bit damp.

Clark sat stiffly under her hands, back ramrod straight, his breathing low and noticeably slowed—controlled. *Good.* She hoped he was nervous.

Riley massaged the sides of his jaw with her knuckles. With the way he constantly ground his molars, she figured he needed it. Strange to think that just a few days ago, she'd had her hand on this same skin with completely different intent, melting against him, opening for him, yielding.

She had to work to knead at the thick slabs of his shoulder muscles, calling on the strength in her hands and wrists and forearms. See? She was totally chill. Clark's was just a body, like any other. Just the body of a man who had thought he could take her down with a few words, an arrogant demand. She dug in her knuckles.

"Is the pressure okay?" He really was tense—his muscles wiretaut instead of supple.

His smooth skin was starting to glisten under her hands. Riley had no idea if he was enjoying this. Or if she wanted him to, even a little.

Clark grunted, the sound rough and guttural, making her belly flutter.

She pressed her thighs together where she knelt, closing her eyes for just a second. It was heady, having permission to touch him, knowing she might grant him some degree of pleasure or relief even as he resented it.

Riley pushed up with her palms parallel on either side of his spine. She was going to win this round. Make him weak.

Leaning forward to whisper in his ear, making sure to scrape her teeth just shy of his skin, "Just let me know if you want it harder."

Clark bent his knee, crossing one leg over the other. "Feel free to go as hard as you like."

Using the side of her hand, she worked at a knot in his back, coaxing the muscle to relax, slow and steady. She didn't have to hurt him to win.

Curse breaking was hard on the body. She knew about muscle systems, about pressure points. What to feel for, how to coax the response she wanted.

After a bit, Riley felt a shift, a release, as she unlocked a sequence down his back.

Clark groaned, letting his head fall forward on his chest, breathing like a wounded lion.

Only because he couldn't see her behind him, Riley smiled a little. "You okay?"

"Grand," he said as the tips of his ears turned pink.

She scritched at his scalp in a way that wasn't strictly about releasing aches, luxuriating as she ran her fingers through the thick, silky strands of his dark hair until Clark sighed, tipping his head back into her hands.

Riley liked him like this, liquid, easy, quiet. It was more difficult than she'd care to admit to keep her thoughts from straying to other noises he might make for her. She squeezed and released where his neck met his shoulder, applying the type of firm pressure he seemed to prefer.

Suddenly, Clark stood up, bringing the couch pillow with him. "I think that's enough."

Riley blinked, coming back to herself. "Was there something you wanted to admit?"

She wasn't born yesterday. Even if he hadn't reached for camouflage, she could see now that his pupils had blown wide, his bottom lip carrying tiny indents from his teeth. He was *affected*.

But fuck. Seeing him so worked up was almost a worse temptation than getting to rub her hands all over him. Getting to breathe in the scent of his body.

Suddenly, she wanted her mouth everywhere her hands had been, wanted to strip off her own clothes and press against him, to have him reach back and yank her into his lap, to writhe while he told her she was right, of course she was right, he needed her desperately, had barely been able to sit still, to keep from howling for how much he had to have her.

She didn't want to stop, Riley realized with mounting horror, even if that meant being right, so she had to get out of here. Now.

"No. Thanks," Clark said, practically shoving her out the door. "For the massage, I mean. I'm much more relaxed now."

"Me too," she called back over her shoulder. "I'm so glad we're not attracted to each other."

As soon as the door swung shut, Riley ran.

Chapter Eight

"This is the worst idea I've ever had," Clark said aloud to the empty room as he tossed the pillow back on his sofa and thumbed open the button on his jeans.

He didn't feel like he had a choice. The only parts of his body that burned hotter than the places where Riley had touched him were the ones where she hadn't. He sucked in a harsh breath through his teeth as the cold air of the room kissed the flushed skin of his hard cock.

Wrapping a rough hand around himself, he squeezed at the base, trying to hold off the sensation that had been building from the moment Riley's eyes had drunk in the sight of his naked chest. She had looked so caught, so helplessly wanton, watching him undress just so she could put her hands all over him.

Clark sank down onto the couch, his knees already jelly, one hand gripping his thigh, the other gathering precome and working it down in loose, easy pulls. Was he really going to do this? Get himself off to the idea of a woman he couldn't tolerate?

His abdominal muscles clenched. One who made him so angry, so senseless, so bloody out of control.

She'd worked him over like a goddess merely to prove that she could. Each stroke of her strong, capable hands its own sweet torture. Riley had coaxed his muscles to unclench one by one, her hands moving without hesitation from his neck down his spine. The steady pace she kept unrelenting. Every tender ministration bringing him another breath closer to his undoing.

Clark shouldn't fantasize about someone who loathed him. It was wrong. Bad.

Hadn't Riley gone out of her way to tell him she didn't want him and never would again?

Just let me know if you want it harder, she'd said, teased.

The silky strands of her hair brushing against his bare back as she leaned over him. Her hot breath falling against the sensitive skin of his nape.

Clark bit his already abused lip so hard he tasted blood, trying not to whimper for her, not to thrust his hips up into his calloused palm. He fought himself the way he'd battled not to beg for Riley's touch to slide lower than his waistband. Or worse, for her to let him touch her—anywhere, everywhere—in return.

Nothing but a lifetime of ruthless, well-honed restraint had kept him playing statue with her hand on his neck, his own breath gone ragged in his ears.

Fuck, fuck.

He squeezed on the upstroke, lengthening his pulls, swiping his thumb across the glossy head. He was so hard. His balls tight, sore. Clark hated how good this felt. How helpless he was to deny himself the terrible indulgence.

Even the way she worked made him want to scream. Had he ever seen anything as sexy as Riley Rhodes with a pen in her pouty, porn-star mouth? Studying like she was ravenous for it. Making connections in seconds. Diving in like she'd conquer any problem, just watch her and wait.

God, he would if she'd let him. Clark was a sick bastard who could come just thinking about how her whole face went rosy with pleasure when she thought she'd solved something.

He fucked his fist, letting himself recall the ridiculous way she applied lipstick, slowing the memory down, zooming in on her shiny, dark pink lips.

In his fantasy he waited until she put the cap back on, touched the corner of her mouth with a single finger to make sure the application was pristine.

Then he stepped in front of her and slowly, deliberately used his thumb to smear the bright, tacky substance toward her cheek.

Get on your knees.

He'd watch her fight the impulse. But in the end, Riley would do it, her eyes flashing as she took him between her lips, ruining her own makeup on his cock.

Clark licked his palm, made his strokes slick, imaging the wet heat of her mouth.

Fine. If he was gonna do this, he might as well do it—

Think about pinning her down on his bed and getting his mouth on her pussy. Having her clench his comforter in her fists. Her legs over his shoulders, her heels digging into his back.

He'd finger fuck her until it was dripping down his wrist. Make her watch, glassy-eyed, while he licked it off. Riley would beg for release, weep for it.

Clark groaned, the sound loud in the camper, obscene in his own ears. He threw his head back, banging it against the side of the camper, stars dancing in front of his eyes. *Shit.* The pain worked for him right now, melded in with all the other good-bad emotions. The wrongness of the orgasm building at the base of his spine.

No. Not yet.

He slowed his strokes to keep from spilling.

She thinks you're awful, mate. His hips hitched. *I am.*

Because just when Riley got close, right on the edge, sobbing for how badly she needed to come, he'd flip her over and spank her, take that ripe ass in hand and make it sting.

Clark would get her to count the strokes. Have her apologize for driving him to distraction. For not taking enough care with herself. For lying to him and destroying his peace.

Even after she finally promised to be good for him, he'd decline to bring her over the edge, instead manhandling her so she straddled his thigh, granting her the small mercy of finishing herself off grinding against his denims.

Riley would think it was punishment, that he refused to touch her. But really Clark didn't trust himself, even in his fantasies. He wanted too much. It was all-consuming, made him forget.

The worst part was, Clark pictured her face as he came, splashing hot across his fist. Her face that first night when he kissed her. The way her cheeks had been crimson from the cold, her hair mussed from his hands, her smile bright and soft and hopeful.

After, as he cleaned up, he told himself he wouldn't do that again. Wouldn't let his body get used to thinking about Riley, associating pleasure with her name.

She was a trap, perfectly set, designed for his undoing. But Clark wasn't an animal.

He wouldn't fall for the honeyed illusion of her. No. He would get up tomorrow, early enough to make up for the progress he lost today. He'd earn back the respect he'd fumbled, slowly but surely.

If he really loved his work, he couldn't risk it again.

His father had gotten him this fucking job, he reminded himself as he brushed his teeth. His father, who'd promised to come visit, to see the progress he hadn't made.

Shame burned hot across Clark's back as he climbed into bed, as he shivered, trying to shake the memory of Riley's hands.

I can prove it, she'd said to him that day with the dagger. And perhaps that was where he'd gone so wrong. Letting her.

Giving her chances to weave a fabrication about curse breaking instead of cutting to the chase and pulling back the curtain. Leaving them both no choice but to confront stark reality. Enough was enough. Already he'd let her go too far.

As talented a pretender as Riley was, Clark couldn't let her act stand unchallenged.

Chapter Nine

Late the next morning, hopped up on a cocktail of resentment and sexual frustration, Riley headed for the pub.

Eilean looked up when the cheerfully tolling bell above the door announced her arrival. "Curse breaker." It was still early enough that the lunch rush hadn't hit, only a few singles sat at the bar with sandwiches. "Done for the day already?"

"Actually, I'm here on business. I was hoping you might be able to introduce me to a local who can tell me a bit more about Philippa Campbell."

Clark Edgeware could suck an egg. Riley didn't need him or his research to figure out this curse. The village was full of people who had grown up surrounded by the lore of the mysterious Arden Castle.

"Ah." Eilean beckoned her farther in with a smile. "So, you've subscribed to the theory of the last daughter, have you? That one was always my favorite as well. I've long suspected the reason it's not the definitive origin story for the curse has to do with the fact that people underestimate a woman's will to survive. Anyway"—she flipped up the side of the bar and slid out from behind it—"you're in luck. Ceilidh's working today." (Eilean took the time to explain that even though it was pronounced like *Kay-lee*, the spelling was Gaelic.)

Eilean led Riley to the back of the pub and introduced her to a tall redhead filling saltshakers. "I'm sure she'd be happy to chat your ear off if you give her a hand."

As it turned out, Eilean was right on all counts. Born and raised in Torridon, Ceilidh Wynn worked at the Hare's Heart part-time while doing her master's in European history at the local university. While Riley helped her restock condiments, she learned that Ceilidh's thesis was actually on the curse—specifically the legend of the last daughter. She'd spent years studying the castle's history and even moonlighted as a tour guide in Inverness in the summer, where she told the story of the curse over and over along with other parts of local supernatural folklore.

"Anyone who doesn't believe in the curse is full of shite," Ceilidh declared after Riley had explained her contract with the land developers and the complication of Clark Edgeware.

Riley agreed, but it was amazing how much more defiant it sounded in Ceilidh's accent.

"This land has always been different. Special." The redhead married two ketchup bottles. "Why do you think thousands of people pass through Inverness every year, coming for a glimpse of an ancient monster or to touch a series of sacred prehistoric stones? It's not just down to Jamie Fraser."

Riley relaxed a little. It was a good point. Even if local legends had evolved into more elaborate or dramatic stories to attract tourism, their origins still lay in this unique historic place and the behavior of the people who lived here dating back to ancient civilizations.

"It's the fairy thing that people get hung up on." Ceilidh nodded sagely. "The fae have been Disneyfied enough that your average Joe pictures Tinker Bell—someone tiny with wings and a magic wand."

Riley knew that phenomenon well. Half the time, when she introduced herself as a curse breaker, she got a Lara Croft or *The Mummy* joke.

"But as far back as the Picts there have been stories about powerful magical beings in these hills." Ceilidh finished with the ketchups, and they moved on to topping up bottles of malt vinegar. "They're always cruel, beautiful, and eager to make a deal with humans only to delight in the suffering that comes when they get their heart's desire."

"My gran did a lot of research on the supernatural." Riley had mentioned the family business when she introduced herself. "And she said one way or another, any kind of magical bargain ends up biting you in the ass."

"She sounds like a wise woman." Ceilidh nodded approvingly at the silverware Riley was wrapping. "Around here we're weaned on warnings about offending the fae, and that's nothing new. Both the Campbells and the Graphms have dead laid just south of here in Tomnahurich Cemetery, under the Fairy Hill. I'm quite certain Philippa Campbell knew the risks when she went looking for the fae—when she made a deal. She just didn't have another choice."

Riley's hands moved in a practiced routine. Knife, spoon, fork, roll. "Are there any accounts of the wording of the deal that led to the curse?"

In curses, everything came down to language. Since the dawn of civilization, language had acted as a primary conduit for magic, a way of realizing the power of intent.

"Not that I've heard." Ceilidh shook her head. "But whatever those words were, they worked fast. Within a fortnight, Philippa had managed to capture Malcolm Graphm."

"Wait, what?"

Malcolm Graphm. She recognized that name from the list Clark had made yesterday. He was the son of the chief and the clan's best warrior. There had even been a portrait of him, an artistic rendering in one of the history books. Riley remembered because he was—while not as hot as Chris Pine when he played Robert the Bruce—definitely pretty easy on the eyes.

"That's where the legend of the last daughter comes from, how Philippa turned from a lamb for the slaughter to a warrior in her own right," Ceilidh said. "Once the remainder of the Campbell forces had fallen, the Graphms sent their best soldier to take her down under cover of night and claim the castle."

"But they didn't account for the curse." Riley loved this part of the job—how real people's lives could unfold with intrigue of mythic proportions. It made the trials of working with the occult, including insults from stuck-up archaeologists, easier to weather.

"Exactly." Ceilidh stoppered the cork on the vinegar with a resounding *smack*. "We don't know exactly how she captured him, but by all logic she shouldn't have been able to—she had no military training, no weapons proficiency that we know of. But accounts from the Graphm side insist that Philippa sent a raven at dawn to their camp, saying she planned to keep their man as a hostage at Arden and warning his clansmen that if they didn't abandon their quest and retreat, she'd slay their leader's beloved son."

For a second, Riley wished Clark could hear this—she'd love to rub his nose in research he'd overlooked because he didn't take the curse seriously—but then she scolded herself for thinking of him at all.

"How long did she hold him for?"

"Almost three weeks"—there was a sad twinge to Ceilidh's voice—"according to her final letter."

"Final letter?" A first-person account, after the curse had been set—Riley hadn't dared hope for such a valuable relic.

"Before she vanished and was presumed dead. A lot of historians overlook it. They think the contents are trivial because she was writing to a friend in the south, nothing but a woman's musings that never reached their intended audience." Ceilidh began placing the silverware packets Riley had prepped. "But it exists. A descendant of the friend found it in the early 1900s and donated it to a national heritage museum. If you take the time and effort to translate the Gaelic, it's actually a pretty juicy read."

"Did she mention the curse?" If so, this might be exactly the missing piece Riley needed.

"I'm afraid not," Ceilidh said. "At least not explicitly. She mostly wrote about Malcolm." She made her accent higher, more distinguished. *"The prisoner vexes me to no end. He refuses to disclose anything useful about his clansmen, instead staring at me with eyes like blazing emeralds, his filthy chest heaving."*

Riley giggled at the impersonation. "Sounds like one of my mom's Highland warrior bodice rippers from the 1980s."

"It gets better! Philippa wrote that for a week, Malcolm made not a sound. He would take neither food nor ale—but then one night, as she's holding a chalice of water to his lips, a wild breeze comes out of nowhere and knocks her hand, spilling the contents down her front. And then—*and this is a direct quote*—at the sight of her gown plastered to her chest, *he growled.*"

"He growled?!" And wait a second, a wild breeze out of nowhere? That sounded familiar. Maybe Riley's jeans going up in flames hadn't been purely accidental. Did the curse have a hand in both events?

"I swear!" Ceilidh laughed. "It's all in the letter. Philippa figured out this massive warrior was hot for his enemy and decided to use it to her advantage. She started undoing her hair in front of him, spending hours combing it out, making him watch from where she'd chained him in the dungeons. She would eat wild cherries while he refused his plate, licking her fingers. She even sprayed her perfume on his neck, so every time he inhaled, he'd have to think about her."

"Wow. This lady is my hero." Mentally, Riley took notes. "She said, *I don't need to torture my enemy with weapons, I will simply ensure he dies from a lethal case of blue balls.*"

"I know. I always get so bummed out thinking about the fact that she must have died shortly afterward."

According to Clark's chart, Malcolm had too. "What do they think happened to her?"

"The Graphms didn't take her warning seriously." Having finished her prep tasks, Ceilidh wiped her hands on her apron. "It's sort of classic, men underestimating a woman to their own detriment. They charged the castle. Both she and Malcolm are presumed to have been casualties in the attack."

"You've said 'presumed' twice now," Riley pointed out.

"Technically, their bodies were never recovered," Ceilidh said. "Not super uncommon, given the time period, but still, I like to think she might have vanished into the hills." She shook her head. "I never understood why the curse didn't protect her."

"She probably didn't explicitly ask for safety." Most people didn't. "Curses are very literal." Riley didn't know anyone who had sought one out and escaped unscathed. She stayed in business because the human heart loved nothing so much as yearning.

Chapter Ten

The ends justify the means, Clark told himself as he finished the sketch of the map. The words that had become a mantra over the last twenty-four hours didn't make him feel any better, but he knew he didn't have a choice. He'd woken up yesterday covered in sweat and shame, Riley's name still lingering on his lips. He couldn't afford to have her around any longer. It was that simple. And that selfish.

After hours of unavoidable contemplation, he no longer thought her a liar—in fact, he'd be the one earning that title after today. Seeing her dedication to research, the range of emotion when she thought she made a discovery—no one could act that well. No. Whether he wanted to or not, Clark now believed that she believed.

And for that reason, the trap he set was a strange kind of mercy. Once she stopped living her family's fantasy, who knew what she could accomplish. He knew firsthand how hard it was to let go of someone else's dream for you. In proving once and for all that curses didn't exist, he would lift the veil on her long-held misconception and set Riley free. At least, that was how he comforted himself.

At the sight of her this morning, striding forward through the mist, guilt rose in his throat like bile.

"Good morning." He steeled his spine and pulled out the paper intentionally folded to look casual from his back pocket. "As a follow-up to our research, I put something together that I thought might be of interest to you."

Immediately, suspicion flared across her gaze, her brows lifting. "Oh yeah?"

Clark knew it wouldn't be easy, selling this story. Despite what Riley might think of him, he'd never developed an aptitude for deception. That's why he planned to stick as close to the truth as possible, to exaggerate a theory that might—in another universe—hold weight.

"There are rumors of an ancient sacred site in the cliffs below the castle. Several of the texts I collected about this region mention it as a place marked by standing stones, where this land's earliest inhabitants would go to commune with a higher power—*the hidden people*, they were called. Many historians assume it as an alternate name for the fae."

He held out the paper to her, pleased to see his hand was steadier than his roiling stomach. "I made a map of where I think the site might be located based on historic accounts."

Riley unfurled the paper, taking her time to read Clark's sketch of the landscape, a path of descent marked winding away from the castle.

"You and your father share a talent for sketching," she said mildly.

The comment took him aback. Clark had expected her to launch into an inquisition.

"He would draw with me, when I was younger." He hadn't thought about that in a long time. It had been ages since he could remember doing anything with his father that didn't involve a lecture. "It was difficult to bring lots of toys to an expedition, but a pen and something to scribble on were always easy to procure."

It had felt like the sun on his face, every time his dad had taken a few minutes out of his busy schedule to sit with him, to sketch a volunteer or the fabric of their tents blowing in the wind.

Riley moved to hand him back the map, but he didn't take it.

"I thought you might want to go with me to explore the area, see if we can turn up anything related to your curse."

That was the plan—take her on a wild-goose chase. Tell her a perfectly ordinary piece of land was sacred and see if she ran with it. If she did, he'd know she was making it up, inventing pieces to fit her story. At that point, Clark would reveal his deception, and Riley would have no choice but to admit she didn't know what she was doing.

"I've taken the liberty of packing some bags with gear."

Scaling those cliffs would be no easy feat. He might be a bad person, but he didn't want her to get hurt.

"Who knows if the weather will hold out"—he winced at the gray sky above—"but I consulted the tide schedule, and we should be all right if we head out soon."

Riley stared at him so hard and so long, he thought she might actually be trying to see through him to the castle at his back. "Why would you voluntarily help me?"

Ah, yes. He'd anticipated this question. She'd snared his previous assistance in a neat little act of manipulation, yet this offer came unbidden. "I know we don't necessarily see eye to eye on everything—"

She made a sound of derision.

"—or much," Clark amended. "But I think given our respective occupations it's safe to say that neither of us can resist unraveling a mystery. I know I've been cross with you, but last night, I found it surprisingly pleasant to share that pursuit with someone again." He might have taken a leaf out of Patrick's betrayal handbook—the only one Clark knew intimately enough to emulate—because that part wasn't even a lie.

Riley was quiet, shifting to stare out toward the crash of the ocean.

Clark figured his plan had fallen flat.

"It is," she said finally, quietly.

"Pardon?"

"Surprisingly pleasant," she repeated, and then after a beat, "Okay. Let's go."

"Right. I'll just grab the gear, then, shall I?" Pressing at a sharp pain in his side as he hurried back toward the camper for the packs, Clark thought he might be developing an ulcer.

It would have been cleaner if the map were a complete misdirect, rooted in no true evidence at all, but of course Clark couldn't bring himself to do that. He hadn't slept last night, instead spending hours going back through his research, following Riley's advice, looking for pieces that didn't fit. As such, the land they trudged down, mud squelching beneath their boots, really was favored as "fae territory" in various fables. Though obviously those stories were all nonsense.

About an hour into the trek, Riley held the map while Clark used his compass to navigate along the false route.

"Are you sure we're going in the right direction?" Riley raised her voice to be heard over the pounding of the ocean against the rocks. "According to your map, we should have come across some standing stones by now."

Right. *Time to execute part B.*

"Oh no." Clark glared down at his compass in his best approximation of horror. "I've just realized the metal in these cliffs could be interfering with the needle." Also true—a problem famous in this part of the Highlands—he just hadn't forgotten.

"Oh. Really?" Riley pushed hair damp from sea spray off her forehead. "Does that mean we're totally turned around?"

"I'm afraid so." Clark rotated the compass, making the needle bounce. "The polarization is shot." Hopefully the poor weather obstructed his face, making his terrible acting easier to swallow. "I'm sorry. I've completely mucked this up."

"It's okay." She adjusted the straps of her pack on her shoulders. "I'm pretty sure I did the same thing to a compass one time, only mine went bananas because of the metal in my underwire."

Through considerable effort, Clark managed not to picture her in the hot-pink bra that had attacked him in her room at the inn.

"Say." He pitched his voice to reflect what he hoped would come across as casual curiosity. "You know how you found that dagger so quickly in the castle?"

"Yeah?" The slight indent between her eyebrows said he'd missed at complete innocence.

"Well, perhaps you could follow that process again out here." He gestured to the cliffside. "After all, if there is a link to the curse among these trails, you should be able to find it, right?"

"I mean." Riley looked unsure, her eyes tracing the rough terrain ahead before looking back over her shoulder at the looming castle at the top. "Technically, yes, but—"

"Fantastic." Clark quickly jumped in. "How can I assist you?"

"Well, ideally I'd have brought the dagger with me."

"I have it." He set down his pack and began carefully moving things aside, looking for the waxed cloth he'd wrapped it in. "I thought you might want to compare the metalwork to any coins or arrowheads we might uncover out here."

"You really thought this whole thing out," Riley said, her gaze noticeably narrowed as she took the artifact from him.

Clark kept as still and silent as he could while she uncovered it.

He had no idea what she'd do next, if she'd fall into the trap he'd laid.

And what if she didn't? What if she called his bluff?

He popped a ginger candy into his mouth against another wave of nausea.

How had Patrick lied to him for six months? More, actually—for however long it had taken him to plot as well? Clark had never had illusions of nobility, but this was awful.

His heart raced. His skin grew clammy.

"Okay," Riley said, more to herself than to him as she held the dagger in front of her, turning it this way and that. "Okay," she said again as she closed her eyes and inhaled, slow and deep.

Was this some kind of calming ritual? Was she trying to meditate?

"This way." She grabbed his sleeve roughly, her eyes popping open as she marched them to the right, her chin lifted and her nose in the air.

They walked farther down the rock face, the map forgotten, and even as stones slipped under their feet, Riley picked up her pace, working to pull more air into her lungs in a way that was starting to trouble him.

"I don't mean to be rude"—Clark lengthened his strides to match hers—"but are you having some sort of asthma attack?"

"I'm trying to catch a particular scent," Riley informed him, not stopping, not even sparing him a glance.

Clark took a deep breath too, letting his chest expand under his waterproof coat.

"All I can smell is wet stone and sea salt." He turned to sniff the air in the opposite direction, but Riley caught his hand this time and yanked.

"It's stronger this way."

Her hand was small and warm in his, and because he was weak, Clark made no immediate move to take his back.

"What does it smell like?" he asked, genuinely interested despite suspecting this might be part of her plan to save face.

"You won't be able to smell it."

Ah! So, he'd caught her.

"My nose works perfectly." Clark put every ounce of British condescension he could muster into his voice.

"I promise," Riley said, ignoring the dark clouds that rolled ominously across the sky ahead as they continued to wind toward the base of the cliff, "that if I tell you, you'll freak out."

"I can assure you that I'm an extremely calm, mild-mannered person." Or at least he had been, before he met her. "Every report I ever got from school called me a pleasure to have in class."

Riley snorted. "I bet." She pulled away to press the back of her hands against her eyes. "Fine. Sometimes I can smell magic."

"You can *smell* magic?" Clark said slowly, and then pressed his lips together, fighting not to let his complete bewilderment bleed into his voice. He'd just told her he wouldn't fly off the handle.

"Sometimes," she repeated, dropping her arms to see Clark's reaction. "But this"—Riley gestured at his sour-lemon face—"this reaction you're having is exactly why I don't tell people."

Well, obviously no one could hear such a proclamation and not regard it with skepticism. Clark was starting to grow concerned about the depths of her self-delusion.

"Look, I can appreciate that it's weird," Riley said, "but it's a family thing. My grandmother taught herself to track curses by their scent signature—it's sort of like a magical fingerprint—and then, when I was old enough, she taught me." She shook her head.

"I didn't even realize how strange that sounds until I was in high school. Lots of people in Appalachia learn to track, to hunt. I just don't shoot what I find."

"To be clear, you're saying you're some kind of . . . supernatural bloodhound?"

"Did you just call me a *dog*?"

Since Clark didn't have a death wish, he quickly pivoted. "What exactly does a curse smell like?"

"It's hard to describe. It's not a normal scent, like rosemary or oil paint or chlorine. It's more like a set of sense memories stacked one on top of another. Like . . . odor vignettes." Riley grimaced at her own metaphor. "Arden's curse smells kind of like blood in your mouth when you bite your tongue—salt and copper—mixed with the ground a second after lightning strikes. Iron. Burning. Earth."

Clark couldn't help himself from trying again, feeling silly as he sniffed the air. "You smell all that now?"

"Yes. Scent memory is hard to hold on to. When I trained with Gran in the forest, most of the smells grew familiar after a while. It was easier to isolate a new signature. But here, everything is new— new air, new flowers, new ocean, new rocks—but the same scent clings to this"—she unhooked the dagger from her belt—"and it's even stronger at the castle."

Clark didn't know what to make of her reaction. Riley didn't look or sound like someone panicking or grasping for straws. She looked damp and slightly frantic, but more determined than ever. Raising her chin to catch the wind like at any moment she might lose the trail.

There was no way she could have known where he'd take her today—so the chances of her stashing something up ahead like she could have planted the dagger at the castle didn't add up. Was it possible his fake map really had pointed them in the direction of something mystical?

With a slightly unsteady hand, Clark gestured for her to precede him. "I guess you'd better lead the way."

As dusk began to fall, the changing light created deeper shadows on the rock. One minute they faced solid granite, dark and un-yielding, and the next—

Riley brought her hand up to shield her eyes against the setting sun. "That wasn't on the map."

The cave entrance must have been carved into the cliff surface by centuries of wave erosion. Clark halted his footsteps.

"I think it's only accessible at low tide." He'd never seen any-thing like it. Grabbing a fistful of Riley's jacket, he held her back. "We can't go in there."

"Are you kidding?" Riley kept walking, towing him along. "We just discovered a mysterious cave at the bottom of the cliff that houses Arden Castle, and it's practically dripping in the curse's scent signa-ture. As a curse breaker, I'm obligated to investigate. You, however"— she gave him a withering look—"do not need to come."

Right. Not bloody likely. A gray haze clung to the opening. And though they weren't terribly high, the atmosphere felt significantly thinner here. It was harder to take a deep breath. He wasn't sending her in alone.

There could be bears or falling stalagmites in there. *Stalagmites? Stalactites?* Clark could never remember the difference. In any case, there might as well have been a neon sign declaring *DANGER AHEAD.*

"Helmets," he said, removing his pack and starting to pull out safety gear. It was the least he could do, considering he might have inadvertently lured her to her demise. "You're lucky I had an extra one in the camper."

Riley knocked his hand away when he tried to do up the buckle under her chin, fastening it herself. "And you're lucky you look like that, because you're a massive dork."

Clark frowned. What? It needed to be snug.

They walked for a while, the tunnel deep and dark enough that even with their headlamps pointed straight ahead all they saw was yawning black abyss. In her eagerness to explore, Riley banged her head twice on low-hanging chamber ceilings.

"Who's the dork now?" He crowed, knocking on her helmet as he passed.

The temperature dropped steadily as they walked farther, the crash of waves growing fainter with each step.

Without the light from their headlamps, they might have overlooked the ravine.

Riley threw out an arm to halt Clark's process, staring down at the abrupt drop-off of the ground at their feet. It looked like some kind of fissure had fractured the stone, leaving a cavity close to five meters deep and perhaps one, one and a half meters wide.

They both stared down where Clark aimed the torch on his helmet, illuminating murky water and jagged rock.

"What do you think?" Riley took a few steps back.

Clark was still peering over the edge. "The fall probably wouldn't kill you, but—"

She must have stopped listening at that point, because the next thing he knew, she'd broken into a run.

"Riley." Clark watched in frozen horror. "Don't you dare—"

But she'd already landed with a gravel *crunch* on the other side.

Glaring at her, he pressed his hand to his racing heart, hoping his knees wouldn't buckle.

"Sorry?" She offered him a weak grin.

"You are not." The scowl didn't leave his face, even as he leapt to follow her.

Clark landed less neatly than she had, rocking forward on his heels on impact, so he had to throw out his hands to steady himself.

"Are you having"—Riley held her thumb and index finger about an inch apart—"maybe this much fun?"

"No," Clark said very firmly, but he didn't think she bought it.

"The curse scent is sharper here," she told him, gesturing at the small chamber ahead.

Clark still couldn't pick up the trail she claimed to follow, but the rock wall a few meters forward seemed to vibrate, almost like when heat rose off pavement in the dog days of summer.

Riley pressed her palm to the wall and closed her eyes. "Not here, not quite."

Walking slowly, she dragged her hand across the rough texture of the stone, over dips and bumps, grooves and edges.

It was the same type of thing she'd done in the tower at the castle, he realized, right before she'd found the dagger. He couldn't comprehend the events unfolding. His brain was an unbroken horse, dragging him along. She wasn't supposed to find anything. Her process shouldn't be repeatable. It shouldn't make sense. Clark *shouldn't* have goose bumps.

Finally, Riley stopped, crouched, moved her hands down to the space where the wall bled into the floor. "Can I see your water bottle for a sec?"

He rushed to retrieve it from the pocket on his pack.

Uncapping the metal canister, Riley poured the liquid against the rock wall, washing away hundreds—if not thousands—of years' worth of dirt and silt.

"What are you—" Clark began, but then stopped because they could both see.

Deep, dark marks scoured the rock face. Etchings. The characters small and precise and dense. Picture symbols, almost like hieroglyphs, some of them burned away by scorch marks.

"Riley," Clark said, bending down beside her, "I think these are really old."

"Older than the castle?"

He nodded, not tearing his gaze away from the symbols. "It looks like the lost language of the northern tribes that built their kingdom in Dark Age Scotland. Who beat back the Romans before they disappeared from record."

"Oh, so like, *old* old." Riley blanched.

He ran his fingers over the marks. "This is unbelievable." He grinned at her, drunk on the discovery. "I wonder if anyone knows this is here."

"What do you mean?" Riley said, each word edged with danger Clark didn't notice until it was too late.

He was too busy thinking about whether he should take out his camera, about whether he could get decent enough pictures in this low light to send to his friend Rodney, who specialized in ancient civilizations of this region. Whether he should get out his phone and call his dad—even though there was no chance he'd have service—

"Clark."

He stilled, hearing the danger now.

"Why are you so surprised?" Her whole body had gone rigid. "You developed the map based on research that identified fae interference in this area, right?"

"Uh," he said, his brain overworked, sloppy, lazy. "Yes. Quite right. I just—well, you see there was some evidence, a few anecdotal references, but I . . . I didn't necessarily . . ."

She closed her eyes. "Wow. I am such a fool." A horrible half smile pulled at her mouth.

It was like watching a mirror or a recording of himself six months ago. Clark knew the symptoms she was experiencing, the disbelief, the way it was almost funny, laughing gas before a root canal.

"You think curse breaking is a farce." Her face shuttered then, became hard, impenetrable. "Of course you didn't expect me to find anything."

"Riley." But what could he say? His gut twisted, the sick feeling returning with a vengeance. He'd eaten all the ginger candy already.

"Did you think we'd wander around in the dark for hours?" She swore under her breath. "I knew something was up when you said the compass stopped working. It was too obvious an oversight. You really constructed this whole elaborate plot to humiliate me. That seemed worth it to you?"

Christ. He was going to be sick.

Clark didn't expect her to understand. She hadn't seen how bad things got after Cádiz. The way he couldn't sleep. Couldn't eat.

Even based on their short acquaintance, he could tell Riley was stronger than him. That she could weather a professional nosedive, losing her family's respect, even the disintegration of the only support system she'd ever known, far better than he had.

He'd tried to spare her as much as he could, by pulling the wool over her eyes privately rather than publicly.

"I'm sorry."

"Are you?" The question was drenched in disdain.

He couldn't hold her gaze anymore. The weight of his own self-disgust threatened to engulf him. Just next to his boot, something small and dark at the very bottom of the wall caught his eye.

"Riley." He bent for a closer look. The set of letters were smaller, fainter, more urgently etched than the symbols they'd first seen. "This is Scots Gaelic."

Bending, he traced the line with his thumb. "See how the carving is shallow? The Picts would have used tools made of silver, would have planned their symbols meticulously, but this is crude, done quickly, maybe even with a rock. Someone else came to this site much, much later.

"*Crìoch air naimhdean*," he read, his voice hoarse and low.

She took out her phone, using an app she'd downloaded the other night for translation.

"*An end to enemies*," she read.

"What do you think that means?"

"I think it's the curse," Riley said, face grim.

Chapter Eleven

Back in her room at the inn, Riley stared at her murder board. Wait, no—her not-at-all-crime-affiliated curse-breaking mind map. *Man, that really didn't roll off the tongue in the same way. Whatever.* After scribbling a rough approximation of the Gaelic words they'd found etched in the cave along with their English translation on a Post-it, she tacked the note up in the center of the board. The scent signature in the cave had matched the one in the castle exactly.

She had it—the language of the curse, the keystone piece to breaking it. *An end to enemies.*

When Riley closed her eyes, she could almost see Philippa Campbell, hiding from her family's butchers, sneaking out under cover of night to scale the dangerous cliffside, searching for a sacred place revered by her ancestors. A fae cave where ancient magic bled through stone.

Something in her bones assured Riley that Philippa had scraped those words into the rock face. Willing them true. A prayer. A vow.

To find that cave—that particular spot—she must have known where to look. And therefore known the risks.

Philippa had chosen in those desperate hours to do what she

must. To put herself at the mercy of a power that local legend promised was both great and terrible.

She'd made her daring into the sword she couldn't wield, her body a vessel for her clan's vengeance.

Riley felt like an echo the choice that was no choice. The helplessness. The ambition. Philippa had come to that cave at the very end of what must have been an exhaustive search for her family as they struggled for so long to find another way to hold the castle—their home.

Even now, tucked under her quilt at the inn—the clock by her bedside flashing almost midnight—Riley still felt the unbridled power of that cave thrumming in her ears.

Born of rock and salt water, carved by the hand of the tides as a monument, that place was proof that even the unyielding could yield.

Thousands of years ago, the people who had left those symbols had marked that spot as sacred, determined to use their tools and their language to bear witness to a force they otherwise couldn't process, couldn't name. Whatever ran through the seams of those rocks had proven both ancient and enduring. And way more intense than anything Riley had ever faced before.

She'd stared at those cave walls, two sets of etchings carved centuries apart, each holy in their own way. And for the first time in a long time, she'd been afraid, not of failing but of falling.

Fresh off another betrayal from Clark that she should have seen coming, she missed Gran like a homesickness for a place she could never return to.

Ever since she was a little girl, even when she hadn't been practicing, Riley had carried the words *curse breaker* like a golden sun inside her chest, warding against rainy days and bad dates and double shifts with terrible tips. She'd been content to wait for fame and fortune, secure in the knowledge that when her chance came to prove what she could do, she'd seize it, make the loneliness of her chosen life worthwhile.

But then she'd come here and met Clark. And just when she'd begun to worry that his doubt was so powerful it would shatter the confidence she needed to succeed, he became the answer. The key.

An end to enemies.

Riley read through her notes again.

Philippa Campbell. Malcolm Graphm. Two forces fighting for opposing sides. Both believing they deserved domain over the castle.

Malcolm with an army at his back, with the advantage of battle training, the resources and privilege of being born a man.

Philippa, alone, the last daughter, force of will her only weapon besides a decorative dagger. She'd outmaneuvered him—almost. Had set the curse in motion, captured a valuable hostage, tried to drive the rival clan away in the only fashion she could fathom. But as Riley had suspected, there was no safety in her magic words. No guarantee against the greed of the men on the other side.

Riley flipped through the moth-wing pages of Gran's journal, looking for an illustration marked by a series of circles, one inside the other. There. And beneath the image, two sentences. *Curses are patterns. Inescapable repetition.*

Setting the book aside, she Googled for the portrait of Malcolm Graphm.

Fuck. They even looked alike. Dark eyebrows. Thin lips. Hard jaw. She hadn't seen it before. Probably hadn't wanted to.

"It's us," she said to the hum of the heater in her room.

The curse had cast her and Clark as modern-day proxies for ancient foes.

An end to enemies.

A second chance to fulfill Philippa's vow for vengeance.

One of them had to drive the other away. The evidence was right there in front of her. Clark goaded by circumstance into creating a fake map he'd hoped would lead her to turn tail.

But Riley didn't scare that easy. No, if the curse wanted them to repeat Philippa and Malcolm's battle to banish each other, she intended to be the last one standing.

Eilean had told her that first night in the pub that the castle found ways to drive away everyone who entered. Riley didn't know if the curse commonly used people against one another to achieve those ends, or if the chance to put her and Clark—with all their similarities to Philippa and Malcolm—at each other's throats was just too juicy to resist.

She slept fitfully that night—too keyed up, knowing what she had to do—and woke reciting the strategies: *Charms, cleansing, sacrifice, ritual.*

Gran had taught her well. "Start small and work your way up by process of elimination."

Plants and herbs pruned from within the closest possible proximity to the curse would be her best bet for making a banishment charm.

As she entered the castle grounds, the sky remained a sleepy gray, the sun barely peeking over the cresting waves of the sea below the cliff. Aggressively thriving gardens stood in stark contrast to the crumbling deterioration of the castle structure. It was like nature slithering forward to erase all evidence of humanity with endless flora.

As she got closer, she realized the view—rows of wild purple heather with Arden lurking menacingly in the background—would have made the perfect setting for one of the romance novels her mom loved. A silly wave of missing her had Riley reaching into her pocket and pulling out her phone to snap a pink-cheeked selfie.

After sending the image, she made her way over to where a cluster of ancient ash trees stood tall and twisting on the edge of the property, their bark so weathered it had begun to calcify in certain places, emulating stone. Riley pressed her hand to a trunk, almost expecting a heartbeat as she tilted her head back to take in the canopy of leaves above. She'd never seen trees like this, never encountered anything that had existed on the earth for so long. To this ash, her life was nothing more than a handful of seasons.

With a sharp pocketknife, Riley carefully carved off a few pieces of dried bark. She made sure to take only chips in the process of natural shedding, borrowing a bit of the deep-rooted tree's strength and stability for the base of her charm.

It had seemed like a game all those years ago. Gran bartering with Riley's adolescent attention span to share what she knew of tapping into the natural world's innate power. Looking back, Riley would give anything for more advice. She'd had to make up so much on her own, trying to fill in the gaps in the journal. Half the time, she didn't know what she was doing.

She tried to be bullish, as confident in her abilities as her foremother, but it was work to harness bravado, constantly trying to mask the fear that deep down she was exactly what Clark and her father before him had said: nothing special, a pathetic pretender.

At least she'd always found spite motivating. The more Clark doubted her abilities, the more Riley had no choice but to back herself.

Besides, she'd effectively created repellant charms in the past, even if the circumstances here weren't exactly the same. Kettle Brook Farms in southeastern New Jersey—the place where she'd gotten the scar on her knee—had almost gone out of business a few years back because of a mysterious blight on their tomato crop.

Not only had the farmers, Fred and Ike, been embarrassed that their Jersey tomatoes disgraced the name—pale and undersized, the flesh unbearably mealy—but they also couldn't afford to weather the financial blow of another season lost to cursed crops. Riley made a face just remembering all the terrible tomatoes she'd tested during the long weeks she'd spent trying to figure out how the husbands had run afoul of dark spirits.

In the end, she planted crimson amaranth along their crop beds for protection, and hung a handwoven wreath of blackberry, ivy, and rowan as a shield above their door. And this year's offering had been different—the tomatoes came in huge and vibrant, fire-engine red, so good you could take a bite of them like an apple, devouring one after the other with just a pinch of salt across the top.

The difference here was that since she was trying to send away a specific person, she needed an identifying marker. In a note that looked to have been added to the journal later, since it was in a different color pen, Gran had scribbled, *hair works—no fluids needed!*

Thank god.

Needing to collect some of Clark's hair (uninvited) wasn't ideal, but at least she'd seen enough episodes of *Criminal Minds* to know what to look for. His hairbrush would be the path of least resistance to securing the goods.

Normally, Riley wouldn't consider breaking and entering a casual part of her curse-breaking practice, but it was kind of hard to feel guilty after Clark's repeated attempts to screw her over. Especially when she considered that he'd made up an elaborate scheme aimed to take advantage of her reluctantly extended trust—which, it was worth noting, was the exact thing he'd accused her of doing in the first place! Pot, kettle—it all came out in the wash.

While Riley waited for Clark to abandon the scene of the heist, aka head inside the castle to work for the day, she continued foraging for other fresh supplies she'd need for the charm.

She couldn't find dill among the overgrown gardens' vast array of flora, but luckily, she'd brought along her collection of dried herbs. Airport security had not loved her collection of vacuum-sealed bags, but ultimately, because of the size and weights, they couldn't find any reason within their jurisdiction to take them away.

Picturing that Ina Garten meme, Riley muttered to herself, "If you can't forage fresh herbs for a charm to repel your enemies, store-bought is fine."

When Clark finally came outside, familiar pack slung over his not-particularly-remarkable-in-any-way shoulders, he looked even more surly than normal. Riley gave a sarcastic little wave as their eyes met, and he dropped his own gaze quickly. Good. She wanted him to know she was still pissed. Even though she'd already ignored him the entire return trek last night and then tossed back his helmet with a little more force than strictly necessary. He looked back at her once over his shoulder before disappearing inside the castle—that same piercing, rebellious pain taking on new dimension in his face. Not that she cared about his emotional wounds anymore. Fool me twice and all that.

Once the coast was officially clear, she headed straight for the side of the camper where she'd seen him leave a window cracked for the cat. After a quick inspection, her hopes for easy entry dimmed. No way was her ass fitting through a space that tiny.

The front door was no friendlier, lock firmly in place. That left one decidedly undesirable option: the escape hatch over the bed.

Here goes nothing.

It was a process. First, finding a set of logs big and sturdy enough to give her a boost so she could climb onto the camper.

Then lying on her stomach and slithering across the top of the thing, her whole outfit going damp from the morning dew covering the metal exterior.

No one ever said curse breaking was glamorous.

The hatch didn't actually open from the outside. But—small graces—Clark had left it cracked, presumably for ventilation. After much trial and error, Riley managed to slide a stick in and flip the latch.

When she finally got the hatch open wide enough, she pitched herself through, falling in an undignified heap onto his bed. Riley sprang up as quickly as possible. For all she had hatred as armor against his beauty, she didn't need to test herself by rolling around with her nose in his sheets.

It made sense to start her search for the brush in the bathroom. Unfortunately, the stray cat had once again chosen to occupy the space, this time curled up in the sink. It gave her the stink eye complete with a brow furrow powerful enough to rival Clark's when she opened the door.

"Don't look at me like that." Riley did her best to return the steely glare. "You're an interloper as much as I am, so just be cool and no one has to know I was here."

As soon as she took a step forward, the cat opened its jaws and started yowling.

"You fuzzy bitch," Riley said, not without some respect.

She doubted the passionate cries would carry all the way inside the castle, but still, she didn't need a feline narc sending up audible signal flares while she attempted burglary.

Quickly backing up into Clark's kitchen, Riley started opening cabinets and lifting the lids on jars, hoping to find some food to bribe the animal into silence.

Unfortunately but unsurprisingly, none of the stuff Clark ate looked very appetizing.

Why did he have so many different kinds of seeds?

Finally, she settled on a banana. After hastily peeling the thing, she offered the cat a piece, which it took only after a noticeable pause that said it was doing her the favor.

Of course, the second its mouth closed around the fruit, Riley realized she had no idea what kind of people food was bad for cats. Her house had never had any pets growing up. Just last summer she'd learned grapes were lethal to dogs after some regular came into the bar sobbing about an incident involving unsupervised fruit salad. *Shit.*

"Drop it, drop it," she said with as much authority as she could muster, pointing to the ground from the safety of the doorway.

The cat covered the part of the banana not currently in its mouth with both paws and hissed.

Great. Now she was gonna have to wrestle Garfield to get the thing back.

"Hey, just relax," she said placatingly, taking a few careful steps toward the sink. "I'm trying to save your life here."

Shocking no one except Riley, the second she moved within claw radius, she received a set of long, mean scratches from her wrist to halfway up her forearm.

Riley cursed, spinning in a circle while cradling her wound, trying not to scream.

Okay, in hindsight, taking food from a wild animal was pretty friggin' ill-advised.

"I deserved that." She whimpered. "I did."

Clearly she had to find some food of equal or greater value to replace the banana.

She must have done something good in her childhood, because way back in the bottom of the fridge, she managed to uncover some plain cooked chicken breast.

Perfect. Riley figured that if cats could eat tuna, they could eat chicken—since tuna was the chicken of the sea. Shout-out to Jessica Simpson and elder millennials.

"Here. Look at this." She shook the Tupperware containing the poultry with the hand on her uninjured arm. "Mmm. Meat." She rubbed her belly, feeling like a clown of the highest caliber.

Once she had the cat's attention, she threw the chicken into the shower, hoping it would drop the remaining banana and fetch.

"Okay, go get it," she coaxed.

What the animal actually did was look at Riley like she was a doofus, which at this point seemed fair. Blood from the scratches had pooled down her arm, catching in the crease of her elbow and dripping to the tile floor below.

Yikes. This place was looking more and more like a crime scene by the minute.

Grabbing some toilet paper, Riley tried to mop up and then stem the flow, wrapping the wound as best she could one-handed.

After that, she went to pick up the chicken from the shower, since Clark might not miss a banana off his counter but would probably notice leftovers randomly flung about his washroom.

Apparently, her interest was all it took for the cat to decide it did want to eat that—*Thank you very much*—since it leapt down from the sink and stalked forward.

Having learned her lesson, Riley got the fuck out of the way, abandoning the bathroom as fast as her legs would take her.

With fingers crossed that Clark kept his brush in his sock drawer or something, she walked back to the bedroom, only noticing that she was leaving a wet trail of footprints when she slid a little on the laminate. *Oh, come on.* Who knew there were so many ways to leave evidence?

Riley might be hot and capable, but she was starting to think she would make the worst criminal ever.

Hopping on one foot, then the other, she took off her boots and set them beside the door.

She'd have to find a way to mop up before she left, but that was fine. Doable. Clark definitely had cleaning products around here somewhere. The air held faint traces of lemon Lysol.

A quick glance at her watch confirmed that she needed to get a move on. It had already been close to fifteen minutes since Clark left. The longer she trespassed, the higher the risk of him coming back and catching her.

Riley canvassed the bedroom as stealthily as possible.

There weren't a ton of places in the compact area for him to keep a brush. He didn't have anything on top of his dresser. With as much detachment as possible, she folded back his sheets and turned over his pillows, scoping for loose hairs, but unsurprisingly, his linens were pristine.

Starting to panic a little now, she yanked open the top drawers of his dresser. The contents were neatly organized by type— undershirts and athletic shorts—though not color coordinated, which she'd half expected.

He did fold his socks. *Nerd.*

When she knelt to open the bottom drawer and caught a glimpse of boxer briefs, Riley couldn't fight the sudden assault of a Calvin Klein ad montage featuring Clark as all the models—pouting, flexing, bending over . . .

By the time she snapped out of that haze, she'd managed to bleed through her makeshift bandage—right onto his underwear. *Oh my god. Red alert! Red alert!!!!*

She tore out the marked pair, shoving them into her back pocket—she would have to dispose of the evidence later—and slammed the drawer closed, jumping to her feet.

Her heart thrashed in double time. B&E was one thing, damaging the man's delicates another.

What a disaster. She would have to find a way to slip him a twenty—or two? How much did it cost for a new pair of Calvin Kleins?

Get it together, she told herself, shaking her head to try to clear it. This was no time to go to pieces. She needed a plan B here.

She paced back and forth, sliding a little in her socks, and then it came to her—*hats*.

Hats had hair in them sometimes—thanks again, Matthew Gray Gubler, for being hot enough to get her through even the more upsetting episodes of *Criminal Minds*.

Riley spun, trying to figure out where Clark might keep knitwear. Surely a man who insisted on carting around not one, but two pairs of caving helmets took care to protect his delicate ears from chilly temps?

Except this room had no hooks. Maybe he kept bins under the bed like her mom? Flattening herself to the floor, Riley army crawled under there. And—aha! Bins! She was a genius. A genius who could barely raise her head under here, but still.

Despite the cramped quarters, she managed to lift the lid on the first plastic container, coughing when the movement released a cloud of dust in her face. Apparently, Clark didn't clean everywhere.

Once she recovered, Riley rooted her good hand around in the bin, going by feel, since she couldn't see much under here. When her hand brushed something that crinkled, she jumped at the noise, slamming her head up against the bed frame.

Ow. Fuck.

Okay, this wasn't gonna work. She could be unknowingly running her hand over crystallized grasshopper guts.

No. No way. She needed to slide the bin out so she could actually look at what was inside.

Scooting backward, Riley managed to get the thing out and, blinking in the sunlight, pulled the lid off.

Oh. Huh. The crinkly thing she'd touched turned out to be a newspaper clipping. Riley was about to move it aside when the black-and-white picture at the bottom caught her eye. That was unmistakably a younger Clark—same brooding expression minus twenty years—standing with a man who, judging by his jaw shape and dark brows, could be his father. Upon closer inspection, he was even wearing the same kind of signature felt hat with a quail feather as the main character in the film from the plane. As she pulled the clipping closer, Riley saw that the image was folded. Carefully, she brought forward the other section, revealing another guy in the picture. Hmm. Maybe a volunteer? Riley scanned for a caption.

> Archaeologist Alfie Edgeware, on-site in Leeds, with
> his sons, Clark (15) and Patrick (19)

Her brain skipped a beat like an old record.

Sons?

Patrick.

"Oh my god."

The camper door swung open, Clark ducking inside. His eyes followed the trail of her boot prints, snagged momentarily on the cat chomping chicken in his shower, and ended on her kneeling next to his bed, storage box open, newspaper in hand.

"What the fuck are you doing in here?" Clark's stance pulled tight with mounting rage. *"Are those my pants in your pocket?"*

Riley couldn't say, *This isn't what it looks like.* It was. He'd caught her red-handed, snooping with intent to steal. *Shit* didn't seem like a strong enough response to her rotten luck at this point.

She sighed. "Sonofabitch."

"I shouldn't be surprised, and yet somehow I am." Clark thrust both hands on his hips. "God, I knew you were . . ."

Somehow, his brows sank impossibly closer together.

". . . bleeding."

Huh? Oh, right. She looked down at the grisly mess of her arm.

"You should be proud. Your guard cat is very effective."

He folded his lips together, breathing deeply once and then again through his nose before pointing at his desk chair.

"Sit," he said dangerously.

Apparently, Riley had less of an iron will than the cat, because she obeyed.

Was he going to interrogate her? Here? Now?

When instead he moved to take out a first aid kit from under the sink, she slumped forward onto the wooden table.

"Don't think this means you're off the hook." He placed the box in front of her and began removing supplies.

Normally Riley would argue that she didn't need fussing over, especially from him, but if Clark wanted to patch her up instead of immediately turning her over to the local authorities, she certainly wasn't in a position to complain.

Besides, now that she'd stopped moving, the scratches stung to all get-out.

"She doesn't usually bite the hand that feeds her." Clark eyed the empty chicken container left on the counter before unwrapping the toilet paper from her arm.

"I tried to take back her banana," Riley felt obligated to explain. "Those aren't, like, lethal to cats, right? Bananas?"

Clark gave her a wry look as he poured liquid onto a cotton ball. "Right."

Phew. At least no one could add cat murder to her list of recent crimes.

Riley eyed the doused cotton ball with anxiety. "Is that gonna sting?"

"Unfortunately"—he swiped the cold compress against her scratches and watched her wince, unmoved—"*no.*"

Yikes. If she had to guess, she'd put his anger at a spicy eight out of ten right now.

"At the risk of aggravating you further by sounding unapprecia-tive, can I ask why you're bandaging me up right now instead of berating me for committing literal crimes against you?"

As much as Riley preferred this response, it didn't make sense. Especially when you considered that just yesterday, he'd been ready to strike against her without more than superficial remorse.

"You didn't take a Hippocratic oath or anything, right? So why nurse me back to health when you could let me suffer? I mean, yeah, you were a pretty massive dick to me yesterday, but I man-aged to forfeit the moral high ground almost immediately."

As he unspooled a length of clean, white bandaging, Riley could tell he was using the action to ground himself. The more she got to know him, the more she recognized how much he resented situa-tions that prodded him into emotional outburst.

When he spoke next, his voice was lower. Not quite calm, but more controlled.

"I'm not doing it on purpose. I've been this way ever since I was a child. Overattentive. A worrier."

Resuming his ministrations, he tucked one end of the bandage under her arm and began wrapping. "My mom's diabetic. And it's fine. She manages it really carefully. But between balancing medications, injecting insulin, monitoring her blood sugar, being thoughtful about her diet and exercise, and juggling doctors' appointments as a full-time barrister—it's a lot."

He reached for a small pair of scissors in the kit and carefully snipped the gauze.

"With his busy schedule, my father has never been a particularly attentive partner," he huffed disdainfully. "So from a young age, I felt a certain responsibility. To check in with her, take care of her, to be ready in case something went wrong."

"Oh, Clark." His obsession with safety no longer seemed like a mere eccentricity or a heavy-handed attempt at control.

"Don't worry. My mum hates it as much as you do." Smiling ruefully as he secured the bandage with a piece of medical tape, he said softly, "There," before clearing away the supplies.

With his back turned, it was too easy for Riley's heart to clench, filling with something almost like tenderness for the apprehensive little boy who had turned into such a careful man.

Once finished, Clark leaned back against the counter and folded his arms.

"Now, are you going to tell me why you broke in here? Were you just looking to trash the place?"

Riley cringed, taking in the trail of destruction she'd left across the camper.

"That was not my intent, no." She really didn't want to share any more details about curse breaking with him, especially when her current strategies revolved around kicking his ass out of here, but she did sort of owe him an explanation.

Damn. She hated feeling guilty so soon after he'd wronged her. No doubt the curse had a hand in whatever urgent impulse had driven him back to his trailer to catch her at the least opportune moment. If she didn't know better, she'd almost swear the malevolent forces infecting Arden Castle enjoyed watching them squirm.

"I needed a lock of your hair," she finally admitted.

"Dare I ask why?"

"I don't suppose you'd believe me if I said it was to wear in a heart-shaped necklace, huh?" Riley couldn't exactly confess she was making a charm to banish him. Despite the spectacular failure of her attempts, she still needed to figure out a way to get him to cooperate so she could do her job.

He didn't smile. "They do say there's a fine line between love and hate."

"I'll clean up all the mess I made." She tried backing into his bedroom, hoping against hope that he hadn't noticed the newspaper she'd dropped on the ground in her surprise when he came back.

"No." Picking up on her ratcheting unease, Clark stepped around her to his bedroom. "Leave it."

Riley's stomach sank as he bent to pick up the clipping. A terrible silence filled the camper as he lingered, crouched over the faded photo.

"Patrick—your partner who betrayed you in Cádiz—" She had to say something, had to admit what she'd seen. "He's your brother?"

"Didn't you know?" Turning, he looked genuinely surprised at the question. "I assumed you'd looked me up on the Internet by now."

"I've been sort of busy." *And trying not to think about you.*

"Cádiz was his idea." Clark stood, the faded print clutched in his hand. "Our father's dream, conquered at last. Patrick had gotten his PhD four years earlier than I did. He had time to apply for all the right grants and permits, so that by the time I finished school I could join him with everything set."

He looked down at the image, running his thumb carefully over the crease between his father and Patrick.

"You might not guess it, but he was trying to do something kind, including me. You see, he'd always been my father's favorite. The perfect firstborn. Talented, decisive, independent. Everyone adored him."

Riley could hear the way he automatically compared himself, unspoken, in the description.

"I don't think it ever occurred to him that we might be caught," Clark said, a hint of fondness soaking through. "He designed the lidar map to buy us time and investment for the resources we'd need to truly find the temple. It almost worked. We got more funding, a bigger crew. The temple might very well sit at the bottom of that bay. But my father's movie put the family in a spotlight even Patrick couldn't anticipate. Of course, industry analysts wanted to look into the research and expedition of Alfie Edgeware's sons when rumors began to circulate that they'd followed in the family footsteps."

Riley's next breath came harsh, the fall of her rib cage painful. It hurt to hear the strange vacancy in Clark's words, the detachment she knew he paid for dearly.

Before, she'd felt bad for him, betrayed by a friend. But this was different.

Riley knew from experience what it felt like when your family failed you.

Suddenly she could smell spaghetti burning on the stove as her dad walked out the door. Her mom chucking his favorite flannel at his retreating back.

"Patrick couldn't stay, after the scandal. He tried. He wanted to fix things, but our dad was relentless." Clark shook his head sharply, cutting himself off. "He's in Japan now. We don't speak much. I'm not sure either of us knows what to say. He sends the occasional letter. Says the mountains are peaceful."

Her arms ached with the desire to reach for Clark, even though she knew it would be unwelcome. Riley had never been anyone's comfort—even her mom didn't take well to coddling—but she felt in her chest the exact kind of wound that she heard in his voice.

The one that came from a blow you never saw coming. Because your older brother, like your father, was someone you believed would protect you.

"I'm sorry." Riley didn't know which part she was apologizing over.

For what had happened to him and his family? For breaking in here? Or for stumbling across a raw truth that he hadn't offered her?

Setting the newspaper down on the bed, he crossed back to the kitchen, pulling something out of a drawer with jerky, urgent movements.

"Cut it," he said, sitting down in the chair she'd abandoned and extending a pair of scissors handle-side toward her. "What I did yesterday, lying to you—well, now you know I understand how it feels to play both parts."

"Clark." She shook her head. "You don't have to—"

"I do," he cut her off. "Trust me, this side of treachery is just as awful. Like missing a step down the stairs and falling the rest of the way. If a lock of my hair will lessen the debt between us, take it. You'd be doing me a favor."

After all the effort she'd gone to today, Riley didn't want to. Things were always off balance between them. This never-ending battle for the upper hand more often than not left her with her head spinning. Desperately trying to remember her goals in the face of Clark's relentless campaign to prove her wrong every time she thought she might understand how he ticked.

But she stepped forward.

Riley didn't get to back off every time the circumstances surrounding a curse made her uneasy. Showing the supernatural forces her stress would be letting them win. Clark might not understand why their respective engagements at Arden seemed impossibly at odds, but she did.

Carefully, she clipped a few strands from where his dark hair curled against his nape before placing them in one of the small bags secured around her belt for gathering herbs.

"Are we even now?" he asked her afterward. "I'm afraid I haven't been keeping proper score."

"We'll never be even." Every time Riley moved against him, Clark found a way to catch her off guard, to slide under her defenses.

Even when he wasn't trying, he made her job harder.

Chapter Twelve

Clark didn't mean to call his dad.

After Riley left, he'd picked up his phone to contact the preservation society, to update them about the cave and the etchings that they (she, really) had found. It was exactly the kind of discovery he'd hoped for when he took this off-color assignment. If those symbols really did belong to an ancient people, the HES would look to secure external funding for an initial investigation. As the person who delivered the lead, Clark might get to spearhead the process or at least take part. Even though now he could hardly summon the exhilaration he knew he should feel at the prospect of such an opportunity.

He must have dialed on autopilot, the newspaper clipping in the back of his mind even as he tried to tuck memories of Patrick neatly away. As he strained to keep Riley at arm's length, if not farther, and failed at that too.

When Alfie answered after two rings, sounding groggy, Clark realized with a jolt that he didn't know where in the world his father was at the moment.

The movie was still launching in new markets. An assistant had emailed over the schedule a while back, but Clark couldn't recall the specifics.

"Sorry," Looking at his watch, he guessed Alfie must be somewhere in Asia. "I didn't mean to wake you."

"'Sall right. Give me a moment to find the light switch."

Clark waited, listening to his dad's mumbled curse as he bumped into the wall, then his yawn.

It was often difficult to get his father's attention, especially now, when he was in even higher demand than usual.

Finally, he settled in with a sigh. "Give me the report."

The words were said casually; his father might have meant anything, a simple sort of check-in. But Clark couldn't help snapping to attention, skipping past niceties into a professional update.

It was a bit awkward, trying to recount the story of discovering the dagger, the etchings, without mentioning Riley, but Clark managed. Thinking about her made his head hurt, threatening to trigger a tension headache, but it was more important to show progress after a month of nothing. Clark had predicted Riley would infiltrate his carefully constructed Path to Professional Redemption™ when he found out why she'd been hired, but he hadn't expected her to dig so far into his personal upheaval. Maybe that wasn't fair; after all, he was the one who'd gone into the family business, ensuring that there were no boundaries between blood and ambition.

"Good, that's good," his father said when he'd finished the summary of his progress. "I'll admit I was getting a bit worried we'd sent you to those fancy schools for nothing."

Clark weathered the graze, barely noticing it.

Alfie Edgeware had come up the son of a butcher and a schoolteacher and almost immediately become exceptional. There wasn't a lot of money in archaeology. His dad had hustled from day one for speaking engagements and later the book deal, had insisted on consulting on the film even though they'd offered him more money to leave the California creatives alone. He'd risen at the same time as the golden age of Indiana Jones, when the world had hungered for a real-life stand-in to the action hero's charismatic mythos, minus the cultural appropriation. Was it any wonder Clark's meager accomplishments seemed like relative failure in comparison?

"You think the symbols are Pictish in origin?" His dad specialized in the broad region of the UK. He'd even done an adjunct stint at St. Andrews on Scotland's ancient peoples when Clark was a boy.

They tossed a few theories back and forth—it was nice, easy— ground they were both comfortable treading. His dad was eager to come visit so they could go back and look at the cave together.

"Family project," he announced absently, checking his calendar and tsking at what he found.

Clark closed his eyes. *Family project.* It's what he'd said, proudly, when they were little—about everything from doing the dishes to building a tree house in the yard. It's what he said when he found out Patrick had invited Clark to Spain.

His dad probably didn't even realize the slip, was already shifting into goodbyes, but Clark couldn't shake the timing of it. Patrick hovering like a specter in the room with him. His letters sitting undisturbed in the box Riley had pulled out earlier—most of them unanswered.

"Right." The phone was hot where it pressed against his cheek.

On some level, maybe this was why he'd called. To remind himself about his dad's expectations and the consequences of not meeting them.

"See you soon."

A single conversation had ensured he couldn't turn tail and run, so the next morning, Clark decided to work in the stables.

There were other interior rooms higher up on his list, but when he got like this—gloomy and agitated—he needed to be outside, to feel the sun on his face. To remember that though he was here to study the dead, he hadn't joined their number and could still change his fate.

Though the frame of the stable was intact—whoever built it had reinforced the wood with stone—its thatched roof had holes that opened to the sky.

Clark used a hand pick and his masonry trowel to break up the soil floor, removing weeds and debris, looking for artifacts that had probably been lost to either looters or the elements long ago. As he worked, he saved organic materials for sampling: seeds, wood chips, bits of charcoal. Occasionally, a sliver of glass or metal. The HES might not even want the stuff, but Clark needed the routine and the carefulness in contrast to how messy and exposed he felt inside.

Maybe if he hadn't dedicated his every waking hour to work, his lack of progress wouldn't feel so dire. But growing up a famous father's overlooked second son had warped his sense of self. Clark grew up defining the relationships in his life by what he could offer people—knowledge or assistance, and on his worst days, borrowed clout.

Especially now, without the halo effect of his father or brother— he knew he had to be the smartest person in any room. Otherwise, no one would want him there.

Another two days passed.

Martin stopped by only long enough to say he was going on holiday to France for a bit over a fortnight. When Clark asked if the investment firm would be sending a replacement to monitor their progress, he laughed.

Apparently oversight of the dilapidated castle was low on their list of management priorities.

It was just as well, since Clark continued to acquire nothing of note from his survey except for a mild sunburn on the back of his neck. He took a small degree of solace in the fact that whatever Riley was trying to do didn't seem to be working either.

Yesterday, she had constructed this thing—it looked sort of like a wreath, only shaped like a triangle—made of twigs and herbs and wildflowers. She kept hanging it in different places around the castle. First the front entrance. Then the back. Even outside the stable at one point.

She tried making it bigger, then switching the direction the point faced, groaning for some reason every time Clark walked past it on his way in or out. Perhaps she was just groaning at the sight of him. He didn't ask.

Though it wasn't her fault, her beauty carried the constant threat of distraction. Both her body, soft and full—as lush as the most indulgent portrait of Venus—and her arrestingly expressive face. Her frustration was so animated—she pumped her arms in the air and stomped away, blowing air through her lips like she was trying to fill a balloon. Clark envied the freedom of her anger. How she trusted herself to show it.

He told himself she was only a woman, like any other. That he could, with a bit of effort, work in parallel to her while remaining calm, cool, and— Dear god did she have to close her eyes as she rubbed sunscreen down her throat?

Needless to say, when she came up to him around noon on Wednesday, a hamper over her arm and a scowl on her face, and said, "I got you a picnic," Clark was more than a little taken aback.

It didn't help that she'd chosen an entirely black spandex outfit today. As if she hadn't messed with his head enough this week. Christ, she was curvy.

"Pardon?" He wiped his damp brow with the back of his hand.

"I did a shitty thing." She toed at a clod of dirt rather than look at him. "And you did a shitty thing too—"

He had. Emotional whiplash from the oscillation between betrayer and betrayed had definitely contributed to his current funk.

"—but I don't like my shitty thing being the last shitty thing that happened. So, here." She held the basket out. "Guilt cheese."

"Is that an American idiom?"

"No, there's really cheese in there." She shook the handle until he grasped it. "Plus sausage rolls, apples, and some grapes."

"No wine?" He opened the hamper, saw a napkin with the pub's logo. "Not much of an apology."

She shrugged. "I don't like you that much."

As Clark laughed, his stomach muscles contracted in a way that felt morosely unfamiliar.

"You already apologized." He knew she felt bad for the other day—and she should, it was a huge violation—but he hadn't expected anything beyond what he'd previously received.

"I know," she said softly, and then louder, "But I'm still trying to break the curse, and you're sort of . . . *in the line of fire*. Usually, people who might get hurt are willing participants. They hire me, so they sign off on the risks. You didn't."

No. In fact he'd done just about everything he could to avoid getting caught in her crosshairs. Not that it had worked.

"So, whatever." She tugged at the bottom of her stretchy shirt. "I guess I feel guilty seeing you walking around all extra mopey."

"It's called brooding," Clark said, standing up a little straighter, "and no one complained when Darcy did it."

"Yeah, well"—she gave him a look just shy of a leer—"that's because Colin Firth had the decency to get his shirt wet."

"I'm waiting to be asked," he said reflexively, forgetting they weren't allowed to flirt the way they had that first night at the pub.

He liked the little blush stealing across her cheeks too much.

"Hey." He nodded at the basket. "Why don't you join me?"

The second the words left his mouth, Clark wished he could snatch them back. He'd found a tiny bit of peace these last few days, even if he hadn't particularly enjoyed it. What was he doing, willfully backtracking for a few kind words and a heated look?

"Like a truce?" Riley said, clearly uncertain.

"Are we still at war?" Clearly neither of them felt particularly comfortable with deception.

"Yes," she said, any lightness from their earlier exchange gone from her face.

"Fine, then." Clark supposed he should be grateful that she held the line when he seemed to struggle with it so much. "Like a truce."

They found a bit of shade under a grove of trees in the courtyard and made one of Clark's tarps into a picnic blanket. He even pulled two beers out of his fridge, bringing them out and explaining, "My contribution to peacekeeping efforts."

In true picnic form, none of the food required utensils, though watching Riley lick cheese off her thumb momentarily made Clark wish otherwise.

"We should play a game," she suggested, stretching out her legs and kicking off her boots to reveal mismatched socks, both navy but one with thin white stripes.

"Like what?" His position on the tarp provided an excellent view from which to admire her legs, if one were so inclined.

After some bickering, they settled on Six Degrees of Kevin Bacon.

Clark was awful.

"What do you mean, *who is Laura Dern?*" Riley's shout scared a family of birds out of their nest. "She was in Greta Gerwig's *Little Women*, *Big Little Lies* on HBO. She was an integral part of a Star War!"

"I've never seen any of those things." Clark popped another grape in his mouth. They were quite good. Tart. Juicy. It was fascinating to see how bothered Riley got over his lack of exposure to American pop culture.

"How?!" She blinked at him extravagantly, dropping open her jaw. "What about *Jurassic Park*?"

The movie with the all the dinosaurs? He supposed it might have been on TV sometime when he was in primary school. "What about it?"

"It's got fossilized DNA in it." Riley put down her apple to smack him on the arm. "As an archaeologist, you should be, like, obsessed with that."

"Paleontology is in an entirely separate field," he said primly, then took a long sip of his beer. "So does your Laura Dern voice one of the dinosaurs?"

"Does she—what— Oh my god, no! The dinosaurs don't speak. Are you from another planet?" Riley gaped at him, wide-eyed with outrage, until he cracked and smiled, and she realized she'd been had.

He'd never really teased anyone growing up. He'd always been too obviously sensitive to invite that kind of playful interaction. Don't dish it out if you can't take it, et cetera. Even Patrick had always gone easy on him, hyperaware that Clark was prone to emotional bruising. He'd looked on with envy while other lads ribbed each other, jostling their shoulders, coming up with silly nicknames.

It was a way of being close he never thought he'd get to experience but had always wanted to. Done right, he thought, teasing gave you permission to take yourself less seriously. Riley did that for him, let him try to do it back.

"I'm not playing with you anymore." She picked up one of his grapes and threw it at him. "It's thankless."

They played four more rounds while they finished their lunch.

By the end of it, Clark's white shirt was covered in grape stains from ones she'd lobbed at him, though he had managed to catch a few in his mouth near the end.

Before he knew it, two hours had passed, and Clark found he'd had one of the best afternoons in recent memory, with this woman who'd actively admitted they'd never be friends.

He was in the middle of an impression of Sir Michael Caine that Riley had somehow convinced him to attempt when a loud hiss came from about a foot to his left.

He scrambled to his feet, scanning the nearby grass for— *Yikes.*

Clark's pulse spiked, a cool tremor shooting across his skin with instinctive revulsion as every one of his limbs seemed to lock at once. *There. Still coiled. A snake.*

"Okay, remain calm." He held out both palms slowly, hoping Riley wouldn't try to move toward the angry reptile, given her propensity for launching herself face-first toward danger. "I've read about it and there's only one kind of venomous snake in Scotland."

Reddish-brown body. About two feet long. Distinct zigzag pattern across the back.

Oh. That was definitely—

"An adder," Riley supplied, not moving, not taking her eyes off the animal.

The snake hissed again, sustaining the sound as it began to slowly unfurl its scaled body. Adders weren't normally aggressive, but not much about this castle was normal.

"Move," she told him urgently as the animal angled itself in their direction.

Clark started backing away, keeping his eyes on the snake, but the animal tracked him, following with increasing speed.

Adder bites don't kill people, he consoled himself. *Usually.* Though apparently they caused excruciating pain.

As if offering a demonstration, the adder opened its jaw, thrusting its head forward with extended fangs.

"You're not moving fast enough," Riley yelled, and when he looked back, she was much farther from their canopy of trees than he expected.

Something was wrong with his feet. They weren't obeying, tangling together in his fear.

I'm going to get bit, he realized a few seconds before Riley grabbed a long stick off the ground and then, tilting her head to judge the angle, lunged, scooping under the snake's writhing form, lifting, flicking, lobbing the adder about ten feet into a set of soft shrubs.

Clark stood as frozen as a statue, mouth open to catch flies.

"Let's go." Dropping the stick, she grabbed Clark's hand and broke into a straight run, bodily dragging him in the opposite direction of the still-spitting snake until they made it inside the gates to lean against the castle's cold stone wall—each of them pulling in oxygen in great heaving gasps.

Clark closed his eyes. "Please tell me you didn't just fling an angry, venomous snake with a stick."

"It was gonna bite you!" she protested. Her face was closer than he'd thought, close enough that he could see the arc of her lashes, the way her incisors were slightly long, how one eye had more gold in it than the other. With most people, the more he got to know them, the less he found them intimidating. Riley wasn't like that.

"Where the fuck did that thing come from?" How had she known how to handle it? Did they have a lot of snakes in South Jersey?

"I think the curse was trying to send us a message." Riley looked up at the castle. "It doesn't like it when we're nice to each other."

As if just now noticing that she still held his hand, she finally released it. For some reason, that kind of thing kept happening.

Clark flexed his fingers. "What do you mean?"

"Think about it. You gave me your gloves; the castle gave you a rash."

"I'm sure it must have had something to do with an external irritant."

"I let you in on my approach to curse breaking," she continued, "and I literally catch on fire."

"Well, you shouldn't have built a blaze in that ancient fireplace in the first place—"

"And now," Riley said over him, "we call a temporary cease-fire and the only venomous snake in Scotland appears out of freaking nowhere."

When he first met her, he'd assumed a curse breaker would be all airy-fairy, but the way her brain worked was consistently scientific. Cause and effect. Process of elimination. The more he spent time with her, the more he understood how she drew in clients. She would have been persuasive, if he hadn't had his guard up.

"Even if you think these events are supernatural in influence," Clark began, "you can't think the curse would be so particular about the way you and I interact."

She might think him self-important, but he and Riley were hardly the first people the castle had tried to banish. For centuries, Arden's lore and the strange events surrounding the property had driven people off. The power of suggestion held tremendous sway.

Riley made a noncommittal noise.

Only once they'd waited long enough to be totally sure the coast was clear did they venture back to clean up the remains of their picnic.

As they were packing up, Clark came across an untouched red thermos he hadn't noticed in the hamper. "Is this yours?"

"Oh, yeah." She tried to shove the thing behind her back. "It's nothing. A cleansing solution. I was supposed to try and get you to drink it."

Clark recoiled. "Not the one you used on that evil Victorian eBay doll from your website?!"

That client testimonial still haunted him.

Prior to curse removal, Wilhelmina Spindlehausen showed the propensity to randomly turn off light switches in any room she occupied. Her glass eyes followed me every-where, and she emanated a chill that could permeate a ten-foot radius.

"No." Riley looked up and to the left. "I mean, I diluted it. Like a lot."

Taking the thermos from her, Clark unscrewed the top, checking to see if the liquid inside bubbled. "It smells like pure petrol."

The thermos had a bumper sticker on the front that read *Stay Shameless.* Certainly a fitting moniker.

"I can't believe you were trying to poison me during our truce." That snake had done him a favor, breaking up the chummy scene.

"Okay, first of all, I didn't give it to you, did I?" She stuck her nose in the air. "And besides, cleansing dolls is one of my most regular sources of income. You'd think the freaky factor was the selling point, but I guess some people bring them home and end up with buyer's remorse."

Clark swirled the thermos. The liquid inside was so aggressively herbal his eyes started to water just from the smell.

"Not for all the gold on god's bloody green earth am I ingesting that." He could admit that whatever she'd used in that salve had proved remarkably effective. But still, a man had limits.

"That's fine." She snatched it back, spilling a little on both of them. Clark was relieved to find it didn't singe his flesh. "I'd ruled out cleansing as a strategy anyway. I'm pretty sure it only works on objects."

He was unreasonably annoyed that she'd had an ulterior motive. It shouldn't sting that she'd done nothing but prove his initial assessment of her correct.

"I suppose it would have been too much to hope your hamper was truly altruistic."

Riley blew out a frustrated breath. "I did pack the basket as a peace offering originally. It just so happened that while I was at the pub last night having dinner, Ceilidh told me about this local wild mint that I thought might work well in a cleansing solution, so . . ." She shook her head. "You know what? It doesn't matter. You and me, we both know we're nothing but the job, right?"

"Absolutely."

Clark said he wouldn't forget they weren't friends, and unlike this brother, he kept his word.

Chapter Thirteen

Riley was starting to think it must be sacrifice. Her charms had flopped majorly. They didn't repel Clark—they didn't even make him pause in the entryway. Cleansing had always been a long shot, and at this point, she was confident she'd made the right call ruling it out. She could, with some moral backbends, justify B&E, but even she drew the line at potential poisoning.

No. Sacrifice made more sense. Not least because the more she got to know Clark, the less Riley *wanted* to drive him away. The process of curse breaking had never felt bad—wrong—before, but this time, every exercise felt like trudging uphill. Obviously she needed to switch directions, and fast.

Sacrifice. She ran her fingertips across Gran's handwriting, the familiar loops and curls across the page—*One thing you value in exchange for another.*

"You're supposed to feel the lack," Riley told her clients. "That's how you know it's working."

And besides, she'd done harder stuff in the name of her professional pursuits than run off some random guy. Telling her mom she wanted to pick up the mantle of curse breaking some twenty odd years after her dad left them over it, for example. But past experience didn't matter. There was something about Clark that got under her skin. He thought her mere presence on the site was such a danger to his career. She might as well prove him right by blowing up his redemption gig.

A combination of bitterness and guilt kept her up at night, even if nothing about her plans seemed to trouble Ceilidh.

"It's like that one Buffy episode where Sunnydale students keep getting caught in a loop repeating the tragic love story of some couple from like the 1950s," she said after Riley updated her on her latest theory regarding the curse.

Ceilidh, Riley had begun to suspect, was a romantic.

"It's not like that, really." Riley had to explain the whole "curses can't interfere with free will" thing again.

It would be easier, actually, if she could turn off her brain and let the ghost of Philippa Campbell choreograph what needed to be done.

"If it's bothering you so much, why don't you just remind yourself of all the reasons you didn't like him before?" Ceilidh suggested, following Riley's complaints about her inconvenient conscience.

And . . . that wasn't a bad idea. Not at all.

The next day Riley set up shop in the room Clark was excavating.

He'd moved upstairs, finally, to one of the south-facing bedrooms. Like all the parts of the castle that backed up to the cliffside, this space had sustained less damage than those that faced the road. All the walls and ceilings still stood in good repair, as well as most of the floor—though some of the wooden boards had warped from water damage. The sagging remains of a bed could be found in the center of the room, the linens so moth-bitten they might as well have been thread.

Operation Roller Skates would serve two purposes. One, she could observe any annoying habits Clark had that she might have missed. Personally, she was hoping for nose picking.

Her second goal was simply to bother him—make sure he kept

up his side of the loathing. Riley would have made a deliberate plan to provoke him if she didn't think simply being herself would achieve the same outcome.

He made her job easier by providing a camp chair that she unfolded with a satisfying snap. She didn't know why he brought it. Presumably he took breaks sometimes. But the thing was pretty comfy and even had a cup holder for her water bottle! Score.

After planting herself in his periphery, she took out a magazine. This shouldn't take long.

She'd worn an outfit designed to provoke him. A white peasant blouse see-through enough that the bra he'd gotten up close and personal with during that trip to her bedroom showed through, plus a pair of ass-squeezing vintage bell bottoms she'd thrifted. When topped off with stiletto boots, the outfit was deliciously impractical, breaking almost every rule he'd given her about proper work-site attire.

Infuriatingly, Clark managed to ignore her for most of the morning, even if he did huff out an irate little breath every time he walked past her chair.

Finally, when she took out the big guns—uncapping a bottle of nail polish that immediately unleashed headache-inducing fumes to touch up her manicure—he cracked.

"Don't you have work to do?" He wrinkled his nose. "A caldron to stir somewhere?"

"I'm not a witch." She didn't practice magic, she tussled with it. There was a difference.

Though on second thought, she wouldn't say no to a cauldron. It would come in handy. She was constantly ruining stockpots cleansing those dolls.

"Could have fooled me," he muttered from where he was sorting through the remains of a dilapidated closet.

Riley smiled as she painted her pinky nail. This was exactly the kind of cranky unpleasantness she'd come for.

Under no circumstances could she allow the animosity between them to fade enough that the curse no longer qualified them as enemies. In fact, maybe she should be even more provocative.

"Clark," she called, finishing off her left hand.

"Yes?" He was in the process of setting up a giant ladder.

Riley could have waited until he finished or offered to help, but neither of those behaviors would have served her objective of raising his blood pressure.

"What would you say are your worst traits?"

He poked his head around the corner to frown at her. "Do people normally offer up this kind of information to you?"

She chewed her bottom lip, considering. "Actually, yeah."

Riley didn't know if it was the bartender thing, or the "men love unloading their emotional baggage on women because they don't feel they have societal permission to form intimate relationships with same-gender friends" thing, or the curse-breaker "I will help solve your problems, even the ones that seem impossible" thing, but she added, "Kinda all the time."

"Well, considering the rocky history of our brief acquaintance, you'll excuse me if I don't jump at the chance to offer you any more of my vulnerabilities."

She felt a twang of discomfort. He was referencing the family drama she'd uncovered. But this was different. They liked teasing each other. They were good at it. And what was more, it was safe. Bickering gave them something to hide behind.

"Oh, come on, it'll be fun," she needled. "Here, I'll start you off. You're overly critical." She began ticking things off on her newly manicured fingers. "A complete control freak, and all of your shirts are just slightly too big."

Clark stared at her, eyes coolly assessing, not picking up his sword right away.

"Oh," he said after a beat, "I see. You're here to satisfy your hero complex."

"My *what*?" Sure, she'd chosen an occupation where she could help people, but so did doctors and teachers and stuff. No one accused them of ulterior motives. "I don't have a complex."

"You absolutely do." He watched her fidget, his face going severe, closed off. "But I'm not interested in being rescued. Thanks."

Riley struggled to reconcile the grating metal of his tone. Her? Rescue him? From what? Being rich and clever and too handsome for his own good?

"In fact"—Clark had worked himself up enough that there were scorch marks high on his cheekbones as he fussed with the ladder—"you might consider that you're the one who needs saving."

"Excuse me. What did you just say to me?" He'd called her every kind of liar, but this was another step beyond.

"You're reckless and obstinate." Clark counted on his hand, mirroring her previous action. "And if I hadn't been at this castle, looking out for you—thankless task that it is—you would have done yourself a serious injury by now, most likely multiple times over."

"Oh yeah?" Riley's temperature rose in alarming spikes. Of all the self-important, hypocritical bullshit she'd heard from him, this was the tops. "Well, you're a villain who thinks he's a victim."

Hurt flashed across his eyes, but Riley ignored it, barreling forward on a lethal cocktail of rage and unwanted lust. This guy? This asshole had to be the hottest man she'd ever seen? Really?

How many times did she have to save his ass before he believed she could handle herself?

She should have let that snake bite him. Should have stood by and watched as he writhed in pain at her feet.

"And you know what else?" Her voice shook slightly with anger, "If *I* hadn't come to Arden, you'd have nothing to show for almost six weeks of work."

Clark seethed, grip on the ladder tightening, his knuckles going white.

Riley thought he might storm out and relished the thought. She'd come for this fight. If she was afraid of getting her hands dirty, she wouldn't be here.

Instead, he stalked closer. "I'm not the only one floundering here, though, am I?" He stood over her, looking down his nose. "When are you going to admit you're completely out of your depth?"

Riley sucked in a breath. He'd struck a nerve she didn't touch, didn't look at. Suddenly, it felt like more than her top was see-through, like he could stare through her skin to her tender, striving heart.

"You might have a few family parlor tricks up your sleeve." His voice wasn't raised, no, it was dark, and low. "But when it comes to actually"—he raised his hands to make fucking finger quotes—"*breaking the curse*—"

That was it. If she had that dagger in her hand right now, Clark would lose more than a button.

"—so far all you've done is drop a priceless artifact *in a fire* and hang a bunch of ugly wreaths. Which, let's add that up, amounts to precisely *nothing*. Hmm." He tapped his chin. "If you can really do what you say, how come everything you try fails?"

He'd said rude things to her before, but those barbs had been easier to dismiss, unequivocally not true.

They knew each other now. These insults weren't shots in the dark. They came after almost two weeks of weighing, measuring, and he'd aimed for maximum damage.

Just as Riley surrendered to her anger, letting it burn up her weakness, her fear that he was right, the clouds shifted outside the window, changing the light in the room. A piece of the ornate crown molding glimmered—winked at her.

Ha!

If Clark thought the worst thing she could do was pity him, he was wrong.

"You wanna talk to me about incompetence?" She pushed past him, purposefully ramming her shoulder into his as she grabbed his stupid ladder. "You've been working in this room all morning, and you don't even know where to look."

The metal ladder made a heavy scraping sound as she dragged it across the floor. Damn. It wasn't terribly tall, maybe eight feet, but the thing was heavier than it looked.

As Riley moved, so did the clouds outside, until the room grew progressively dimmer, the sun all but blotted out. By the looks of it, Arden Castle was in for a storm.

"What do you think you're doing?" Clark stomped over.

"Your job, only better than you." Hand over hand, she started to climb.

"Oh, excellent," he said sarcastically. "Scale a rickety old ladder in heeled boots *inside a castle notorious for freak accidents*. That'll end well."

Despite his protests, he reached out to hold the base, stabilizing it.

"What's possessed you this time? Oh. Let me guess. Smelled sulfur again, Lassie?"

Riley knocked on the part of the wood she'd seen illuminated, going up on her toes as she tried to hear if it was hollow.

Clark warily eyed where she was prodding. "Do be delicate, that could very well be remnants of the original design—" he said just as she curled back her arm and struck her elbow through the weakest spot in the wood.

While she yelped—that hurt more than she'd anticipated—Clark massaged the bridge of his nose with the hand not holding the ladder.

"Tell me truly. Are you or are you not the personification of chaos?"

Ignoring him, she rooted around in the hole she'd created. There must be something up here. The light had been so odd, such a tantalizing temptation.

"I can't tell if there's something back here." She leaned on one foot to get her hand deeper.

"Riley, you really shouldn't—"

"I'm fine." She shushed him.

"Did you just— Never in my life . . ." he muttered.

After a few more minutes of failed inspection, she deflated. "I guess there's nothing here."

Her cheeks burned. All her instincts had told her to climb up here to prove Clark wrong. Now it felt like the curse laughing at her expense.

She'd been so sure she'd have this moment of triumph, whipping out another artifact. Instead, all she'd delivered was another dramatic act of failure.

Clark was going to be even more insufferable now.

Riley moved to step down but before she could even lift her foot to descend the first rung, Clark cut in, "Be careful."

"I am," she said, realizing in the same moment that her sleeve had caught on the splintered wood of the hole.

Oh, perfect—Riley leaned back and forth, trying to create enough leverage to pull free, but the gauzy fabric just tangled worse.

Sure, why wouldn't her strategically selected outfit turn on her too? Why shouldn't the curse make her into even more of a spectacle?

"Don't yank at it," Clark scolded just as the material gave way with a violent-sounding tear.

Her stomach plummeted as she went rocking backward, her equilibrium thrown.

Riley had that terrible moment of knowing she was gonna fall right before she went down.

But instead of the cold hard floor greeting her, she tumbled backward into Clark's arms, her body landing against his with a loud *thwack*.

He kept his footing, barely, stumbling back a few steps with his arms around her waist.

"Easy, now," he said, and Riley realized she was trembling.

Must be the adrenaline.

"You're all right." Spinning her around, Clark patted her hair back from her face with one hand, keeping the other in place to steady her. "I've got you."

"I think you were supposed to drop me," she said weakly, once she'd regained control of her hectic breath.

"It's too late for that now," he said seriously, but his lips curved up. "I could have a bit of a grope, if you'd like." He slid his palm from her waist toward her thigh. "Split the difference?"

He was trying to make her laugh, and it worked, warmth chasing away the lingering bitterness of fear.

"You can let me go now," she said softly, not really wanting it. His hand was huge on her hip, not groping despite his words, but there. Lingering.

He was looking at her mouth, his own breath unsteady. "Can I?"

Who knew what might have happened if a great crack of thunder hadn't startled them apart? A second later, a brilliant flash of lightning illuminated the entire room.

Uh-oh.

They both turned toward the window as rain began to smack against the glass.

"Oh, crap." Walking back to the inn in this mess was not gonna be fun.

By the time they got outside, the low ground had already begun to flood, wide puddles gathering as streams of water ran down the muddy earth.

By the time they'd taken ten steps beyond the parapet, they were both soaked to the skin, and freezing liquid had seeped through the fake-leather soles of Riley's boots.

More thunder clapped and a lethal-looking lightning bolt cut across the cliffside to cast a spotlight on the comically exposed path back toward the inn.

Clark raised his voice to be heard over the sounds of the storm.

"Camper on the grounds is starting to look pretty smart all of a sudden, isn't it?"

The wind swallowed her answering profanity.

Chapter Fourteen

Riley dripped on the ridged rubber entrance mat while Clark unlaced his boots and then hurried forward, muttering about fetching towels. She toed off her own shoes beside his. The muffled sounds of the storm raging outside made the interior of the camper—warm, dry, and alarmingly intimate—feel like a hideaway reminiscent of pillow forts and tree houses.

What the hell had just happened? One minute she was torturing Clark, the next she was in his arms. That wasn't supposed to happen. They weren't supposed to almost kiss. Why did the curse destroy all her best-laid plans?

"Here." Clark tossed her a beige towel, avoiding looking directly at her.

Staring down, she realized it might be because water had turned her already thin top fully translucent. *Whoops.*

"We'll both need to change, I expect." He plucked at where his soaked denim work shirt had plastered itself to his chest like it paid for the privilege. "I can get you some dry things."

When he returned with a navy sweater and gray sweatpants, items that would hang loose on Clark and hopefully cover her curves, he looked as freaked out as Riley felt.

"I'm, uh, not sure what you'd like to do about underthings." Clark made a valiant effort to speak to her left eyebrow. "I could—"

"I can go without," she cut him off. The last thing she needed was to have the black briefs she'd seen in his drawer pressed against her.

"Right." Clark looked slightly dazed. "I suppose I better leave you to it, then." He turned. "The bathroom's clear. Cat must have found somewhere else to camp out. I'll be in the bedroom. With the divider closed," he finished awkwardly.

Riley waited until he'd managed to get the flimsy plastic barrier hooked before heading into the tiny bathroom and unbuttoning her jeans.

It was surreal to be undressing within five feet of Clark, knowing he was doing the same, even if they couldn't see each other.

The plywood door of the bathroom was thin. Could he hear the slide of her zipper? The *shush* of wet denim clinging as it slid down her thighs?

She had goose bumps all down her legs, no doubt from having been soaked to the skin for so long.

Moving to the sink, she did her best to squeeze the water out of her clothes before hanging them in the shower. Hopefully they'd dry enough for her to be able to wear them home when the storm let up.

Naked and shivering, she reached for the sweater Clark had given her. The interior of the camper was warmer than outside. But try telling that to her nipples.

She sighed as she pulled the soft material over her head, trying in vain to pluck at it so it wouldn't settle too closely against her unbound breasts. Wow, it wasn't scratchy at all. This must be a rich-person sweater. A quick peek at the label confirmed: one hundred percent cashmere.

Okay, time for the sweats. Shaking the pants out, she held them against her legs. Riley gave it fifty-fifty odds that she'd get them on without splitting the seams. Besides a penchant for curse breaking, she'd inherited Gran's "birthing hips" and an ass to match. Carefully, she shimmied the pants up. While they stretched intensely across her thighs and stuck like cling wrap to everything else, she got them on thanks to the elastic waistband. *Phew.*

Another bolt of lightning cracked across the sky, making her jump.

There wasn't room in the shower to hang her towel. She'd have to ask if there was somewhere else she could put it.

"Clark?" Riley knocked gently against the divider to his bedroom. "Yes?"

She assumed that meant *Yes, I'm fully dressed*, so she pushed back the divider only to find it very much did not mean that.

She caught him in profile, and for a second the inside of her brain was just *Thighs, thighs, thighs.* All that taut muscle cut in harsh, heavy lines.

Riley licked her suddenly parched lips.

"Do you mind?" Clark said blandly, sounding more bemused than offended at her attention.

Oh, fuck. She covered her eyes with her hand.

"Sorry." *That's good, Riley, get caught ogling the enemy.*

There was a sound of material in motion as he resumed dressing. Then, "All done," he said softly.

When Riley lowered her hand, he wore a tattered rugby shirt and dry jeans, his feet bare.

"I have your towel." She held it up as evidence.

"Thanks," he smirked, taking it and spreading the material across the back of the chair in the corner. "Do you need anything else?"

"No. Thank you," she said awkwardly. He'd already been more generous than she was comfortable with—there was no missing the way her curves were making his nice clothes beg for mercy. "I just need to figure out something to do with this." She lifted her sodden mass of hair that had started to soak through the shoulder of his sweater.

Clark looked up from where he was hanging his towel. "I could plait it for you, if you like."

"You know how to braid hair?"

He raised one shoulder. "My nan likes it done."

"Oh." She refused to find that endearing. "Okay, then. I guess, if you don't mind?"

"Have a seat." He gestured to the foot of the bed.

Riley made her way over and tried to sit as primly as possible for someone whose brain had melted to goo at the sight of her nemesis's hairy quads.

Clark grabbed a comb from one of the cabinets built into the bookshelf (*So he does have one*) and then, standing behind her, proceeded to part her hair.

The first press of the comb's teeth set off her already tingling nerve endings. Riley made herself hold still, keeping her back straight in a callback to his posture when she'd given him a massage.

With their positions reversed, she couldn't help noticing that for all she'd been trying to break him then, he was careful with her now. Starting at the ends of her hair, patiently working his way through snarls. No matter how many times she pushed him, how many ways she tried to prove she didn't want coddling, he always found a way to be careful with her. That, more than his condemnation, was hard to shake.

For a few breaths there was nothing but his presence at her back, large and close and warm, and the gentle tugging of the comb at her scalp. Riley didn't know whether to laugh or whimper. It was maddening, having this man she wanted to loathe constantly find ways to burrow beneath her defenses.

Clark's knuckles brushed the sensitive arch of her neck as he sectioned off her hair for the braid. Riley's lips parted. Even though he couldn't see her face, she felt so exposed, here in his bed, wearing his things, letting him touch her.

She tried to calm herself by taking a deep breath, but of course these clothes smelled like whatever fancy organic detergent he used—fresh but not floral, with a lingering hint of the sunscreen and bug spray he wore. Summer scents that made her think of grilling and swimming and heated, glistening skin.

While he constructed the braid in quick, sure strokes, she sat there helplessly, trying not to focus on the dexterity of his fingers. When the next tug on her hair pulled sharply, Riley let out a soft gasp.

"Sorry." Clark immediately relaxed his grip. "I'll be more careful."

"Don't bother. I like it," Riley blurted without thinking.

There was a heavy pause.

Her pulse began to match the wild riot of the storm pounding against the metal roof.

There's no need to get embarrassed, she told herself, fighting off a mounting urge to panic. So she liked a certain kind of sex. So what? She knew this about herself and had for a while. It wasn't a big deal.

And sure, it required a partner with certain complementary inclinations, but Riley didn't expect Clark Edgeware to give her what she needed.

He was English. His people had practically invented repression.

Except he was slowly wrapping the tendrils of her hair more firmly around his fist.

"Do you?" The words fell like velvet against the skin he'd exposed at the back of her neck.

This time when he pulled the pressure was deliberate. A test.

Riley shouldn't do this.

They'd been in a constant power struggle since they met.

He thought she was beneath him.

She wanted to be.

"Yes," she said, heart thrashing inside her chest.

"How much?" The question wasn't breathy. He didn't just want to hear her say it—though she assumed there was an element of that. No, Clark asked like a scientist—curious, assessing. Like he wanted to know precisely how to make her hot.

"Just . . ." Riley closed her eyes for a second, gathering her strength. "*Harder.*"

He placed one knee on the bed beside her and leaned forward until his back almost covered hers and his face was just above her left shoulder.

"Really," he said, low, interested. Not a question.

Clark used his grip on her hair to tilt Riley's face toward his, until only a handful of inches separated their lips and her scalp stung.

"Tell me to stop." The rough stubble of his permanent five-o'clock shadow lay in vivid contrast to the soft invitation of his mouth.

Riley stared into his eyes, defiant. There was nothing he could do to her that she couldn't take.

His breathing had shifted, his chest rising and falling under the rugby shirt with exaggerated movement. Clark moved his mouth to the underside of her jaw and planted the faintest, barely there kiss.

"Tell me you don't want me." The command was gravel rough, grinding. As harsh as the hand in her hair.

"No." Riley relished the refusal, leaning forward so the tension from his grip grew even tighter as she closed the distance between them.

Clark pulled back from the kiss almost immediately, his eyes wide, shocked. He hadn't thought she'd go through with it. Had assumed this, like so many of their interactions, was another game.

This time when he laughed, it was soft, dark. "You'll be the death of me yet."

The proclamation seemed to unlock something inside him. When he kissed her after, there was nothing tentative about it. He took her mouth like it belonged to him. Like all of her did.

His lips should have been poison with the way she went dizzy, pliant in an instant. Nothing should feel this good. Each press and slide of his tongue going straight between her thighs.

They kissed the way they did everything, a heady give-and-take.

Clark slid his free palm from her jaw slowly down her throat, the touch light, caressing, to rest between the wings of her collarbone. He sucked her bottom lip, bit the swollen curve. More than a little bit cruel.

I'll pay for this, she thought, and, determined to get her money's worth, closed her eyes against a shiver.

The scent of his skin, the warm weight of his hand on her chest, the way he held her hair. It was all terrible and exquisite.

"Riley." Clark scraped his teeth against the hinge of her jaw. "Let me leave a mark."

She nodded, the movement limited by his grip, ready to spread her legs just from the way he said her name.

He raked her from head to toe, assessing. "Where?"

Riley imagined her naked skin marked by imprints of his desire.

She was an agent of her own destruction. As reckless as he'd said.

"Anywhere." She breathed hard in and out through her nose, feeling positively feral. "Anywhere you want."

The most severe parts of his face—the slash of his dark brows, that hard mouth—pulled wicked with delight.

Riley expected him to go for her neck, to leave his first bruise where it would be most visible as a conquest, but Clark brought his lips to the meat of her shoulder instead and sucked, hot and hard on the tender skin.

"I can't believe I've got you in my bed, bare beneath my clothes." His voice was low and incredulous, something like starry-eyed delight underpinning the words.

"And?" Even though fighting for the upper hand seemed vaguely insincere at this point, Riley could at least make him work for it. "What do you plan to do with me?"

Clark reached between her legs and pressed the rough ridge of his knuckles against the thin inseam of his sweats. "Take you apart."

Riley's back arched. She brought her hands to his shoulders, biting her lip to silence a moan.

It wasn't her fault. How dare he turn hair braiding into foreplay?

Clark let her rock back and forth against his fist, working her hips in tiny circles, seeking friction.

Riley wanted to come so bad she couldn't see straight. She recognized every terrible instinct inside herself—to whimper, to mewl, to beg.

But she wouldn't. She pressed herself harder against his hand, working her hips. If she had to get herself off, just like this, even, she would.

Clark watched her face. "I can't believe you're gonna make it this easy on me."

Heat flooded her cheeks.

And, okay. No. Riley refused to be the only one unraveling. She yanked his sweater over her head with one hand, using the other to force him to sit back.

For a long moment he just looked at her, breathing hard through his nose.

Her nipples tightened under his gaze, so fast it almost hurt.

Clark swore as he moved to cup her breast, testing the weight in his palm. His thumb grazed her nipple, back and forth, maddeningly soft.

"I told you what I like," Riley said, shivery and impatient. She wanted that spike of pain to clear her head, to give her back some sense of herself. Here, in his bed, where she felt so dangerously adrift.

He closed his thumb and index finger against the tip of each breast but didn't apply any pressure, just held. "You did, didn't you."

Without changing his previous grip, he managed to pinch the bottom of her breast between his middle and index finger, hard enough to bruise.

Her head tipped back, her mouth falling open. The sensation was good, but not enough.

"Christ, you're responsive," he said, practically to himself.

Eyes closed, Riley panted, "Is that the best you've got?"

She opened her eyes to find his burning as he shifted his hold, applied pressure from a different angle. Sharper. More intense.

He kissed her neck softly as the pain bloomed. "You wish."

She did make a noise then, something hysterical, caught between a laugh and a whine.

He thought she was a joke. Riley could picture him saying, *You know, if you'd just give up this silly little curse business, I might take you out on a second date.*

Her throat ached, her voice gone hoarse from holding back. "This doesn't mean I like you."

"You don't have to like me." Clark released her breast to smack between her spread legs. "You're about to soak through the pants I just gave you."

He tutted between his teeth.

Riley gasped. It could have been outrage. Wasn't.

"Aren't you?"

He did it again. Harder.

The sting was so good and not enough.

As always, Riley hated when he was right. "If you care so much—"

She moved to push the pants off, but Clark caught her wrists.

"Oh, no, sweetheart." He guided Riley onto her back and crawled on top of her, his knees on the outside of her hips.

She looked up at him. At his wide-set eyes and slightly-too-big ears, features that rather than detracting from his beauty only served to enhance his allure—made him distinctly, humanly lovely. Why did a false endearment prick at her like nothing else? Because she'd never had a true one, probably never would.

"I'm not your sweetheart." Holding Clark's gaze felt like staring at the sun, risking permanent damage for the chance to know something brilliant.

"No." His mouth was a harsh line as he brought his knee between hers, pushing the damp fabric of the sweats tighter against her. "But you'll let me wreck you anyway, won't you?"

Riley shuddered. She shouldn't allow him this much, but he was giving her what she'd craved for so long. Since she knew what sex was, what it could be. He was right; having this, from him, was ruinous.

Clark pulled the lobe of her ear into the wet heat of his mouth, sucking, before nuzzling at her pulse point. "Let's see exactly how much of a mess I can make of you."

When he moved to kiss her lips, she turned at the last second, deciding he couldn't have everything.

"You're still mad?" He laughed helplessly against her neck. "Oh, that makes it even better."

Riley's blood boiled as she squirmed beneath him. A part of her she'd never indulge craved violence, wanted to shove her elbow up into his stupid smug face.

You could fuck someone and still loathe them. People did that all the time.

He smiled as he brought his teeth down against her nipple. "I'm gonna suck bruises across your sweet tits until you're panting, writhing—begging me to hurt you just a little bit longer."

"Do it, then," Riley grunted, thighs clenching from the image alone.

He could have her body. It wasn't like it was her heart.

Clark pushed her breasts up and together, kissing across the tops of the soft swells almost reverently. His nose was cold where it brushed against the seam of her cleavage.

"Can still smell the rain on you," he said, surprisingly tender.

And oh no. None of that.

Riley arched her hips up, trying to grind against his knee again, but he dropped his hands to her waist, keeping her back flat to the bed as he rubbed his stubbled cheek against the underside of her breast, over her ribs. Watching as she pinked up from abrasion.

"Hurry up," she made herself complain. And it was true at least that for all his dark promises he'd barely even bitten her yet.

Until, *oh.*

His teeth closed against the thin skin behind her ear. Then high on her breast. Then over the hollow of her throat.

Unsurprisingly, Clark was methodical in his approach, mapping his marks across her chest, down her belly, removing her pants to canvas each of her thighs until the pleasure and pain blended in her nerve endings. Until he'd left a blistering trail across her body. Until he had her trembling below him.

She'd never been edged like this. To the brink. Over and over. Tears leaked from the corners of her eyelids.

Clark rubbed at them gently with his sleeve, placing featherlight kisses over their tracks down her cheeks and chin.

He sat back on his heels, giving her space. A moment to breathe.

"Is it too much?" he said, soft, serious. "Do you want to stop?"

Riley shook her head, panting against his pillow. "I'll fucking kill you."

Clark smiled, brushing a tendril from his half-undone braid away from her sweaty temple. "You've really got a perfect face, huh?"

Riley held her breath. She could handle herself, barely, when he was being crass or cruel. But he shouldn't be allowed to pretend to care about her when he didn't, not really.

It was fucked up that back in the castle earlier, while she'd been up on a ladder plotting to destroy him, Clark had been making sure she didn't fall.

"Well." He pulled his hand back, looking at the comforter for a moment like maybe he'd thought of something fucked up too.

But then he made a show of clapping his hands, loud enough to snap them both out of it.

When he spoke next his accent was stronger, rougher. "Are you finally ready to come, then? Been waiting on you ages."

Riley let out a choked laugh-sob.

"You're awful," she said softly, eyes closed tight, body strung like a bow.

"Most of the time," Clark whispered as he finally, *finally* slid his hand between her legs, his touch light, appraising.

He whistled at what he found. *"Riley, you dirty girl."*

If he hadn't given her two thick fingers at that moment, she might have smothered him with a pillow.

Clark was exactly the same person in bed as he was out of it: cocky and controlling, mocking and self-congratulatory. The difference was, here Riley liked it.

"Your whole body's blushing." He remarked casually as his fingers pumped inside her.

Riley reached for her clit, flicking hard and fast, desperate to end this.

"Impatient?" Clark bent his neck to watch their hands working together. "That's cute." He brushed his ring finger against where she was already stretched. "You want another?"

Her toes curled, she was close, so close. "I want you to stop talking."

He chuckled darkly—"Liar."—and curled three fingers inside her as Riley worked her own hand, fast, unrelenting.

She'd set out to make him her enemy this morning and come up short, but Riley could hate him for this—for how good he made her hurt, the way he drew pleas from her bitten-red lips.

"I hate you," she told him, low and fervent, as it all crashed down. As she came longer and harder than she ever had in her life. "God, Clark. I hate you so fucking much." Riley savored the words along with release.

When she finally stopped shaking, Clark groaned, sliding his fingers slowly out of her, bringing all three to his mouth and sucking them clean. With his other hand, he palmed the obscene bulge in his jeans.

He stared down at the sweaty, tumbled mess of her, lingering on the marks he'd made with his mouth. "God, look at you."

She slid one palm against his tensed abdomen, under the rugby shirt, to trace the lines of muscle that pointed toward his pelvis. "Why are you still wearing all of your clothes?"

When he didn't seem inclined to stop looking at her long enough to disrobe, Riley pushed his shirt up as far as she could in this position, trying to reveal his bare stomach, his chest. Dark strands dusted from his collarbone to below his naval. Riley wanted to run her mouth all over him until his eyes rolled back in his head.

"Happy now?" His breath came in harsh gasps as he worked himself over his jeans.

"No," Riley said, tugging at his waistband. "Take your pants off."

"I'm close," he warned her as he shoved down his jeans and, with a groan, wrapped his hand around himself.

Because there was no justice in the world, his cock was as gorgeous as the rest of him. Riley blinked, dazed, as he pumped himself over her.

He reached out with his opposite hand to circle one of the sets of teeth marks on her breast with his fingertips. "Let me come on your tits."

"Yeah, yes," she sputtered, trying to sit up a little on her elbows. God, she wanted him to. What had he said earlier? *Let's see exactly how much of a mess I can make of you.* She'd do anything to make him lose control the way she had.

Riley gorged herself on the way he looked—teeth clenched, neck straining, thrusting into his fist like he couldn't wait to bring himself off. Had she ever seen anything as sexy as this man?

When he caught her looking at him, Clark sped up his thrusts.

"Oh," she said, a Cheshire-cat grin spreading across her mouth. "You like being watched."

His abs tensed as he blushed all the way down his chest.

Riley had just come. Her body was still wrung out, flushed, but, well, wasn't that interesting. *I wonder if . . .*

"Who knew"—she held his gaze—"that you were such a *slut*."

Clark swore as he splashed come across her chest, already running his hand through it, painting over her nipples and her steadily blooming bruises.

Riley pressed her knees together and struggled to catch her breath. She looked down at her own body. The sight was so deliciously obscene, she already knew she'd come again later thinking about this.

"I'll, uh, get you a new towel." Clark hauled himself up, looking a little flustered in the aftermath of his orgasm.

Right. God, she was in a camper, in the middle of a thunderstorm.

She let herself fall back on his sheets, wallowing in the disaster of it all.

Eventually, she'd have to walk back to the inn wearing whatever lingered from the physical remnants of their passion. If that wasn't cursed, she didn't know what was.

Riley needed to regain her composure and stat. She'd let this happen. Fine. It wasn't ideal, but she could handle it. And she needed to because she wasn't the only one in danger here.

In the end, when Clark took his pleasure, he had looked at her like he was . . . lost. Like Riley was the only thing anchoring him to the earth. And she wasn't. Couldn't be that. Not for Clark. Not for anyone. She'd never been more sure than she was right now.

Curses didn't understand the concept of pain or mercy. They were destruction, unrelenting. And she'd made a vow to her family and to herself to meet them in the arena. To break them by whatever means necessary.

Sacrifice. Not just Clark as a forfeit, but herself.

Because she wanted this—the afterglow, beyond. She couldn't lie to herself anymore. Tonight he'd left marks on more than her body.

Riley wanted Clark. With all his flaws. With hers.

She ignored the knot in her throat. The sudden wave of dizzying nausea.

Curse breaking was more than her job. It was her calling. Her purpose. She didn't get to quit because it got harder. Because the cost became personal. She couldn't be good for him. But she could be good at this.

One of her first clients had been a painter who'd lost his muse. They'd tried everything else: charms, cleansing, rituals. Nothing worked.

You'll have to give up the thing you're most afraid to lose, she'd said, as kindly as she could.

He hadn't painted for a year. Said it ached, every day. *I'm alive but I feel like I'm dead.*

You have to have faith, she'd tried to console him, *that sometimes the hard thing, the thing that seems impossible, is the only way out.*

It had come back eventually, the muse, the art. Riley had never asked him if it was worth it, the dead year. She'd been too afraid of the answer.

Clark deserved better than her anyway. She hoped that after this he'd find someone who'd never try and hurt him. God knew they'd be less trouble to look after than her.

He came back holding a damp washcloth. His jeans were still undone, sitting low on his hips, and the collar of his shirt was stretched away from his neck. Riley could almost see where she'd touched him, as if he'd walked away from the bed just as marked as her. Dread pooled like iron in her stomach.

The curse had led her to an opportunity she never would have considered on her own, the chance to climb into his bed, to get naked with him. To slink past defenses, leave him armorless.

Philippa Campbell had captured Malcolm Graphm. *The thing that seems impossible.*

"Riley?" For a minute he looked like he wanted to clean her up himself, but then Clark held out the cloth. "Are you all right?" He sounded concerned, nervous. "Do you want some water?"

Don't you dare cry, she told herself. *You owe him that, at least.*

She took the washcloth, stalling. "I'm okay."

Riley knew how to reject someone. To make it clear they didn't stand a chance with her. She worked in a sports bar in South Philly. It was kinder to be ruthless, to cut to the heart of the issue, leave no ambiguity, so the worst part could be over as quickly as possible.

Come on, she told herself. *You know what you have to do. How to do it.*

The cruelest thing you could say to someone was the cruelest thing they said to themselves.

"You knew, didn't you"—she made her voice steady—"on some level, that Patrick had lied in Cádiz."

Clark froze.

"What?"

Was that the manipulation he'd accused her of? If she hadn't earned the insult before, it would be harder to argue after tonight.

Riley had forgotten—had willfully let herself forget—that the double-edged sword of making Clark her villain would cut both ways.

"You pay too close attention." She sat up, crossing her arm across her tacky chest. "You wouldn't have missed something that big. Your gut would have told you to investigate, to help."

"You're truly unbelievable." There was genuine incredulity in Clark's tone, though he'd managed to shutter his face. It was the kind of thing he might have said to her as a compliment ten minutes ago, along with all the other lust-induced nonsense he'd spilled against her skin. No one would mistake the meaning now.

An end to enemies.

She swallowed against the lump in her throat. "Do you think on some level you wanted to see him fail? To lose your father's trust? Break his heart? So that you could finally know what it felt like to be the favorite?"

He'd schooled his features into a mask of coolness, but he wasn't particularly good at holding his temper. His eyes flashed with mounting fury. "Is everything a game to you?"

Riley turned away, running the washcloth over herself, quick and perfunctory. She'd shower and apply salve when she got back to the inn, could whisper sweet nothings to herself as she fell asleep. Riley pulled back on his sweater. She wasn't going to voluntarily fight topless. She found his sweats under the bed, stepped into them despite the mortifyingly damp inseam.

Clark was beautiful in his anger, clenched fists and steel jaw.

He'd been mean to her earlier because she'd asked him to. This was so different.

Riley brought her hand to his cheek, the skin burning hot under her palm. She traced her thumb over his lips, those lips that had kissed and caressed her, that had brought her such lethal temptation.

He closed his eyes, practically vibrating with the effort it took to hold himself still under her palm.

Come on, she urged herself. *Finish it.*

He'd given her all the tools. All she had to do was make it official. Make him hate her.

"But it didn't work, did it?" she whispered, unable to speak the words even a decibel louder. "You're still not good enough."

The harsh bark of his laughter rang in her ears as he pulled away, pacing for the entrance to the camper and opening the door. Outside, the storm had exhausted itself, stalled to a slow pitter-patter.

Clark walked out and into the darkness, leaving Riley alone in his home.

This time when she cried, he wasn't there to dry her tears.

If through her terrible treatment, Riley managed to drive Clark away—the curse wouldn't be the only thing she'd broken tonight.

Chapter Fifteen

Clark couldn't get the taste of Riley out of his mouth.

He'd been so foolish. So bloody eager. Desperate enough for her after prolonged exposure, all that frustrated wanting, that he'd ignored every warning sign. Told himself it was just sex. Nothing to get worked up over.

It was pathetic the way she'd made an absolute mug of him. In his bed, he might have been the one on top, but Riley had him eating out of the palm of her hand.

He'd expected her to strike against him, just not like that. Not then.

Riley had gotten close to him only long enough to find his weakest spots, waiting for the perfect opportunity to go in for the kill.

It was even more humiliating, somehow, that he'd tried his hand at deceiving her only last week and failed so spectacularly. Apparently six months of moody reflection and self-flagellation had taught Clark nothing about betrayal. Riley hadn't slipped past his defenses; he'd lowered them for her willingly, practically fell over himself to do her bidding.

Hadn't he been drawn to her—a moth to a flame—the first night they'd met? Was it any wonder, then, that in trying to touch her he'd gotten burned?

At least now he was well and truly done. Clark should thank her for knocking some sense into him. Under no circumstances would he allow himself to go near Riley Rhodes again. If that meant abandoning his camper in the middle of a terrible storm, so be it. His entire home smelled of her anyway. *Of them.* It would take days to air out.

Instead of finding somewhere dry to sleep, he'd gone back to the castle and worked, shivering through the last howls of the rain. The survey grounded him. Demanded exertion, concentration. With tools in hand, all that mattered was completing the assignment. Clark labored until his body mirrored his emotions—wrung out, used.

When he'd finally gone back to the camper after dawn, it was empty except for the full kind of silence that came after a violent storm. He yanked a comb through his hair until he looked like a man who didn't know the word *ravished.* Shaved with savage precision. Cinched his tool belt and relaced his boots.

Clark wasn't born yesterday. He understood casual sex. It wasn't like he thought Riley was his girlfriend or something because she let him put his mouth on her. But he certainly believed that when you got naked with someone, you should treat them with respect. Part of that unspoken covenant meant not throwing their worst insecurities in their face before the come had even dried.

His face heated. Clark knew he had a filthy mouth in bed, but that was different. He could let himself go carnal, unfiltered in the heat of the moment, when blood abandoned his brain for more urgent demands. Riley brought it out in him like no other partner, daring him at every turn to show her how base he could be. He found her responses—equal parts yielding and resistance—singularly addictive.

But he couldn't have let her into his bed without a considerable degree of trust. That offering mattered—to him, at least—when they'd done nothing since they met but break faith with each other. He'd thought that if nothing else, their interaction last night had been honest. To know she could lie so well about something so raw only made him fear her more.

No one had ever seen him as clearly as Riley. Frankly, he'd never wanted them to. All the effort he put into controlling his temper, keeping up appearances, hadn't stopped her from finding his weak spots.

Clark loved being a little bit mean to her in bed—it made both of them hot. But last night, after, when she'd gone for his throat, he'd seen how desperately she wanted him to fight back and declined to give her the satisfaction. He didn't understand what had changed. Why she'd turned on him so suddenly. Had she confused the boundaries between bedplay and real life?

He told himself it didn't matter why she'd done it—determined not to care.

Gathering his tools and supplies, Clark made his way down to the dungeon, an area he hadn't explored yet. Unsurprisingly, the cramped space was exceptionally dark, not to mention damp, the dirt floor flooded from the storm.

Clark reckoned Riley wouldn't follow him down here, now that she knew he could resist her baiting. What fun was a dog who wouldn't fetch?

As he descended the stone steps, the wrought-iron door of a cage that took up the entire room swung, creaking, in the cold morning breeze. Inside the cell, runoff from the damp soil rushed toward a drain in the corner. Clark tried not to think too hard about all the other fluids that might have been spilled here over centuries as he stepped inside.

It was macabre, but he loved dungeons. They held so much des-

perate emotion. And desperate people thought most about leaving
a mark. That thought harkened back to something Riley had said
early on about this castle and curses, but Clark shoved the memory
away, unwilling to admit she'd polluted his mind.

Moss grew between the thick gray slabs of stone in the walls, the
scent of undergrowth mingling with other minerals in the air. He
searched methodically for loose stones, hoping to find a hiding
place left by one of the dungeon's former prisoners. According to
his research, Malcolm Graphm was the most famous man held
here. As far as Clark could tell, he'd also been the last.

It was slow work. Occasionally, he'd find a piece that shifted at
his touch, but more often the deterioration came from age rather
than intent. Still, determination fed him better than any food. He
needed to find an artifact of his own today, something untouched
by Riley and all her confusing theories.

Finally, at ground level, his eyes snagged on something. It was a
collection of lines scraped into the iron cage that looked like they
might be . . . tally marks? And then, as he wiped away layers of dirt
and dust, underneath the count, tiny, was a line of Gaelic.

Bho a bilean, bàs

Immediately, he thought of the cave, though the etching here
looked different, thin and slanted, and when Clark translated the
line he didn't see an immediate correlation.

His phone showed the phrase in English. *From her lips, death.*

"Tell me about it, mate." Clark could feel the prisoner here in
this dank cell, trapped but methodical, counting the days, hoping
for rescue. Unsure if they'd make it out. Leaving a last word the
only way they could.

When the walls yielded nothing else but dust, Clark went to

work on the ground. Shoveling gave him an outlet for his anger. It was harder to think when all his muscles strained, working together to sift through the long-dormant earth.

A few minutes in, the tip of the shovel hit something. The clink of metal on metal in his ears was like crawling to water after days wandering in the desert. Clark's pulse kicked up. *Could it be? Salvation?*

He didn't care what he'd found. Let it be a chamber pot. All he wanted was to have something to show for coming here beyond emotional bruises.

Dropping the shovel, he got down on his hands and knees. The wet earth soaked into his pants as he gathered coarse soil between his fingers, too frenzied for gloves or even tools. Carefully, Clark swiped at the surface of something dark and curved in the ground. Whatever the object, it had been crafted in heavy metal.

When he'd cleared away enough of the surrounding dirt, he pulled out a coil of iron chain made up of thick interlocking rings about twice the length of his forearm. At either end, he found manacles—oblong and thick, each of the bands close to eight centimeters wide.

Clark tugged the artifact carefully from the ground. The manacles were unlocked, and he made sure not to press them closed in his inspection. He'd never encountered a pair this old. The ironwork was masterful, like the dagger they'd found but much less ornate, designed for service rather than aesthetics. His hands tingled where he held the artifact, excitement shooting up his spine like an electric current.

How strange, that a pair of manacles could offer him his escape. For surely Clark could go now. Take these directly to the HES for lab testing and analysis. He wouldn't have to stay here, with Riley. He could abandon the memory of her, his foolish fantasies.

A sick sort of euphoria settled over him instead of the usual sense of pride that came after a find. He documented the scene, collected soil samples, and snapped photographs, all with shaking hands. When Clark finally packed up to leave, he took the manacles with him. Since Riley had joint jurisdiction over the dagger, he'd get Martin to deliver it to the lab at some point in the future. Whenever she left.

He hurried up the steps on his way out. He was so close, almost in the clear when—there she was. In the entrance hall, backlit by the setting sun.

All evidence that Clark had ever touched her was neatly obscured by dark jeans and a long-sleeved crewneck. The hair he'd had his hands in last night flowed loose, freshly washed, over her shoulders.

After a lingering beat between them, she opened her mouth, then closed it as her eyes fell to the dirty manacles in his hands.

"What are you—"

"I'm going," he said, cutting her off. "Leaving Torridon."

Who cared if he hadn't finished surveying the entire blueprint of the castle? A man had limits. Plus, both Martin and the HES wanted this assignment done ages ago. They'd all be relieved to hear he'd finally agreed to leave.

Riley nodded, tightly, her face unusually pale. "And you're leaving because of me?"

He could have lied. But what was the point of being kind? She didn't even like it. "Yeah. You win."

The announcement didn't seem to please her.

"I suppose"—she wrapped her arms around her stomach—"nothing I could say would change your mind?"

He frowned. She must have woken up guilty, to even offer.

Clark thought about it—Riley asking for forgiveness. Riley saying she wanted him. Riley begging him to stay. While the images conjured brief flashes of emotion, none of it moved him enough to change his mind.

"That's right." He'd learned his lesson. He wanted an end to this and had grabbed the first meager opening he found. "One artifact isn't much to show for six weeks on-site." As he held up the manacles, Clark could hear his father's voice in his ear. "But perhaps I've always been more cut out for desk work."

He stepped forward, past her. Was almost at the door when she said—

"Clark, wait."

He paused but didn't turn. "If you're going to take back what you said last night, don't bother."

"I'm not." The signature defiance that had been missing in her so far this morning crept into the statement. "I was just going to say that even if it's true—everything I said—about your brother, your dad—you're wrong about what makes someone worthy."

"*I'm wrong?*" He had to laugh. If this was her attempt at an apology, it was as awful as her pillow talk. "Those are the last words you had to have?"

"Yes."

He did turn then to sneer at her. Of all the wretched games . . .

"I'm trying to say—I want you to know . . ." She ran a hand through her hair, making it wilder than it already was. "You're good. A good person. And you'll be good—the same amount—whether you're a famous archaeologist or a disgraced layabout or god forbid you join a band." She pulled a truly appalling face at the last.

Clark, like most people, couldn't properly hear praise, but Riley

hadn't delivered it that way. *You're wrong*, comforting in its famil-
iarity, had ensured her other words came in at normal volume instead of muted. *You're good.*

He didn't know if this was her attempt at an apology. If her
conscience demanded she balance the scales a little before he left.
But Clark heard the conviction in her tone. Strong, steady. Aimed
like an arrow straight for his soft, smushy insides. She meant it.

This time, when he played back the accusations she'd hurled at
him last night, he heard them slightly differently.

They were still a blatant attempt to wound him. A callout of his
selfish desire to be seen, to be loved, to make his father proud even
if it came at Patrick's expense.

Clark had carried that rotten thought as long as he could remember. He'd tried to bury it, to shrink and ignore it. But it was
part of him. Like a small, dark spot on his heart. The subject of
constant shame.

He'd spent thirty-odd years trying to hide this . . . *this failing.*
Before today, he couldn't imagine anything worse than having
someone, practically a stranger, see.

But now, if Riley thought—like she'd said—that somehow despite his moral deficiency, he was good . . .

Not that he could be, if he atoned. *He was*, she'd said, *already.*

In ways that transcended what he could accomplish.

Clark didn't like her in that moment any more than he had this
morning. But it was true that she'd already gotten what she wanted—
he was leaving. She had no reason to lie.

Even if she had only handed him a parting consolation prize,
Clark thought he'd like to keep it.

He held her gaze, allowing himself one final indulgence after a
hard week, a hard month, a hard year. "Joining a band is the worst
occupation you can imagine?"

Her lips curved into the ghost of a smile. "There is literally nothing more awful than having someone sit in front of you with an acoustic guitar and play a song they just wrote. It should be illegal. Where am I supposed to look? Your hands? Your mouth? What if it sounds terrible? I don't wanna tell you."

There was something painful in the way she uttered the hypothetical. Though she obviously meant *your* in a general way, the words left too much ambiguity for his fragile ego. *Your hands. Your mouth.*

Darkness descended upon them. The last sliver of sun must have slipped beyond the horizon. A strange fluttering noise drew their attention upward, to where all of a sudden the ceiling seemed to be shifting, breathing. Undulating, almost as if . . .

"Are those . . ."

"*Bats*," Riley said a few seconds before him.

When the wave of tiny black animals crested and crashed, nothing stood between him and their shining eyes and minute fangs. Dropping the manacles, he dove to his belly on the ground at the last possible second.

The colony's airstream ruffled his hair as they escaped out into the evening.

"Quite the farewell." Riley got to her feet gingerly.

Clark stayed on the ground, trying to wrestle back control of his breathing.

"Here." She offered him a hand up.

He didn't take it. The last thing he needed was to touch her right now.

Following his rebuff, Riley moved to pick up the manacles instead.

"It's fine. I've got it," he said churlishly, reaching for them himself.

As they each extended their hands, going for opposite circlets, two consecutive *clicks* cut the air.

"What the fuck?" Clark pulled his ensnared wrist back, only getting about ten centimeters because Riley was attached to the other end of the manacles.

"Oh no." She started pulling too. "Oh no, no, no," she said in time with the metal chain clanking as it extended and contracted between them with the force of her attempts to free herself.

They both yanked in opposite directions, swearing, disbelieving, until their wrists turned red, sore.

"Riley," he said finally, trying to ground himself as his brain screamed. "Do these manacles have that curse-scent-signature thing on them?"

She nodded, biting her lip.

Bloody hell. "Why didn't you say something?"

"You told me you were leaving!" Her eyes were saucer wide. "I thought it was about to go away."

"Well." He gestured at the cuffs. "You're the curse breaker. Undo it."

"Me?" Her voice had risen an octave. "I'm not Magneto. I can't control metal."

Clark closed his eyes. How had they come to this? Ten minutes ago, he'd been imagining how many sausage rolls he was going to pick up from the first Greggs he passed on the way back to England.

"No." He tried to school himself to patience. "I mean use that framework you're always blathering on about. Charm it, cleanse it. Whatever nonsense you have to do, I don't care. Just fix this."

He could not be chained to her. He just couldn't. He was leaving. Clark was never, ever going to see Riley Rhodes again.

"The artifacts are just an extension of the curse," she said, looking more freaked out even than he felt. "Until I break it . . . I think we're stuck."

"No. That's unacceptable." He tugged her forward. "Come along. I've got a series of picks in my kit."

Something would work. It had to. He'd saw the chain links off with a nail file if he had to, priceless piece of history be damned.

Chapter Sixteen

Riley leaned against Clark's desk, racking her brain, trying to figure out what the fuck was going on while he attempted his fifth (increasingly more frantic) lock-picking solution.

She didn't get it. He'd been ready to leave. Had said himself that she'd driven him away. Yet the manacle around her wrist acted like a metaphorical horn blaring *YOU GOT IT WRONG*.

Her head throbbed. Had she really hurt Clark for nothing? It wasn't like she'd felt noble or anything before. She just hadn't realized she could feel worse.

That was until Clark jammed a penknife into his palm while attempting to MacGyver the lock mechanism.

"Fuck." He brought the injured hand to his mouth.

"Don't do that." Riley walked him to the sink, flipping on the tap to rinse the cut instead. "You know, for someone who fusses over everyone else's wounds, you could stand to be a little more careful with your own."

She hadn't actually meant for that to be a metaphor, but . . . *yeah*.

Grabbing the first aid kit he'd used to tend to her cat scratches (her right arm had really gotten the shit end of the stick this week), she took out a Band-Aid, pulling the thing open with her teeth.

"Listen, maybe we should call a locksmith," she suggested while

Clark tolerated her awkward attempts to apply the bandage with her nondominant hand.

"The type of drill they use would completely decimate the integrity of the artifact," he said, as if Riley should know exactly how locksmiths worked. "We need something custom forged to unlock the device without damaging it beyond repair."

"Fine, then." She released his hand and tossed the plastic wrapper. "Let's call a blacksmith."

Those were the people who forged metal, right? Were they still around, like as a profession? She kinda assumed they were an old-timey relic like apothecaries.

After much agonizing and several "bracing" cups of tea, Clark agreed to call a colleague who studied ancient metalworking to see if she knew anyone who could help them.

"I'm going to tell her the question is theoretical, all right?"

Riley looked up at the wariness in his tone. He'd managed to say very little to her in the last few hours of forced proximity, but this sentence in particular seemed to cost him.

Clark was embarrassed, she realized, in addition to generally not wanting to be anywhere near her. That made sense now that she thought about it. As a curse breaker, zany shit happened to her all the time, but getting physically restrained by one of the artifacts he'd discovered was probably a first for Clark . . . though surely not for archaeologists in general?

"Understood." She gave him a salute, feeling the bizarre need to make as much use of her free hand's range of motion as possible.

Who knew how long they'd be stuck like this? Riley was very carefully avoiding her water bottle, since there was no way she and Clark were on good enough terms right now to discuss a system for when one of them had to pee.

It took a fair amount of conversational sidestepping, but eventually his colleague referred them to a friend of a friend who—good news!—could forge them a key. Unfortunately, the blacksmith (they did still exist) would have to come up to take a mold and couldn't arrive from Manchester until tomorrow at the earliest. And that was after Clark had offered to pay an exorbitant price for a rush job.

He made her sit while he transferred money for their rescue on his laptop. Apparently, he couldn't concentrate with her *looming over him*.

This was so inconvenient. She wanted to be back in her room at the inn. It was harder to brainstorm without being able to look at all the pieces. Riley went back to the language of the curse. *An end to enemies.* Language was always the key, no pun intended.

Assuming the power in the cave had fae roots, the curse might be wilier than most. Perhaps the wording was a trick? A play on words, even. Riley considered different interpretations. Really, this shouldn't be that hard.

An end to enemies.

End seemed like the option with the most opportunity for interpretation. Hmm. If the curse didn't want her to get rid of her enemy by driving him away, how else was she supposed to end him? Death was still, obviously, not an option. Besides the fact that Riley would never murder someone (despite her emotional dependence on *Criminal Minds*), it didn't fit. If the curse wanted to hurt them, it would have by now.

They'd survived its ominous influences—many of which could have been lethal—relatively unscathed. At least physically. The curse had caused plenty of mischief since its inception, but thinking about it now, she couldn't recall any record of fatalities on-site in three hundred plus years. No, she didn't believe the curse wanted anyone six feet under. Instead, it seemed to be trying to send them signals, nudges in the right direction.

She turned to Clark. "What's the opposite of enemies?"

"Huh?" Repeated urgent clicking and his refusal to remove his eyes from the computer screen said PayPal was giving him trouble.

"I'm doing the crossword on my phone," she fibbed, holding up the device that had been sitting next to her on the armrest. It didn't seem like a great time to explain the whole "I tried to drive you away because I thought that was what the curse wanted but now I need to rethink my strategy" thing.

"I haven't the faintest idea," he snapped, and then, after a moment of reluctant pondering, "Does *friends* fit?"

Oh. There was an option that never would have occurred to her.

Was that plausible? Could you end your enemy by turning them into something else? She guessed so. Though she couldn't see Philippa Campbell and Malcolm Graphm setting aside their families' blood feud to bond over— *Actually, what do friends bond over? Hobbies? Entertainment properties?*

"Do you—" There was no way Clark watched *Criminal Minds*. *CSI* was way more evidence oriented.

The computer made a *womp* sound. "Riley, figure it out yourself. I'm clearly busy."

Right. Something twisted in her chest. Clark would make a good friend. For someone else. He was loyal to a fault, strangely considerate, funny sometimes—mostly by accident.

But, of course, after what they'd done to each other, he and Riley could never go back.

As night fell, it became harder to avoid the looming presence of his bed and all that had occurred there—both decadent and devastating.

"Why don't we stay in my room at the inn tonight?" At least the mattress was bigger, and neither of them had made the other moan in it. "We can get dinner at the pub on the way."

Her belly had not enjoyed "working" through lunch, but asking Clark to stop and make her a snack while he wielded various sharp objects had seemed like pushing her luck.

Reluctantly, he agreed. Probably half because he hadn't had time to change his sheets.

Anyway, they went.

"Could you please stop drawing attention to yourself?" Clark gritted his teeth the second time Riley knocked over the saltshaker.

"Sorry," she said, using her free left hand to set the shaker back beside its peppery fellow. "These things"—she jangled the cuff on her right wrist—"are heavier than they look."

Contrary to what he seemed to believe, she wasn't actively trying to humiliate him.

Besides, in her opinion, the reception to their manacled appearance at the pub had been downright mild. A few stares, a few chortles behind raised hands. One good-natured scolding that they shouldn't involve bystanders in their kink games without informed consent. No big deal.

Eilean wasn't even working tonight. Riley could just imagine what the no-nonsense bartender would make of Clark trying to block their chain-linked wrists behind a propped-up menu. Luckily for him, it was Ceilidh who appeared at their table wearing an apron and carrying a notepad.

The redhead raised an eyebrow at their joined wrists, but when Riley mouthed, *Don't mention the handcuffs*, she pivoted quickly.

"Are you both ready to order?"

"Definitely," Riley said. The sooner they got this over with, the better. "I'll have the balsamic spinach salad without onions, please, and a side of fries."

Clark ordered his usual burger and "the largest glass of whiskey you can legally serve."

After Ceilidh scribbled their requests on her pad and returned to the kitchen, Riley leaned forward to whisper conspiratorially, "People will lose interest if you stop looking around like we're about to dine and dash."

"Fine." He stopped peering at the tables around them and leveled the force of his gaze on her.

Uh-oh. She realized her mistake as mounting silence grew between them. It was the first time since they'd been chained together that neither of them was occupied with a task.

Sweat began to gather on her lower back. What were they supposed to do for the fifteen or twenty minutes it took for their food to come out? They didn't even have drinks yet—Ceilidh appeared to be swamped at the bar—so Riley couldn't pretend to be occupied with taking a sip or plucking at her garnish.

There was nothing for it. She was going to have to talk to him.

The trouble was, she had no idea what to say.

Thanks for the great sex last night. Sorry I tried to make you feel like shit about yourself after.

Yeah, no.

It would have been clean, at least, if *You're a good person* had been the last thing she ever said to him. Frankly, she hadn't even planned on admitting that much. After last night, she wasn't supposed to say anything to Clark ever again. She'd hoped (mostly hoped) to find him gone this morning when she returned to the castle.

But of course, there he was in the entranceway, all handsome and stoic and wounded, and as she watched him leave, Riley couldn't help herself.

To be fair, it wasn't supposed to matter what she said at that point—he'd openly admitted nothing that came out of her mouth could make him stay.

What she'd said hadn't even been a compliment, not really. She'd just stated a fact. It didn't make up for the way she'd broken the sacred code of postcoital interaction, not even close.

That hadn't been her aim. Riley just wanted—needed, for some reason—Clark to know. He'd gone his whole life thus far believing he had to be useful in order to be wanted. What if no one else ever thought to correct him? The idea made her irrationally angry . . . even if she was the asshole who'd tried to use his misconception against him.

God, no wonder Clark had nothing to say to her. Everything he'd shared—no, everything she'd barged in and yanked out of him—Riley had thrown back in his face at the coldest opportunity possible. He'd been open with her, more vulnerable than he had to be, trusting her, even though she'd never been brave enough to do the same.

The least she could do was try to even the score between them a little. Riley couldn't change the way Clark's dad treated him or what had happened with his brother, but he didn't have to feel like he was the only one at this table who had been measured by their kin and found wanting.

She gathered her resolve. "Do you want to know the worst thing about me?"

"Excuse me?"

"You can say no," she rushed to assure him. She wasn't trying to trauma dump or whatever the kids called it these days. "I just thought you might feel a little better if you had some leverage on me, you know, after I . . . *you know.*"

His mouth twisted like he'd bitten into a lemon.

Riley was sure he thought the offer was silly, or worse, insulting. "Sorry, never mind. I don't know why I—"

"Go on, then." He motioned with two fingers for her to proceed.

Oh.

"Okay, so . . ." She realized she didn't have a lead-in. No disrespect to Clark's trauma confessions, but they had come with those handy visual aids.

"Um, my dad left, when I was nine— This part is backstory, for context," Riley clarified, intimidated by Clark's perfectly stoic expression. "Anyway. So, yeah. As it turns out, my mom had kept the whole curse-breaking thing a secret from him and he didn't find out until after Gran died when she left me a bunch of her practitioner materials."

She could still remember her dad sorting through the carefully wrapped contents of a cardboard box that had come back from West Virginia after the funeral. The way his face had gone white and then red.

"He, um . . . didn't like it. He said Gran was unnatural, and my mom and I were tainted by association."

Riley wished Ceilidh would bring her water. For some reason her throat hurt, though she was barely speaking above a whisper.

"There was a lot of screaming and big sweeping hand gestures after that. And then . . . that was it. He just stopped loving us. At least, that's what he said. For context."

"That's enough." Clark's expression was complicated, restrained, but what killed Riley was how gentle he'd made his voice. "You don't have to keep going for my sake."

"I think I do." It felt good—scary but good—to air out the place inside of her that had been shut up dead for so long.

Had Clark experienced a fraction of the same relief with her? She hoped so.

"The worst thing about me"—Riley took a deep breath—"is I didn't have to make the choice. My mom made it for me. And I love her for that. So much. But . . ."

Jordan Rhodes might not have chosen to pursue the "family talent." She might have left Appalachia and her mother behind to make her own path. But no one, including—*perhaps especially*—a husband, had ever stood a chance of shaming her for where she came from.

Late that same night, after they'd cleaned up the dishes and lay together in Riley's twin bed, she'd explained as best she could that Daddy's anger hadn't been about them, not really. Had promised that even though it was just the two of them now, they'd be okay.

Riley had believed her.

"But . . ." Clark prompted when she'd sat silently for too long.

"I can't help but think sometimes that if he'd asked me . . ." Riley fiddled with the stitching along the edge of her napkin. "As much as I love my gran, love curse breaking . . . I think I would have given them both up."

Her cheeks heated in shame from the traitorous thoughts. "If it meant I could have had a dad, that my mom wouldn't have had to do everything on her own."

Clark clenched his fists suddenly, the movement made more prominent by the way the iron chain jerked between them in response.

Riley raised her gaze. Was he okay?

Slowly, he relaxed both hands until his palms rested flat on the table.

"It's not wrong," he said, his voice tight, "for a child to want to be loved and accepted by their parent." Clark shook his head a little. "You can see it clear as day when it's someone else's family instead of your own."

In the low yellow light of the bar, his troubled eyes looked more green than gray.

"Your father failed you. And he failed your mother. Not the other way around."

Riley swallowed. Nodded. It was how she felt about his father. His brother, in a different way.

In fact, as she sat there, the mirror image of his pain and hers cracked her open a little down her sternum, until it felt like her guts might spill out onto the table.

"By turning curse breaking into a career, you're defending your mum and your gran. Their choices. Their power." Clark stared at her intently, in that way he did sometimes that made her feel like a butterfly pinned for his inspection. "You've been defending them your whole life."

"Yes," she said, holding his gaze even though it felt intense, too raw.

When Ceilidh rushed over to drop two plates in front of them, they both jumped a little in their chairs.

"Sorry, sorry," she said, grabbing their drinks from an equally frazzled-looking colleague and placing those down too, fast enough that some liquid sloshed over the sides. "I just realized, I think I mixed up the tickets for tables seven and eight."

She shot concerned glances at a pair of couples near the front. "Do you guys need anything else?"

Clark peered first at his burger and then at Riley's salad. "Didn't you say no on—"

"We're all good," Riley cut him off. "Go check on those tables." She shooed away the younger woman with her free hand.

After Ceilidh had scampered off, Riley nudged the pile of cara-
melized onion on her plate, wielding her fork awkwardly with her
left hand. *Damn*. They weren't just on top. They had been mixed
into the salad. She might have managed to pick around them if she
could use her dominant hand, but alas . . .

"It's fine," she told Clark, who had made a far wiser choice for
his meal in a sandwich he could hold in one hand, though, she
noticed, he'd yet to reach for it. "I'll just eat the fries."

He frowned. "Do you want me to call her back?"

"Oh no. I would rather die," Riley said sincerely.

The frown, impossibly, deepened. "Are you allergic to onions?"

"No." She just hated the texture. Leave it to onions to ruin her
attempt to feed herself something green.

Clark beckoned the offending plate forward. "Give it here."

"What are you gonna do?" Riley swore if he draped his napkin
over it like a shroud or something she would drag his snooty ass
right out of here.

He raised his fork as if there was no doubt his order would be
followed. "I'm going to pick them out, obviously."

"You're gonna pick out my onions," she said, disbelieving.

"I am if you'll push the bloody plate toward me." He glared at
the manacle chain between them. "Afraid my reach's a bit ham-
pered at the moment."

"That's okay." Riley pushed the plate to the side instead. "You
don't have to."

She didn't want him putting himself out just because she'd told
him a sad story.

"Riley," he said dangerously. "I'm going to pick out those onions
whether you like it or not, so I suggest you hand me your plate before I have to stand up and make a scene." He put his free hand on
the edge of the table like he was threatening to scoot his chair back.

She didn't smile, but it was a near thing.

Clark picked out her onions with the same steely-eyed diligence he applied to every other activity, placing them on his own napkin, as far away from her as the table would allow.

"There." Job done and her plate returned to her, he sat back in his chair and finally reached for his burger.

It was probably cold by now.

Only when he raised his eyebrows at her did Riley realize he was waiting for her to try the salad. She did, quickly.

"It's good." She would have said so either way after that, but it was true. The acid in the dressing cut nicely through the richness of the goat cheese. "Thank you."

"You're welcome," he said, and finally satisfied, took a bite of his own food.

Riley couldn't help the strangest rush of . . . she didn't even know the word for this feeling. It was what happened when she saw a picture of a puppy. A kind of squeezing sigh.

Which was ridiculous. *Girl. It was a pile of onions.*

He'd even been surly while completing the task. Did his lips fold down naturally, or had they gotten stuck that way after thirty-odd years of repeated use?

A few minutes later, Clark raised his chin toward the bottle beside her elbow. "May I borrow the malt vinegar?"

"Oh, yeah, sure." She moved to grab the condiment as Ceilidh sped toward their table, gushing an apology about onions, her eyes immense and panicky.

"Please don't worry about it," Riley rushed to assure her.

"Oh my god." Ceilidh bent her knees and opened her arms for a quick hug. "Thank you for not being the third person tonight to scream at me."

The angle of the embrace was wonky, considering Riley only

had one arm available and was currently holding the vinegar, but she'd been there, the middle of a shift when nothing was going right and someone, anyone, was generous about it. Riley raised her arm and hugged back, trying to position her hand so that she didn't boink the poor waitress in the head with the bottle. "It happens to everyone, seriously—"

Ceilidh bumped the vinegar with her shoulder as she pulled back. The next thing Riley knew, insanely pungent liquid was pouring over her neck, down her chest, seeping into her shirt.

She tried to stop it, but her other arm couldn't reach, and now Ceilidh was trying to help and getting it all over herself too. Clark jumped to his feet, yanking Riley around in his effort to grab the bottle, all three of them slip-sliding on the wet wooden floor.

By the time they finally set it to rights, the entire bar was staring.

Riley winced, for both herself and for Ceilidh, who was having a truly terrible night.

Only when she'd sent her friend back to the kitchen to change— one of them had to stay and work, after all—did Riley, belly full of dread, make herself look at Clark, mentally preparing for his scorn, but instead . . . he had his face in his hand, his shoulders shaking.

What the hell? Was he so mortified of the spectacle he was cry- ing? Sheesh, he wasn't even the one who'd gotten wet.

But no, wait, he was making little undignified hiccuping sounds.

"I'm sorry," he said, gasping for breath. "Not laughing at you—" His speech died off in another bout of helpless laughter. "You don't look that bad, really."

Riley rolled her eyes. It was nice, unexpected, to hear him laugh.

"I'd offer you my napkin," he said as she wiped ineffectually at her shirt with her own, which was so wet it was crumbling, "but you see"—he tried and failed to smother another helpless giggle—"it's got onions in it."

"You're such a jerk." But brightness cracked between her ribs. And then she was laughing too. "God, Clark, I *stink*."

That set them both off in a new bout. Clark was going to fall out of his chair.

"I'm just glad," he said, and swiped at a tear that had appeared in a corner of his eye, "that we already agreed to sleep in your bed."

Chapter Seventeen

The first thing Clark noticed upon entering Riley's room at the inn was that her murder board had expanded significantly. The second thing he noticed was that it now had his face on it.

"Uh, so . . ." She tried to place herself in a way that obstructed his view, an act that was complicated by the fact that he was taller than her and they were chained together. "I normally work alone, right? Like totally solo. But since the curse has sort of aggressively insisted you and I are linked . . ." She gave him a weak smile. "Linked," she repeated as she held up her manacled arm, "get it?"

When Clark simply tried to sidestep her, she rushed to continue, "I guess I better fill you in on my working theories, or, in light of recent developments, lack thereof."

"Where did you even get that picture?" It looked to have been taken at some kind of event. He was wearing a tux, but it wasn't a posed step-and-repeat kind of thing. He wasn't even looking at the camera.

"Google. Obviously."

"Oh, obviously," he repeated, mimicking the flat way she said the word in her accent. "Why am I up there? And is that— My face is circled." He pointed.

"I was getting to that." Riley walked them over to stand right in front of the wall that now stretched well beyond the original board—that Sellotape was going to peel off the wallpaper when she took it down, no question—but she blocked the part with his face on it with her body.

"The board is divided into different sections arranged chronologically."

Yes, Clark could see that. To the far left was the curse-origins section he'd seen the first time he was here, now filled out with corresponding information.

It read a bit like a game of Cluedo. "Philippa Campbell (who) in June 1779 (when) at the cave by the cliff (where) because a blood feud had wiped out her family and threatened her home (why)," though instead of a weapon Riley had listed that Gaelic sentence they found in the cave: "*an end to enemies* (how)."

"Not much progress on that first section, aye?" He made a clicking sound with his tongue. "Didn't you suss all that out ages ago?"

Clark wanted to make sure she knew that just because they'd had a laugh and he'd removed her onions didn't mean he'd gone soft for her again.

"Yes," she deadpanned, "thanks so much for pointing that out."

The next bit said *Curse Evidence* with a section tagged *Artifacts* and an instant photo of the dagger underneath.

Doesn't respond to fire, cleansing, or charms, she'd noted in the photo's white space. Beside it, a Post-it read, *belonged to Philippa?*

While Clark scanned the next few items on the wall, Riley grabbed a pad of fresh notes off the nightstand and scribbled *manacles* before throwing it up beside the dagger.

"Oh, good. If you hadn't written that down, we might have forgotten about them."

Riley drew a cartoon penis and promptly stuck it to his chest.

"Very mature," he said, removing it and shifting his gaze to the section labeled *Events*.

"When did you encounter stinging nettles?" he asked in the same moment that a phantom itch manifested on his hand. Clark scratched at it mindlessly. He still had some of her salve left . . . "Oh, you wily minx."

"Are you talking about me or the curse?"

"You." He'd known it hadn't made sense for the dagger itself to have caused the rash, since Riley had never developed it despite handling the artifact plenty over the last week and a half.

"Just checking." She smiled.

The rest of the events he recognized—*fire, snake, ladder, storm*.

Riley said the castle didn't like it when they were chummy, but looking at the list again, Clark wasn't so sure. Maybe it was because he physically couldn't escape her at the moment, but another observation jumped out at him almost immediately.

"You realize that every one of these disasters resulted in us putting our hands on each other in some fashion." He tried to sound calm about it, even though inside he was railing.

Riley had assured him the curse couldn't impact free will, but his attraction to her certainly felt otherworldly, almost mandated. It would be a relief to blame the way he couldn't resist her on something, anything, other than his own terrible taste in who to trust.

"What?" Riley practically croaked. "No. No way. Come on. We haven't touched *that* much." But she stared at the list too now, likely playing it all back in her head the way he was.

Riley backing him against the wall with the dagger pointed at his throat, him throwing her to the ground when her clothes caught flame, the way she'd grabbed his hand to run from the snake, him catching her as she fell from the ladder, their rain-soaked bodies in his bed.

"The opposite of enemies," she said slowly, and then much faster, "Holy shit. I have to call my mom."

"Pardon?" He barely had time to read the name of the last section, *Attempted Strategies*, and see that she had notes under *Charms*, *Cleansing*, and did that say *Sacrifice*?

Clark leaned forward trying to make out the words—the woman had abominable handwriting—he thought it said something about *away*—when she pulled him aggressively toward the desk where she'd deposited her mobile upon their entry.

"Mom," she said when someone on the other line answered. Riley turned her back to Clark as much as she was able and kind of cupped her hand around the mouthpiece.

Why had she gone red all of a sudden?

If he hadn't been intending to eavesdrop before, Clark certainly was now.

"Hi. Um, so this is kind of random, but you know those romance books you're always reading where one person, like, killed the other person's family and at first the protagonist is like, 'Watch out. I'm gonna bathe in your blood,' but then when they end up in a sword fight a few chapters later it's suddenly extremely erotic?"

Excuse me?

Her mother must have answered in the affirmative because Riley nodded her head.

"Okay, yeah. What's that called, again, like the trope or whatever?"

After another murmured sentence, Riley's high color drained. "And just to clarify, when you say *lovers* that can mean like sex, right?"

Sex?!

"Shoot. That's what I was afraid of." Riley bit at the thumbnail on her right hand. "All right. Thanks, Mom. Yeah. I gotta go. I'm actually a little tied up right now."

She made eyes at Clark like, *What? The joke was right there!*

"I'll call you tomorrow, okay? Love you too. Bye." She put down the mobile looking shell-shocked, almost afraid.

"What was that about?"

Walking them awkwardly over to the nightstand, Riley opened the drawer and removed a faded leather journal. "I, uh, just need to check something."

Clark bet that was the book from her gran. It looked well loved, and he noticed Riley's note-taking method—the pages so marked by Post-its that the padded width stretched the heavily creased spine.

"You know, you don't have to worry about this," she said as she flipped through the pages with increasing speed. "It's just some silly curse-breaking stuff. In fact, why don't you look at your phone for a little." She eyed his pocket meaningfully. "Maybe watch a funny video on YouTube?"

Please. The only things he watched on YouTube were archaeology seminars and season recaps of *CSI*.

He arched his neck to see what she was looking at.

"Listen." She chewed her bottom lip. "I don't want you to get the wrong idea."

"The wrong idea about what?"

He finally spied the page over her shoulder, and . . . *Oh*.

The title was *Sex Rituals*, and the opening began, *Like all bodily fluids, semen can be a potent part of* . . . Clark stopped reading, looked up, faintly seeing stars.

"Is that . . . are you . . . er, doing *that*, much?"

"No. No, no." She shook her head for good measure. "I'm not. I *wouldn't* with a client. That would be inappropriate. And like I said, I work by myself, so no. I've never." She moved her eyes meaningfully toward the book. "In fact, I've never even read this section before. Not exactly something I really wanna think about Gran exploring, ya know?"

Clark did. His nan had plenty of beaus in her retirement community in Kent. He certainly didn't linger on their extracurricular activities.

"But now you think Arden's curse might require . . ."

Nettles, fire, snake, ladder, storm, manacles. Had all these dangers actually been an unseen power using disaster to usher them together like some kind of malevolent matchmaker?

"I don't know." Riley returned to the Philippa section of the murder board, once again tugging him along, and took down a printout of a photocopy of what looked like a letter. "There might be some historical evidence to suggest the curse has a history of encouraging blue balls." She winced, passing him the paper so he could read for himself.

According to this firsthand account, Philippa Campbell had taken Malcolm Graphm prisoner and found some *creative* ways to torture him.

"*From her lips, death,*" he said, suddenly remembering the sentence he'd found in the cell.

"What?" Riley frowned, "Does it say that somewhere?"

"No." He lowered the letter. "In the dungeons of the castle, that sentence had been carved in a cell right next to scratch marks from a prisoner tally. I saw it just before I found the manacles."

"*From her lips, death,*" she repeated. "You think those could have been Malcolm's last words?"

"As far as we know, the curse has prevented anyone else from holding the castle long enough to take prisoners since he died."

Between the two of them, they must have turned over every scrap of documentation that referenced Arden.

Riley tapped her foot. "So, do we assume he was referring to Philippa? To her dooming him with the curse?"

"Possibly, or . . ." How to say this without giving himself away? "It might refer to the dangerous temptation of an ill-advised kiss."

"Oh," Riley said softly. Her foot stopped moving. "Right."

Why did she have to have the perfect mouth? Hadn't Clark endured enough trials in his thirty-two years? All he wanted was to hate her, and if he couldn't manage that, then at least the universe might have allowed him indifference.

"Wait," he said, "earlier, you asked me about the opposite of enemies. That wasn't for a crossword, was it?"

Riley quirked said perfect mouth like she was trying to decide how much to reveal. "I'm almost certain that *an end to enemies* is the language of the curse. Which means to break it, that vow must be fulfilled." She took a long breath. "I thought, until very recently," she said ruefully, "that meant one enemy had to conquer the other—send them away."

Away. His eyes went back to the handwriting underneath the word *Sacrifice* on her board.

"But most accounts assume Philippa and Malcolm were both killed by his clansmen. They couldn't break the curse from beyond the grave. So . . ."

"Who are the enemies?" A rising sickness in his gullet told him he already knew the answer.

"Um." Riley covered her face with her left hand. "I don't really know how to say this."

There was a picture of him on that board.

All her antics of the last week . . . breaking into his camper, requesting a lock of his hair, the cleansing solution she mixed for him to drink. Yesterday—her inescapable presence. The persistent questions targeted to poke at him. That incredibly distracting outfit.

What had Philippa wanted with those words, *an end to enemies*?

To drive the Graphms back, hold the castle unchallenged once and for all.

"We've been trying to get each other to leave"—the manacle weighed heavy against his wrist—"and it hasn't been working."

Riley spun the cuff around her own arm.

Unbidden, a vision of her in his bed came back to him. He'd thought the darkness in her eyes as she tore him apart last night had been nothing but malice, but perhaps he'd mistaken something else: grim determination, even regret?

"I did what I thought it would take." She made herself meet his eyes. "I don't expect you to forgive me."

Clark didn't know if it made him feel better or worse to hear that the attack had been strategic, calculated to achieve some greater end than wounding him. Of course she would prioritize breaking the curse over his feelings. It was her job.

His eyes fell to the journal still open on the nightstand.

Sex rituals.

"That's clever, actually. The opposite of enemies is lovers." Clark joined Riley in sweating. "But if that's the requirement, we've already . . ." He raised his arm to wave off the end of the sentence and—mortified—realized he was accidentally gesturing to her chest.

After what they'd done last night, it was pretty ridiculous to find himself circumspect now, but his facilities had been significantly weakened over the course of this conversation. Besides, even if he was a . . . *god help him, freak in the sheets*, he was still a gentleman in the streets, thank you very much.

Riley looked thoughtful—and, thank goodness, distracted.

"What if the sex has to actually take place *in* the castle—or maybe the curse only recognizes certain types of intimate interactions?" She shook her head. "I need to read more about it."

Clark fought to keep composure amid his rising internal temperature. "You're saying this curse might have antiquated ideas about what acts would qualify us as paramours?"

Riley gave him a sardonic grin. "I'm saying I think the ancient, horny fae magic might not be satisfied until you rail me."

"Jesus." Clark went as tongue-tied as a blushing schoolboy.

"Hey," Riley jumped in, "I certainly don't define *sex* by penetration. But"—she shrugged—"it's a three-hundred-year-old curse. It stands to reason we might be operating under a less-than-progressive definition of *lovers*."

The idea that the castle wanted . . . *that* sent a bolt of awareness through his body. Clark didn't know whether it was from interest or a primal survival warning to run.

Riley must have seen something troubled in his face because she reached for his arm. "Oh, god, Clark, listen, I would never, ever ask you to do that. After last night, I know you wouldn't," she said firmly.

Reaching for the book, she flipped the pages again. "I'm sure there's something else in here I can try."

"Something else. Right." He'd stop thinking about taking her from behind any minute now.

Partially out of curiosity and partially to distract himself, Clark made himself consider the work that must have gone into compiling a journal that massive.

Her gran had seemingly dedicated her entire life to the study and practice of curse breaking, taking care to record all she could in order to pass down the legacy to her kin.

That kind of commitment, the pursuit required for such an endeavor, was even more impressive when you considered that unlike fishing or cartography or even lidar technology, curse breaking was a practice without an established history.

Chasing after such a polarizing calling must have required a massive leap of faith, especially for a woman back in—what, the 1920s? 30s?

"Riley, how did your gran—sorry, what was her name?—how did she become a curse breaker in the first place?"

She looked up, evidently surprised that he'd asked.

"June," she said softly, as if talking about her family even now brought up dormant emotions. "Her name was June, and she was born in rural Appalachia. Into a small mining community."

Oh. He'd expected she came from near Philadelphia, like Riley.

"I've always found Appalachia fascinating."

The bedrock of the mountains was 480 million years old. It was one of the most ancient and mysterious geological artifacts in the world.

"Do you know those mountains predate the dinosaurs?"

"Yeah." Riley grinned. "My mom likes to remind people that her hometown is older than Saturn's rings when they sass her about her accent."

Clark had begun to recognize the particular kind of softness born of—he suspected—love and pride that entered her voice whenever she spoke of her mum.

"But she left?"

Riley nodded. "She moved away when she got a scholarship to go to college—that's where she met my dad—but even though she never studied curse breaking, she did kind of go into the other branch of the family business."

He raised his brows. "What's that?"

"Midwifery." Riley put the book back in the drawer. "My mom's a nurse in obstetrics and gynecology, but my great-grandmother, and her mother before her, they served in a long line of midwives in the mountains. So much of the land out there is isolated, almost inaccessible, trapped as it is in valleys and ridges. It's hard to get to a hospital."

She sat on the bed, eyeing the spot beside her until Clark did likewise.

"Our family brought generations of children into the world. And because the women in the community trusted them so much, they began to show up asking for help with problems beyond babies. By the time she was nineteen, Gran was the person everyone in town came to with their troubles."

Clark had never heard Riley talk like this—effusive but tender, almost shy.

She was quick to share stories about her clients or to defend her decisions, but he rarely heard her describe anything personal. This easy, reverent storytelling about her matrilineal line came in such sharp contrast to the stilted, painful way she'd revealed her father's betrayal at the pub.

He found himself so hungry to know her in this way he physically stilled, terrified that if he moved too much, he'd spook her into stopping.

"At first"—Clark exhaled when Riley continued—"she just listened, or if it made sense, she'd give them a tonic or balm like the salve I gave you, something simple with ingredients mixed to bring healing or comfort, to soothe or fortify. But then one day, the sheriff came knocking at her door." Riley's face grew somber. "There had been a terrible cave-in at the mine. And June's sweetheart, the father of the child she was still carrying, he was one of the men down there, trapped."

Riley twisted her hands together in her lap, the movement flowing like a current through the chain to Clark.

"For a long time, Gran wouldn't tell me the story. But finally on my eighth birthday, she let me stay up until midnight, and we huddled together under a blanket as she explained."

At the slight tremor in Riley's voice, Clark had the terrifying impulse to close his hand around hers. But he knew the most he could offer her was his attention, so he merely nodded, encouraging her to go on.

"Twelve men, some of them still boys, really, were slowly suffocating under miles of rocks and soot. Helpless, they screamed into the earth their anguish, their anger. And as each of them perished, their pain became a curse—whether they'd meant to create one or not."

Clark's throat tightened. He could only imagine the complete horror—both for the men and for their families—knowing they were down there but unable to save them.

"The land around the mine began to change after they died," Riley said. "The soil turned black, frozen. Nothing would grow. Soon after, the water in the streams dried up. Animals began to starve. Those who could packed their belongings and left, but Gran stayed. All those tunnels, the network of the mines—she was afraid of how far the curse could spread. Her community had nowhere to turn for answers. You can't fight a curse with rifles or fists. So they did what they'd always done—came to Gran and begged her to fix it."

To take on such an immense, oppressive force, especially believing its origins were supernatural . . . as much as Riley didn't want to claim her hero complex, clearly it was inherited.

"Gran wrote a counter curse that she refused to repeat, said she couldn't, not again, but she told me she'd gathered all the loved ones of the lost. Took them to the entrance of the mines, where they'd laid their joined hands upon the ground and repeated her chant.

All the love those men had lost, the comfort they sought in their final moments, poured back into the earth—a ritual to mirror the curse's origin. Gran said everyone felt it, the moment when the curse ended. It was a kind of quiet, she told me, a kind of peace."

There had been so much confession between them in the last twenty-four hours. All of it felt tremulous, dangerous. A different kind of dare.

They were each trapped by fortune's cage, the bars constructed of legacy and obligation, aptitude and determination. After tonight, Clark could see in her eyes the same heartsickness that he carried, the kind that came from tamping down and tamping down a longing to be accepted. Only unlike him, rather than courting approval, Riley spat in the face of societal norms. No one could reject her, because she existed in a singularity, isolated and enshrined by abilities others couldn't access.

He'd thought at first that she relished that position, that she'd manufactured it, but after tonight, he knew he'd been wrong. She was born a curse breaker, and any further branding was an attempt to claw back agency from a calling that had stolen her chance at a more ordinary life.

Clark bowed his head. Riley had offered him something fragile here, a piece of her heart. He wanted to believe in the practice she'd dedicated her life to, but how could he?

They were at an impasse bigger than a contrast in temperament or working style. It was like she could see colors he couldn't, and Clark only knew how to follow his own eyes.

"It's a lot of responsibility, curse breaking." He wanted to acknowledge the bravery, the commitment that she and her Gran both displayed, even if he couldn't offer more. "And it's impressive. People place control of their future in your hands."

Riley shook her head. "Curse breaking isn't about control."

"What's it about, then?"

The lingering happiness around her mouth turned gentle, secret. "Hope."

"Hope?" The word caught in his chest—a concept that seemed flimsy only until you lost it.

For all Riley's attachment to the occult, hope was an exceptionally mortal concept. A belief in better, knowing that your ability to effect change was limited. Clark, who had spent his whole life wanting—to be seen, to be special—found himself forced more often than not to use grimacing determination as a proxy.

Hope. It was the exact right word for Riley's particular brand of determination and persistence.

For three hundred years a curse had plagued Arden Castle. The woman before him might be the first to challenge it directly—to try to fix it. One way or another, Clark knew she'd be the last.

"So . . ." Riley said in a way that made it clear he'd been silent for an usual amount of time. "Should we, like, brush our teeth and stuff? It's pretty late."

Ah. Clark checked his watch and saw the hour dashing toward midnight. The sun had set hours ago.

"I suppose we should get to bed." As he stared down at the looming piece of furniture, he gulped.

Though he'd packed a bag to sleep here, Clark hadn't actually engaged with the reality of climbing under the sheets chained to Riley. Of trying to *sleep* next to her. You couldn't maintain your defenses in sleep. What if, in the midst of a dream, *he tried to cuddle her*?

Completely unaware of his crisis, the woman causing it sniffed her collar.

"Ugh. Okay, that's it. I can't stay in this disgusting T-shirt a moment longer."

Clark jerked his head to stare at her. "What do you mean?"

"Well, I'm not gonna sleep doused in vinegar," she said, as if this were a foregone conclusion. "I assumed that since you're, uh, shall we say *familiar* with the impacted area of my body, it wouldn't be a huge deal if I just—" She made a Hulk shirt-ripping gesture.

Panic must have registered on his face because she lowered her arms sheepishly.

"Or I can totally keep it on if you'd be more comfortable?"

"No." Clark was gratified to hear his voice come out even. "No, don't be silly. Of course you should change."

"Oh, thank god," Riley said, sagging in relief. "I'll grab the scissors for you right now."

Scissors? Oh. Right. She couldn't remove the T-shirt over her head because of the manacles.

"Are you sure you don't want to cut it yourself?"

"Well, yeah." She tried bending to demonstrate how the angle wasn't going to work.

In the loo, they fetched the small—tiny, really—pair of scissors she kept in her makeup bag. *So much for getting this over with quickly.*

Riley stood with her back against the sink, with Clark facing her. He could see himself in the mirror—he looked fucking terrified.

Starting at the bottom, he carefully pulled the fabric away from her skin with his opposite hand as he sliced through the saturated cotton. The soft skin of her belly was warm against the back of his knuckles.

As each snip of the scissors exposed a little more of her, Clark pressed his molars together, reminding his brain that this wasn't a prelude to anything. He really needed to see a dentist after this trip.

By the time he reached her collar and parted the stained fabric,

Riley's chest had begun to rise and fall with slightly greater frequency. She must be nervous.

At least she still wore one of those soft, cloth bras, the kind without underwire. He didn't know the name, but it was like a bathing suit, he told himself. Nothing particularly illicit about that.

Unless her tits were sore from his mouth, her nipples too sensitive for lace.

Clark was still standing close enough that he couldn't really see her exposed skin below the neck—a blessing, if temporary. He cut the sleeve from her collar down her arm and freed her of the garment.

"You can cut the bra too," Riley said easily. "The vinegar bled through, but at least I got it from the clearance bin at Target, so no great loss. That way I can give myself a little sponge bath before we go to bed."

A sudden, vivid visual of her running a washcloth over her chest, water dripping from her nipples, made Clark fairly faint. They were chained together, for Christ's sake. Even if he didn't see it, closed his eyes, turned away, he'd hear it. The wet swipes across her naked skin.

Damnit. It was too close a counterpart to the way he'd anticipated clearing his spend from her body after they'd been together in his camper. Clark had wanted that chance to linger over her body—to worship the marks he'd laid across her skin.

Fuck. *The marks.* If he looked down, he'd see them.

He was already hard.

"Riley." He almost said *I can't do this.* It was too much. Being this close. Knowing it was temporary. Everything about her undid him.

"Yes?" Her lips were shiny; she must have run her tongue across them. God, he wanted her mouth again. Wanted his hands in her hair. Needed everything he'd had the other night—but more.

He hadn't known last time that it was the last time.

"Nothing," he said, and lifted the scissors again. Comparatively, the bra was quick, three snips before her breasts were bare for him. And even though he knew it was wrong, Clark did look then. At the expanse of Riley's smooth skin from collarbone to navel. At every place he'd laid claim to while he had her underneath him, pliant and gasping for it. Each point of possession carefully placed so they'd linger like this, pale but present. The memory of his teeth.

If things between them were different, he would have loved tending to her this morning. Running an ice cube in a trail from one mark to the next, chasing the drops of melting water down her stomach with his tongue. Letting her tight nipples go from cold to warm in his mouth.

Enough. He tore his gaze away, made himself turn so he couldn't look anymore even if he wanted to. Staring at the tiles of the wall, he forced himself to start counting them, trying to hide the fact that he'd lost control of his breathing somewhere.

After a long moment where there was nothing in his ears but ringing, Riley turned on the tap. She must have done what she'd said. At least the air went from smelling like a chip shop to smelling like hand soap, lavender maybe. Clark was grateful for the small mercy that she hadn't reached into the shower for her shampoo. If forced to think about lube right now he might actually cry.

Riley grabbed a towel and wrapped it around herself until she could pull out a clean shirt—something she called a tube top, which had no sleeves, so she could step into it and hike it like a band around her chest. She changed her trousers too, to sleep shorts, very quickly. Despite his grim efforts, Clark caught a glimpse of mint-green cotton panties out of the corner of his eye.

"There, I'm decent," she announced when she'd finished.

Clark couldn't say the same. All he could do was hope she mistook his silence, his refusal to meet her eye, for priggishness as they finished their nighttime washing up.

Riley tucked her toothbrush inside her cheek. "Are you gonna sleep in your clothes?"

Normally he didn't, but if he took off his denims right now, she'd know just how calm he wasn't.

"Yeah." He tossed his floss in the bin. "Might as well."

Finally, they lay down with as much space between them in the bed as the chain would allow. It wasn't much.

Highland chill crept in through the inn's double-paned windows. Despite the sturdy quilt, it was an effort not to curl toward the beckoning warmth of Riley's body as the temperature in the room dropped increasingly lower.

Even with his eyes closed, Clark couldn't pretend he was alone. His brain kept zooming in on the sound of her breath or the slight dip in the mattress when she shifted.

To keep his mind in check, he considered the curse.

He'd been so sure, back when Riley found the dagger, that she was a schemer taking advantage of a piece of local folklore that had gotten out of hand. But then when he tried to catch her in a lie about her abilities, she'd led him to that cave, where it became harder to reconcile what he saw in front of him with what he thought he knew.

He was chained to her in an ancient set of iron manacles facing a mounting pile of evidence he couldn't explain away. And she'd introduced the tantalizing possibility that somehow sleeping with her might satisfy some supernatural mandate.

What was a scientist to do?

The idea spread like a vine in his brain. He had the chance to test a working theory and have Riley in his arms for one more night. Clark could see for himself what it meant to attempt to break a curse.

He'd get to kiss her. His cock throbbed against his zipper. *Be inside her.*

His mind and body were in agreement: the offer was too tempting to resist.

"Riley." He turned to her. "Would you do it?"

"Do what?" Her voice was a whisper, the shape of her next to him a moonlight-drenched outline in the dark.

"Would you let me"—*Don't say it like that, you utter knob*—"would you have sex with me again to break the curse?"

"Um." She curled her free hand under her cheek. "I guess, assuming you were willing, I would."

Just from that hardly eager declaration, he had to dig his nails into the meat of his palm.

"It wouldn't be the hardest thing I've tried," she said, her voice so close, he knew he could take the chain between them and haul her to him. Could fill his hands with her sweet curves in an instant.

"We'd both know, I suppose," he said, "that the only reason we were doing it was to test your theory." *Tell me I'm wrong. Tell me you want me beyond your job. Beyond sense.*

"Absolutely." She raised her head to nod at him, cautious optimism in her voice now. "That would be one hundred percent crystal clear. Honestly, it probably wouldn't even be very sexy, if that makes you feel better. Since it's for the ritual, you could think of it as sperm donation, almost!"

"Good idea." *So much for the remains of his ego.* "I'll try that."

"Are you saying yes, then?" Riley sat up against the headboard. "You'll do it? You'll help?"

As if taking her to bed was some bloody act of charity instead of a privilege.

"Yes," Clark said into the darkness. "As long as we both go in with the proper boundaries, I don't see how it could hurt." He was such a fucking liar.

The next thing he knew, there was a heavy metallic *click*.

Chapter Eighteen

You're a fucking professional. Act like it. Wait, that wasn't right. Riley wasn't a *fucking* professional. Just someone who happened to need to fuck as part of her job. *Shit, it still sounds like—* The point was, she could remain detached about this ritual. She would treat it like every other slightly off-center strategy she'd ever attempted in the hopes of overthrowing a curse—trusting her instincts and going forth with conviction.

Needless to say, she was giving herself a pep talk on the way to the castle. It had been three days since the manacles released them. Three days since Clark had stared down at their miraculously free wrists and said, "Well, you've got to admit that seems like an encouraging sign."

The blacksmith who'd taken the train all the way to Inverness was less than pleased to be told her assistance was no longer needed upon arrival. But once Clark assured her he wouldn't be pressing for a refund, she decided to sign up for a loch tour and made a holiday out of it.

After so much prolonged exposure to one another, Clark and Riley both agreed that taking some time apart to regroup made sense before they attempted the ritual. She would read and research while he drafted his report for the HES.

Gran had left some interesting theories about sex rituals to consider, and cited plenty of external sources, but no two curses were the same. The more Riley read, the more apparent it became that she would have to develop something from scratch.

Once she'd done so, she realized they'd be lucky if they were ready to attempt this thing before the week was out. Even with Clark helping, it required a surprising amount of prep work.

They were meeting now to iron out their game plan.

Riley wasn't nervous. She was sweating because her sweater was too tight.

When she'd sent a text yesterday that put him in charge of location scouting, Clark suggested they reconvene in his first choice—the great hall. After a bit of awkward pleasantries better suited to strangers than people who had seen each other naked and would again, they finally got down to brass tacks.

"Okay." Riley paced in front of the camp chair where Clark sat. "So, the central goal of the ritual is to prove we're not enemies, right?"

"Hmmm?" There was a crinkling of plastic as he pulled a Clif Bar out of his pocket.

"Clark." She stopped pacing to snap at him. "Seriously. I need you to buy into this whole thing. It's not gonna work if you're expecting us to fail."

She already had enough doubts about letting him into her process, giving him so many opportunities to mock or dismiss her ideas well before she took her clothes off.

"I'm committed." He made a show of shoving the granola bar back in his pocket to demonstrate. Then, his voice serious, he said, "Go on, I promise I'm listening."

"Fine." Riley didn't really have a choice but to take him at his word. "The ritual I've written has four steps, each one designed to show the curse that we've abandoned our hostility toward one another. It's all about demonstrating trust, and"—she wet her lips—"tenderness."

There was no getting around that last part; she'd checked.

"It won't be easy to pull off. There's a lot we'll need to set up, and once it starts, if either one of us balks, it could blow the whole thing."

Clark pulled out his notebook and uncapped the pen tucked inside. "What do you need me to do?"

As Riley outlined the steps of the ritual, she made sure Clark had an opportunity to weigh in on and agree to each act. By the end of it, she actually felt confident that his questions and suggested tweaks had made things better.

Well, mostly she felt confident.

"Are you sure you can build a tub using raw materials from a garden supply store and the remains of one of those old stoves in the kitchen?" She frowned down at the sketch he'd done of a proposed design.

"You just worry about your part of the list"—he closed his notebook with a clap—"and I'll worry about mine."

"Okay." She sighed. "Then there's just one more thing."

"Hmm?" Clark began packing up, folding his chair and shoving it into its little carrying bag.

"I think it would be best if you didn't masturbate leading up to the ritual so that we can make sure you have, you know, *enough stuff*."

His head shot up, "Are you implying that I underperformed in that area last time?"

"No," she rushed to assure him, trying not to dig up that memory. "Trust me. You were very . . . effective."

She covered her eyes as he smirked.

"I'm just trying to cover all our bases."

"Whatever you need." Clark hitched the strap of the bag higher on his shoulder and gave her a once-over that teetered on the edge of a leer. "It's my pleasure to be of service."

Oh, for fuck's sake. What was that saying? Hoisted by her own petard?

The next day, she recruited Ceilidh to help hunt down her half of the supplies.

"An enemies-to-lovers sex ritual with a smoldering Englishman?" The Scotswoman groaned. "Why are the requirements of your job so much better than mine?"

They bought salt in bulk and gathered rowanberries, going back to Ceilidh's little flat to cook the vivid red fruit down, low and slow, for hours, trying to get the consistency right. They ended up adding some wild honey from a local crofter. It perfectly cut the tartness, turning the bubbling ruby mixture sticky and just shy of syrup-thick. Riley stuck her finger in the cooling concoction and brought it to her mouth for a lick. *Perfect.*

By Wednesday, they were almost ready. Clark assured her that even though an issue with a valve had "thrown a spanner in the works," the tub would be ready the following night.

The last thing to do was have the slightly awkward but necessary conversation about protection.

While Clark chopped firewood, they ran through STI testing (good to go) and birth control (Riley's IUD). It all felt very mature, as close to professional as they could make it.

Finally, the day of reckoning arrived with everything prepped, carefully outlined. There was nothing left to do but *it.*

Thankfully, they'd agreed to wait until sundown. Cover of darkness just seemed like it would make things slightly less awkward.

Riley didn't mean to be late, but the rowanberry mixture had to be fresh and the stove at Ceilidh's decided to act up at the last minute. By the time she finally got dropped off at the castle, Ceilidh laying on the horn and shouting, "Happy boning!" as she peeled out, Riley could see from the warm orange glow on the stained glass windows that Clark had already arrived.

She expected to walk in to flashlights and lanterns, but instead found— "Holy shit, Clark."

He'd put real candles in the chandelier, and more in the few surviving wall sconces. The effect created just the right play of light and shadow to bring out the room's faded glory.

"It's beautiful."

When she finally managed to stop taking in the ceiling and the walls, she saw what else he'd done. In the cleared-out center of the room lay a clean canvas tarp. On top was the mattress from his camper, covered in fresh sheets and blankets, piled with all the cushions she recognized off his couch. To the side sat a neat stack of towels, a big flask of water, and two metal cups.

Riley pressed a hand to the squeezing in her chest. "You made it nice."

She knew it wasn't a romantic gesture. He was practical and safety oriented. He probably didn't want to break his back rolling around on the cold floor in the dark, that's all. No doubt he would stop in the middle of sex to lecture her on the importance of hydration.

"Thank you," she said anyway, meaning it. The gesture felt like flowers before a date—no, actually, better. It felt like someone caring about her comfort. Like Clark wanting her to know she was worth the effort.

"Yes, well, just because we have to strip down in the middle of a crumbling castle doesn't mean we have to be uncomfortable the entire time." He stood with his hands behind his back, his face giving nothing away. "The tub was the real achievement."

Oh! She hadn't even noticed. But there, in the corner. The rig he'd built was impressive, a structure of stacked bricks that looked almost like a pizza oven with a grate, a chimney she recognized from her very memorable foray into the kitchen, and a large metal trough on top.

Riley walked over to dip her hand in. The water was hot, not quite scalding but definitely toasty, with billows of steam wafting up into the chilly air.

"It'll cool as the fire underneath burns down," Clark said from her side, "but that should still give us plenty of time."

"This is incredible." And she meant all of it, but mostly him doing this for her. With her.

The smile he gave her then was small, almost shy. "Do you want to unpack your things?"

Oh, yeah. She had a bag over her shoulder. Right.

First, Riley laid the salt circle for protection, creating a wide arc around the entire room. Then she carefully set the rowanberry mixture next to the bed, since they wouldn't need that for a bit.

When there was nothing left for her to arrange, she turned to where Clark was leaning against the wall, arms crossed, watching her work.

"Last chance to back out." Riley was only partially joking, only partially talking to him.

The night held a kind of crackling potential, the scent of ozone stronger in this room than any other and growing as the minutes passed.

"We've run through everything twice," Clark said, serious eyes, serious mouth. "It's a good plan. Highly considered, but simple."

"You shouldn't be the one comforting me." It scared her more than she wanted to admit that there was no way for her to do this alone.

"I don't mind." He tucked a strand of hair behind her ear.

Riley couldn't tell if it was supposed to be mocking or conciliatory—the way she might have been if he'd been the one who had to ask her for help.

Selfishly, she was glad his part came first.

He'd dressed casually, as she had, knowing what was coming.

Had she never seen him in a T-shirt before? The plain white cotton looked thick, definitely not the kind that came in her preferred Hanes three-pack, and the simple cut highlighted the raw beauty of him. Short sleeves cut high on his biceps hugged the curves like they knew how lucky they were.

"Ready?" Her voice came out high. They'd barely started and already her heartbeat was as frantic as the wings of a caged bird.

Clark gave her a slow, easy nod, grabbing a towel and walking over so he stood next to the tub.

Here goes nothing, she thought as she went to her knees in front of him. At least she could hide her face while she untied his bootlaces.

Undressing the enemy was a callback to ancient custom. A way to show they came together without weapons on their person, concealed or otherwise.

She got his boots off and then his socks, then decided to stand and do his shirt before working herself up to his jeans. Riley needed to remove everything. He couldn't help.

Even though the air outside was chilly, the residual heat off the water created an almost sauna-like quality in the air. Everything felt a little bit dreamy. The smell of wood smoke, sweet in her nose, comforting and familiar.

By every rational metric, she should have been better prepared to see his chest this time. But as the white cotton of his T-shirt came over his head, as it dropped to the ground, she wasn't. This was just the beginning, seeing him bare, of what they'd do tonight, but the way looking at him made her feel wasn't the kind of thing you got over.

Not just because he was beautiful. Riley knew he worked hard for the layers of taut muscle, the harsh definition, but he'd be just as lovely soft and rounded. It came down to the way he held himself. The strength in it. Patience in his stance. A quiet openness that rolled off him and put her somehow more at ease.

She made quick work of his jeans, the expensive briefs. He was half-hard already, she noticed with a pleasant stomach flip. Though, to be fair, that likely had more to do with her request that he *delay gratification* than anything Riley had done or was about to do.

Turning, she gave him her back so he could unzip her dress. It was nothing special, an LBD by the most literal definition only, A-line with a modest V-neck. She'd packed it for Scotland only in case her new employer wanted to take her to tea. She wore it tonight to make it easier on him, one less piece to take off.

Clark slid down the zipper in a single long, careful pull, but he had to help the fabric over her hips, his palms sliding down either side of her thighs until the dress pooled around her ankles.

"Damnit, I forgot to do your shoes first," he said, low and frustrated. She could tell it was genuine oversight by the way his ears burned as he knelt in front of her.

If this were another night, in another universe, maybe he wouldn't wait to finish undressing her. Maybe he'd lean forward— it wouldn't be more than a handful of inches—and kiss the arc of her hip, nothing but the gossamer thin tights between her body and his lips.

Already she was glad for the cool air chilling her fevered skin.

He discarded her boots, more neatly than she had done with his, taking the time to fold her dress and lay it on top of them so the dark material didn't touch the floor.

The problem with rituals was that you had to go slowly, methodically. It would be so much easier to lose herself if Riley could speed things up. If this could have been wild, messy. She'd happily sacrifice the skin of her back for Clark to take her against the wall, if it meant she didn't have to pretend tonight was purely professional for her. If she didn't have to hide that she'd never wanted anyone more.

Despite Clark's repeated claims that she loved risk, she really didn't. Sure, she was impulsive, but that was different, action without thought. Risk was calculated. Riley had never been any good at the thinking part.

Clark, on the other hand, had never done anything without analyzing it to death first. That must be why he seemed so much more in control of himself tonight. Aside from a slight staccato increase in his breathing, it barely seemed to bother him at all, how slowly he rolled down her tights, having to work to stretch the silky material over her ass and the curves of her thighs before she could finally step out of them. Meanwhile, the anticipation was killing her. So when he said, "Looks like you wanted it to be nice too," while running a finger under the lace band at the top of her prettiest pair of underwear, she trembled.

And when he pulled the elastic forward and let it snap back against her skin, she almost screamed.

"You're supposed to be demonstrating your affection for me," Riley hissed.

"I am," he said innocently before sliding her underwear down.

Clark stood to slip one of her bra straps off her shoulder and then the other, testing the engineering of the balconette style that even on its best day functioned more as decoration for her breasts than support.

"This is me appreciating your efforts."

He undid her bra in the back before hooking a single finger between her breasts and, pinning her with his gaze, tugging the whole thing off.

"You've got the easier part." His voice was darker, deeper than the sky over the ocean outside.

She assumed he meant what she'd thought earlier, that surrendering yourself to serve someone was easier than the reverse, but then he finished.

"I have to wait ages before I get to touch you the way I want to."

They made their way over to the tub, where Clark lowered himself in until he was submerged up to his sternum. Almost immediately, his golden skin took on a rosy blush. The bricks below had kept the water plenty hot.

He splashed his chest, brought his legs up so his feet hung off either end of the basin.

"Tell me again what this part symbolizes."

Riley had seen his notes. She knew that he knew. Either he wanted to fill the heavy silence in the room, or he needed to remind them both why they were here.

"I'm attending you." She poured a handful of his expensive orange pepper soap in her hands and rubbed down his arms. "To show I don't hold myself superior."

"Ahh yes." He relaxed deeper into the steaming water, getting the hair at his nape damp as he reclined, grinning. "I remember now."

In truth, it was no kind of hardship to learn the ridges and hollows of him. To get to trace his outline with soap-slick hands. This was different from the massage she'd given him, when all she wanted to prove was how much she didn't care, didn't want him. Now the dare was letting him see that she liked making him feel good. That doing so brought her pleasure, her eyes growing heavy-lidded, her tight nipples pressed against his back as she leaned over him.

She wasn't being careful, in any sense of the word. Water trailed down her forearms and splashed her neck, so that even though she stayed outside the tub, her body still got damp, warm. Steam curled the hair at her temples, made her loose bun fall until she had to reach up and tug out the elastic, letting the blond strands float around her shoulders.

Riley allowed her hands to fall beneath his waist only briefly, enough to count but not to tease.

From the way he exhaled low and even as she kept moving down his legs, Clark must think she did it as an act of mercy.

She did, but not for him.

"The water's still warm," he said when she'd finished. "If you want to have a go, I'll scrub your back."

But that wasn't how the ritual went, so she tossed him a robe from her bag—not a ceremonial one but fluffy and white, the kind you get at a spa—and pulled one out for herself. Ceilidh insisted Riley buy them when they went to a big-box store to get the salt.

No one's getting shagged if you freeze your bits off.

Riley made a mental note to buy her something nice for being such a wise and good friend.

They sat on the edge of the mattress, and Riley unscrewed the jar of rowan she'd prepared. Clark would eat from her hand, a symbol of trust—since the raw berries were poisonous.

Dipping two fingers in the ruby glaze, she held them out to him. He could have easily licked it off, but with a hand around her wrist, Clark took both her fingers on his tongue and closed his mouth.

Riley made a noise, a telling noise, at the wet heat as he flicked across the sensitive pads of her fingertips. Clark just held her gaze, his full of promises, all of them obscene. After an indecent amount of time, she pulled her hand back.

It could have been done then. That was enough and all they'd outlined, but Riley didn't want to stop. She reached for the jar again, using her ring finger this time to gather more of the sticky, sweet gloss and spread it across first her top then her bottom lip.

The second she finished, Clark surged forward to capture her mouth. Groaning like he'd been waiting for permission. Using his teeth like he remembered what she liked.

He kissed her and kissed her, greedy long after the tart flavor of the rowan left her lips.

When at last he did lean back, gasping, trying to catch his breath, his lips were stained. Hers must match. Placing one hand on the back of her neck, Clark ushered her onto her back, bracing on his arms over her.

They hadn't practiced this next part. Her notebook simply said . . . *and then we have sex.*

Riley couldn't find anything to suggest that a particular speed or position was required. It should work as long as he came inside her, as long as she let him.

He pushed her robe open all the way down her front before carefully drizzling a line of rowan glaze between her breasts, using his mouth to chase the slow drip all the way to her navel.

She arched into him—knowing that if she had brought him poison berries, at this point, he'd be sick.

Even when he'd caught every trace of the mixture, Clark kept kissing her. Hotter. Lower. Sliding his hands under her ass, spreading her legs so he could fit his shoulders between them.

"Let me," he said against her inner thigh, and he could have meant anything.

Riley nodded until she could find her voice. "Yeah, yes."

As his dark head ducked to taste her, Riley whined. She'd wanted this but would have never dared ask.

With everything between them, she expected him to tease her, draw it out, make her whimper again, but he didn't. Instead, he sucked her clit straight into his mouth, rubbing his knuckles below, checking, making sure she was wet enough to take it before he curled his fingers inside her.

Oh, god. It was fast in a way that she liked. The stretch tight but not too much.

She slid her hands into his hair, urging him on, holding him close. You'd think she'd never done this before from the way she was acting. She had, but not like this—not with someone she thought might hate her. Someone who she'd handed the worst of herself. Who kept, despite her protests, treating her kindly through all of it.

"Clark," she said, for both of them, confirmation, claiming.

His fingertips were leaving bruises on her thighs. Unlike last time, she didn't think he realized. He moaned into it, like this was as good for him as it was for her, though Riley couldn't imagine.

When she came the first time, thrusting up against his mouth, she assumed he missed it. Clark didn't let up at all, kept pumping his fingers inside her, kept his mouth on her clit.

"Hey." Her voice was wrecked. She had to try again: "Hey, you can stop. It's all good. I already . . ." but that just made him moan and go at it harder, hiking her leg over his shoulder. And that— that was . . . the second time hit so hard, so fast her vision swam.

Since Clark still didn't stop—didn't look like the idea had occurred to him, even though she'd been loud—*louder*—Riley had to dig her heel into his back a little.

"If you want me to make it to the main event, you gotta quit it."

He raised his head, licked his lips, said, "Sorry," a little rough, a little sheepish. "Sorry, I just like it." He wiped his mouth with the back of his hand.

"Fuck." If Riley thought she was in danger before . . .

Clark's eyes closed when she slid her hand down to reach for him, yanking at the knot of his robe until it came undone. He tipped his neck back, veins straining, at the first stroke of her fist on his cock, breathing through his nose, startled, urgent.

Riley tried to mirror the grip, the slide, he'd used on himself, before, but he shook his head almost immediately after she sped up.

"I can't." He wrapped his hand around hers, stilling her movement.

For a second her heart stopped.

But then he said, accusatory, helpless, "I've been hard for you for *a fucking week.*"

And oh. OH.

Whatever control he'd had before was gone. He held his back so straight it looked like it might snap.

Riley lay back down until her shoulders hit the mattress and pulled him forward so he covered her with his body, his dick pressing hard, insistent against her hip.

Clark cupped her cheek, looking at her in a way that made her feel desperate, so she kissed him again, whimpered against his mouth because she needed this and she shouldn't, wanted him when she couldn't.

If he'd been snarky again, she would have liked it. But right now, the gentle way he ran his hands through her hair, petting down her throat, his scent everywhere—spice and orange and the salt of his sweat—was better. More. More than she'd asked for, more than she deserved.

He was heavy on top of her, a good kind of crush as he moved a little, rubbing against her, making himself wait. Riley wrapped her hand around him again, positioning him as she raised her hips.

His mouth opened over hers as he pressed inside, pushing when she clenched, her body adjusting to the stretch as she gripped his shoulders.

This time, as he started to thrust, it was him whispering, "Fuck." Syllables dragging across his tongue. And then her name, almost angry, like she should have told him it would be this good, only she didn't know. Had thought she'd be prepared, but she wasn't.

You're a curse breaker, she told herself. *This is a ritual*. But it didn't matter, not as he kissed the fluttering pulse point at her neck.

His chest slid against hers as he worked his hips, faster now, his hand on the inside of her knee, pressing out, opening her up.

She couldn't come again, her body so sensitive, spent already. She'd fly into a million pieces, combust in Clark's arms. But if he realized, he didn't care, because he reached between them, pinching her clit while his hips snapped, the rhythm unrelenting.

Like so much else he'd given her, it was a gift, after all, to have no choice but to fall apart.

This time he felt it when she came. She knew because Clark let his head fall forward, burying his face in the crook of her neck as his thrusts finally went uneven.

As she stroked his back, taking him through it, Riley wanted to hold on to things she couldn't have, things that had never been hers but felt like it. Now, in this moment as he spilled inside of her, as every candle in the room flickered, once, twice, a third time before they all snuffed out in unison.

"Hope you enjoyed the show," Clark panted into the darkness.

They'd pulled off the ritual perfectly. But as he reached for her hand, brushing his thumb across her knuckles as they lay together under the sheets, Riley thought, *Maybe it won't work, even now.* Because it was clear to her in that moment that she'd never managed to hate him, not really, not even once.

Chapter Nineteen

Someone was knocking on the door of Clark's camper, ruining what had been up until then a very pleasant dream. Except—Clark peeled one eye open—he wasn't in the camper. And there was a warm body curled across his chest, strands of hair that didn't belong to him half in his mouth. And—he sat up urgently—*the knocking wasn't knocking.* It was footsteps through the entrance hall, getting louder, closer.

"Hey!" Riley complained loudly, having woken at Clark's abrupt movement.

"Hello?" his father called back as he appeared in the great hall's entranceway.

His eyes blew wide for one terrible second as he took in his son, his son's companion, the bed, their precariously covered nudity.

Immediately, he spun to face the wall. "Er . . . you lot all right?"

Clark scrambled to his feet, hopping around on the cold stone floor trying to get to his pants, stubbing his toe on a loose slab.

"Not exactly what a father expects to find when he drops in on his son at work," Alfie called, his voice loud enough that he was likely trying to cover the sounds of frantic dressing.

Father? Riley mouthed at Clark, hastily wrapping a sheet around herself.

"On second thought, I'll just wait in the entrance room, shall I? While you sort yourselves out." Alfie ducked back the way he'd arrived.

As soon as his footsteps faded Riley rounded on Clark.

"What the flying fuck is your dad doing here?"

Clark didn't even have time to think about how gorgeous she looked, sleep mussed and barefaced, midmorning light making her skin luminous. Okay, so he had a little time.

"He said he wanted to stop by the site when I spoke to him a few weeks ago. I'd completely forgotten." In all fairness, there had been rather a lot going on.

"Be with you in just a mo'," he called to his dad. Realizing that he'd yanked his T-shirt on backward, Clark had to do it again.

"He's gonna think you joined a cult." Riley gestured to the broken ring of salt, the melted wax from the candles, the crimson stain from where they must have knocked over the rowanberries at some point, her arm moving like an irate air hostess pointing out the various emergency exits.

A cult sounded like a rather sensible cover-up for what he'd actually been doing. Clark couldn't imagine his father taking well to the idea of a mystical sex ritual, especially at his place of work.

Speaking of. "So, did last night . . . umm . . . do anything?"

You know, besides threaten to transform him body and soul.

Riley paused, closed her eyes, as if checking in with her senses.

"No." She shoved the nest of her hair out of her face as she bent to pull on her boots. "I don't know what's going on. The candles flickering and then snuffing out right as we . . . *completed the ritual* seemed like a positive development, but the scent signature hasn't changed this morning."

Well, Clark couldn't say he was totally put out. As soon as Riley broke the curse, he'd never see her again. That proposition was becoming rapidly more threatening than any of the other terrors the castle had thrown at them.

"Listen." He reached for her elbow without thinking, but when her eyes fell immediately to his hand he backed off. Apparently whatever permission he'd had to touch her last night had been revoked. Good to know.

"I was just going to say, before we go out there, please, whatever happens, don't let my father ask you too many questions."

His dad was curious by nature and virtue of occupation both, and he picked apart living people with the same precision as he applied to the dead. At some point, Clark assumed he'd suppressed his sense of empathy in order to better enable him to pluck out little pieces of people's hearts, taste them, and categorize their contribution to society.

Riley tucked her hair behind her ears. "Why would he wanna ask me questions?"

Clark had never seen her so fidgety. It made him almost calm in comparison—like the universe was out of alignment unless they were opposing forces in some capacity.

"You won't be surprised to hear that I don't get caught in compromising positions that often. At least, not like this." It was why Patrick had been frozen out while Clark was merely put on a tighter leash. His father didn't believe him capable of deception or, in this case, reckless disregard—because he didn't expect much of anything from Clark.

Not to mention, the way I look at you is obvious. "My father will assume, I'm afraid, that this mess was all your doing."

By the time they were decent enough for the entrance hall, his dad had worked himself into a theory. Clark could tell by the way he studied Riley, his head tilted just so. The same expression as when he picked up his trowel for a delicate extraction.

Riley hugged the wall on her way out, like she thought she could slip past without a formal intro, but his dad cut that off at the pass, striding forward with his signature rakish grin.

"Apologies for disturbing you this morning." Alfie Edgeware wore his gray hair comfortably, his cheeks sun-browned, each of his fine lines well-earned. While all the Edgeware men shared the same bone structure, his father's face had more character, scars and pockmarks that make him rugged—approachable—to Clark's pretty. "I've been on a lot of work sites over the course of my career, but as it turns out an old man can still be surprised. I'm Alfie. Clark's father."

He used the title, Clark knew, not as a primary identifier, but under the assumption that his reputation preceded him.

"Riley." She held out her hand, back straight.

His dad slid his leathery grip into hers, raising a brow like he expected to hear more. A last name. A form of relation. But Riley, clever girl, gave nothing away.

"Nice to meet you." She didn't sound particularly pleased. "If you'll excuse me, I need to get back to my room at the inn." Riley dipped her head in a way meant to signal her exit, but her approach misfired—the obvious withholding snared his dad's attention.

"If you're only in town for a visit, you should join me and my son for lunch. I've arranged for a private tour of a distillery on the Isle of Skye. It's a once-in-a-lifetime opportunity."

All of this was news to Clark—and Alfie to a tee. Find something local and exclusive, enjoy handing it out like a benevolent king, repeat.

"I appreciate the offer." Riley looked to Clark, holding his gaze to confirm she understood the earlier directive not to give his father an in. "But I'm afraid I'll have to pass this time."

Once again, she made for the door, but this time Alfie turned to

Clark. "Surely this lovely young lady hasn't tired of your company already?"

The most surprising thing about the comment was that Clark wasn't ready for it. The smarting meanness of the words, belied by a chipper tone.

Last night, he'd gone into it promising himself he'd leave nothing on the table. That meant prying himself open for Riley, inch by inch. Even his father's unexpected arrival hadn't managed to close everything back up.

He was already trying to think of an excuse, but Riley didn't bother when she cut in.

"Actually." Clark knew that little half smile. He'd seen it right before he found a dagger pointed at his heart. "You know what? I am available."

Clark stepped between them, just in case, as he led the way out.

A few hours later, after he and Riley had had a chance to shower (her) and panic (him), his dad drove them in his rental car out to Skye. The gorgeous drive included rolling green hills, misty moors, and the loch—as mysterious as it was vast. Not that Clark could appreciate any of that.

He kept waiting for an axe to fall, his palms so sweaty they left damp spots on his dress slacks. But his father must have wanted the benefit of eye contact for his interrogation, because he kept the conversation light—chatting about people he'd met abroad, something funny someone said to him on the plane, the perils of jet lag.

Even the tour of the distillery went off well. The charming owner showing them different kinds of casks, where they processed the grain, large pieces of giant metal machinery that looked like alien robots as described in a sci-fi novel he'd read recently. Not until they'd gotten seated around a high top in the luxurious private tasting room did things start to go downhill.

The owner brought out a leather-bound menu of all the different varietals and vintages on-site. His father surveyed it before ordering a round of something old and expensive for the table.

"Doesn't matter how many times I come to Scotland," he confided after the man left, passing over the menu now that he'd already ordered. "I've never been able to develop a taste for the stuff."

"You're drinking the wrong kind." Riley skimmed a finger down the selections. "Next time try something less peated and you'll enjoy it more. The flavor is richer, caramel instead of smoke."

With the beckoning of a hand, she summoned the host back to order her own drink.

"Whiskey's an acquired taste." Riley passed the menu back to his dad. "It's misplaced machismo that convinces men they have to prove themselves by putting back Lagavulin sixteen."

Alfie blinked.

Clark tried to remember the last time someone had explained anything to his dad, gently chiding.

"You're probably right." His father's smile was bemused. "Know a lot about whiskey, do you?"

"A fair amount," Riley said. "I've been a bartender for over a decade, and I've got a particular affinity for scotch."

Nicely done. She'd managed to neatly neutralize the subject of her occupation.

"Is that so?" Alfie leaned back in his chair. "In that case, I insist you pick out my second glass." By grace of his warm chuckle, the question didn't come across as condescending. Still, a test given in good faith was equally revealing.

Riley agreed, no hesitation, then debated with the server about the merits between a sherry and a calvados bourbon-cask single malt before making a selection.

"It's beginners' whiskey," she told his dad when it came out in a highball glass, neat, "but it's also amazing. No compromise."

After swirling the selection and taking a healthy swallow, Alfie closed his eyes and shook his head. "Fuck, that's brilliant."

Unlike Clark, who wouldn't have been able to resist beaming, Riley merely nodded, though he could tell by her eyes that she was pleased her choice had passed muster.

Part of his father's allure was how he made you feel—important, exceptional—when he wanted to.

Clark wouldn't tell her the fall from that feeling was swift and steep. She'd never have a chance to find out.

"Tell me more about you," his dad said to Riley. "You're American?"

"I'm from South Jersey, right outside Philadelphia," she confirmed, and acquiesced by telling him about her hometown—apparently it was "a pillar of American diner culture," something Clark had never heard of, but now wanted to experience with a kind of desperate curiosity.

As the conversation went on, Clark realized he'd never seen Riley so mild-mannered. It was jarring. He wasn't sure he liked it.

At first, he attributed the shift to her being uncomfortable, but when it didn't go away after a second glass of whiskey, he changed his mind. This was her making an effort. Not for Alfie. Clearly her opinions on his father hadn't swayed from her initial assessment that first night at the bar. No. From the way her eyes kept slipping in Clark's direction, she must be talking about herself and listening to his father prattle on about the one time he'd visited Atlantic City for *him*. Because she knew how much he prized his dad's good opinion.

Clark had to fiddle with his napkin about that for a while.

When Riley got up to use the washroom, Alfie nudged his son's elbow.

"Relax. I like her." He smiled into the drink she'd picked. "You should bring her around to the house sometime. She can have that bottle of scotch my publisher sent me."

Hang on. Were Riley and his dad . . . getting along?

A sudden daydream montage assaulted him—Riley burning a pudding she wanted to take to Sunday dinner. Her kissing him after he bought a replacement. Riley shooting darts at his father's local. Lord knew she could hold her own against the old blokes when it came time to trash-talk. Clark wouldn't mind watching, fetching her drinks. Talking her down when she lost and subsequently challenged her opponent to a fistfight. His father and Riley on a family holiday, bullying him to do something horrible like cliff dive.

He chewed the inside of his cheek. The addition of Riley, of anyone, wouldn't replace Patrick's absence.

For the first time in a long time, Clark missed his brother and found the feeling untainted by any sense of resentment, betrayal, or guilt. Perhaps it was because he'd learned recently how easily fear could convince you that the right thing to do was lie even to people you respected and cared for in order to protect them, to protect yourself. He couldn't pinpoint the exact moment, maybe there wasn't one, instead a handful of small shifts that had somewhere on the grounds of Arden Castle finally resulted in release. He'd forgiven Patrick. Realizing it felt like taking his first deep breath after six months with a head cold he couldn't kick.

Clark had always been a second son, but today he saw the potential in it.

"Always thought you could do with a bit more messing about." His dad ruffled his hair. "Looks good on you." He pulled back, tilted his head again. "You look happy."

Before Clark could even process that comment, what it meant, his dad launched into a story of one of his own exploits featuring his infamous coalition of mates named Dave. Though this particular tale—how the middle-aged man Clark knew as "well-behaved Dave" had earned the now-retired moniker "rave Dave" by passing out in a puddle of sick during an underground punk gig—was new.

Clark laughed, breathless. This was the kind of messy, embarrassing story you told a friend, someone you saw as a peer, not a kid.

By the time Riley returned and they ordered a last round, he couldn't believe how well the outing had gone. Had he ever felt this relaxed around his dad? Yes, the whiskey played a role, but it was more than that. Riley provided some kind of magical buffer, smoothing out the harsh edges they usually caught themselves on.

Under the table, he nudged her knee with his.

"Thanks for this," he said when his dad got up to speak with the owner.

She gave him this look out of the corner of her eye, soft and private, and shrugged.

"The pair of you won't believe this," his dad said, startling them as he returned to the table. He braced his hands on the back of his chair. "Apparently, there's some horrible person at Arden Castle masquerading as a curse breaker—whatever the fuck that means."

Shite. Clark might take the easy way out, let the comment lie with a noncommittal "Is that so?" but Riley wouldn't. She'd have no problem barreling in, telling his dad exactly what she did and why, gloriously righteous, as ever.

Yes. Any second now. She should be . . .

But her knee went jittery next to his. And when he looked over, she had her eyes firmly planted on the tablecloth.

Clark didn't understand. After all those times she'd told him off, defended her family and her craft, why would she sit there now and bite her tongue about what she did?

Then, something came loose in his chest, some vital part. Riley biting her tongue, he realized, was a choice. An offering. For what he'd done for her last night. As if anything on Earth could have kept him away.

"Well?" His dad looked between them, nonplussed but still jovial. "Have you heard anything about it?"

Clark could sit back, do nothing. They could move on, end the evening on a high note. Lord knew he had enough experience disappointing both Riley and his dad.

Except. Even if Riley could reconcile letting this moment pass unacknowledged, Clark couldn't. Couldn't stand her having to hide, to make herself smaller, for anyone.

She sat there bracing herself, expecting no support, no defense—nothing from Clark. She hadn't even bothered glancing at him—that settled it.

"I'm not sure why you're so surprised," he said before he had a chance to overthink it. "Surely you've heard of Arden's curse? There have been accounts of mysterious malevolent activity on the grounds going back several centuries."

"Don't tell me you're caught up in this, Clark?" The temperature in the room fell several degrees as his father stared at him. "I raised you to know better than to believe in that kind of foolish deception."

"You raised me to be a researcher." Had fed him and Patrick both on a strict diet of logic. Built their household at the altar of science. "And I'm telling you there's something more than the power of suggestion going on at that castle. A curse is at least a viable theory."

Riley raised her head, caught his eye like, *Are you sure you know what you're doing?*

His father didn't notice, focused solely on his son as his cheeks hollowed with anger.

Clark never contradicted him. Not as his son. Not as a scientist.

"Rumors like this, of supernatural forces, they're toxic." Alfie kept his voice low, controlled, but on the chair back, his hand curled into a fist. "You'll forgive me if I prefer to put stock in fact rather than fearmongering."

"But you're an archaeologist. You know fact is nothing but our best approximation of the truth." He'd expected pushback, but to ignore even the possibility . . . *"The world is flat. Earth is the center of the universe. An atom is the smallest building block of matter.* If history has taught us anything, it's how often we get it wrong."

Clark found, to his surprise, that he wasn't just arguing for Riley's benefit. He believed the words coming out of his mouth. An argument crafted just as much for himself, two weeks ago, as it was for his father now.

"You believe that a place can be sacred, right?"

"I do." His dad had worked on enough temples, enough tombs. "For a specific group of people."

"Well, those places, they're the epicenter of powerful emotions, existing together in a single space, year over year, and they leave behind a certain energy. We can't name that feeling, that power, but we still recognize it exists."

His father's nostrils flared. "I can't believe this. I'm telling you that there's a person preying on the ignorance of rural villagers, hawking services they can't possibly deliver—and you're saying you believe *curses* have some logical explanation?"

Under the table, Clark gripped his chair seat. Losing his dad's approval so soon after earning it felt like a car crash in which he was somehow both driver and spectator. But he refused to let Riley sit there and listen to someone else's father spew the same ignorance as her own.

"I'm saying that much of the universe is unknowable."

Riley put her hand over her mouth, whispered, "Well, I'll be damned."

Part of Clark did want to drop it then. See if maybe they could steer things back into a pleasant, placid direction over a round of digestifs. He could salvage the situation, have his dad go back to smiling at him.

In the end, he didn't get to choose. Alfie had to have the last word.

"You listen to me." He pointed at Clark. "If you run into that curse breaker, let him know I think he's a dirty crook."

"You know what." Riley got to her feet. "He doesn't have to. Because it's me." She did a little wave. "Hi, I'm the curse breaker."

That drew his father up short. "I thought you were a bartender?"

"I'm both." She smiled tightly. "It's sort of a hyphenate situation."

He turned to Clark, mouth twisting with distaste. "So that's why you've bought into this thing. For a bird."

Ah, yes. Here was his father's signature brand of takedown.

Only, Clark wasn't a boy anymore.

"Actually, no," he said. "It simply seems to me like spectacular arrogance to assume that anything I can't prove is impossible."

Color rose in his father's cheeks. "Are you calling me *arrogant*?"

"Clark," Riley said. "It's fine, you don't have to—"

But this wasn't just for her benefit anymore.

He held his father's glare. "Yes, sir."

Alfie took out his wallet, threw a tenner down on the table.

"I should have realized." He laughed, the sound hollow. "You've always been easily led."

Riley sucked in a breath.

Two birds. One stone. Clark had to hand it to him.

His father managed to take every major mistake he'd ever made and sum them up in one neat, biting remark while simultaneously insulting Riley's integrity.

After the door to the tasting room slammed, they sat in silence for seconds that seemed infinite.

Well. He'd been close to getting his father's acceptance there for a minute. That was something.

"You okay?" Riley pulled her chair back out, folding herself down neatly and crossing her arms.

"Sterling." Clark drained the dregs from his glass before propping his elbows on the table and lowering his head into his hands.

"He thinks he knows you, but he doesn't." Her voice was low, gentle. "It's not weakness. The way you trust people."

Clark looked up, folded his hands together, at a loss. "How can you say that after what just happened?"

It was like a bad play. How many times was he going to appeal to his father for acceptance, affection, before he realized Alfie wasn't capable of it?

"You know what he's like." Riley stared at the door his father had stormed out of. "You knew the risk in standing up to him. But you were giving him a chance. To be better."

She turned to Clark. "It wasn't an accident or oversight." Like everything about her, the words were clear, definitive. "You're braver than he is."

Clark swallowed, sat there, tried to make himself hear it. "I don't know what's more disconcerting, when you're cruel to me or when you're kind."

"I think you like a bit of both," she told him, gunning for a smile.

He nodded seriously instead. "It depends on my mood."

Clark knew his father criticized because he cared. Because he thought Clark needed pushing and prodding to live up to his potential. Inside his dad's head lived a relentless taskmaster and Alfie Edgeware credited that harsh, wily animal with his success. Knowing didn't stop the rush of nausea.

"I suppose we've only got one real option now."

"Yeah." Riley took out her phone. "I'll order an Uber."

"No, I meant we pull out the big guns. Break this fucking curse."

Her brows rose. "I'm listening. You got an idea?"

Clark smiled, surprised that he could. "It just so happens, I do."

Chapter Twenty

Apparently, for archaeologists, "pulling out the big guns" meant "using your academic credentials to get access to a university's rare books room, even if said rare books room was technically closed to the public due to ongoing renovations."

Or at least, that was what Riley had taken away from Clark's call to the head of the collection at St. Andrews.

"We're in." He'd grinned as he hung up, looking only slightly wild-eyed from where he sat beside her in the back of a very expensive Uber on their return trip to Torridon. "A security guard will be there at ten a.m. tomorrow to meet us."

"Great." Riley hadn't totally understood the plan at that point, but he looked so adorably eager. After his dad had been such a horrible monster—like so bad that for a few hours she was glad her own dad had had the decency not to stick around—she would have gone pretty much anywhere that made him smile like that.

When she got back to the inn, after she did all the normal face-washing, teeth-brushing stuff—Riley put on her pj's and called Ceilidh to see if she'd want to take the train with them in the morning to visit the collection. As far as she could tell, Ceilidh was the only person who loved old books more than Clark.

"Damnit, I've got class," her friend moaned. "Can you just take pictures of everything? Like just all of it?"

"Oh, sure," Riley agreed. "That shouldn't be a problem. Clark said they only have like two hundred thousand books in there."

Ceilidh made another sound of excruciating pain. "Don't rub it in, you horrible woman, or I won't let you take my car and you'll be stuck on the bloody train for one thousand years."

Riley laughed.

The following morning, Ceilidh not having made good on her threat, Clark and Riley met the surly security guard after the four-hour drive.

"Don't get yourselves locked in." The guard ushered them through a very old-looking door. "The knob will lock automatically behind you, and my shift ends in an hour." His bushy white mustache twitched. "I won't come back."

"Noted, sir," Clark held the door for Riley, who tried to nod in a way that conveyed her utmost respect for academic institutions, their employees, and procedures as they walked inside.

"Whoa." She hadn't had a firm vision for a rare books room, having never visited one or really thought about them existing before, but even with some scaffolding and tarps covering parts of the space, the massive room at St. Andrews was majestic.

Riley couldn't help stopping to take a deep inhale of the sweet, dry scent of preserved paper. America had a lot going for it, as far as she was concerned, but *man*, Europeans really took the cake when it came to old stuff. And gun laws. But that was a different story.

It wasn't just the books that were old here—it was everything. Her mom would have called the space handsome. It had all the HGTV stuff she drooled over—high, vaulted ceilings, crown molding.

Clark made a beeline for a computer desk in the corner, a man on a mission, but Riley just swiveled her head, taking in the books in all directions, including up.

Some had spines bound in cloth or leather, some books were skinny, and some were extraordinarily fat; volumes lived in little families. There were books under glass, their pages open to show the gilded, hand-painted illustrations.

"Holy smokes." It was the first time she'd thought about a university as more than just somewhere to go to get a degree that let you make more money. This place, this room, kept so many centuries of knowledge—it hurt her heart that she only got access for a few hours.

She envied Clark the way he didn't even blink when they walked in. This was his world. Of course he'd feel at home here.

Riley found him bent over a keyboard. "It was nice of you to bring me here."

Before she came to Scotland, she'd thought working alone made her stronger. Now she wondered how much she'd missed out on by not asking for help sooner.

As Clark looked at her, the determined frenzy he'd been in ever since his dad left lifted. His eyes warmed. "Do you like it?"

"How could I not?" She'd already passed several sections she wished she could linger in. Books on botany and mysticism and geology.

Clark smiled and then pointed at the screen. "I think you're about to like it even more."

She leaned forward to read over his shoulder. *"History of the Clan Graphm: from public records and private collections, compiled by Amelia Georgiana Murray MacReive. Published in 1790."*

"Why didn't you collect this as part of your first round of research?" It seemed promising. A study of clan life before, during, and right after the events of the curse in 1779.

"It came up in my initial searches, but because of the condition of the book you can't remove it from the collection." He pointed to a note in the catalog. "Let's just say I was less incentivized to make the trip out here when I looked a few months ago."

Riley nodded. She recognized the same fierceness in his face from when he'd defended curse breaking at the restaurant. They were here because of his father. Because Clark was finally striking back against a lifetime of tyranny.

He hadn't developed a newfound belief in her calling beyond her request and a sense of obligation. Clark didn't feel, as she did, that they stood at the precipice of something ancient and powerful. So close—if they could push through this last stretch—that they might have the unique ability to fix something that had been broken for so long. As much as Riley wanted to believe he was really in this with her, she didn't dare hope.

Look at Gran and her mom. Curse breakers didn't get partners, romantic or otherwise. They got adventure and adrenaline, gratitude when they did a job well. And if Riley could help it, they got paid.

The way Clark's father looked at her, like mud under his shoe, wasn't an anomaly. His whole circle of gentleman academics would turn up their noses at her family legacy. Clark might be willing to fight for her once, but she couldn't see him signing up for the job full-time.

Following the tracking number, they found the book tucked away in a special temperature-controlled cabinet, its spine bent and peeling with signs of wear. After taking special care washing and drying their hands, they took the text over to one of the room's glass tables and pulled out two chairs.

"Something weird, right?" Clark looked to her for confirmation after they sat down.

"Right," she said, resisting the impulse to reach over and smooth a wayward curl back from his forehead. *Gross.* When had she turned so mushy? When had this man become so . . . dear?

Several hours and one neck cramp later, Riley realized the book was full of weird things. The problem was none of them felt particularly useful. Plus, there was only one book and two of them so they kept bumping shoulders and thighs, as they leaned over trying to read the fine, faded print.

She took back her assessment of Clark as helpful. He was outrageously distracting.

Every inhale brought her lingering traces of his wintergreen shaving cream. She kept looking at his jaw. Which inevitably led to looking at his mouth.

Then Clark would catch her looking at his mouth, and say, "What is it?"

And she'd have to make up something, pretending she'd been lost in thought about crop patterns or methods for roof thatching. It was a whole mess.

But it wasn't her fault. She didn't know what the rules were between them anymore.

They'd done this whole ritual that, even if it didn't break the curse, still cemented them as intimate. Riley felt like she *knew* Clark, his body, his mind. Like he belonged to her, only he didn't.

Now, all this banding together to prove his dad wrong, or everyone wrong in Riley's case, it had a way of making it seem possible that— *Hey, wait a minute* . . .

"Clark." She fumbled for his arm while keeping her eyes locked on the book. "Look at this wound report."

"Really? Wounds?" He turned green around the gills. "Must I?"

"You must." Riley pushed the book closer to him. She supposed not everyone grew up studying their mom's medical journals as a hobby. "It's an excerpt of a field medic's record from right after the Graphms took Arden. And see here? It says the patient—a scout—died after he was attacked with an unusual instrument."

"Right," Clark said, still looking at her, clearly lost. "Are you sharing simply because you're excited by blood sport?"

"What? No." She slapped ineffectually at his hand. The man had picked a fine time to stop paying attention to detail. "Would you just read it?"

Chin in hand, Clark bent over the passage, "All right. It says the wound came about after the scout entered the castle's guard tower— Oh." He raised his head. "That's where you threatened to stab me—this is sort of nostalgic. Look how far we've come." He smiled fondly.

"Would you just keep reading," Riley urged, massaging her temples in an attempt to remain calm.

"Not up for a bit of reminiscing, I see." He bristled, somehow becoming more British in the gesture. "Well, fine. Fine, where was I?" Clark made a show of returning to reading. "Ah yes. Here we are. *Scout entered the guard tower*, blah blah, oh here's something, he was actually stabbed in the back of the neck by 'a dagger of unusual design'—hmmm—and the medic notes that because of the length and width of the blade that must have caused the wound, the attacker needed to possess extraordinary skill to severe the spinal cord in a single blow." Clark turned to her. "You believe this man was attacked with the dagger you found in the castle?"

"It sounds like it, doesn't it?"

"I need to read more." Clark pored over the rest of the text for several moments, making little *hmm* noises and shushing her every time she tried to ask him a question before finally he sat back and crossed his arms. "It doesn't make sense."

"What doesn't?"

"Well, aside from the fact that it's unlikely Philippa would have possessed the physical strength or training to make such an attack, I can't see how she would have gotten close enough to the scout to make a strike at such short range. Here, stand up." He grabbed both her hands and hauled her to her feet. "Okay, you're Philippa. You stay there."

After placing her, he jogged about fifteen feet away.

"I'm the scout. This is roughly the distance from the end of the guard tower to the end of the staircase."

Riley squinted, trying to remember, but that seemed rightish. "Now what?"

"Now try to stab me in the back of the neck with your dagger."

She judged the distance between them. The blade they'd found couldn't be more than eight inches. Riley walked toward Clark. Because the tower was circular, and the staircase entrance exceptionally narrow, she didn't see how she could get behind him.

"You can't, right?" Clark mimed unsheathing something from his hip. "Plus, I've got a sword. There's no way you're getting close enough."

"Unless . . . unless I'm not Philippa. What if I'm Malcolm?" This time when she approached, Riley held one hand behind her back.

Confused, Clark let her get within arm's reach. Instead of extending the dagger, Riley opened her other arm, embraced him, and only when he reached for her—automatic, unthinking—did she drag her opposite fingernails across the back of his neck, the faintest proxy for a blade.

"Malcolm was a hero to his clansmen. Their favored son." Clark shivered. "They wouldn't have expected to find him waiting in a guard tower, not when he was supposed to be in the dungeons. The scout would have been surprised, would have greeted him as a lost brother."

"Especially if he appeared unarmed." At this rate, she'd have to send the writers' room at *Criminal Minds* a thank-you email. "Philippa's dagger would have been easy to conceal until the precise moment when he needed it."

Clark's heart raced, a mirror of her own where their chests pressed together.

"It was always strange that Malcolm died in the siege, and no one ever said how, or why. But if, at the very end, he betrayed them, they wouldn't have wanted it known. The Graphms would have done everything they could to hide the record. Would have burned any trace of warrior accounts, but something like this"—he broke apart to rush over and tap the medical report—"they might have missed."

Riley stared down at the page.

"I don't understand. He was barely there for three weeks. I thought they might have been hot for each other, sure. But for Malcolm to turn on his clan for Philippa." She blew out a long breath. "Was it Stockholm syndrome? Like are we talking a full *Beauty and the Beast* situation here?"

"No," Clark said, surprisingly quick, surprisingly sure. "I think he fell in love with her. I mean, look what we know even centuries after her death. She was brave. Determined. Clever."

He laughed, looking wondrous. Looking at Riley.

"He was probably terrified at first, of how caring for her, wanting her, put him at her mercy," she mused.

Two things are bound into repetition, Gran had written, *history and curses.*

"*From her lips, death*," Clark said, "of all he knew, all he was."

Riley hadn't seen it. Hadn't wanted to. It was right there in the word—*lovers*.

She clenched her hands into fists.

"No one falls that fast." Especially women who knew better, who'd seen it all go to pieces in an instant.

Clark looked her dead in the eye. "Of course they do."

No. Not now. Not this. Riley took one step backward, then another, kept going until her heels hit a bookcase at the far end of the room.

He shouldn't be allowed to look at her like that, like he knew her. Saw how scared she was. Wanted her anyway.

In stories, when a prince fell in love with a commoner, happily ever after was assured because "the end" was only the beginning. It was a load of narrative hand-waving if you asked her. Things only seemed like they'd work out because the protagonists had never been truly tested.

Where was the proof they could survive the trials of everyday life? What happened the first time she embarrassed him in front of his society friends? How would his face look when the scullery maid took the prince home to her dingy kitchen and cheap IKEA mattress?

"You're letting all this talk of fairy tales get to you."

"Am I?" He wasn't moving but Riley could feel the space between them like a current, calling, beckoning. Any moment she might fall under. "Tell me you don't feel it."

"I don't feel it," she said in an instant, loud, ruthless.

But Clark just leaned back against the desk, crossed his long legs at the ankles.

"I don't believe you."

Heat flared in her face. The audacity to not take her at her word. When she needed him to!

He truly was the most infuriating man. At least anger felt safe, hot and powerful. Riley clung to it, wrapped it around her shoulders like a blanket.

"How would you like me to prove it?" She'd go pick up someone at a campus bar, would call any one of the contacts in her phone labeled *Absolutely Not*. Bring her a pen and she'd sign the legal oath of his choosing.

The bastard didn't want any of that.

"Kiss me," he said, his deep voice a siren song.

Riley's knees wobbled. "What? Why?"

"Because there's nothing left to hide behind."

Riley huffed. She didn't back down from a challenge. Every day, she went toe-to-toe with ancient evil. She certainly wasn't afraid of a man, even this one.

"We're half a day from the castle. The curse," he told her. "If you're not falling in love with me, fine. Kiss me," Clark repeated, "and then we'll both know."

Fine. She marched over, grabbed a handful of his sweater, and pulled him in.

He might be expecting a peck, but she kissed him fully, filthy, tongue and teeth. Riley kissed him like they'd never have sex again and he was gonna regret it for the rest of his miserable life. She brought her arms around his neck and pretended it wasn't because her own knees were shaking.

Clark stood there and took it, opened his mouth for her, let her rub against him, and the whole time he met her lips with control, soothing her into some semblance of a rhythm, petting her hair back from her face, smiling against her frantic lips like he'd won.

They kissed until all she could hear was the blood pounding in her ears, the hectic rhythm of her own breath.

"There," she said, panting, stepping away only when she couldn't keep from melting against him a second longer. "Ha! See?" Her voice was somehow both hoarse and too high. "What did I tell you? I'm good. I'm totally good."

Clark stood there, sweater rucked up, hair mussed from her hands, his mouth red, lips kissed swollen and—her brain almost exploded—shoved his hands in his pockets.

"Well?" she demanded. "Aren't you going to say anything?"

Riley needed him to fight with her right now more than she needed oxygen.

A beat of silence passed. Then another.

"Clark," she warned, the tug of the ocean at her waist, her chest, her throat, "if you don't say something . . ." She pressed a hand to her tingling lips and then, realizing what she'd done, yanked it away. "I—I swear, I'm gonna leave."

He wasn't right. They weren't—they couldn't be.

She just had to hold it together until she got back to the village. There, she could get a second opinion. That's right. She grabbed her coat off the back of the chair, gathered her bag. All she needed was some external perspective, a few alternate explanations.

Riley could count on Ceilidh. As a researcher specializing in the curse, she'd have some sensible explanation for why Clark's conclusions were silly. They'd laugh it off. They had to.

Hating Clark was one thing. It didn't feel good, but it also didn't feel like diving off a cliff. This—*this theory*—demanded she disregarded all sense of self-preservation.

Clark, the son of a bitch, kept standing there, checked his watch as if he was expecting the bus.

"You think I'm joking?" She turned and walked backwards toward the exit, waiting for him to break. "I'm not." She patted her pocket, heard a reassuring jangle. "I have the keys."

Any second now, he'd see sense.

"I will totally leave you here." She was almost at the door. "You'll have to hitchhike home. And even though you're handsome, no one is gonna pick you up because you have a terrible personality . . ."

Oh, who was she kidding?

Later, if anyone asked, she didn't run to him after that. Didn't throw herself into his waiting arms with such force that he said "Oof" into her neck as he bent, smiling, to nuzzle her jaw.

"You better keep that mouth occupied," she warned him. "If I see one hint of a smirk, I'll—"

Clark caught her chin in his hand and tilted her face up to his. "You'll what?"

"Fall in love with you," she finished, and this time when she kissed him it was soft. Hopeful. She kissed the corner of his mouth that marked his scowl. Then his often-furrowed brow.

Riley gathered his hands in hers, large, warm, rough, and kissed his knuckles. Then turned them over and kissed each palm.

"Promise me," he said, barely a whisper. "You're not just saying it because you think it'll break the curse?"

"I promise." Riley rubbed her thumb across his cheekbone. "Like you said, we're half a day away from the castle." She tucked herself under his chin, held on tight. "This is just us."

Clark stared at her for a moment, like he was trying to make sure she was real.

"In that case," he said, a little breathless, a little giddy, "I love you."

Even after all the lead-up, the words still took her aback. Riley hadn't known how much she wanted to hear them. How much she wanted them to come from Clark. How much she kept from herself, because wanting it scared her.

But now. She carried his love for her in her chest. As if she'd swallowed the sun. And all she could think was *I hope it's the same for him. That he doesn't just hear the words, but that they stay somewhere safe behind his ribs—a light that doesn't burn out.*

Chapter Twenty-One

"I'm sorry," Clark said when he grew hard from all the breathless necking. He brushed his lips across her temple, hiding his rapidly heating face. They were in public, for Christ's sake. Besides, he was cheapening the moment.

Only, Riley didn't seem to think so.

"I'm not." She trailed her hand down his chest to cup him through the fabric of his wool trousers.

Clark couldn't help himself; he bucked into her palm.

"What are you— We *can't*." Because it wasn't so much that he didn't know what she was suggesting as it was that he found himself utterly scandalized.

The wooden floors underneath their feet were original to this very old, very important academic institution.

"Sure we can." Riley undid the top button of his shirt and licked the exposed hollow of his throat.

"Someone could come in here," he said helplessly.

The idea spiked his pulse, made his whole body overheat.

Riley still had her hand on his cock, her thumb circling the head through the rough fabric, barely-there pressure.

"Yeah." She went to her knees in front of him, holding his gaze. "They could."

Clark sagged against the bookshelf at his back as she pushed his shirt up to ghost her blunt fingernails over the hair below his navel. Goose bumps spread from the point of contact, making him shiver. She tugged down his zipper very slowly, as if waiting for him to stop her.

He didn't.

Smirking like she knew exactly how hot the threat of discovery made him, Riley flicked open the button on his pants, wrapped her hand around his bare cock, and kissed the tip.

Clark had never—*oh, god*—never done anything like this. Never broken a rule—*a law*, he corrected with a heady jolt—certainly not on purpose.

Riley must have assumed as much, since she sat back on her heels, licked her perfect pink lips, and raised her eyebrows like it was Clark's call whether or not she'd suck him off in the bloody rare books room.

"Please." His hands went to her hair, threading through, gentle but sure, urging her forward. "God, Riley. Please."

Her little smile in response was wicked. Wanton. Said she knew she was his bloody wet dream. On her knees. In a library.

Clark was so hard as she slid down his length, the tight, slick heat of her mouth almost too much already.

Even though Riley must have known he was in a bad way from the hectic pace of his breath, from the way his thighs tensed as he leaked against her lips—as always, she didn't take it easy on him. There was no starting slow to warm him up. No, she went ahead and tongued the slit straightaway, squeezing around the base, setting a rhythm that had Clark biting his lip ruthlessly to keep from crying out.

He brushed his thumb across her round cheeks as they hollowed, working for him. The risk of this made everything more intimate. Their secret.

As the shuffling of footsteps and faint strains of conversation drifted in from the hallway through the gap between the wooden door and the floor, he tensed even further, balancing on a razor's edge for control, pleasure and fear zinging up and down his spine in equal measure.

He wouldn't last like this. No chance. And as much as he'd love to spill in her mouth, he needed to be inside her knowing it wasn't for a ritual or some game between them.

Gently, he pulled Riley to her feet, kissing her, sucking his taste off her tongue before tucking his throbbing cock up under his waistband and walking her backward until her knees hit the table where they'd been studying.

He thought for a moment about making a grand sweeping gesture, knocking everything to the floor like in a movie, but he didn't want to damage a piece of the collection—and their notes were really important—so he quickly, carefully, gathered all the materials in his arms and deposited them safely on a chair in the corner while Riley gazed at him, looking amused, looking—incredulously—charmed.

When the table was clear, she hopped up on it, spreading her legs, beckoning him between them. Clark went, got his hands underneath her shirt to rub the silky skin of her back before moving to caress her breasts over her bra.

Once again, the style didn't seem engineered for much besides driving him mad, the cups cut so low they barely covered her nipples. Wanting a proper look, he peeled her top off.

Fucking hell.

She practically spilled out of the dark fabric. All he had to do was thumb at it to have her popping out into his hands.

Riley gasped when he tugged at her nipples. Gently at first and then, gradually, harder. She'd asked for it rough in his camper, but he didn't know if that was more about the mounting animosity between them at the time, the way she didn't want to want him.

He kept his eyes on hers, monitoring her response as she arched into his hands, hitched her legs around his waist, and ground against him.

After nuzzling at an almost faded bruise beneath her collarbone, Clark pressed his teeth over the mark, biting again, some primal part of him insistent, possessive.

Her breath hitched, nails sinking into his shoulder blades.

When he finally got a hand beneath her skirt, he closed his eyes and groaned, the questions of if she liked this, and how much, answered definitively.

Clark pulled her underwear off and shoved them in his pocket, while Riley hiked her skirt to her hips. He ran his fingers back and forth over her, smearing wetness up and over her clit in tight, quick circles until she clenched, quivered.

"Please." Riley reached for his cock. "I can't wait anymore." She wasn't trying to be quiet at all, like she didn't care if someone heard them, as long as he kept touching her.

Despite how worked up she was, it took them a minute to get him fully seated. Once they did, Clark had to breathe through his nose, counting backward from ten, trying to get a hold of himself so he could make it good for her.

Displaying absolutely no sympathy for his struggle, Riley gripped his ass and tilted her hips up, taking him as deep as she could all at once.

He braced one hand beside her on the table for leverage, the other cradling the back of her skull, before bringing her mouth to his so he could kiss her as he started to thrust.

The table legs stuttered against the floor as they rocked together. A steady *thump, thump, thump* that went to his head, made him woozy.

"You're so fucking sexy." He took her bottom lip between his teeth until she whimpered. "I almost want someone to walk through that door right now, see you like this—clothes half undone, gorgeous tits bouncing, pussy so wet for me you're gonna leave a mark on this desk."

"Clark, Jesus." Riley squeezed her thighs around his waist, locking her ankles behind back. "When we first met, I thought you were *repressed*."

Laughter made his strokes stutter.

He brought two fingers to Riley's lips, gently pushing inside so they rested on her velvet tongue.

"I was a lot of things before I met you."

She sucked the way she'd taken his cock earlier—eager, her dark eyes heavy-lidded.

When he slipped his hand out of her mouth, trailed his fingers down her chin, her neck, they left the faintest trail. A straight line to where his hand came to rest at the base of her throat.

Riley's eyes fell shut for a moment, her lips parting, before she placed her own palm over his and—locking their gazes, pressed gradually, shifting his grip until his hand was applying the barest pressure on either side of her throat.

Clark stilled his hips, holding inside of her, bracing everything in his body, trying not to spend.

"Is this okay?" Riley let go of his hand to stroke his face, to run the backs of her knuckles across his tensed brow.

Leaning back a little, Clark looked down as she tipped her chin up, giving him an unobstructed view of how she trusted him—completely.

"Yes. God, yes." He pulled back, sank forward, gave her exactly what she asked for. Exactly what she needed.

They'd been rough with each other, parried for control both physically and emotionally, but this wasn't that. He'd never felt anything like the sense of staggering wonder that came from being this close to someone you cared about so much, having it feel somehow impossible and right at the same time.

"I can't believe I found you," he said quietly, as she tumbled over the edge, falling apart in his arms. "I can't believe you're real."

When at last he gave himself permission to come, the pleasure was so intense—staggering—his vision swam. Every other time with Riley had been good, better than good—the best he'd ever had—but this? This was different.

Just for us, she'd said.

He'd been happy before. Had won an egg and spoon race on sports day in primary school. Rode horses with his mom in the Lake District, her whoop of joy loud in his ears. He got into Oxford. Bought the camper and built the bookcase of his dreams with his own two hands.

None of it felt quite like Riley Rhodes in his arms, telling him she loved him, whispering it over and over against his lips, his cheek, his jaw. Like holding her, kissing her, without worrying it would be the only time he had permission—or the last.

Chapter Twenty-Two

They spent the night in a cozy rental cottage not far from the St. Andrews campus. With its rounded doorways and low ceilings, the place reminded Riley of a hobbit hole.

Clark bonked his head carrying in the pizza they ordered for dinner.

"This crust is terrible," Riley said as she took a second slice. (Hey, it was still pizza.) She curled her legs up on the couch, her feet resting against Clark's thigh where he sat beside her. "Come to Philadelphia and I'll show you a real pizza."

"All right," Clark said easily, smiling at her as he picked off a mushroom and popped it in his mouth. "I will."

Her pulse spiked.

"Really?" She lowered the slice back to her plate. Had he just casually announced he'd come visit her in America?

"Yeah," he said, and then slightly less sure, "if you'll have me, that is."

She broke into a grin. "I'd love to have you."

Clark kept his eyes on her as he took a long swallow of his beer.

"Oh, shut up." Riley watched his throat bob and tried not to think about what else he might like to get his mouth on, lest she crawl across the sofa and ruin dinner.

(He did eat her out later. First in the shower, on his knees, and then again in the bed with his arm across her stomach, saying, "One more. Give me one more," in a rough, desperate way that ensured she did.)

Only after the fact did Riley realize the curse didn't come up once all night. It wasn't on purpose, not a rule or even something either of them seemed to actively avoid—there were just so many other things to say.

Once they'd packed up the food, Clark insisted on asking her questions "now that he could." He held her socked feet in his lap, tracing her arches with his thumb.

"What's your middle name?"

Against her will, Riley giggled.

"Olivia." It was very her—very them—to cover this stuff only after they'd bared their emotional and physical scars.

It made her feel good, *cherished*, that he seemed so hungry to know her. Not just the curse-breaking bit, but who she was beyond that. All her boring stuff seemed interesting to him.

"When's your birthday?" She volleyed back when it was her turn.

They found out they were born on opposite ends of January— him on the fourth and her on the twenty-seventh.

"Maybe we could have a joint party." She wanted to be brave, like him, saying he'd come visit. "Split the difference and do it somewhere around the fifteenth?"

At the implication that she wanted to make this work, keep it going, figure out the future even if things got messy—Clark glowed. There was no other word for it. His eyes and cheeks and smile all radiant.

Riley rubbed at the corner of his mouth, savoring it like a sap.

"I'm really glad we decided to stay here tonight." Not least because if anyone in the village caught them gazing at each other like this, she'd expire on the spot.

"Wait." He dimmed. "Would my father be allowed to come?"

His tone made it clear he thought Riley might refuse.

She wouldn't.

"Yeah, of course." Clark got to decide his relationship with Alfie. Riley would have his back.

He stroked her anklebone. "He loves buying presents, so that'll put him in a good mood. And my mum is the best. She's going to crochet you an awful hat or a pair of socks—she does them while they wait for deliberations in court."

"I would be honored." She was glad that even after the disastrous first interaction with his dad, he wanted her to meet his mom. To fold her into his life and vice versa.

Maybe if they were in their twenties, it would seem too soon to be talking about this kind of stuff, but they weren't. They both had a strong sense of self, they knew what they wanted, what they valued.

Riley hadn't hoped love would feel like this, hadn't let herself. Outlining a future with someone she loved, she didn't kid herself that it would be easy, and she knew Clark wouldn't either—come on, he was the most fastidious, considered person she'd ever met— but even though they didn't get into the complications of visas and time zones tonight, she knew they'd figure it out.

They were a good team.

On the way back the next morning, they picked up takeaway as a thank-you for Ceilidh, bringing it around when they returned her car. Riley felt alarmingly adolescent sitting next to Clark on the sofa telling her friend, sheepishly, about their discovery at St. Andrews and the new plan to break the curse over curries.

Clark filled in when she got tongue-tied about the personal

part, put his hand on her bouncing knee, the pressure warm, reassuring.

Alarmingly, Ceilidh was so happy for them she burst into tears. Suspicions of her being a romantic: confirmed.

She dabbed at her eyes with a takeaway napkin. "So you'll join hands in front of the castle and declare your love?"

Riley nodded. That was as far as they'd gotten on the drive back.

"Are you going to sprinkle salt again or bathe each other or . . ." She made a vulgar hand gesture.

Riley tore off a piece of naan and threw it at her.

"No. This time, I think we need to figure out a way to honor the fae."

The way Riley saw it, the curse had lasted a long-ass time, causing tons of strife and mischief that their ancient supernatural catalyst might not be so eager to relinquish.

"Our best chance of avoiding any last-minute mystical tomfoolery is to design a ceremony with a proper amount of fanfare to send off a sacred power. Basically, I gotta learn about local fae customs—STAT."

"Oh. Well, I'll help." Ceilidh dunked the piece of naan that had landed next to her elbow into her curry. "Actually. The villagers here know all kinds of fae customs and stories. Why don't we invite them to participate? The children can gather flowers to scatter." She chewed thoughtfully. "Ohh, and we can get Eilean to bring mead. Fae love mead!"

It was a brilliant suggestion. Even if Riley had never before broken a curse with an audience.

"You don't think people would mind?"

"Are you joking?" Ceilidh wiped off her hands and reached for her cell phone. "This curse has been terrorizing our village for three hundred bloody years. Now that someone's finally come to vanquish it, the least we deserve is a proper festival. I'm going to make a garland for your hair."

She mumbled names, presumably scrolling through her contacts.

Riley turned to Clark, who was quietly eating his biryani. "What do you think?"

She wasn't the only person participating in this ritual.

He lowered his fork, looking surprised to be consulted. "I think you'd look very fetching in a garland."

"No." Riley rolled her eyes. "I mean about making the ceremony public."

"Oh. Well, as a former skeptic," he said, taking a sip of water, "I think it's a splendid idea. You've faced so much doubt and opposition. Why shouldn't more people come and see what you can do?"

"Seriously?" It had been less than a month since he thought she was the worst kind of scam artist, only a week since he'd tried to disappear behind a menu at the Hare's Heart, ashamed to be chained to her in public. "You, Clark Edgeware, want to intentionally set up a spectacle?"

He gave her a half smile. "Just this once. I'll admit I would respond differently if it was the first time we were telling each other how we felt, but we've already had our private moment."

Ducking his head, he looked adorably embarrassed. Riley knew he was thinking of what had come after. Man, she couldn't wait to continue corrupting him.

"And hey." He regained his composure. "We could invite journalists from Inverness. If they can get out of bed for every would-be Nessie sighting, they can sure as hell come see a professional curse breaker at work."

"I don't know." Riley traced a painted flower on the edge of her plate. In theory she should jump on the suggestion. But what if she messed up somehow? Did she really want professional documentation?

"Press would be good for business, right?" Clark's voice was gentle but firm. "Pretty soon you'll be done with this job and looking for your next. You should get as much credit for overcoming Arden's curse as you can."

Right. If this worked, she'd fly home. Back to the hustle. It was easy, while working on an assignment, to get swept up in the problem-solving and the intrigue. But every time an adventure ended Riley had to face down the reality of tax forms and mounting bills.

Her mom called the week after a project wrapped "the grays." When Riley wasn't quite blue, but fell into a sort of doldrums. Eating dry cereal out of the box and watching reruns until her bank account ran low enough that she had to put on eyeliner for a shift at wing night. She didn't really want to go back to that, but she didn't have a choice.

At her prolonged silence, Clark tilted his head. "Isn't that what you were after when you first got here—legitimacy, a way to make a name for yourself as a curse breaker?

That had been her goal. But now maybe she wanted more.

"Can't we just call them after? When we're sure it's worked?"

"In that case, how would we prove that you're the one who broke it?" Ceilidh snapped off a piece of papadum and popped it in her mouth. "Don't let the conservativeness of this one"—she clapped Clark on the back, making him momentarily choke on some dal—"put you off a little high-risk, high-reward situation."

Clark looked prim at what was, admittedly, fair criticism—even if it came from someone who had only technically been introduced to him twenty minutes ago.

"Okay." Riley was helpless to resist the combination of their enthusiasm. "Fine. Let's do it."

"Good." Ceilidh picked up her phone again. "Because Tabitha McIntyre already agreed to make the honey cakes that have been in her family for twelve generations and my cousin Lachlan is going to bring his fiddle. You're about to see what a celebration looks like in the Highlands, *lassie*."

Riley took her friend's hand across the table and squeezed. "Thank you. For everything. I couldn't have done this without you."

"Pishposh." Ceilidh squeezed back. "We'd all run out of hope before you came. Now look at us."

Hope. Riley had almost forgotten what it felt like.

She'd never had this many people behind her. Friends. A partner. A whole community.

Still, something in her gut was restless at the idea of performing, literally putting her feelings for Clark to the test in such a public stage.

Later, as they lay under her quilt at the inn, Clark kissed her.

"Come on, considering everything we've already been through, what's the worst that can happen?"

Chapter Twenty-Three

High on the exquisite cocktail of new love, Clark convinced himself that nothing could go wrong.

It took about a week to get everything set up with the village. The more people who heard about the impromptu festival, the more they wanted to contribute.

There wasn't much for Clark to do, his part firmly set, so he finished up his survey, worked on his report for the HES. He ended up packaging his results through the lens of the castle's potential ties to mysticism, an angle that never would have occurred to him previously. Even though his search hadn't turned up many artifacts, he hoped that by weaving in the etchings they'd identified in the cave, he might convince the HES that Arden warranted additional research and preservation efforts.

Still, the calm he'd wished for, once it finally arrived, made Clark oddly jittery.

Riley was the same, her hands and mouth in constant, frenetic motion. When she wasn't coordinating fae offerings, they went off-site to distract themselves. Hiking and taking the bus out to local museums. Places they could find quiet together. It helped, eased the tightening in his chest. But even though neither of them brought it up, they were still having sex like they were running out of time.

The morning of the ritual dawned bright and clear. By noon, a local crowd had gathered on the castle lawn, people spreading blankets across the grass. Rich, warm spices filled the crisp air—clove and cinnamon and ginger—along with peat smoke from the bonfires. Eilean passed out mugs of mead to the adults and hot chocolate to the children while a man who must be Ceilidh's cousin played the fiddle, his bow moving fast enough that the strings blurred.

There were honey cakes and iced buns arranged on trays as offerings for the fae and ribbons wrapped around the ash trees to mark the occasion. Children and adults alike chatted with their friends and neighbors. A buzz of excitement hummed in the air, everyone dazzled by the idea that they'd come to witness a once-in-a-lifetime supernatural event.

When he met Riley in the entrance way, Clark could tell by the care she'd taken with her clothes, the extra makeup on her face, that she was nervous.

"Everything's going to work out," he told her, adjusting the garland of pale purple heather that sat at her brow. "You've done all you can to prepare."

"Thank you." Her smile was wan, her eyes jumping back to the crowd. "It's just—there's a lot of people out there."

At first, he thought this wasn't like her—the nerves, the concern about what others might think—but Clark knew that Riley had always felt like an outsider, that she faced near-constant ridicule and rebuff for her work. The more people who knew about what she did, the more people who could reject her. She must have always feared this on some level, even as she'd worked to grow her business—the difference was now she was letting him see how she felt, trusting him enough to lower her guard.

"Hey." He pressed a kiss to her temple. "You can do this."

Riley gritted her teeth in an approximation of a smile as someone started snapping pictures of them with a mounted flash. "How do you know?"

"Riley." He bent his knees so she'd meet his eye. "Because it's you."

Going over to his bag, he pulled out a tissue-paper-wrapped parcel. "I was going to give this to you after but . . ."

She took the gift and unwrapped it carefully, slipping her fingers underneath the tape so as not to tear the paper.

"Clark." Riley gasped, looking down at the handsome, leather-bound notebook he'd gotten custom made from a local artisan a few days ago. A near-perfect match to the one she had from her Gran, only new.

"It's for your own observations. You're an expert, just like your gran, and you'll want to pass down what you've learned—"

She cut him off with a kiss, so Clark guessed she liked it.

A little while later, they took their positions in front of the castle entrance.

The music faded to a stop, the crowd growing still, hushed as they took out the cursed artifacts.

Clark held the manacles, and Riley the dagger. In addition to honoring the fae, they wanted to remember Malcolm and Philippa, their bravery, their doomed love.

They carefully arranged the metal objects in the grass and then Riley placed a length of woven rope around them, the interlocking knots symbolizing remembrance, the reunion of their spirits, now protected for eternity.

At her cue, the children, rehearsed and eager, scattered wild-flowers over the arrangement—thyme and thistle—the blooms falling like teardrops, like rain.

The crowd seemed to vibrate with energy. It was as though Clark could feel them, the way he felt the earth under his feet, the looming stone of the castle at his back.

Hope was in the air. All these people, gathered for the chance to see a wrong righted. To see someone change things. To beckon in a new future for their home, one full of potential unhindered by ancient feuds and spilled blood.

As Riley turned and reached for his hands, Clark felt a bit like he was getting married in front of witnesses. The idea made him significantly less uncomfortable than it should.

"Ready?" She steeled her shoulders.

Clark nodded and squeezed her hands as a breeze came in from the east, random and extravagant and somehow familiar.

The force of the sudden gale made the trees sway, startling birds from their nest. Spectators sat up on their knees, turning and pointing as leaves gathered on the wind, swirling until the foliage circled him and Riley like some kind of cocoon.

"The weather patterns in this castle don't seem strictly natural," he said, gazing over either shoulder at the swirls of forest green and crimson and umber as they whipped by, blowing Riley's hair against her cheeks.

She smiled. "I think it's a good sign."

He worked to block out the spectators, the press that had arrived with cameras and microphones extended. To focus only on Riley, to let his love for her flow through him like water, to feel her love for him from the place where their hands joined.

"Shall I?" Clark had to raise his voice to be heard over the whooshing of the air around them.

At her nod, he took a deep breath.

Clark had been lost when he came to Arden. Not just for six

months. No. He'd been lost for so long that he'd stopped wishing to be found.

He'd feared Riley when they first met. She'd made him so angry, so frustrated. Had seen him before he knew he wanted her to.

Even then, Clark had wanted her, not just her body; he'd needed to care for her.

Her laugh in the dark. Her fierce determination. The way she hummed absently sometimes while she worked.

Clark had spent his life studying how other people lived and loved—all of it filtered through the distance of time. He'd preferred emotions muted by soil and centuries.

He'd been avoiding this. Missing this. What a sodding shame.

"I love you," he said, loud, clear. It felt different, *good different*, to get to say it first. "I love you," he repeated, softer, an indulgence.

"I love you." Her voice was quieter—sweeter, he thought—but just as sure.

A cheer broke out from the crowd. The fiddle picked back up, fierce and celebratory. People raised their glasses, knocked them together with such exuberance that liquid sloshed over the rims.

The breeze stopped, and for a second the leaves froze, seeming to hang in midair, before all at once the foliage fell to lie limp on the ground at their feet.

A wave of confusion washed over him, followed by dread. He leaned into Riley. "The scent?" But he already knew.

She shook her head. "No change."

Her eyes slid to the press person in the first row. He'd turned to his camerawoman, whispering in her ear.

"Damn." Clark hadn't truly thought about, hadn't let himself imagine, how damning the framing of a story around failure could be to Riley's reputation.

Either she's deluded or she's a charlatan. That was what he'd convinced himself because the truth was harder to buy, less convenient.

Now the same conclusions would run online, come up when you searched her name.

"Riley, I'm sorry. I shouldn't have pushed you into this."

Ceilidh crouched before a disappointed child, consoling. Across the lawn the mood had rapidly dampened. He wanted to believe the villagers were still on their side, but Clark knew this didn't look good.

When the man with the press badge started toward them, Riley yanked Clark deeper into the castle, tucking them into the hidden alcove off the entranceway where they'd stowed their bags.

Immediately, she went for Gran's journal, taking it out and flipping through the pages in a crouch.

"We're missing something. I don't know if we're supposed to make the vow at the cave instead of in the castle. Or we're supposed to do it in tandem instead of one after the other? There are too many variables."

"We'll figure it out." He'd go talk to the crowd; tell them they'd try again shortly. If nothing else, Clark knew how to manage a scandal. You had to get out there. Get ahead of it.

He felt oddly calm. Not afraid in the same way, though he realized belatedly any negative press coverage here would likely include his name as well.

How could he fear a false narrative when he'd seen for himself how foolish it was to get Riley and her work wrong?

"Fuck." She covered her eyes with her hand. "I don't want to be, but I'm embarrassed."

"It's all right." He crouched beside her. "Trial and error, right? It's all part of the process."

"This is the second ritual I've gotten wrong."

"Well, I can't say I minded with the last one," Clark said, trying to make her smile.

It didn't work.

"I'm supposed to be a professional," she said softly, "an expert," playing back his words to her earlier.

"You are." He stood and pulled her to her feet. "Don't let a bunch of random people get in your head."

"It's not just them." Riley bit her lip. "I've never done this before."

Clark wrapped his arms around her until she sagged against him.

"What? Broken a curse?"

"No," she said into his chest. "Fallen in love. How many more times am I allowed to get it wrong before you lose faith in me?"

He ran his hand over her hair. "Oh, my darling."

She pulled back just a little. "That's the first time you've called me an endearment that wasn't meant as an insult."

"I'm afraid you'll have to get used to it."

Considering what had happened with her father, Clark was disappointed though not surprised to find Riley believed his support for her was fragile.

"Okay, that's it." He stepped back so she could see him properly. "I need to tell you something. I'm not sure I'll ever fully believe in curses. It doesn't matter how much I observe or experience, there will always be a tiny part of my mind that's looking for alternate explanations."

"What?" Riley frowned. "Then what are we doing here? Why did you say all that stuff to your dad about being open and then campaign to invite all those people out there to witness—"

"I believe in *you*," he cut in. "In your ingenuity, your problem-solving, your courage and commitment." He stroked her cheek. "In your big heart and impossibly hard head."

Riley closed her eyes, leaning into his palm.

"I will love you," Clark promised her, "even if you never break another curse. *Even*," he repeated, "*if you write a song and want to sing it directly in front of me.*"

She blinked up at him. "That's quite a promise."

"Yes, it is." One he couldn't have made if Riley hadn't helped him face his fears, his shame.

His mobile rang, startling them both.

"Just a second." Clark fished it out of his trouser pocket. *Unknown number.*

"Hello?"

"Mr. Edgeware? This is Helen from the HES," a voice said around static. The service in the castle was terrible.

"Oh, yes, Helen. Hello." He owed her an email. Perhaps several. When had a job not been the most important thing in his life? Clark felt equal parts guilty and glad.

He walked farther into the castle to get away from the rising din of the disappointed crowd. "What can I do for you?"

"Unfortunately, I'm calling to inform you that we are immediately suspending your assignment at Arden Castle."

He'd been expecting these words, feared them, for months. Still they took him completely aback.

"What?" He plugged a finger into his ear. "Sorry? May I ask why?"

"I'm afraid I can't disclose the committee's decision-making process. But I believe someone"—this she said with telling pity—"may have informed them you weren't the right fit for this assignment."

Who would call the HES? The second the question entered his mind, Clark knew the answer.

Helen said other things, something about collecting his last paycheck. He couldn't hear very well.

Months of work, his new proposals, all dead on arrival.

Helen cleared her throat. "Do you have any other questions?"

Clark didn't. *Not for her.*

After they hung up, he laughed, hard and painful, until tears cut at the corner of his eyes and he had to lean against the wall to keep from sagging to the floor.

He taken this job to try to repair his reputation. To regain his father's esteem.

Only to now have Alfie snatch the opportunity away. The sheer irony of it all.

"What's going on?" Riley had come to find him, concern clear across her features.

"Oh, nothing." Clark wished he could say he was surprised, but it was almost textbook Alfie. He'd gotten his son a contract and when he no longer felt Clark deserved the favor, he'd taken it away. "My father's just had me fired."

Over the course of his lifetime, Clark had resented plenty about his dad. He resented when he wasn't home. All the attention he gave to people who weren't his family. His casual brand of cruelty. But right now, Clark resented his dad most of all for taking him away from Riley when she needed him.

He wouldn't have left if she hadn't made him.

"Go." She pushed gently at his chest. "Don't let him get away with this."

Three weeks ago, he'd feared this exact scenario—mucking up this job, disappointing his father—more than almost anything.

When Patrick had first suggested Clark join him in looking for the lost temple, he'd balked, said no. *I'm not interested in making a fool of myself chasing a myth.*

Patrick had smiled at his censure.

That, right there, he said, pointing at Clark's scornful face, *is exactly why you're going to come along. Anything you react to that strongly has something you need buried beneath it.*

He'd been right then, as he was now.

"It's the end of my contract, not the end of the world." Clark found he wasn't lying. His priorities had unlocked, shifted, in the last few weeks. Riley had shown him no amount of professional success determined your worth.

"It's not about the job and we both know it. Go," she said again, softer this time. "I'll hold down the fort. I promise I handled my fair share of angry crowds before I met you and I can handle them now."

So Clark went.

Chapter Twenty-Four

Dusk had fallen by the time Riley got done dealing with the fallout of their failed ritual. There weren't many positive side effects of having a bunch of hometown sports teams that constantly fumbled the bag at the end of the season, but at least Riley knew how to corral disappointed drunk people after a long-sought victory was snatched from underneath their noses. Soothing ruffled feathers was far from her favorite part of her job, but with any luck, she'd done enough damage control to avoid negative Yelp reviews.

It wouldn't have made that big of a difference, she told herself as she kicked off her shoes in her room at the inn, *if she and Clark had been able to break the curse in front of that crowd.*

Most people wouldn't be able to tell, at least not right away. That was the trouble with contracting on public curses instead of private ones—Riley had to figure out how to prove she'd earned her fee when the only evidence of a broken curse was its absence.

She took off her bra and sat on the floor, leaning back against the bed frame as she pulled out her phone.

Her mom picked up after the third ring.

Instead of a normal greeting, Riley said, "Do you think our family is cursed to die alone?"

She didn't mean to spring something so heavy on her unsuspecting parent. Especially not at—she checked her watch and winced—eight in the morning. It just came out. All of Riley's finely honed "bad bitch" bravado crumbling at the sound of her mom's voice.

Jordan Rhodes didn't respond right away. Instead, Riley could hear her dragging out a kitchen chair, plopping herself down with a sigh.

"What happened?"

"I fell in love." The admission came a little breathless.

She and her mother talked about love sometimes. The surface details of other people's relationships—a neighbor's new beau and whether it would last, actors with enough onscreen chemistry that they must loathe each other in real life. But it had been a long time since they'd had a reason to discuss it like this—when it was close and disruptive and precious.

"Ah." Riley could hear her mother's knowing smile all the way from New Jersey. "The infuriatingly handsome Englishman, huh?"

Now that they were together, Riley wanted to argue with the shorthand she'd been using to summarize Clark for weeks, but yeah—still true. Sometimes his face made her want to punch his mouth with her mouth. She groaned instead.

"I'm so happy and also such a mess."

"Sounds about right." Her mom hummed a little. "Come on, enemies to lovers. It's right there in the label. Don't tell me you didn't see this one coming."

Truthfully, Riley hadn't. There had seemed like too many good reasons why it shouldn't work between her and Clark. They came from such different worlds. Had complete opposite approaches to how to handle pretty much everything. They'd hurt each other on purpose. But most of all, Riley had used curse breaking to keep people at arm's length for so long.

"I didn't think I was capable of it."

Her mom went quiet, long enough that Riley pulled the phone back from her face to check the call hadn't disconnected.

"Mom?"

She blew out a long breath. "I fucked up."

"What?" Riley picked at a loose carpet fiber. "What do you mean?"

"I mean . . ." Her mom sounded tired, or like she was getting a cold. "I grew up without a dad, so I thought—*I let myself think*—that you not having yours wouldn't be so bad."

"Mom," Riley said fiercely. "No. We never needed him."

They didn't talk about her father. Not since that night when Riley was nine. It wasn't that she'd never been curious, never had questions, but asking had always felt to Riley like some kind of betrayal—like simply speaking his name would suggest her mom wasn't doing enough, didn't love her enough when the exact opposite was true.

"Curse breaking and romantic partnership are not mutually exclusive," she said in that "you'd better hear this" Mom Voice, and then, softening again, "I'm sorry if I gave you that impression."

Hurting her mom, especially by accident, made Riley feel like her chest was collapsing. But now that this conversation was out there, she had to keep going. Had to lead them out, through.

"But you kept it a secret. Told him Gran was a seamstress. That I spent my summers helping her cut cloth."

She could picture her mom at the kitchen table, running her fingers over the familiar wooden grooves, trying to pick her words.

"I kept curse breaking a secret from him not because I was ashamed of Gran or of the practice, but because I was ashamed of myself for abandoning it."

"What?" Riley had never considered that. Her mom had always seemed so at peace with her decision. And while she'd been supportive about Riley picking up the family mantle later in life, she'd never shown any signs of wishing she'd done the same.

"When I was growing up, before I left for school, I trained the same way you did. I wasn't a natural the way you are, and I didn't have your drive, but I think mostly, I'd watched my mom pour everything she had into it—solving other people's problems—for what always seemed to me like little recognition or reward. I didn't feel prepared at twenty-two for the degree of resilience curse breaking requires. Fuck, at *fifty*-two I still don't."

Lacking a teleportation device, she settled for FaceTime.

When her mom switched the call over, she was still wearing her flannel pj's. A mug of coffee was steaming at her elbow.

"Mom," Riley said, staring down at her phone, trying to make her tone firm, her own version of Mom Voice. "I swear you're the most resilient person I know."

Her mom covered her face with her hand, then took a long sip of her coffee before she said, "Thanks, kid.

"You know what I've realized? It didn't matter in the end if I chose curse breaking or not." She lowered the mug. "I used to read her journal when you were at school or asleep. Looking for a way to be close to her. Looking for advice. And I realized, all those pages of reflection and advice, all the cross-outs and footnotes. Gran didn't care in the end if either of us decided to follow in her footsteps. She wanted us to know her. And she wanted us to believe in our ability to change things, to help people."

In that moment, staring at her mom's face, still slightly puffy from sleep, Riley knew the answer to a question she had never asked. *Did you ever worry that you made the wrong choice, sending him away?*

There was never a choice. The right person didn't make you choose.

"I miss you," she told her mom. "I miss Gran too."

"She'd be so fucking proud of you, kid." Her mom beamed. "Almost as proud as me."

Riley started to cry, a big noisy sob into her hand. She had to get up and grab tissues from the bathroom. Had to put her mom on mute while she blew her nose like a trumpet.

"I'm kind of floundering at the moment," she admitted.

Now both of their faces were puffy on the screen.

"I used to worry about failing at curse breaking a normal, reasonable amount, but now my personal life—this man I really care about, that I want to figure out a future with—is involved, and for the first time it's like I have a partner."

Clark and breaking the curse. Two things she wanted that had become hopelessly entangled.

"And now all of a sudden, I'm not in total control anymore. We have to trust each other. He's there up close for every mistake. And it sucks because I want to impress him. As shallow as that sounds."

"Sounds like love."

"I've never had more to lose." It was frustrating. Terrifying. And part of her did desperately want her mom to step in and somehow make everything better.

"To your credit, you've never shied away from a situation that demanded a leap of faith, but in some ways, when it comes to finding a partner, that's the easy part. There's no time to think. For better or worse it's over quickly. But if you want to make love last, you have to take smaller steps, match your pace to someone else's well enough that you can hold their hand."

"What if you do all that, you match their pace, but it still doesn't work out?"

"Then it doesn't work out."

"Okay," Riley said, frustrated, "well, what if that hurts like hell?"

"Then it hurts like hell."

Fuck. Riley wrapped her arms around her thighs. "Things were simpler—worse, but simpler—when I thought we were cursed to die alone."

"Well, you know what Gran always said." Her mom took another sip of coffee. "You're cursed as long as you believe you're cursed."

Chapter Twenty-Five

All it took was a quick call to his father's assistant to find that Alfie hadn't gone far. He'd booked a room in Inverness. Had stayed waiting in the wings, ready to give Clark a good lecture as his career, once again, took a hit.

At the hotel, when he told the desk clerk he was visiting Alfie Edgeware, the man offered to send him up along with a complimentary tea service.

Normally, Clark got anxious before seeing his dad. His belly filling with the kind of jittery pre-exam nerves where you tried to remember what you knew, to keep your mind sharp, ready to respond in a way that showed you to your best advantage.

He didn't feel like that now. Instead, an odd calm settled over him. Like his center of gravity had shifted, stabilized.

Riley was right. He knew what he needed to do.

Alfie's suite was twice as large as Clark's camper and included an abundance of tacky gold accents. As Clark held the door, the hotel server shuffled forward to settle a laden tray on the table in front of his father, who sat reading next to the window. Only after Clark had tipped the man and seen him out did Alfie fold his newspaper over one of the velvet arms of the reading chair he occupied and look up.

"I was expecting you sooner."

"Funny. I just received your summons." Without waiting for an invitation, Clark settled himself in the opposite chair. "Don't you think we're all getting a little old to be involving public institutions in our family squabbling?"

"I would have ordered you off the site directly if I'd thought you'd listen." His father helped himself to a butter biscuit. "You should thank me for handling the matter discreetly before the HES found out you were taking your trousers down on their dime."

"Given the circumstances to which you're referring, I think you'll agree discretion is no longer my primary motivation."

His father tugged at the sleeves of his neatly pressed dress shirt, undoing the cuffs and folding them back as if to imply an ease that didn't exist in the rest of his suddenly tense posture. He might have expected Clark to show up here today, but not like this.

"Here's what's going to happen." Clark leaned forward to pour the tea from the handsome china set. "First, you're going to apologize for treating me like a child or someone who works for you—since I am neither."

Setting down the pot, he added milk into his father's cup until the color resembled Cadbury milk chocolate—the exact shade of Alfie's preference.

"Then you're going to make things right with the HES. I don't care how you do it, but I suggest starting by admitting you made a mistake."

Alfie didn't usually take sugar, but he liked it, so Clark dropped in a cube before lifting the saucer to stir.

"Then, finally," he said, swirling the silver spoon, "since at that point you'll have earned my magnanimous forgiveness, we're both going to make amends with Patrick, since you're too bloody proud to do it yourself." He extended the steaming cup to his father. "Tea?"

His father took two sips, staring out the window at the drizzly afternoon, before replying. "I don't see any reason I should apologize to Patrick."

Clark sighed. "As your son, I shouldn't have to tell you this, but in fact it's wrong to shove your child out of your life because you're ashamed of them."

Really, Clark owed his mother a tremendous amount of gratitude. Without her patient, generous, forgiving rearing, who knew how awful he might have ended up?

He'd asked her once, after his father had forgotten her birthday for the second year in a row, why she stayed with him. *Your father is a great man*, she'd said with a sad smile. *And I've never been able to stop myself from believing that with our help, he could also be good.*

Clark poured himself tea, dark and sweet. "What Patrick did—falsifying those scans, lying to the industry—it was wrong. And I know it tarnished your sterling reputation, but it's past time that we both forgave him, especially since he obviously did it in a misguided attempt to make you proud."

Alfie set down the cup with rattling force. "I'm not mad about what he did to my name. What I can't forgive him for is what he did to yours."

"Excuse me?" Clark paused with his cup at his lips. "Please tell me I misheard you." He lowered his tea, slowly. "Because it sounded like you've been going to bed at night blaming Patrick for deceiving me and then waking up the next morning to tell me how weak I am for believing him."

Sometimes the truth was so obvious, so annoyingly right in your face the whole time, but you couldn't see it yet because you hadn't done the work, hadn't cleared the way.

His father was the oldest son of a butcher. The first Edgeware to attend university. And he'd picked archaeology. It must have seemed so flimsy to his family, so silly and self-indulgent. He'd gotten famous off his first expedition—one where he'd been hired to carry another man's bags. He'd never even gone back to Manchester to clear out his rooms, had simply sent for his car.

"Neither of us will ever be good enough for you. At least, not while we're trying to be."

Clark thought he had learned the mistake of making his dad his hero after Alfie had let him assist on a summer dig in northern France. They'd faced miserable weather for days—rain and hail and winds so sharp they stole the breath from their lungs—and his dad wouldn't sleep. The project fell behind, and Alfie didn't trust anyone else to manage the troubleshooting. He kept the crew out in unsafe conditions, but even when they mutinied, seeking shelter, his dad stayed in the dirt, furious and focused.

Clark had stayed too, even though he couldn't appease his father, could barely hold a trowel with the way his hands shook from cold, exhaustion, and fear. He remembered the harrowing moment of looking into his dad's wild eyes and realizing Alfie Edgeware was flawed—as human as anyone else.

A decade later, Clark could finally see the wounds behind those flaws. See the boy who wanted so desperately to earn the rank and renown he'd stumbled into. Who didn't trust that he was worthy or even truly wanted. A crushing sort of helplessness came with the knowledge that Clark couldn't fix his dad.

But he could fix the way he responded to him.

Could make sure that whatever next choice he made—in occupation or partner or haircut—he did for himself.

"I suppose this new bullishness is the work of that girl." His father folded his arms. "The one you thought was magic."

Not a denial, but Clark hadn't expected one, wouldn't have wanted it.

He couldn't help it, he smiled at the description. It sounded so innocent in ways Riley wasn't—painting a picture of someone who chased shooting stars and tossed coins in a fountain. But digging into the etymology of the word, *magic* meant *transformative*. And in that way, the adjective fit perfectly.

"Some of it's her fault," Clark said finally. Whatever Riley was, whatever she did, she'd changed him. "But I don't think we should give her all the credit."

By falling in love with her, in striving to be worthy of her love, Clark had grown to see himself differently.

"You always do this." Alfie shook his head. "You find a way to follow the person with the worst idea."

Clark magnanimously translated that in his head to: *I wish the people you trusted took a bit more care.*

His father frowned, making the lines on his face more pronounced. "I'm afraid she'll hurt you."

The comment might have fallen with a note of irony, considering the source, but loving Riley had helped Clark understand his family a little better.

Somewhere on that cliffside in Torridon, he'd accepted the fact that he adored—senselessly—complicated, extraordinary people. People who were exceptionally hard on everyone, but most of all themselves.

He liked the striving in their mistakes, the messiness of their attention, the unvarnished surprises revealed by the way they approached everyday life.

Clark loved the fierce way they loved him: like they wanted to protect him even when they couldn't.

"We all hurt the ones we love," he said, softly, pointedly. "It's why we must learn to make amends."

A joke about Riley breaking both curses and hearts came to mind, but Alfie wouldn't appreciate it, so instead Clark said, "I'm made of tougher stuff than you think."

His dad was many things: proud and gruff, charismatic, yes, and even caring, in his own way.

"I love you," Clark told him. "I'm grateful for all you've done for me."

His father, sensing more to come, seemed to brace himself.

"But I don't owe you a career you admire or a partner you approve of. I need you to hear me, really hear me, when I say that I'm through having my life measured and weighed against your ambition." He took a breath in and let it out slowly. "And if you can't accept that—and don't change how you treat me—I'm done."

Color rose in his father's cheeks. Clark expected another outburst, like the one they saw in Skye. Though he expected this time his father would order him out instead of leaving, since this was his hotel room, after all.

"It's your choice. Accept your sons, warts and all, or lose us both."

The sunlight from the window cut across Alfie's face, making him look somehow both older and younger than his sixty-five years.

"All right," he said finally, and then leaning forward, grasped the teapot, offering to top off Clark's cooling cup.

It was more concession than Clark had ever had from him, more than he'd seen him give to anyone personally or professionally.

All right. The love in that single phrase beat like bird wings in the space between them, steady and climbing, soft but hopeful.

"I hear you." He set down the teapot and sat back in his chair. "We'll call Patrick."

"All right," Clark echoed, thinking it just might be, after all. Alfie Edgeware had a history of making good on slim odds.

If the last few months had taught him anything, it was that just because something hurt didn't mean it wasn't healing.

Chapter Twenty-Six

After hanging up with her mom, Riley decided, for the first time since she'd arrived in Torridon, to take a night off from curse breaking. Both she and Clark had already battled professional setbacks and difficult family conversations today. They deserved a little R&R.

After treating herself to a long bath and a face mask, she swung by the local grocery store before it closed and picked up supplies for a romantic dinner. Well, her idea of romantic anyway—since it was red wine and mac and cheese. Each in boxed form, as was her preference.

She did also, virtuously, pick up a few heads of broccoli, thinking of Clark's affinity for fiber. The desire to care for a man might be new, but Riley was pretty sure she was killing it.

Even if she secretly hoped Clark would make a comment about boxed wine being lowbrow so she could whip out all her favorite facts about how many high-end vintners had embraced the model to optimize both sustainability and production costs. If instigating opportunities for harmless, heated banter with her boyfriend was wrong, she didn't want to be right.

When she arrived at the camper, she found Clark sitting at his desk with his laptop open in front of him.

"Hey." He'd changed into a faded long-sleeved T-shirt and gray sweatpants—so at least they were on the same page about the leisurely direction of the evening.

"Prepare yourself for a culinary feast," she told him, dramatically displaying the cloth bag of groceries hanging over her shoulder like Vanna White.

"Not sure there's another kind . . ." he teased.

"Don't be fresh," Riley warned, even though she loved the haughty twist of his mouth, "or I won't show you all four of the ingredients I purchased."

"Wow," he said when she'd finished laying them out on the coffee table. "Thank you. I'd make a joke about how there's no dessert, but I think we both know what I'll be doing with my mouth after dinner." He folded his hands in his lap primly.

"Someone's in a good mood," Riley said gleefully. "I take it the conversation with your dad went well?"

He proceeded to fill her in while she poured them both wine.

Even from their brief interaction, she knew that Alfie Edgeware had a keen, innate understanding of people, how they worked. He would understand that he couldn't bully Clark now that his son had stopped living and breathing for his approval.

And if he forgot, Riley would be there to remind him.

When he finished, she wished she knew how to say *I'm really proud of you* without sounding condescending. But since she didn't, she just handed him one of the glasses and placed a kiss on his cheek.

As they both took a sip, the screen of his computer caught her eye.

"What are you looking at?" She leaned her chin on his shoulder to snoop. "Is that— Do you just peruse Google Maps in your downtime?"

Scattered across America and Western Europe, little flags in different colors had been added, along with what looked like notes. Riley hadn't even known that feature existed.

"No." Clark huffed like he'd never done anything so dorky in his life, even though she could clearly see he had another open tab where he'd paused a multipart documentary about something called "non-market-rate housing."

"I simply thought I'd do some research about other sites with evidence of ancient curses." His voice held a hint of defensiveness. "Obviously, after you're done here, you'll need to figure out where to go next, so . . ."

"Wait, you made this for me?" Riley's heart squeezed. "Holy crap. You really are sugar." After peppering kisses along his rough jaw, she leaned closer, squinting to read the small location names near the flags. "Well, what are you waiting for? Show me what you've got."

As Clark clicked to zoom in on the nearest flag, his gentle blush perfectly complemented the traces of crimson lipstick she'd left on his face.

"Based on what I've read so far, this one looks rather promising."

"That one, really?" Riley squinted. "Isn't that like southwestern France?"

"Yes."

"Uh, okay, small problem there." Riley laughed. "I don't speak French."

"Oh." Clark pulled her into his lap so her legs were across his. "Well, I suppose I just thought"—he pressed his forehead into her shoulder—"that might be okay, because I do."

Riley caught his face in her palm, not letting him hide. "Are you saying you'd go with me?"

"If you wanted," Clark said, his beautiful eyes impossibly earnest.

"You see, I have this camper. I believe you're acquainted with it. And as you know, I'm between jobs at the moment."

They both knew that was temporary. Especially with his dad's promise to sort out the situation with the HES. No, this was a choice. To leave the field he'd loved since he was a boy, the one he'd stuck with when it would have been so much easier to quit.

"Are you sure you want to take a detour from archaeology just when professional redemption is finally within reach?"

Clark's gaze fell to the corner of the desk where an earlier copy of his final report on Arden Castle sat with his notes scribbled in the margins.

"I went into the field for two reasons that have nothing to do with my family," he said. "The first is, I love the mystery. Searching for clues, putting the pieces together. You've seen all the pulp novels. I think we can both agree curse breaking delivers on that count in spades?"

Riley nodded. A couple months with her and he could live out all his fantasies about Hardy Boys hijinks.

"The other is company. I love the collaborative, sleepaway camp feeling of being on a dig, everyone working together, taking care of one another. After Cádiz, I didn't just lose Patrick. I lost everyone. And I wasn't sure I could get back there, to that place of trusting someone I worked with so completely. But that's how I feel, working with you."

She knew how much it meant to her, to share this family practice she'd long ago convinced herself came part and parcel with alienation. Riley hadn't considered that it might mean just as much to Clark.

"I feel that way too," she said softly.

"I hope you'll agree I have applicable skills." He must have mistaken her sudden shyness for lingering reluctance because the next thing she knew he was *listing them*. "Obviously I have extensive experience with research and excavation, but I also excel in map reading and—"

"Stop trying to sell me." Riley grinned so wide, it was a wonder her mouth didn't swallow her whole face.

"Are you saying I'm hired?"

It was a good thing she hadn't bothered putting on underwear before coming over because the cheeky smile he was giving her right now would have melted them clean off.

"I'm saying let's go to France."

"Well, good. Glad that's settled." He nuzzled her neck. "Imagine how difficult it would be to break a curse if you didn't speak the right language."

Speak the right language.

"Oh my god." Riley shoved to her feet. "Clark, you absolute, perfect genius."

"What just happened?" His brows came together.

Riley kissed him smack on the lips before patting her pockets frantically. "Where's my phone? I need my phone."

After a few seconds, she remembered she'd tossed it in the bag with the groceries. Fumbling open the trusty translation app, Riley keyed in the words racing through her head with unsteady hands.

"Okay, yeah," she said when the translator populated. "We're definitely gonna have to pull up some pronunciation tutorials on YouTube."

Forty-five minutes and two boxes of mac and cheese later, they had the sentence down pat.

"Do I need to change?" Clark looked down at his sweatpants despairingly.

"No. We delivered all that fanfare this morning. The fae got their festival. There's only one thing left to do."

One missing piece.

When they entered the castle, a trail of moonlight greeted them, illuminating a path up the central staircase. The curse, probably tired of waiting for them, must have decided they needed a map.

This time while they climbed to the guard tower, Clark and Riley held hands.

She had never been up here after dark. The view was enough to steal her breath. For once the night sky was clear, a perfect black canvas for twinkling constellations. Waves crashing against the cliffs enveloped them in a bittersweet soundtrack of ascent and retreat.

It was impossible to stand here now and not think of Malcolm Graphm. How torn apart he must have felt waiting for the attack of his own people. He might have stood at this window, given a signal for Philippa to run as his clan descended. She might have looked back at him, just once, hoping he'd make it out to follow her while knowing every odd was stacked against them.

It was hard to blame the curse for campaigning for a happier ending. Maybe even ancient supernatural forces needed hope in the face of relentless death and destruction.

Riley stood in front of the beam where they'd found the dagger lodged.

She hoped Malcolm's last thought was of love. The kind of impossible love that challenged everything. Even death.

Turning to Clark, she held out her hand. "Ready?"

They took their places.

Without the hum of the crowd, the pageantry of the swirling leaves, Riley could give herself fully to the feeling of his hand in hers. The air crackled, restless, around them, making the back of her neck prickle like pins and needles.

It turned out, the curse did want a kind of sacrifice, just not the one Riley first assumed. She didn't have to hurt Clark, or even herself. Instead, the curse asked her to cast aside the belief she'd clung to for so long like a security blanket—that she had to choose between calling and partnership.

It was like the universe wanted her to know that the sense of peace she strove to deliver wasn't just for other people. It was for her. And Clark. And maybe, after tonight, in some small way for Philippa Campbell and Malcolm Graphm.

Riley had never had any particular aptitude for languages, but as she made her vow to Clark in the Gaelic words they'd practiced, she felt them deep in her bones.

"Tha gràdh agam ort."

There was something amazing about looking at someone you'd once thought you loathed and realizing how wrong you could be— about other people, about yourself.

"Tha gràdh agam ort," Clark said back, his low voice becoming a tether between her restless heart and his.

As the last syllable fell from his lips, Riley held her breath, pulling Clark forward and wrapping her arms around his neck, the foot of space between them suddenly too much. When she let herself inhale, deep and long, there was the scent of stone and mist. Of cobwebs and dust. There was Clark's detergent. The warm orange spice of his shampoo mingling with the faded perfume at her wrist.

Nothing else.

"Clark." She leaned back to tell him but saw tears tracking down his stubbled cheeks.

"What is it?" She dried the damp skin gently with her knuckles, a pit forming in her chest. "What's wrong?"

He turned to kiss her hands as they stroked his face.

"I could have missed this."

She didn't understand. "Missed what?"

Clark brought her hand to his heart. The beat was even, steady, under her palm.

"I felt it."

"What?" Her mouth fell open on a gasp. "You did?"

It wasn't that unusual for someone to experience a curse in the moment it broke. Occasionally, one of her clients did. But most of those people had lived with the oppressive weight of malevolent power in their lives for years.

She had never considered that Clark—who had been so adamantly opposed to the idea of supernatural forces less than a month ago, who earlier today had told her might never be able to fully believe—could have a similar response.

"It's the stomach-swooping, breathless, terrifying thrill that happens at the top of a roller coaster, that single frozen second at the peak right before you descend. The release of all that buildup, the mounting pressure. The hardest part is over—you're already falling, but it's okay. It's good. It's what's supposed to happen." He frowned. "Is that—does that sound right?"

Riley nodded against his mouth, already on her way to kiss him.

As it turned out, sometimes what you needed was someone who brought out the worst in you. There was a gift, she realized, that could only be exchanged between former enemies—permission to forgive yourself. Because if someone could see all your failures and faults, could actively seek out every possible reason to dislike you, and somehow still come around in the end, well, maybe your worst wasn't so bad after all.

The next morning, Riley and Clark woke up to find that for the first time in three hundred years, indigo angel's-trumpet had bloomed on the grounds of Arden Castle.

Epilogue

"**I** can't keep having this same fight with you. I'm at my wit's end."

Clark came out of the shower to find Riley arguing with the cat, who seemed to have gone into a protective crouch over a bunch of bananas.

"We just bought you all those cans of fancy French cat food," she continued, a note of imploring in her voice. "The least you could do is let me try to make this bowl of steel-cut oats less boring."

"Félicité," Clark said sternly.

At the sound of her name—or at least, at the sound of his voice, since he wasn't sure the cat had actually accepted their adoption so much as she'd enjoyed the camper enough to stow away in it when they left Scotland—Félicité turned and, blinking innocently at him, abandoned the fruit as if she'd suddenly lost interest.

"I never should have let you give her a French name," Riley grumbled, retrieving her prize and returning to breakfast prep. "I can't even pronounce it."

"Sure you can." He came over and wrapped his arms around her waist, then softly said the word against her neck.

Riley leaned back against him, arching to encourage him to kiss her pulse point, and reluctantly repeated, "Félicité."

Clark had no shame. He got a silly thrill every time she said it in her terrible accent. It meant *a very great happiness*—a feeling he'd become increasingly acquainted with in the eighteen months since they'd left Arden Castle.

After exhilarated local press swore in print that they'd seen the land of Arden Castle change overnight, the story of their curse breaking got picked up internationally. Interview requests and assignment inquiries came pouring in from around the world.

Even Clark's father had been begrudgingly intrigued. He offered to introduce them to his literary agent—suggesting that their story might work "if appropriately adapted for fiction audiences, of course." They'd politely but passionately turned him down.

After the dust settled, Clark and Riley had followed their original plan to the Dordogne region of France, chasing a lead that guided them to the Lascaux caves where Paleolithic paintings had sparked rumors of mysticism for over fifteen thousand years. (Riley assured him that both of the curses he'd been exposed to having ties to caves was nothing more than coincidence.)

Unfortunately, getting extended access and proper resources to investigate such a unique and treasured historical site required calling in a few favors.

For example, the clanging noises and intermittent cursing coming from directly outside their window this morning suggested Clark's father was already up and wrestling with his snow-climbing equipment.

Though they'd simply asked for his endorsement with the French Heritage Society, in order to secure the proper permits, Alfie had insisted on "supervising" this phase of research firsthand. Clark suspected that his father was experiencing a mounting sense of FOMO that other people were going on potentially dangerous adventures without him.

A bit later, when Clark had managed to get dressed and Riley had finished her breakfast, a pounding on the camper's front door preceded it flying open.

"Oy. Would you lot quit faffing about in there?" Patrick, decked out in full winter regalia, stepped inside. Behind him, Clark could see that once again it had started to snow, turning the mountainside into an endless sea of white. "I don't know how much longer I can keep Dad from leaving without you. The man keeps muttering that we're wasting daylight."

"Wind your neck in," Clark hollered back, though he couldn't fully suppress the desire to grin that came at seeing his brother hale and in the flesh. "We're coming."

After returning to Europe following reconciliation with his father, Patrick had agreed to come out to France. He was helping them use a handheld lidar device to create 3D scans of the cave so they could better study the extensive ancient markings.

The "family project" was going a long way toward repairing relationships between the Edgeware men. And while Patrick had turned down his father's somewhat reluctant offer to have his PR firm "quietly" work on a "professional rehabilitation plan," he was considering trying to teach once he got a bit more settled back in the UK.

Spotting Riley, his brother straightened up.

"Good morning." *The wanker even made his accent more posh.* "Say, will Ceilidh be joining us on the trek today?"

He'd been introduced to Riley's tiny redheaded friend—who had come out for a weekend visit—last night when they'd all gone to dinner at the nearby mountain chalet where she was staying.

"No." Riley smirked, probably picturing the way his brother had chatted Ceilidh's ear off all evening. "But I told her we'd meet her after for fondue."

"Brilliant." Patrick ducked out again with a tiny sigh.

Riley laughed after him. "Have you ever seen a man go so completely to pieces over a woman he just met?"

Clark gave that remark the only reply it deserved: a long, heated look.

"Oh," she said, flushing prettily. "Well, I guess it runs in the family."

Acknowledgments

Writing books is the best, scariest job I've ever had. *Do Your Worst* would not have been possible without the support of the following people.

Jessica Watterson. Thank you for always making yourself available for a phone call and for holding space as I found a path to publication that would enable me to keep writing from a place of joy.

Kristine Swartz. Thank you for all you've done to shepherd this book. Even more, thank you for the grace you've granted me as a writer while I continue to find my footing in this craft and in this industry.

Hannah Engler, Mary Baker, Kristin Cipolla, Yazmine Hassan, and the entire Berkley team. Thank you for your warmth, enthusiasm, and the tremendous skill with which you help my work reach readers. I look forward to every email, every call, and, of course, every taco I get to share with you.

Lauren Billings and Christina Hobbs. The two of you are my North Star in so many ways—in how to be good to people, in how to advocate for myself, in how to mentor, and in how to chase joy. I'm so grateful for your guidance and for your friendship.

Sarah MacLean. I would follow you into battle. Thank you for giving advice in the exact way I prefer to receive it: direct, hilarious, warm, thoughtful, and as an invitation to be brave.

Margo Lipschultz. Thank you for, in the dark days of 2021, treating me so delicately and generously, but still telling me what I needed to hear.

Leigh Kramer. Thank you for delivering such a considered sensitivity read.

Rachel Lynn Solomon, Mazey Eddings, Susan Lee, Alexa Martin, Charlotte Stein, Denise Williams, Tessa Bailey, Meryl Wilsner, and KT Hoffman. Thanks for making the solitary endeavor of writing less lonely and the public endeavor of publishing less soul-crushing.

Sonia Hartl, Meg Long, and Ellen Lloyd. Thank you for generously reading the shelved (for now) book before this book. *Do Your Worst* might not exist if not for the kindness and advice you extended to me then. You are each so dear to me.

Lea. Thanks for guiding me through breakthroughs, on the page and off.

Jen. Thank you for helping bring out the best in this book and in me as a writer.

Quinn, Marisa, Emily, Ilona, Dave, Ryan, and Frank. Thanks for always being down to brainstorm in the group chat. I'm still really sad I couldn't figure out how to make Clark's butt tattoo work. It was not due to a lack of our collective effort.

Alexis De Girolami. You're an incredible friend and an incisive critique partner. I love making margaritas, watching campy movies, and going on vacation with you. Thank you for being there for me through thick and thin over the last few years. I can't imagine them without you. Please move to Philadelphia. 😉

Ruby Barrett. You're the only audience I write for every time.

Thanks for holding my hand from 3,341 miles (*sorry*, 5,377 kilometers) away.

My family. Thanks for letting me steal away during vacations and holidays, for setting up desks for me in your homes, for constantly worrying about how stressed I get but supporting my writing career all the same. I love you all so much.

Romance readers and reviewers. I will never stop being humbled and blown away by those of you who go out of your way to recommend my books. Thank you for sticking with me through my gap year. You make all the difference.

My husband, Micah. You once bought me a vintage writing desk you couldn't afford. Even though we'd only been dating for six months. Even though I hadn't finished a book yet and for all you knew might never finish one. I get as much comfort from your boundless faith in me as I do in the knowledge that you'd love me, just the same, if I never wrote anything.

When the man of her dreams ran a hand across his devastatingly handsome face and said, "I have to tell you something, and I don't want you to freak out," Clara Wheaton considered, for the first time, the alarming possibility that she could get dumped by someone she'd never managed to date.

She cursed her wicked ancestors as she glared at the pineapple-scented air freshener hanging from the rearview mirror of Everett Bloom's Jeep Wrangler.

No matter how many lines she'd fed her mother's friends back in Greenwich about "pursuing fresh career opportunities," she'd moved across the country because part of her believed she stood a chance at winning Everett's heart after fourteen years of pining.

"I rented my room out for the summer," he said, the words both gentle and firm, the way someone might confess to a child that Santa wasn't real.

"You . . . rented your room?" Clara's response came slowly, comprehension dawning with each syllable. "The one you offered me two weeks ago?" If he hadn't been driving, and her mother hadn't made her memorize the etiquette of Emily Post in her adolescence, she might have lunged at him.

She'd broken the lease on her apartment in Manhattan, left

behind her friends and family, and turned down a curatorial internship at the Guggenheim. All for . . . nothing?

Even compared to generations of storied Wheaton family scandals, surely this nosedive into misadventure could claim a land speed record.

The palm trees they passed along the freeway mocked her, a hallmark of the Hollywood happy ending slipping between her fingers.

She hadn't even unpacked her suitcases . . . an undigested airport pretzel still floated somewhere below her diaphragm. How could Everett already be saying goodbye?

"No, hey, wait, no. I didn't rent *your* room." His signature lazy smile—the same one she'd fallen for the moment his family moved in next door all those years ago—dropped back into place. "I rented the master. The band got an offer to go on tour last minute. Nothing too wild, but we're opening for a blues band outside Santa Fe with this crazy cool sound, and Trent bought a sick van to haul the equipment . . ."

His careless words sent her straight back to high school. How many times after his social standing skyrocketed in tenth grade had Everett canceled plans with her in favor of band practice? How many times since then had he looked over her shoulder instead of into her eyes when she tried to talk to him?

No one would believe she'd earned two advanced degrees from Ivy League institutions only to end up this stupid.

"Who rented the room?" Clara interrupted his detailed description of the tour van's vintage fenders.

"What? Oh, the room. Don't worry. He's this super nice guy. Josh something. Found him on the Internet a few days ago. Very chill." He waved a hand in her general direction. "You're gonna love him."

She closed her eyes so he wouldn't see them roll toward the sunroof. No matter how many times she considered the lengths she would go to in her quest to finally win Everett Bloom's affection, she'd never imagined this.

He turned the car onto a street proudly sporting a rainbow crosswalk. "Listen, I'll drop you off and give you my keys and stuff, but then I gotta head right out. We're supposed to be in New Mexico by Friday." The last traces of apology ebbed with his words.

Clara watched his fingers, the ones she'd often imagined running through her hair in a tender caress, resume their furious beat on the steering wheel. She searched for any trace of her childhood best friend underneath his aloof veneer and came up short.

Pain burned beneath her breastbone. Somewhere in her bloodline, a Wheaton had crossed Fate, cursing his descendants to pay the price. That was the only explanation for why, the one and only time Clara had taken a leap of faith, she'd landed with a spectacular belly flop.

She dragged a deep breath into her lungs. There had to be a way to salvage this whole thing.

"How long will you be gone?" If there was one thing she'd learned from her ne'er-do-well family, it was damage control.

"Hard to say." Everett pulled the Jeep up to a Spanish-style ranch in desperate need of a new coat of paint. "At least three months. We've got tour dates through August."

"Are you sure you can't wait a few days to leave?" She hated the note of pleading that bled into her question. "I don't know anyone else in Los Angeles."

A face from the past, blurry through the lens of adolescent memory, flashed through her mind before she pushed it away. "I don't have a job here yet. Hell, I don't even have a car." She tried to laugh, to lighten the mood, but what came out sounded more like a grunt.

Everett frowned. "I'm sorry, Cee. I know I promised to help you get settled, but this is a huge break for the band. You get that, right?" He reached over and squeezed her hand. "Look, this doesn't have to change the plan we made. Everything I said over the phone is still true. This move, California, getting out from under your mother's thumb . . . It'll all be good for you."

He held his palm out for a high five in a long-familiar gesture. They might as well have been back in homeroom cramming for the SATs. Reluctantly, she completed the unspoken request.

"L.A. is summer vacation from real life. Relax and have fun. I'll be back before you know it."

Fun? She wanted to scream. Fun was a luxury for people with less to lose, but like generations of Wheaton women before her, Clara resigned herself to silent fuming instead of confrontation.

If a friend had told her a week ago that they planned to move across the country and give up a better life than most people could lay claim to for a shot with a guy—even a particularly handsome guy—Clara would have invested significant energy into trying to stop them. *That's insane*, she might have said. It's always easy when the shoe is on the other foot. No one from Greenwich knew the consequences of an ill-conceived impulse better than a Wheaton. Unfortunately, like grain alcohol, unrequited love grows more potent with time.

Everett unloaded her bags from the back of the Wrangler and hugged her—too tight and too fast to provide much comfort. "I'll call you from the road in a couple of days to make sure you're settled." He fumbled with his key ring.

Clara stared at her own hand with detachment as he pressed the small piece of metal into her palm. The urge to run, primal and nonsensical, sang under her skin.

She had two choices. She could call a cab, book a seat on the next flight back to JFK, and try to rebuild her old life, piece by piece.

Or she could stay.

Stay in this city she didn't know, live with a man she'd never met, without a job or friends, without the clout her family name commanded on the East Coast.

The Greenwich gossip hounds would salivate over her disgrace. She could already picture the headline. *No Longer "In Bloom," Careful Clara Shacks Up with Stranger.*

Not this time. She straightened her shoulders, smoothed her shirt, and ran her tongue over her teeth to ward off rogue lipstick. You only got one chance to make a first impression.

The heavy thump of Everett's car stereo pounded in her ears as he pulled out, but Clara didn't turn to watch him drive away.

Paint peeled back from the faded door when she pressed her palm against it. *Damn.* The society pages were going to have a field day with this one.

Bracing herself, Clara entered her new home the way soldiers enter enemy territory: with light footsteps, eyes mapping the terrain, and elbows tucked tight against her body.

Plush carpet muted her heeled sandals as she surveyed the living room. Without rose-colored glasses crafted by over a decade of repressed lust, the space left much to be desired.

She ran a fingertip through the blanket of dust coating a bookcase in the corner. An odor of decay wafted from abandoned takeout containers littering the coffee table. Clara tried to inhale through her mouth.

Underneath her foot, something crunched. Kicking up her heel, she identified the remains of a potato chip.

Despite the stench and the mess, the little house radiated a retro coziness that stood in direct contrast to both her family's sprawling colonial in Connecticut and the cramped Morningside Heights walk-up she'd rented near campus.

The faded wallpaper exuded kitschy charm, fighting for her affection, but she couldn't shake the crushing weight of her disappointment. Clara wiped off the seat of the sofa before sitting down.

"So this is how it feels to be well and truly fucked."

"I get that a lot," said a low voice behind her.

Clara sprang to her feet so fast she stumbled. "Oh . . . um . . . Hello." She scrambled to stand behind her massive wheeled suitcase, creating a fifty-pound shield between her and the man standing in the doorway separating the kitchen and the living room.

He leaned against the door frame. "I don't suppose you're robbing me?"

When Clara frowned in confusion, he gestured to her ensemble.

She lowered her chin and scrutinized the sleeveless black turtleneck and matching skinny jeans she'd picked out that morning. Sometime in her midtwenties, she'd traded the Argyle and houndstooth of her youth for a closet full of well-tailored monotone basics. Unfortunately, it seemed black clothing, while widely considered slimming and chic in New York City, was the preferred attire of home intruders in Los Angeles.

"Er . . . no." Clara tugged at her collar, glad, in retrospect, that she'd suffered the indignity of touching up her makeup in the tiny airplane bathroom while one of her fellow passengers pounded on the door. "I'm Clara Wheaton," she said when silence lingered.

"Josh." He closed the distance between them, offering her a handshake. "Nice to meet you."

When their hands came together, she inspected his fingernails as a bellwether for his personal hygiene habits. Neat and trim. *Thank goodness.*

After five seconds, Josh raised an eyebrow and Clara released his hand with a sheepish smile.

Despite his impressive height and the fact that his shoulders had filled most of the door frame, she didn't find him intimidating. His rumpled clothes and the mop of overgrown blond curls suggested he'd just rolled out of bed. Striking dark brows should have cast him as surly, but the rest of his face resisted brooding.

He was cute but not quite handsome. Not like Everett, whose mere presence still made her speech falter after all these years. Clara accepted this small form of mercy from the universe. She'd always found it impossible to talk to handsome men.

"Nice to meet you," she echoed, adding, "Please don't murder or molest me," as an afterthought.

"You got it." He raised both hands in a helpless gesture. "So . . . I guess that means we'll be living together?"

"For the time being." At least long enough for her to develop a contingency plan.

Josh peered into the open door of the bathroom. "Where's Everett? He didn't stick around to get you settled?"

Clara's shoulders crept toward her ears. "The band needed to get on the road right away."

"Pretty crazy, huh? Them getting invited to tour last minute?"

"Yeah." She fought to keep the bitterness out of her voice. "Wild."

"Worked out for me, though. I couldn't believe the lowball rent Everett asked for on a place this nice."

Clara decided not to mention that Everett had inherited the house, free and clear, from his grandfather and likely only charged enough to cover the taxes. She massaged her temples, trying to ward off a monstrous headache. Whether it came from stress, jet lag, or dying dreams, she couldn't say.

The longer she stood in this house, the more real the nightmare became. She sat back down on the couch when her vision swam.

"Hey, are you okay?" Her new roommate came to kneel in front of her, the way adults do when they want to speak to a small child. Clara glanced away from where his thighs strained the seams of his jeans.

He had a spattering of freckles across the bridge of his nose. She focused on the one at the very center and spoke to it. "I'm fine. Just reckoning with the consequences of a multigenerational family curse. Pretend I'm not here."

You'd think decades of old money and carefully monitored good breeding would weed out the Wheatons' notorious inclination toward destructive behavior, but if the recent arrest of her brother, Oliver, was anything to go by, the longer their lineage grew, the grimmer the consequences of their behavioral missteps.

Comparatively, she'd gotten off easy with an old house and a broken heart.

Josh wrinkled his forehead. "Um, if you say so. Oh, hey, wait here a minute."

As if she had anywhere else to go.

"I think I've got something that might help." He strode into the kitchen and returned a moment later to press a cold can of beer into her hands. "Sorry I don't have anything stronger."

Clara wasn't much of a beer drinker. But at this point, it couldn't hurt. She popped the top and took a deep slug. "Blech." Why did men insist on pretending IPAs tasted good? She dropped her head between her knees and employed a deep-breathing technique she'd observed once when accompanying her cousin to Lamaze class.

"Hey . . . uh . . . you're not gonna toss your cookies, right?"

Bile rose in the back of her throat at the suggestion. This guy was about as helpful as every other man she knew. "Perhaps you could say something reassuring?"

After a few seconds, he blew out a breath. "Your body destroys and replaces all of its cells every seven years."

Clara sat up slowly. "Okay, well"—she pursed her lips—"you tried. Thanks," she said with dismissal.

"I read that in a magazine at the dentist's office." He shot her a weak smile. "Thought it was kinda nice. I figure it means no matter how bad we mess up, eventually we get a clean slate."

"So you're telling me in seven years, I'll forget the fact that I uprooted my entire life and moved across the country because a guy who's not even my boyfriend encouraged me to, and I quote, 'follow my bliss'?"

"Right. Scientifically speaking, yes."

He had nice eyes. Big and brown, but not dull. They looked warm, like they'd spent time simmering over an open flame. *Cute but not handsome*, she reminded herself.

"Well, okay. I was expecting a banal detail about your job, to be honest. But not bad for off the top of your head." She wiped her hand across her mouth and handed him back the beer.

"Somehow I don't think hearing about my job would reassure you." He took a long sip from her discarded can.

Guess that answered the question of whether Josh was the kind of roommate who would eat her leftovers. "You're not a mortician, are you?"

He shook his head. "I work in the entertainment industry."

Figures. Clara immediately lost interest. The last thing she needed was some wannabe filmmaker asking her to read his screenplay.

Josh gave her a blatant once-over. "You're not what I expected."

Well, that makes two of us, buddy.

She'd expected to live with Everett. She'd pictured the two of them cooking dinners together, their shoulders touching as they worked side by side. She'd imagined watching action movies deep into the night like they did back when they were thirteen, only this time instead of separate sofas they'd curl up together under a shared blanket with glasses of wine.

This house should have set the scene for their love story. Everett should have written a song in that window seat inspired by their first kiss.

Instead, she got to share a toilet with a stranger.

Clara stood up and shook off her unfulfilled wishes. "What do you mean?"

"I'm surprised a girl like you"—he gestured to her Louis Vuitton luggage—"would slum it with a roommate in a place like this."

Clara gathered her dark hair over one shoulder and smoothed the tresses. "I received the luggage as a gift from my grandmother." She lowered her eyes to the carpet. "I took the room because I'm between jobs at the moment." The lie sat sour on her tongue and she quickly swerved back into truth territory. "I've known Everett forever. When I graduated a few weeks ago, he offered me his spare room."

"Oh. A graduate, huh? What were you studying?"

"I recently completed my doctorate in art history," she said with as much bravado as she could muster. As a kid, she'd dreamed about making work of her own, but eventually, she'd realized art required exposing parts of herself she'd rather keep hidden—her hopes and fears, her passions and yearning. Analysis and curation let her keep art at arm's length while using school as a way to extend the exit ramp to adulthood.

Josh smirked. "Is that like a special degree they only give out to rich people?"

Clara ground her teeth so hard she thought she heard a *pop*. "Let's keep the interpersonal chitchat to a minimum, shall we?"

She grabbed her purse and hunted for her move-in checklist, finding it buried underneath her airplane pillow and first-aid kit. Clara had compiled the six-page document to include all manner of questions and instructions on what to look for to know whether a new home was up to code in Los Angeles. Holding the document made breathing a little easier.

When she looked up, Josh hadn't left. "Please don't take this the wrong way, but frankly, Everett didn't tell me he had to go out of town until right now, and no offense, I'm sure you're probably nice, but this"—she gestured to the space between them—"falls a little outside my comfort zone."

"Hey, me too." He put his hand to his heart. "I've seen a lot of made-for-TV movies, you know. You're exactly the kind of pint-sized, tightly wound socialite who goes crazy and paints the walls with chicken blood. How do I know I'm safe from *you*?"

Clara cocked her hip and stared at the over-six-foot man across from her. His threadbare T-shirt, featuring a vintage picture of Debbie Harry, barely obscured his muscular chest and broad shoulders. "You're honestly worried about me?"

His eyes sank to the move-in checklist in her hand. "Oh my God. Is that laminated?" He looked positively delighted.

"My mother got me a machine last Christmas," she told him defensively as he took it from her for further inspection. "It prevents smudging."

He pitched his head back and laughed. A loud rumble without a trace of mocking in it. "'Check the water pressure on all taps for inconsistency,'" he read from the sheet. "This is too good. Did you write this yourself?"

"California is known for its propensity toward forest fires. You have to document pre-move-in conditions to arm yourself for possible insurance claims. The smoke damage alone—"

He laughed some more in what she deemed a rather overblown display of mirth.

Clara snatched back the sheet. "Should we discuss some house rules?"

Josh's eyes twinkled. "Like no parties on school nights?"

"You're right. *Rules* sounds a bit aggressive. I'm thinking more along the lines of guidelines for harmonious cohabitation. We might as well make the best of a bad situation."

Josh straightened up. "Of course. I'm afraid you'll need to make the first rule, though. I'm out of practice."

"Well, for instance, Everett mentioned a while back that the lock on the bathroom door doesn't work. So until we can have that fixed, I suggest we employ a three-knock strategy."

"Why three?"

"It would be easy to miss one or two knocks . . ." She spoke to the beat-up coffee table. "If you were in the shower, for example."

"Well, we wouldn't want that, certainly."

She looked up to find his whole body changed with the tilt of his lips. Goose bumps broke out across Clara's arms despite the balmy June afternoon. Josh had some kind of magnetism she hadn't noticed before. Even when she went and stood behind the couch, putting a physical barrier between them, her body hummed *closer, closer, closer.*

"Hey, listen. You don't need to guard your virtue from me, okay?" Josh dropped the charm like someone shrugging out of a jacket. He must have noticed that the energy between them had shifted from playful to something meatier.

"I'm taken, so you've got nothing to worry about. I'm only living here until I can convince my ex-girlfriend to let me move back in.

She's a tough nut, but I'm sure I'll be able to wear her down in a week or two, and then I'll be out of your hair for good." He broke the news in the practiced gentle tone of someone used to getting people's hopes up and having to let them down easy.

"Oh," Clara said, and then as she caught his meaning, "No." She crossed her hands in an X. He had the wrong idea. Obviously. She wanted Everett. Had loved him almost as long as she could remember. She didn't even know this guy with his ripped jeans and his bed head. "Of course not. I didn't think that you'd want to . . ." She waved a hand down her body and stuck out her tongue in disgust.

His eyes followed the path she'd tracked. "Wait a second. I didn't mean I wouldn't want to under different circumstances. You're very . . ." He held his hands out in front of his chest like he was assessing the weight of a pair of overripe melons.

Clara's eyes went wide.

"Oh God. I can't believe I did that. I'm sorry. I just meant that you . . . um . . . what's a respectful way to say . . ." He put his hands back up.

Blood rushed to her face. "I got it."

"Right. Sorry. Again." He shook his whole body like a wet dog. "Besides, I thought for sure you and Everett were a thing. The way he talked about you, it definitely sounded like you two had history."

At the mention of her beloved, the faded bruises on her heart bloomed anew and throbbed. She didn't know how much to share without seeming pathetic. She and Everett certainly had history, even if the romantic part was one-sided.

Something in the earnest set of Josh's brows gave Clara the impression he could handle more than the sugarcoated version of her past with Everett—more than the BS stories she'd given her friends and family back east, so they wouldn't judge her or worry about her rash decision to up and move.

For some reason, she found herself spilling her guts to this unkempt stranger. "Everett and I grew up together. Despite living on different coasts for almost ten years, we've kept in touch with phone calls and visits. I don't know if you got to know him at all, but he's this amazing mix of sweet and smart and funny—"

"And he encouraged you to drop everything and move out here only to abandon you the first chance he got?" Josh arched an eyebrow.

Clara took a step back. The truth stung. "That's not exactly what happened. I know how this looks." She lowered her voice, embarrassed at how she'd let it climb in volume. "But when Everett called a couple of weeks ago and painted this picture of life in L.A., all sunsets and ocean air and people who don't have to wear mouth guards at night because they can't stop stress-grinding their teeth . . ."

A dimple appeared in Josh's left cheek.

"I know it sounds stupid, but it seemed like a sign or something. This felt like my chance. At love, adventure, happily ever after, the whole Hallmark thing."

"Let me get this straight. You, a woman who created a laminated move-in checklist, made a huge life-altering decision based on a hazy sign from the universe?"

Clara shrugged. "Haven't you ever done something stupid to impress someone you liked?"

Josh plopped down on the sofa, propped his feet on the coffee table, and crossed them at the ankles. "No. Never."

"I think you mean 'Not yet.'" Clara grabbed the handles of her rolling suitcases. "So which one of these bedrooms is mine?"

Photograph by Sylvie Rosokoff

Rosie Danan writes steamy, bighearted books about the trials and triumphs of modern love. Her work has been optioned for film as well as translated into nine different languages and counting. When not writing, she enjoys jogging slowly to fast music, petting other people's dogs, and competing against herself in rounds of *Chopped* using the miscellaneous ingredients occupying her fridge.

CONNECT ONLINE

RosieDanan.com

🐦 RosieDanan

📷 RosieDanan

Ready to find
your next great read?

Let us help.

Visit prh.com/nextread

Penguin
Random
House